The Siren and the Deep Blue Sea

Also by Kerrelyn Sparks:

How to Love Your Elf

The Siren and the Deep Blue Sea

kerrelyn SPARKS

KENSINGTON BOOKS
www.kensingtonbooks.com

KENSINGTON BOOKS are published by

Kensington Publishing Corp.
119 West 40th Street
New York, NY 10018

All Kensington titles, imprints, and distributed lines are available at special quantity discounts for bulk purchases for sales promotion, premiums, fund-raising, educational, or institutional use.

Special book excerpts or customized printings can also be created to fit specific needs. For details, write or phone the office of the Kensington Sales Manager: Kensington Publishing Corp., 119 West 40th Street, New York, NY 10018. Attn. Sales Department. Phone: 1-800-221-2647.

Kensington and the K logo Reg. U.S. Pat. & TM Off.

ISBN-13: 978-1-4967-3007-7 (ebook)
ISBN-10: 1-4967-3007-7 (ebook)

ISBN-13: 978-1-4967-3006-0
ISBN-10: 1-4967-3006-2
First Kensington Trade Paperback Printing: September 2020

10 9 8 7 6 5 4 3 2

Printed in the United States of America

To my father, Les, aka the Mighty Oak.
Knowing that you were proud of me
meant the world to me.
I will miss you more than I can say,
and I love you now and forever.

Acknowledgments

As the last book in the fantasy world of Aerthlan comes to a close, I would like to thank all the people who made it possible for this journey to reach its final happy destination. Many thanks to editor Alicia Condon for gifting these last two stories with her wonderful skill and talent. Another big thank-you to everyone else at Kensington Publishing: Alexandra N., Alexandra K., Jane, Lauren, Elizabeth, Carly, and everyone else working behind the scenes. Thanks also to my agent Michelle Grajkowski of Three Seas Literary Agency for always being there for me.

I would like to invite everyone who has enjoyed this series to go to my website at www.kerrelynsparks.com to experience the interactive map! You'll be able to travel around Aerthlan and visit the different places that you read about in each book.

On a personal note, I wish to thank MJ and Sandy, the best critique partners/best friends on Earth and Aerthlan. And my love and gratitude to Brody's number one fan, my husband, Don, who has been complaining for years that Brody does all the work but never gets any action.

And finally, I am grateful for all of you reading this—my fabulous readers who have embarked on this journey into Aerthlan and stuck with it to the end. You're as loyal, clever, and courageous as any heroes or heroines I have ever imagined. May you always feel Embraced.

Prologue

In another time on another world called Aerthlan, there are five kingdoms. Four of the kingdoms extend across a vast continent. The fifth kingdom consists of two islands in the Great Western Ocean. These are the Isles of Moon and Mist. There is only one inhabitant on the small Isle of Mist—the Seer.

Twice a year, the two moons of Aerthlan eclipse each other, or as the people call it, embrace. Any child born when the moons embrace will be gifted with a magical power. These children are called the Embraced, and traditionally, the kings on the mainland have sought to kill them. Some of the Embraced infants are sent secretly to the Isle of Moon, where they will be safe.

For many years, the Seer predicted continuous war and destruction across the four mainland kingdoms. But not anymore. Now he claims a wave of change is sweeping across Aerthlan, change that will bring peace to a world that has known violence for too long. And it is happening because of five young women from the fifth kingdom: Luciana, Brigitta, Gwennore, Sorcha, and Maeve.

The women were hidden away as infants on the Isle of Moon, and there they grew up as sisters. They knew not where they had been born, nor if they had any family. They only knew each one of them was Embraced.

This is Maeve's story.

Chapter 1

Maeve glanced at her two eldest sisters as a startling realization popped into her mind. Luciana and Brigitta
had everything a woman could wish for. They were queens.
They were powerful, smart, and beautiful. They had lovely children and handsome husbands who were admirable rulers. So
how on Aerthlan had they become so incredibly boring? Good
goddesses, she was tempted to scream!

For the last two hours, Luciana and Brigitta had talked
about nothing but babies. Feeding a baby, weaning a baby,
bathing a baby, dressing a baby. Weren't there more important things to discuss? For example, where the hell was their
friend Brody? He'd been missing for almost two months.
Why hadn't he let anyone know where he was going?

It was so aggravating! The blasted man had a history of
keeping secrets. At first, he'd led everyone to believe he was
simply a dog shifter. But then they'd learned he could shift
into any animal he liked. And recently, they'd discovered he
was able to talk while in canine form. What other secrets was
he hiding?

Unfortunately, all her thinking and worrying had not
yielded any results other than to make her tired and weary. In
frustration, Maeve let her gaze wander aimlessly about the
elegant cabin of the Eberoni royal barge. It was decorated in
the country's official colors of red and black: a thick red car-

pet and big, comfy chairs and footstools upholstered in red velvet; a carved black table laden with cold meats, fruit, and pastries. It was the most comfortable way for her pregnant sisters and their young children to travel. The mothers' soft droning voices and the gentle sway of the barge had caused the little ones to fall asleep on cushioned pallets.

Maeve stifled a yawn. After leaving Wyndelas Palace, they had traveled for three days to reach the town of Vorushka, where they had said good-bye to their sister Gwennore. Then they had crossed into Eberon so they could board this barge on the Ebe River. Maeve was exhausted but far too worried about Brody to take a nap.

Luciana and Brigitta's conversation took a sudden turn for the worse as they delved into the pitfalls of training a child to use a chamber pot. With a groan, Maeve lurched to her feet. *I can't bear it any longer!*

"Sweetie, are you all right?" Luciana asked.

"Ye look a bit flushed," Brigitta added.

"I'm fine." Maeve wandered over to the table, but nothing looked appealing to her. She'd hardly eaten at all the last few days.

"You'll feel better once we're back home at Ebton Palace," Luciana announced. "No doubt there will be a dozen suitors waiting for you at the pier."

Maeve winced. Why were her sisters so eager for her to marry?

Luciana leaned close to Brigitta and whispered in a voice loud enough to be heard, "Maeve has become extremely popular of late."

"I'm not surprised," Brigitta whispered back. "She's grown into such a beauty."

Maeve rolled her eyes. Right. As if all those suitors were interested only in her appearance, not the fact that all four of her sisters were now queens.

"I know of at least one duke, three earls, and a dozen or so barons who claim to be smitten with her," Luciana continued.

"Oh, my!" Brigitta clasped her hands together. "A duke would be perfect!"

Maeve sighed. She didn't want a duke. She wanted a dog.

Luciana chuckled. "I wonder if the duke will be dressed in purple or green?"

Maeve stiffened at the reference to the Telling Stones. The number three; the colors purple and green. Those were the stones that had predicted her future.

And she hated it. She hadn't wanted to play the Game of Stones. In fact, the stones had only fallen out of the chalice because of her refusal to play. So maybe they didn't count?

But the pebble marked with the number three seemed too fitting to discount. There were only three members left in the Circle of Five, a murderous group intent on taking over the world. No one knew who the first two members were, but no doubt the Chameleon was the third. And three also matched the number of kings the evil shifter had killed: Frederic of Eberon, Gunther of Tourin, and Petras of Norveshka.

The Chameleon had caused trouble in Woodwyn, too, shifting into a dragon to kidnap their sister Sorcha. Whoever he was, he had proven impossible to catch since no one knew what he really looked like. Only Brody could identify him by his scent.

But what had happened to Brody?

"Excuse me." Maeve headed toward the door. "I think I'll take a turn on the deck."

"No doubt the fresh air will do you good," Luciana said as Maeve slipped out the door on the barge's port side.

Closing her eyes, she lifted her face to the warm sun and took a deep breath. A summer breeze feathered her cheeks and brought several scents to her nose: the sweat of hardworking sailors, the earthy smell of nearby farmland, and most importantly, the familiar scent of the Ebe River.

All her life, she'd felt a strange connection to bodies of water. She'd always known whenever a storm was brewing over the Great Western Ocean. And she'd been able to communicate with seals and other creatures of the sea.

Now that she was able to actually shift into a seal, she was even more attuned to water. With just a sniff, she knew which ocean, which river, which lake, even which well a sample of water came from. More than that, water had become a second home to her, as comforting as her bedchamber at Ebton Palace.

The river called to her, inviting her to jump in and shift. Let the water carry her weight, buoy her burdens, and wash away her worries. *Not now.* She opened her eyes and glanced up at the sun. It was high in the sky, so it had to be almost noon.

She wandered toward the bow of the barge, passing by the sailors who stood at the railing, using poles to keep the vessel floating down the deepest channel of the Ebe River. Eberoni soldiers, under the command of Colonel Nevis Harden, stood watch every few feet. Nevis and his troop had met the women and children this morning in Vorushka and would see them safely down the river. Once they arrived at Ebton, a troop of Tourinian soldiers would be waiting to escort Brigitta north to the capital of Tourin, where she ruled with her husband.

For the last three years, Maeve had been living at Ebton Palace. Although she was happy to be with her eldest sister, she always missed the other three something terrible. And so, she'd been delighted when they had all been reunited for three weeks at Wyndelas Palace in the elfin kingdom of Woodwyn. There, the fourth sister, Sorcha, had married Brennan the elfin king and become his queen. The three elder sisters had stayed for the entire three weeks, but their husbands had returned to their countries and royal duties after a few days. It hadn't taken long for Luciana, Brigitta, and Gwennore to complain about how much they missed their mates.

But did no one miss Brody? Maeve stopped at the bow of the barge and searched the sky. Sometimes, Brody took the shape of an eagle. But not today. The sky was clear.

She shifted her gaze to the river to see if she could spot any otters. While living at Ebton Palace, she'd used this river as her place to shift into a seal, and every month on the night of the full moons, a river otter had come to play with her. It was Brody, of course, although the fool had never realized that she knew. She'd kept waiting for him to admit what he was doing, but he never did. It was another one of his blasted secrets.

Even when she'd shifted for the first few times on the Isle of Moon, he had come to keep her company in the form of a seal. He'd always been there for her. Every month.

Except the last one. Where the hell was he?

And why was this stupid barge going so terribly slowly? She needed to do something to find Brody. But what?

Once again the water called to her, and she was tempted to shift. If she swam really fast, she could beat the barge to Ebton Palace. Wouldn't that give her sisters a shock! They thought she could shift only when the moons were full.

It had bothered her for years that Brody could shift whenever he wanted while she couldn't. So, in the privacy of her bedchamber, she'd used her bath time every evening to train herself. For the first week, she'd only succeeded in getting her feet to morph into flippers, but now, she could become a seal whenever and wherever she wanted.

She hadn't told anyone yet. She had wanted Brody to be the first to know.

With a groan, she turned and paced toward the back of the barge. Why had the purple and green stones tumbled from the chalice when it had tipped over? Those colors meant nothing to her. Now a blue stone—that she would have liked. Brody had the prettiest blue eyes she'd ever seen. Or at least she could have picked black and white, since he spent most of his time as a furry black-and-white dog with a black patch surrounding his left eye.

She stopped at the rear end of the barge and planted her hands on the railing. Instead of worrying over a few silly stones, she should deal with reality and figure out what to do. She wasn't a child anymore, in spite of what her sisters thought. In a few months, at the Autumn Embrace, she would be twenty years old.

Something bumped against her skirt, and with a jump she glanced down at the furry black-and-white cat rubbing against her legs.

"Oh, you gave me a start." Her eyes narrowed on the cat's face as it looked up at her. Blue eyes. Just like Brody's. Her heart leaped up her throat. "Brody, is that you?"

"It's called a cat," a wry voice announced, and she glanced up to see Colonel Nevis Harden approaching. He smiled at her. "The sailors keep her onboard to catch mice."

"I see." To hide her embarrassment, Maeve leaned down to rub the cat behind its ears.

"I heard something interesting this morning." Nevis stopped beside her at the railing. "Apparently, on the way to Vorushka, you asked several farm animals if they were Brody."

Maeve straightened, her face growing warm. "I had good reason to suspect the cow. He was black and white spotted."

Nevis's mouth twitched. "So are a lot of cows. I take it the pig was black and white, too?"

She gritted her teeth. "Yes. But I fail to see why this is so amusing. Brody has been missing for almost two months, and no one seems the least bit concerned."

Nevis's smile faded. "We *are* concerned."

"Then do something!"

"Such as?" Nevis gave her a frustrated look. "Brody can

shift into a bird or beast. He can fly over mountains and swim across oceans. How on Aerthlan would we ever find him?"

"But he could be in trouble. He might need help."

"If he's in trouble, he can shift into some sort of creature and escape." Nevis folded his arms as he leaned against the railing. "Try not to worry. I've known Brody a long time. It's not uncommon for him to disappear for a few months."

"But he—" Maeve stopped herself before saying that he'd always made time to see her on the night of the full moons. That was their secret time together, and she didn't want anyone else to know.

"But he always comes back," Nevis finished for her. "And he usually has some important information. He's simply doing his job as a spy and investigator."

Maeve knew what Brody did for a living, but not much more than that. "Do you know where he came from originally?"

"Not sure where he grew up." Nevis dragged a hand through his hair, and for a few seconds, the scar on his forehead was visible, one he'd received years ago from his best friend Leo's lightning power. "Brody told me once that he has a mother and a sister, but I don't know where they live."

"How did you meet him?"

"Hmm." Nevis's eyes narrowed as he thought back. "It was the summer of the year 691. Brody was sixteen. Leo and I, twenty-one. There was a severe drought that summer, and with no lightning storms, Leo's power was completely depleted, leaving him vulnerable to attack. My father and I were extremely worried about him. Then, one day, this scraggly dog wandered into camp, looking half-starved. I gave him a bone from the commissary. Then he followed me into my tent and shifted. Scared the crap out of—oh, no offense, my lady."

"Go on," Maeve urged.

"He said his name was Brody, and that he'd just spent a

month at Ebton Palace, listening in on King Frederic's secret meetings. You know who that was?"

"Yes." Maeve nodded. King Frederic had been Leo's uncle, and he had feared Leo because of his Embraced powers. Feared him enough that he had tried his best to get his nephew killed. And when Luciana had been betrothed to Leo, she'd also become a target.

"So I gave Brody some clothes and took him to see Leo and my father, the general," Nevis continued. "They hired him on the spot, and he's been working hard ever since. Not just helping Leo, but the other kings on the mainland, too."

"I knew about that last part." As far as Maeve was concerned, Brody was the unsung hero of all the changes that had happened over the last few years. "It upsets me that no one seems to realize how valuable he is."

Nevis scoffed. "If you value him so much, why do you keep calling him Julia whenever he's a dog?"

She winced. "I-I had my reasons, but I'll stop doing it." At first, it had been an honest mistake. Brody made such a pretty dog with his long, silky fur and bright blue eyes, that she had assumed he was female. But later, after she knew the truth, she'd continued to call him Julia. For deep down inside, she'd wanted to annoy him.

The blasted man had a habit of ignoring her. Whenever there was a ball, he'd dance with her sisters but not her. He hardly even talked to her. She would have thought that he hated her, except for the fact that he always showed up on the night of the full moons as a seal or otter to play with her. That had to mean he liked her, didn't it? So why did he avoid her when he was human?

"You seem to have lost most of your island accent," Nevis observed.

She nodded. "While I was living at Ebton Palace, Luciana encouraged me to improve my diction." No doubt so she could attract a noble suitor. "Where do you think Brody could be?"

Nevis shrugged. "My guess is he's investigating the secret Embraced army that Lord Morris talked about before he died."

She stiffened. "*What?* An Embraced army?"

Nevis's mouth dropped open. "Oh. Oh, shit. I-I thought you knew. All your sisters know. I thought they . . ."

"No." Maeve gripped the railing hard. "They didn't tell me."

Nevis winced. "Sorry."

"What is this Embraced army?"

"I don't think it's my place to say anything." He made a quick bow. "I should check on my soldiers. Good day, my lady." He strode away, disappearing around the side of the cabin.

With a groan, Maeve propped her elbows on the railing. Of course her sisters hadn't told her. She wasn't a queen as they were. During the few days when all four kings and their queens had been in Wyndelas Palace, they had closeted themselves in the royal privy chamber for private discussions. Maeve hadn't been invited. After all, she didn't have a country to protect. She understood that, but even so, it was aggravating to feel left out.

It was a feeling she'd struggled with since childhood. Not that she was ignored. Her sisters had doted on her as the baby of the group. But it had always been clear that the eldest two, Luciana and Brigitta, were the best of friends. And the next two, Gwennore and Sorcha, were equally close to each other. Maeve was always the baby. The fifth wheel.

And now she felt even more left out. Her sisters and their husbands had become an exclusive group she could never join. There was only one kingdom left on Aerthlan, the island kingdom of Moon and Mist, and it already had a queen and an heir. So Maeve would never be a queen like her sisters.

She closed her eyes briefly. *There's no point in feeling sorry for yourself.* Being a queen didn't matter to her. What was important was that Nevis had given her a big clue. An Embraced army?

When she opened her eyes, she noticed the ripples coming from the barge and undulating their way to the riverbanks. Cause and effect. Lord Morris had claimed there was an Embraced army, and Brody had disappeared searching for it. Since he hadn't returned, it seemed likely that he hadn't found the army yet. Had Lord Morris been speaking the truth, or had he taunted them with lies before dying?

She recalled everything she knew about Lord Morris. Before Leo had become king, when King Frederic had ruled Eberon, Morris was his chief counsel and the head of the Church of Enlightenment. In those days, the kings on the mainland feared those who were born Embraced, so they had them hunted down and killed as infants. That way, the Embraced children could never grow up and use their magical powers to usurp the royal thrones. In Eberon, it had been Morris's job to eliminate the children.

But once Morris had become a member of the Circle of Five, had he realized that keeping the Embraced children alive could help the Circle take over the world? Had he hidden the children away to train them as an army? Was the widely believed story that the Embraced children had all been murdered actually a lie?

It wouldn't be the first time that Maeve and her sisters had come across that sort of falsehood. Growing up in the convent on the Isle of Moon, they had always believed that they'd been hidden away because they were Embraced. But in the last few years, they'd learned that this was only partially true. There had been other reasons. Luciana had been sent away because she was a twin. Brigitta's father had gotten rid of her to make everyone believe she was dead. Gwennore had been taken away to punish her mother for giving birth to a half-breed, and Sorcha's mother had been trying to protect her from the plague.

At the convent, Mother Ginessa had told the five young girls that they were orphans. For her elder sisters, that had also proven to be a lie. What other falsehoods would they discover?

As she did every day, Maeve wondered if she would ever know the truth about herself. She had no idea where she had come from. The nuns at the convent had estimated that she was nearly a year old when she'd been left in a basket by the front gate. That had been midsummer, so from then on, the nuns had celebrated her birthday in late summer. But no one knew why she had been abandoned, so they had assumed she was Embraced like her adopted sisters, and that her actual birthday must be when the moons embraced in autumn. That theory had proven correct when, at a young age, Maeve had displayed the odd gift of being able to communicate with the seals that lounged about on the nearby beach. Then, at the age of sixteen, she'd shifted for the first time into a seal.

This was one of the reasons she'd always felt close to Brody. His past was mysterious, too, and he was also an Embraced shifter. Because of a witch's curse, he could maintain human form for only two hours each day, and unfortunately, he spent most of that time in secret conferences with Leo or whichever king he was currently helping. So it was only on rare occasions that Maeve saw him as a human. When he wasn't looking, she would study him intently, memorizing every bit of his handsome face and lean, strong body, so she could keep the image in her mind until she saw him again.

She wandered slowly back to the cabin and stopped by the door. When she'd left, the door hadn't latched properly, and now the gentle sway of the boat had caused it to swing halfway open.

"I don't think the Embraced army could be in Eberon." Luciana's soft voice filtered across the cabin. "The land is all cultivated. There would be no place to hide."

"Rupert is having the mountains in northern Tourin checked," Brigitta said, referring to her husband by his pirate name. "But I don't think anyone could be hiding there. The lords in the highlands are very loyal, and they would have reported anything odd to us."

"I suspect there are vast areas of wilderness in Norveshka," Luciana continued. "But Silas is having his dragons survey every inch. And Aleksi is scanning the remote areas in Woodwyn."

Maeve sighed. Her sisters were no longer talking of babies. Had they been waiting for her to leave so they could discuss business matters?

She leaned against the cabin wall, thinking. If she had to hide somewhere, where would she go? The mainland kings would know if an army was hiding in their countries. Was there somewhere else? When Brigitta's husband had been a pirate, he'd hidden on a secret isle he'd named after himself. Could there be other islands in the Great Western Ocean?

A faint memory stirred in her mind. Over a year ago, while searching for something new to read in the library at Ebton Palace, she'd come across an extremely old book written in a form of the Eberoni language that was so archaic, it had taken her over an hour to decipher it. But once she'd started to understand it, she'd become fascinated with the story it told.

According to the old book, an ancient continent had existed in the Great Western Ocean, and the culture there had flourished long before the primitive people of Eberon had learned to even count the years. It had been the year 699 when she'd found this book, so she figured that this ancient land had to date back over seven hundred years.

The continent, Aerland, had been a place of magic with sorcerers so powerful that the rest of Aerthlan had quaked in fear of them. The ancient race had worshipped the twin moon goddesses, and that had made the sun god, the Light, seethe with anger and jealousy. In a fit of rage, the Light had struck several volcanoes on the continent, causing them to erupt all at once in a massive explosion. Earthquakes had added to the devastation and after a few days, most of the ancient continent had collapsed far below the sea, and most of the people had perished.

There had been a map in the book, and after studying it, Maeve had suspected that the Isles of Moon and Mist were all that was left of the ancient continent of Aerland.

Could there be other islands? As soon as she arrived back at Ebton Palace, she would search the library for this book. And then, tomorrow, she would travel to the Isle of Moon. The nuns at the convent transcribed books, so they had a huge library. She might find more information there. And she could ask the seals at the nearby beach if they knew of any other islands.

Her breath caught. She could also go to the Isle of Mist and ask the Seer if he knew where the Embraced army was hiding. He might even know where Brody was.

Finally. She took a deep, satisfying breath. Finally, she had a course of action to pursue. It was so much better than sitting around worrying.

She strode into the cabin.

Luciana spotted her. "Oh, the air must have done you good. You look much better."

"I am better." Maeve stopped by the table of food and began loading a plate. Now that she had a plan, her appetite had returned.

"Ye should try the cherry tarts," Brigitta suggested. "We were just talking about how yummy they are."

"I know what you were talking about." Maeve gave them an annoyed look. "You should have told me about the Embraced army. And that Brody is gone because he's looking for it."

Luciana's and Brigitta's mouths fell open.

"Well..." Luciana winced. "We didn't want you to worry—"

"I'll worry more if I'm kept in the dark!" Maeve set her plate down with a thud. "Did it never occur to you that I hate being left out?"

Luciana and Brigitta exchanged looks, then turned to her with apologetic expressions on their faces.

"I know I'm not a queen, and I never will be," Maeve continued. "But that doesn't mean I don't care about you or your countries. I want to help."

Luciana sighed. "I'm afraid there's not much we can do."

Brigitta nodded. "It's frustrating for us, too."

"I believe there is something I can do." Maeve put a cherry tart on her plate. "I want to go back to the convent. Can you arrange passage for me to leave tomorrow morning?"

Luciana sat back with a shocked look. "Why? Are you not happy at Ebton Palace?"

Brigitta winced. "Are ye angry with us for not telling you everything?"

Maeve shook her head. "There's something I want to check in the convent library."

"Is it that urgent?" Luciana rose to her feet. "I was thinking of hosting a ball for you. And having my seamstresses make you a beautiful new gown. A sea-green color that would match your lovely eyes."

"Chee-ana." Maeve used her nickname for her eldest sister. "I don't need a ball. Or a new gown. And I'm not angry." She was determined. If the Embraced army was hiding somewhere in the Great Western Ocean, then there was no one better suited than she to track it down. She could finally put her Embraced gift of seal shifting to a good purpose.

And with any luck, she might find Brody, too.

Chapter 2

"Be careful with that," Maeve warned the sailors as they carried a large wooden crate toward the naval ship. "There are wine bottles inside."

"Aye, my lady." The two men crossed the gangplank to the ship, then carefully set down the crate.

It was the next morning, and Maeve was eager to set sail for the Isle of Moon. The ship had arrived at dawn, the smallest of the Eberoni naval vessels. Small enough that it could navigate down the Ebe River to the palace, but sturdy enough to cross the Great Western Ocean. It was the same ship Maeve and three of her sisters had taken from the Isle of Moon four years ago when Brigitta had been kidnapped. Maeve was happy to see that Captain Shaw was still in charge.

After arriving at Ebton Palace the night before, she'd hurried to the library to locate the old book. Then, back in her room, she'd packed it and some clothes for the journey. A few simple gowns would suffice. No need for fancy clothes and headdresses at the convent.

At dinner in the Great Hall, she'd learned that Luciana had been equally busy arranging gifts for Maeve to take to their childhood home, the Convent of the Two Moons. There was a crate of wine from the duchy of Vindalyn, another container of fresh fruits from southern Eberon, and some soft woolen blankets fresh off the looms of the Ebton Palace workroom.

Now that the last of the crates were safely onboard, Maeve was ready to go.

Luciana hurried down the palace steps. "Wait!" She joined Maeve on the pier, pressing a hand to her chest as she caught her breath. "Oh, I was afraid you would leave before I could tell you good-bye."

Maeve blinked away some tears. She was going to miss her eldest sister. In fact, she couldn't remember ever being away from all four of her sisters before. "We talked for a long time last night."

"I know." Luciana gave her an exasperated look. "All my attempts to convince you to stay were in vain. Are you sure you need to do this?"

"Aye."

Luciana's eyes narrowed. "You're up to something. I know it. Promise me you'll be careful."

"I will." Maeve wondered how much her sister had figured out. Luciana hailed from a long line of witches who could predict the future, although her talent usually came out only when they were playing the Game of Stones. "I'll be sure to give Mother Ginessa and all the nuns a hug from you. They'll love the presents you're sending."

Luciana sighed. "I wish I could go with you, but . . ." She placed a hand on her swollen belly. "Leo and I agree that it's not safe for you to go alone—"

"I'll be safe with the nuns," Maeve insisted, knowing very well that her investigation would probably lead her away from the security of the convent. But she didn't want Luciana or anyone else to know that. They would try to stop her for sure. "I'll be fine."

"You'll be a target," Luciana said sternly. "There are still a few pirates out there. And a few members of the Circle of Five. There are any number of people who might try to hold you hostage in order to control the kings and queens who love you as a sister."

Maeve stifled a groan. Was she only important because of the royals she knew?

"So Leo and I have asked Nevis to go with you." Luciana glanced over her shoulder. "Ah, he's coming now."

Nevis? Maeve grimaced as she watched the large, muscular colonel descending the stairs from the palace. He was not going to let her do what she wanted. "Chee-ana, I don't want a bodyguard."

"Too bad." Luciana gave her a wry look. "If you want to use my ship, you'll accept my terms."

Maeve huffed. "I'm almost twenty years old, and you're still bossing me around."

With a smile, Luciana pulled her into a hug. "I know you get annoyed when I still try to mother you. But to me, you have always been my first baby."

"I know, I know." Maeve hugged her sister back. "Try not to worry about me."

Luciana stepped back, her eyes glistening with tears. "I hope you find Brody."

Maeve winced. Luciana had guessed one of the purposes of this trip.

"Your Majesty, my lady," Nevis said as he approached. He was in his uniform as a colonel, a knapsack in one hand and small leather folder in the other. "I hope I didn't keep you waiting." He lifted the leather folder. "Leo just gave this to me. A letter for Queen Esther."

"You're going to meet the queen of the Isles of Moon and Mist?" Maeve asked.

Nevis nodded. "After I make sure you're safely ensconced at the convent."

"We're asking the queen to ally her islands with the kingdoms on the mainland," Luciana explained. "So far, she's ignored all our gestures of friendship." She turned to Nevis. "I had several packages taken onboard, gifts for you to give the queen. They're the ones wrapped in red and black silk."

"I will deliver them with your sincere greetings," Nevis assured her, then went over to talk to Captain Shaw.

This was good news, Maeve thought. Nevis wouldn't be by her side the entire time. She'd be able to slip away.

"We're ready to set sail," Captain Shaw announced. "All aboard!"

"Good luck." Luciana hugged Maeve once more.

Ignoring the sting of tears, Maeve hurried across the gangplank. She headed straight for the quarterdeck at the back of the ship, and as the ship drifted slowly away from the pier and down the river, she waved at Luciana.

A tear rolled down Maeve's cheek as she realized her sister was remaining on the pier until the ship was out of sight. She wiped her cheek and squared her shoulders. This was not the time to look back, but to move forward with her life.

She strode toward the front of the ship, and her heart began to race. Finally. She was off on her very own adventure. *Brody, I'm coming! Wherever you are, I will find you. And I'll find the Embraced army.*

An hour later, her excitement had dulled to barely veiled impatience. It had taken far too long for the ship to reach the mouth of the Ebe River and start its journey across the Great Western Ocean. And all her pacing up and down the deck had not caused the ship to sail any faster.

After another hour of pacing, she strode up onto the quarterdeck for the tenth time. "We'll reach the convent tonight, won't we?" she asked Captain Shaw.

"No, my lady." He gave her a sympathetic look. "I'm afraid going west means we're traveling against the wind and ocean currents. We won't arrive till tomorrow morning."

Tomorrow? With a groan, she turned to look out over the ocean. Nothing but dark blue waves as far as she could see. It was a shame Brigitta's husband wasn't here. Rupert had the Embraced power of controlling the wind. He could blow the ship to the Isle of Moon in just a few hours.

"Isn't it great?" Nevis sat on a nearby trunk, happily munching on an apple.

"What could possibly be great?" Maeve grumbled.

"This. Doing nothing." He finished the apple and tossed the core overboard. "I haven't had a day off from work in years."

She sighed. While other people had been busy the last few years, she'd had nothing to do. She'd read books, learned new dances, attended balls, and played in the Ebe River once a month in seal form—in short, she'd done nothing of any importance. Now that she finally had a goal, it was aggravating that she couldn't get straight to it.

"You should rest, my lady," the captain suggested. "We've reserved our nicest cabin for you belowdecks. I've had some food left there for you."

Rest? From doing what? Waking up and getting dressed? She feigned a smile. "Thank you, Captain."

She hurried down to the cabin and closed the door behind her. "Dammit!" she shouted, using one of the unladylike words she'd learned from her sister Sorcha. What on Aerthlan would she do while she waited? It seemed as if she'd spent her entire life waiting.

In just a few seconds of pacing, she completed a circle around the small cabin. The room was much the same as she remembered: a round table with four chairs, a sideboard stocked with fruit, cheese, bread, and wine, a narrow bed, and a window seat looking out the ship's aft. On the trip four years ago, Brigitta had settled in the window seat, refusing to play the Game of Stones with her sisters. She'd been spooked, Maeve recalled, and rightly so. She had been kidnapped soon afterward.

Maeve paused by the table where she'd played with her sisters to pass the time away. They'd been especially silly with their predictions in a vain attempt to cheer up Brigitta.

Oh, dear goddesses! Maeve's breath caught. At the time,

they had joked that Sorcha would end up with an elf. How strange that their jest had come true!

And what had her stones been? Maeve glanced at the window seat. She'd sat there next to Brigitta. *"My prediction was the best,"* Maeve had boasted. *"In four years, I'll meet a tall and handsome stranger with green teeth, purple hair, and three feet."*

Green, purple, and three? A shudder ran down Maeve's spine. Out of the forty Telling Stones, what were the chances that three of them would repeat like that?

She shook her head. It wasn't an exact match. She had picked four stones that day—four, three, purple, and green. This last time, she'd ended up with only three stones. She'd missed repeating the number four.

But four years had passed.

Coincidence, she told herself. *Superstition.* She couldn't let the Telling Stones frighten her as they had Brigitta. Even though all the predictions for Brigitta had come true.

"Damn," Maeve muttered as she paced around the cabin once more. There was no reason for her to get spooked. Luciana was the one who predicted the future, not her. She didn't have the blood of witches in her veins.

Or did she? Maeve stopped with a jerk. She really didn't know.

There was no point in wondering about the unknown. She opened her bag, which a sailor had deposited at the foot of the bed, and took out the book she'd borrowed from the Ebton Palace library. She hadn't had much time to look at it the night before.

Sitting at the table, she carefully examined each page. Once again, it took some time for her to adjust to the archaic language. And once again, she became thoroughly engrossed in the old story. Imagine the terror, she thought, of suddenly realizing that your world and everyone you knew and loved was coming to an end. A violent end. An entire continent gone. An entire race perished.

She closed her eyes, mentally picturing the chaos. People dashing about, searching in vain for a way to escape, and when that failed, a safe place to hide. The earth beneath her feet shook, and buildings crumbled around her. Fires broke out. Smoke and volcanic ash darkened the sky. Frantic screams and mournful wailing echoed around her. Mothers desperately tried to shield their children from suffocating ash. The children's cries wrenched her heart. Her eyes stung.

It hurt. The heat was singeing her skin. Roasting her. She couldn't breathe.

A knock at the door jolted her out of her thoughts.

"Maeve?" Nevis cracked the door open and peeked inside. "Oh, you're awake. I thought you might be asleep. We haven't seen you in hours."

She blinked and looked around the cabin. Hours? When had the room grown so dark?

Nevis came in, carrying a lit lantern. "The sun is setting. I thought you might need this." He latched the lantern onto a hook in the ceiling. "And the galley has some stew if you're hungry for din—oh, you have plenty of food." He wandered over to the sideboard. "Didn't you eat?"

"Ah, no." Maeve took a deep breath. Good goddesses, what had happened? She'd been so immersed in this book she'd missed the midday meal. "I'll eat now. Would you like to join me?"

"Sure." Nevis grabbed a pewter plate and helped himself. "What have you been doing?"

"I was reading a book." She wandered over to the sideboard to load her plate. "An extremely old book I found in the library at Ebton."

"Mmm." Nevis made a garbled noise as he stuffed some cheese into his mouth that sounded like, "What's it about?"

"Aerland." She selected some sliced roast beef, cheese, and an assortment of fruit.

"You mean Aerthlan?" He poured himself some wine.

"No, Aerland," she corrected him. "It's an ancient continent that used to exist in the Great Western Ocean."

He snorted. "Right." He set his plate and cup of wine on the table. "Is this the book?"

"Yes." Maeve filled a cup with wine and winced as her hand trembled. She was still flustered. How had half a day passed by unnoticed? And why had her imaginings seemed so real? She drank some wine to get rid of the sting of hot ash in her throat.

"How the hell did you read this thing?" Nevis asked. "I can't make out a single word."

"It's an ancient form of Eberoni." She glanced over her shoulder and smiled. "Plus, you're looking at it upside down."

"Oh." He turned the book around to face him.

He was still standing there, staring at it, when she set her cup and plate down and took a seat.

She sipped more wine. "Is it making sense now?"

"No." He gave her a wary look as he sat down. "Not at all."

She popped a grape in her mouth. "Don't let it concern you. I grew up learning all about languages at the convent. No doubt your education focused on weaponry and military tactics."

He snorted. "Is that your polite way of saying I'm an idiot?"

"No!" She chuckled, but her laughter faded away when he kept staring at her strangely. "What is it?"

"I'm actually well educated. Leo and I grew up together and shared a tutor." He motioned to the book. "I could study that for a year and it would still be gibberish."

She shrugged. "I guess I'm good with languages."

"You communicate with seals, don't you?"

"Yes."

"How?" He leaned forward. "Did you find a book titled *The Idiot's Guide to the Language of Seals*? I'd like to see it. It would be perfect for me."

She gave him a wry look as she bit off some roast beef. Maybe this wasn't a good time to admit she could talk to most of the sea creatures. "I've been able to do it for as long as I can remember, so it never felt strange to me. In fact, the real shock came when I realized that no one else could do it. It's part of my Embraced gift, I suppose."

"Right." He tapped the old book. "I think there's more to your gift than you realize."

She swallowed hard. Was there some sort of connection between the old book and her gift? Was that why she was so drawn to the ancient legend?

Nevis stuffed a small loaf of bread with roast beef. "So, what's the plan?"

"Excuse me?"

"You're looking for the Embraced army, right?" He bit into his sandwich. "And Brody, too. You have an idea where he is?"

Maeve sighed. "I'm not sure yet, but one thing is certain. You're definitely not an idiot."

By the time Brody finished his flight to the Isle of Mist, he was utterly exhausted. He hit the beach with a clumsy landing, then rolled as he shifted from eagle form back into his human body. Damn it to hell but his arms and shoulders were aching. Breathing heavily, he sprawled onto his back.

For close to two months now, he'd spent his days in flight, searching in vain for any sign of a hidden army. At night, he'd scrounged about as a dog in search of food. There had been a few minutes each day when he'd been forced to return to his human form, not that it had helped matters. He'd learned the hard way that men from any country did not appreciate a stranger sauntering into their village naked. Women were much more openminded about it, but that only irritated the men more. Sometimes, it was simply safer to remain a dog.

And now he lay on this secluded beach. Muscles aching. Stomach empty. Full circle, he thought. How many years had it been since he'd washed up on this beach naked, starved, and exhausted? Four—no, fifteen years ago. And he'd been more than exhausted. He'd been terrified. Distraught. Devastated.

With a groan, he sat up and gazed out at the ocean. The old feelings of guilt still needled him, even though now, as an adult, he understood that there had been no way a ten-year-old could have saved his father and older brother from drowning in the middle of the ocean.

Brody closed his eyes briefly to stop the horrific memories from playing out in his mind. There was nothing he could have done differently. He would have perished, too, if he hadn't been able to shift into a seal.

He'd barely made it here to this beach. After shifting back into human form, he had lain here, broken in body and spirit. How could he wish for life after seeing his father and brother drown? The entire crew had died, their bodies floating amidst the wreckage of the destroyed ship.

How had the ship cracked in two like that? There had been no enemy ship on the horizon. How could he keep on living when he was the only one who had survived? He'd cried until there were no tears left and he'd become nothing but a drying husk under the summer sun.

Then the Seer had found him. Carried him back to his cottage. Cared for him. Educated him. Taught him that life was still worth living.

With another groan, Brody rose to his feet and stretched his sore muscles. Hopefully, the Seer was doing all right. Brody wasn't sure how old the man was exactly, but he had to be close to a hundred. The last time Brody had come, several months ago, he'd noticed that the Seer was moving very slowly. His eyesight had dimmed over the last fifteen years. And his visions had come less and less frequently until nine years ago when they had stopped completely. Penance, he had called it. His punishment for the terrible crime he had committed.

That had always confused Brody. For he'd never seen the Seer commit any crimes. Hell, the man begged for forgiveness if he had to kill a chicken for dinner. He was the gentlest soul Brody had ever known. And he'd become a second father to him.

So, in order to help the Seer, Brody had left the isle nine years ago to become a spy on the mainland. Then he'd reported back to the Seer, so the old man could continue to make his living by foretelling the future. No one had to know that the Seer's predictions were now based on Brody's information and not on any visions.

Brody trudged into the ocean and washed the sand off his bare skin. Then he followed the beach to a rocky outcropping that hid the entrance to a cave. In the dim light, he located the trunk where he kept dry clothes and shoes.

After he was dressed, he returned to the beach and the path that wound up the bluff and across the windswept moors to the solitary stone cottage. Mist hovered in patches over the green grass, blurring his vision, but he didn't need to see well. He knew which direction to go. He knew where every rock and boulder lay so he could avoid stumping his toes. He knew every inch of this isle. Just as he knew his way around the cave. The Seer had always sent him there to hide whenever anyone came to visit. It was better, the Seer had told him, for everyone to believe that he was dead.

Brody had always suspected the Seer knew a great deal more than he was willing to tell. But Brody could forgive him for that. It had been the old man's way of protecting him.

The sight of smoke curling up from the stone chimney

made him smile with relief. The Seer was alive and well. He was probably cooking himself dinner.

A stone wall surrounded the cottage, intended to keep the deer on the island out of the garden, even though its low height had never stopped them from jumping over. In the last few years, though, Brody had rarely seen any deer.

As he unlatched the gate, a rusted hinge gave out and the gate toppled over. With a prick of guilt, he propped it against the wall. He should have come here more often. The garden was a mess, filled with weeds and spilling over the flagstone path to the door, which badly needed a fresh coat of paint.

"I'm digging up an onion, not a place for you to poop," a grumbling voice announced across a patch of mist.

Brody walked toward the voice and soon saw the brown hooded cloak that the Seer always wore outside. The old man was hunched down, digging onions and carrots from the ground while an orange tabby cat insisted on getting in his way.

"Shoo, Trouble," the Seer fussed at his pet as he pulled an onion from the ground. "Ah, this is a good one." He dropped it into a basket, then fondled the tabby's ears.

The Seer had acquired the cat two years ago. Brody suspected the old man had been lonesome after he had left. But after the cat had ripped the Seer's best blanket to shreds, it had acquired the name Trouble.

"Seer," he called softly, so he wouldn't alarm the old man. The tabby arched his back and gave him a menacing look.

"Oh, you've arrived." The old man straightened slowly and glanced at him with a yellow-toothed smile. "I knew you were coming. That's why I'm making a big pot of soup." He reached a trembling hand for the basket and stumbled.

"I'll get it." Brody grabbed the basket with one hand and steadied the Seer with the other. "Soup sounds wonderful. I'm starving!"

The Seer chuckled as Brody led him into the cottage. "You're always starving."

Brody set the basket on the table next to a knife and wooden chopping board. One glance around and he could tell the cottage hadn't changed at all since he'd first arrived fifteen years ago. A big stone fireplace dominated one wall with the table and chairs close by. The wall to the right held shelves of books, while the wall to the left had shelves for cooking utensils and food. The front door was there, close to a large sink with a water pump. The fourth wall had two small beds, one in each corner. One for the Seer, and one for Brody.

"I've been cleaning—can you tell?" The Seer removed his hooded cloak and hung it on a peg by the door, while the cat took a swipe at it. "I knew you were coming."

"How?" Brody noticed an inch of dust on the bookshelves, but didn't mention it. After all, the old man could hardly see.

"I had a vision!" The Seer smiled proudly. "In fact, I had three of them."

Three visions? "When did this happen? I thought you stopped seeing the future years ago."

The Seer's smile faded. "That's right. I did." He shuffled slowly over to the table to retrieve a carrot and onion from the basket, then washed them off at the sink.

Brody frowned. Was the Seer's mind fading? Was he living in the past? Now that he had removed the voluminous cloak, Brody could see how terribly thin the old man was. His skin had a grayish tint and his long silver hair was lank and dull.

"I believe the visions were a parting gift," the Seer mumbled as he dropped the vegetables on the table and collapsed into a wooden chair. The orange tabby curled up around his feet.

"A parting gift for whom?" Brody winced as he saw the

Seer use one trembling hand to place the onion on the chopping board, then reach for the knife with his other trembling hand. "I'll do that." He grabbed the knife and began slicing.

"Thank you." The Seer sat back with a long, weary breath. "Plucking the chicken and digging in the garden wore me out."

"Maybe you should lie down. I can finish the soup." Brody scraped the chopped onion into the big pot that hung over the fire. A whole chicken was inside, boiling in a broth spiced with garlic and herbs. His stomach growled.

"Can't sleep," the Seer grumbled. "Don't want to miss seeing my daughter."

"What?" Brody brought the chopping board back to the table.

"My daughter is coming. That was my second vision."

"What daughter? I didn't know you ever married."

"I didn't." The Seer sighed. "Before you came here, I used to see her in visions. But then, my visions stopped. Punishment for my crime." Tears filled his cloudy eyes. "I was told that she'd died. I was afraid it was true."

"Who is she?" Brody sliced a carrot.

"So beautiful," the Seer whispered, closing his eyes. "Even more beautiful than her mother."

Brody frowned at the old man, who seemed to have drifted off. In the fifteen years that he had known the Seer, the man had never once mentioned a woman or daughter. Maybe he was remembering something from long ago? If he'd fathered a child when he was a young man, then that daughter could be fifty or sixty years old now. "When is she arriving?"

The Seer opened his eyes and a tear ran down his face. "I'm not sure. I hope she makes it here before I die."

The knife tumbled from Brody's hand. "Don't say that! You're not going to die."

"I am. It was the third vision. I saw my burial."

"Enough!" Brody slapped a hand on the table. "You didn't see anything. You don't have visions anymore, remember?"

"It was a parting gift. My parting. I saw you digging my grave up on my favorite bluff overlooking the ocean—"

"Stop." Brody hated how weak his protest sounded.

The Seer reached across the table and touched Brody's hand. It was meant to be a squeeze, Brody realized with an aching heart, but the old man didn't have enough strength in his fingers to accomplish it.

"I saw you kneeling in the rain and crying," the Seer continued. "Don't let it sadden you. None of us can live forever."

Brody drew in a shaky breath. "You should lie down and rest. You've overworked yourself because of this stupid soup—"

"That reminds me." The Seer motioned toward the pot. "You should put the carrots in."

Gritting his teeth, Brody took the chopping board over to the fireplace and shoved the sliced carrots into the soup.

"When I die, my daughter will inherit my gift."

"What?" Brody turned toward the Seer.

"That is how it works with my people."

"What people?" Brody stalked back to the table and sat across from the Seer. "You've lived here alone for as long as anyone can remember. Except for the years that I lived with you."

"I am the last living male of my race. An ancient race of sorcerers. My father was a Seer, and his father before him. When my father died, the gift passed on to me. And now my daughter will receive it when I die."

"You're not going to die!"

Another tear rolled down the Seer's wrinkled cheek. "I'm not afraid of death, boy. I'm more afraid that you will hate me when you learn the truth."

A chill skittered down Brody's spine. "What are you talking about now?"

More tears fell and the Seer leaned his bony elbows on the table and cradled his head in his hands. "My crime. I have to confess it to you before I die."

"You're not dying!"

"I've been dreading this moment for fifteen years. I'm so sorry. Everything that happened to you—it was all my fault."

Brody sat back. "How could it be your fault, old man? You didn't destroy my father's ship. You didn't cause everyone on-board to die. You didn't put this damned curse on me!"

The Seer crumpled, his head falling onto the table as he cried, and instantly, Brody regretted yelling at him.

"I'm sorry." He touched the man's back and winced at the bones he could feel beneath his skin. "Don't do this, Seer. Go to bed and sleep. You'll feel better—"

"I was here alone from the age of twenty-five," the Seer mumbled through his tears. "So many years of loneliness. So many years of despair. I saw no one for months at a time. I only saw death and destruction every night in my visions. They tormented me. Haunted me. I thought I would lose my mind."

Brody rubbed the man's back. "I'm sorry. It must have been hard for you."

The old man lifted his head. "But then, all of a sudden, I had a good vision. I saw a change come over Aerthlan. Peace and prosperity took the place of violence and bloodshed."

"That is good." Brody wondered if the Seer had seen what was happening now.

The Seer shook his head. "No, it was bad. It taunted me. I could see the peaceful time in the future, but still, day after day, war and destruction wreaked havoc on the world. In my despair, I thought I could no longer stand by while innocent people were dying."

He sighed. "In the end, it was my own vanity that caused my crime. I thought the good vision had been given to me because I was the one who could make it happen. If I was in charge, I could bring peace and prosperity to the world."

"In charge?" Brody sat back, his nerves tensing. "You mean you wanted to rule the world?"

"It sounds terrible, doesn't it?" The Seer slumped lower in his chair. "But at the time I thought it would be all right if I could rule with wisdom and kindness. Certainly better than the constant death and destruction I kept seeing every night in my visions. And who would be better equipped than I to see what problems might arise in the future? I would be able to solve those problems before they even happened."

Brody swallowed hard. "But you didn't do it . . ."

"Then she came." The Seer pressed a hand to his chest and grimaced as if he were in pain. "She was so beautiful. In my loneliness, I opened my heart and mind to her. And she told me I was right. I was meant to rule the world. She would help me."

An alarm went off in Brody's mind.

"She knew powerful men on the mainland who would help me. Men who were sick of war and death. A kindly priest from Eberon and a general—"

"No!" Brody lurched to his feet, causing his chair to fall over with a clatter. A priest? Was he referring to Lord Morris? General Caladras? "What are you saying, old man? What did you do?"

The Seer's hand clutched his shirt as he grimaced once more in pain. "I am the first member of the Circle of Five."

Chapter 3

B rody paced about the garden. *Not the Seer. Not the man who saved me. Not the man who has been like a father to me.* He didn't want to believe it. He didn't even want to hear it. He'd stormed out of the cottage, unable to listen to any more.

"It's bullshit," he said softly. The old man was losing his mind and spouting nonsense. He'd spent too many years alone with his horrific visions. It would be enough to drive anyone insane.

But the Seer had lost his visions. Punishment for his crime— the creation of the Circle of Five.

"No!" Brody clenched his fists. Anger replaced his shock, and he stalked across the garden, ready to punch something. How could the Seer have done such a thing?

But what had the old man done? He'd never hurt anyone. Dammit, he'd never even left the island.

Brody slowed to a stop. Why was he angry at the Seer? It was the other members of the Circle who had usurped his idea for their own selfish purposes. No doubt, the other four members had never intended to let the Seer be a benevolent ruler. They had wanted the power for themselves. And if they had taken over the world, they would have killed each other to be the last man standing.

A crashing sound came from the cottage, and as Brody

turned toward the door, the orange tabby ran out and meowed at him.

"What have you done now, Trouble?" Brody asked the cat
as he walked back into the cottage. "Seer!"

The old man had collapsed on the floor next to the table.

"Seer?" Brody rolled him onto his back. The old man's
skin was ashen, his sunken eyes closed, his breathing shallow.
"Don't die on me now." When he picked the Seer up, his
heart ached at how light the old man was. He gently deposited him on his bed.

The Seer moaned and opened his eyes.

"I'm here." Brody enveloped the old man's hand in his own.

"I thought you'd left me," the Seer whispered. "I thought
you must hate me."

"No, no." Brody sat on the bed beside him. "How can I stay
angry with the man who saved my life? Don't worry about anything. I'll nurse you back to health, just as you did me."

The Seer's eyes filled with tears. "You are the best thing
that ever happened to me. You and my daughter."

Brody blinked away tears. He could only hope that this
mysterious daughter would make her appearance soon.

The Seer drew in a long breath that seemed to rattle in his
chest. "When you washed up half-dead on the island, I realized my mistake. The people I had trusted were evil. And that
was when my visions started to fade. I no longer deserved the
gift, not when I was so guilty."

"You're not guilty, old man. You simply wanted a better
world. There is no crime in that. It was the other members of
the Circle who used your idea for their own selfish gain."

The Seer gave him the hint of a smile. "You were always a
good boy, Brody."

He winced. "Not that good. I know you're not up to it,
but I need to ask you some questions."

The Seer shook his head. "Too tired. The answers are in my journal."

"Where is that?"

The Seer's eyes closed and for a terrifying second, Brody thought he was gone. "In the hiding place," the old man whispered.

That didn't help much. "You may not know this, but two of the Circle members are dead: Lord Morris and General Caladras. The Chameleon is left." Brody grimaced. "And you. Who is the last member?"

"Cahira." The Seer's voice was so faint, Brody wasn't sure he'd heard it right.

"A woman?" Brody asked. Oh, right, it had to be the woman who had seduced the Seer and said she would help him. "Who is she? Where is she?"

"She . . . she lied to me," the Seer whispered. "Told me our daughter was dead."

"She's the mother of your daughter?" Brody asked. Then this daughter couldn't be that old, after all.

The Seer squeezed Brody's hand slightly. "Please look after my daughter."

"Of course." Although Brody had no idea who or where she might be. "Is she with her mother? Where can I find Cahira?"

"No need to look for Cahira." The Seer coughed. "She will find you."

"How?"

"Saw her last week. She . . ." The Seer paused for a moment, breathing hard. "She thought I was too sick to live alone. She's sending a ship here to take me to her castle."

"She has a castle? Where? And if she was so worried about you, why did she leave you here?"

"She didn't come . . . in a boat."

"What? Then how—" Brody stiffened when, suddenly, the Seer gripped his hand with a surprising burst of strength.

"You must take my place," the Seer ordered. "Pretend to be me and go to her castle."

"But . . . what about you?"

The Seer let go of Brody's hand and his eyes grew unfocused once again. "I will not be here."

Brody blinked away tears. He wanted to object, but he could see that the Seer was telling the truth. His death was coming soon. "I don't want to impersonate you. We always agreed that it was morally wrong for me to pretend to be another person."

"You must." The Seer's eyes closed. "You must."

Brody suppressed a groan. Only once in his life had he ever tried to shift into another person's image. At the age of eleven, he'd thought it would be funny to impersonate the Seer, but his jest had not gone well. The Seer had scolded him, explaining how harmful it was to steal a person's identity. Brody had accepted the Seer's words, but it wasn't until much later, when he saw the damage the Chameleon was causing, that he understood how evil it truly was. He didn't even want to try it. Wouldn't that make him just as bad as the Chameleon?

"Seer," he began, but realized the old man had lost consciousness. He leaned over and could barely hear the dying man's shallow breaths. With a sigh, he straightened. There was nothing he could do but wait.

He stood and paced around the cottage. Then he remembered he needed to find the journal. For the next hour, he alternated among three things: checking on the Seer, stirring the soup, and searching for the journal. He looked everywhere, but couldn't find it. Finally, he helped himself to some soup and gave the cat a bowl of chicken meat and broth.

The Seer kept breathing, and Brody realized it would be a long night. If the Seer needed any assistance, Brody would have to be in human form to help him. With less than an hour left of his allotted time to be human, he needed to be careful how he spent it. So he shifted into a dog.

With a screech, the cat jumped straight into the air.

"But I'm a friendly dog," Brody growled at him.

The cat hissed and hunched his back, his fur bristling.

Brody sighed. It was going to be a long night. He curled up on his bed and kept watch.

Sometime, just before midnight, the Seer's breathing stopped. Brody sat up, listening carefully. He shifted into human form and sat on the Seer's bed.

"Seer?" Brody's eyes filled with tears. The man who had been a father to him was dead.

Onboard the Eberoni ship, Maeve turned over in the narrow bed as a tingling feeling started in her head and crept down her spine. Ignoring it, she fell back asleep.

She was floating in the air, surrounded by mist. As she moved slowly forward, a patch of wispy clouds parted before her and she saw a green island surrounded by a narrow belt of turquoise sea. White sandy beaches. Bluffs of long green grass rustling in the breeze. As the sun rose in the east, horizontal rays shot through the mist, and when the light hit the grass, the morning dew sparkled like a sea of stars.

Just as she was thinking what a lovely island this was, a film of mist drifted in front of her and obscured her vision. Still, she floated toward the island, aware somehow in her dream that time was passing. Then the mist parted, revealing a man alone on a bluff. He had a shovel and was moving a pile of earth back into a hole. A grave.

It started to rain, but still the man worked. His shirt and breeches grew wet and stuck to his skin. He was tall, lean, and muscular. His black shaggy hair swooped forward, hiding his face. He tamped down the last of the dirt, then began to pile stones on the grave. With the last stone in place, he collapsed onto his knees. When he lifted his eyes to the heavens, his hair fell away from his tear-stained face.

Brody.

Maeve woke with a jerk and sat up. The cabin was dark, the only sounds the creaking of the ship. She rubbed her brow as another strange feeling swept through her head. It made her feel light, as if she were floating on the sea.

She shook her head. It was probably just a reaction from sleeping on the ship. But the dream had seemed so real. An island. Mist.

Was Brody on the Isle of Mist?

Unable to sleep after her dream, Maeve eventually gave up, got dressed, and went up onto the quarterdeck. Only a helmsman was there at the wheel. Captain Shaw and Nevis were both asleep, so she sat on top of a trunk and entertained herself by gazing at the stars. The two moons, Luna and Lessa, were almost full. Tomorrow night she would be able to shift at the beach near the convent. She smiled to herself. It would be good to see her seal friends again. She'd missed them.

Her smile faded, though, as she realized tomorrow would mark a full two months since she'd last seen Brody. The sun peeked over the horizon, and the sudden burst of light made her remember the dream she'd had. What if it was more than a dream? Could Brody be on the Isle of Mist right now, digging a grave? For whom? As far as she knew, only the Seer lived there.

She recalled once again how Brody looked while in human form. Nevis and Leo liked to tease him for having hair like a girl's, but it wasn't all that long, only to his shoulders. According to Brody, his time as a human was so limited, he never wanted to spare the few minutes it would take to chop off a few inches. Maeve had always wondered if his shaggy black hair was as soft and silky as his fur when he was a dog.

It was amusing, now that she thought about it, that no one thought twice about giving canine Brody a pat on the head or a rub behind his ears. She'd certainly hugged him, petted him, even cooed to him that he was such a pretty dog. Good goddesses, she would be far too shy to touch him like that when he was human.

But Brody never objected to being petted. Was it the only affection the man ever received? Was his life a lonely one?

Maeve sighed. A few times she had caught a haunted, sad look in his beautiful blue eyes. Whenever he became human, the black patch of fur that surrounded his left eye as a dog was transformed into a small freckle at the outside corner of his eye. The only freckle on his face. It always drew her attention, making her want to touch it, kiss it . . .

"You're up early," said Captain Shaw, interrupting her thoughts as he joined her on the quarterdeck.

"Oh, good morning." She jumped to her feet. "Captain, would it be possible to take me to the Isle of Mist later today?"

His bushy gray eyebrows rose in surprise. "I suppose so. Queen Luciana asked me to take you wherever you wanted."

"Oh, that's wonderful. Thank you!"

"What's wonderful?" Nevis asked as he climbed onto the quarterdeck. His brown hair was sticking out in odd directions and he needed a shave. "I hope it's breakfast."

"Breakfast should be ready soon," the captain told him.

"Land ahoy!" the man in the crow's nest shouted.

"There." Captain Shaw pointed northwest, where a strip of land could barely be seen. "The Isle of Moon. We should reach port in a few hours. Excuse me." He strode toward the helmsman to give directions.

Nevis scratched at his whiskers. "Good. That gives us enough time to eat."

Maeve gave him a wry look. "You seem to think about food quite a bit."

"This is muscle not fat." He patted his torso. "And you never told me what was so wonderful."

"The captain has agreed to take us to the Isle of Mist later today."

Nevis snorted. "Why are we bothering to go there? No one lives there but—oh, I see. You're planning to ask the Seer where Brody is."

She nodded. "And the Embraced army."

Nevis shrugged. "I guess it's worth a try. Actually, I've always wanted to meet the Seer."

"Me, too." She took a deep breath. "I think Brody might be there."

"What?" Nevis blinked. "Why would you think that?"

"I saw him there . . . in a dream."

Nevis scoffed. "Right."

"It seemed real."

"Most dreams do. But they're just dreams."

Maeve shrugged. "You don't have to go if you don't want to."

Nevis gritted his teeth. "I'll go."

She crossed her arms, frowning. No doubt, Nevis didn't appreciate being her babysitter. He was a colonel in the army, after all. But she didn't care for this situation, either.

A light rain began, and with a muttered curse, Nevis excused himself and went back to his cabin. Maeve followed more slowly, recalling how it had rained in her dream.

Two hours later, the ship dropped anchor in the bay of the port town of Luna. The capital of the Isles of Moon and Mist, it was named after the larger of the two moons. The rain had stopped, so Maeve brought her bag up on deck. Luna looked much the same as the last time she'd seen the town. Queen Esther's castle, named Lessa Castle after the smaller of the two moons, sat on a hill overlooking the port. The gray stone castle looked a bit dreary compared to the surrounding cottages, which were painted in shades of peach, shell pink, green, and blue.

On the ship, sailors worked around her, stacking the crates she would take to the convent and the packages Nevis would present to the queen. They lowered the boats so they could row the packages ashore.

Nevis met her on deck, looking much better now that he'd combed his hair, shaved, and put on his uniform. "All right, this is the plan."

She sighed. Instead of Luciana bossing her around, now Nevis was doing it.

"After we go ashore, I'll hire a wagon and take you and the crates to the convent," Nevis explained. "Then, I'll go to the castle to meet the queen. About midday, I'll pick you up and bring you back here for the voyage to the Isle of Mist. I just have one question. Do you think the nuns would feed me lunch?"

Maeve snorted. Nevis definitely had his priorities. "Yes, I'm sure they will."

"Excellent." Nevis clapped his hands together. "I've already checked with Captain Shaw. He'll be ready to sail this afternoon." He turned to the sailors and told them to start unloading the packages.

Using ropes and pulleys, the sailors lowered half of the packages into one rowboat and the other half into a second one.

Maeve leaned over the railing to watch and grinned when a seal broke through the turquoise water and barked at her. Was it one of her seal friends? Or perhaps . . . "Brody, is that you?"

"It's just a seal," Nevis muttered.

"I have good reason to suppose it could be Brody," Maeve insisted. "He sometimes takes the form of a seal."

Nevis shrugged. "I thought you said he was on the Isle of Mist."

True. Maeve smiled to herself. If her dream had been correct, she would see Brody this afternoon.

* * *

As Brody set the last rock on top of the pile of stones he'd laid on the Seer's grave, another wave of grief crashed over him, doubling him up. It had started raining earlier, and he could no longer tell whether it was tears or raindrops that slid down his cheeks to splatter on the ground.

The stones were gray. The sky was gray. They were as bleak and cold as the hard knot of pain lodged in his heart. The old man had been a father to him for fifteen years. Longer than the ten years he'd had with his real father. And his older brother.

Brody's mother was still alive, but she'd wept so much when he'd told her about the curse that it had ripped his heart to shreds. He'd realized then that he couldn't live at home. He couldn't subject his mother to the pain of seeing him trapped in the body of an animal day after day. So, he had sworn to her and himself that he would find the witch and undo the curse. Only then would he be able to return to his mother and sister.

But he'd lived with the curse now for fifteen years. More than half of his life. For the last nine years, he'd hunted for that witch. And he'd failed.

He was a human who couldn't be human.

He fell to his knees, then looked up at the heavens as more tears ran down his cheeks. "Why? What have I done to deserve this?"

There was no answer. There never was.

With a sigh, he wiped his face. Was this what the old man had seen in his third vision? He'd seen Brody by his grave, crying. A prick of guilt jabbed at him. Instead of mourning as he should, he was indulging in self-pity. Dammit.

If the Seer was here, he would have slapped him back to his senses. *Don't waste your time, boy, lamenting the past,* the old man would have told him. *You can't change what happened in the past, but you can change the future. So get off your ass and keep trying.*

Over the years, Brody had heard that advice over and over again. Was that what had happened to the old man? Had he taken his own advice so seriously that he'd tried the change the future?

Brody leaned forward and rested a hand on one of the rocks on the Seer's grave. It was cold and slick from the rain. "I won't tell anyone." *I'll never tell anyone that you were the first member of the Circle of Five, that you created that villainous ring of bastards.*

Another tear rolled down his cheek. "I never did enough for you, old man. Raising me was hard, I know." At the age of ten, Brody had recovered physically from the disaster that had caused so much death and left him cursed, but mentally and emotionally, he'd been filled with anger and despair. And the only one available to lash out at was the Seer. But the old man had always treated him with love and patience.

"You helped make me the man I am today." Brody shoved his wet hair out of his face. "So, rest in peace. I'll never tell what you did. I'll protect your reputation. It's the . . . only thing I can do for you now, old man."

He rose to his feet and carried the shovel back to the cottage. When the boat from Cahira arrived, he would board it disguised as the Seer. Then, once he was rid of Cahira and the Chameleon, the Circle would be completely gone. No one would ever know that the Seer had conspired with the others. He would be remembered simply as the kindly old man who had shared his visions with the world.

So what should he do, Brody wondered, while he waited for that ship to arrive? Oh, he still needed to find that journal. Could he search for it in animal form? He'd used up most of his allotted time as a human in order to bury the Seer.

He dashed into the cottage, stripped and shifted into his most comfortable animal form, the shaggy black-and-white dog. The cat hissed at him, but he ignored the tabby and dug around in the garden. No journal there. And it wasn't inside the cottage. He'd checked that thoroughly the night before.

Dammit, where would the Seer hide such a thing? The old man had never been the sort to hide anything. It had been Brody who had hidden himself when anyone came to the island.

Was that what the Seer had meant? Brody's hiding place? He hurried to the beach where he had landed the day before and trotted into the cave. After rooting around, he found nothing buried there. He eyed the trunk that held his spare clothing. Could it be that simple?

He managed to open the trunk and dug through the clothes till he reached the bottom. And there, he found a leather-bound book. The journal! He grabbed it in his teeth and headed back to the cottage.

As he crossed the highest point on the island, he paused to look around. There, to the south, was that a ship? It seemed to be headed straight for the Isle of Mist. Was it the ship Cahira had sent? Or perhaps it was the Seer's mysterious daughter whom the old man had claimed was on her way.

He ran into the cottage to drop the journal on his bed, then dashed out again, turning into a pelican. As he flew toward the ship, he noted the red-and-black flag flapping in the wind on the mainsail. An Eberoni ship? What was it doing here? He drew closer and noticed two familiar people at the bow. Maeve and Nevis? What the hell were they doing here? And damn, but she looked more beautiful than ever.

The wind was whipping at her braid of long black hair, loosening tendrils that curled around her face. Her delicate black eyebrows always made a startling contrast to the pale creaminess of her skin. And the natural pink color of her lips.

She was stunning. She'd always been stunning. Fortunately, he was usually in dog form, so no one questioned the amount of drool coming from his mouth.

He dropped down lower and passed over the ship so he could hear them talking.

"Look! There's another one." Maeve pointed at the ocean, where a shiny black seal had just surfaced.

"It's not Brody," Nevis muttered. "How many times do I have to tell you that?"

Maeve sighed. "I know. I'm just so terribly worried about him."

Worried? She was worried about him? Brody tipped to the side and landed clumsily on deck. He hopped out of the way when a sailor nearly kicked him, then flapped his wings to lift himself up onto the railing not far from Nevis and Maeve.

"Seems to me that you're more than worried," Nevis mumbled. "Brody's on your mind all the time."

Maeve blushed. "I just hope he's on the Isle of Mist. Or, if he isn't, that the Seer will be able to tell me where he is."

Brody waddled along the railing so he could get closer. Maeve had come all this way to look for him? Damn.

"And I hope the Seer can tell us where the Embraced army is hiding," Maeve added.

Brody flinched and one of his webbed feet slipped. Splat. He hit the deck hard. Dammit to hell! What was Maeve doing? She shouldn't be involved in this. It was too dangerous! She should be safe at Ebton Palace. Why the hell had Leo and Luciana let her come here?

Apparently, his fall had made too much noise, for Maeve and Nevis spun around and spotted him. He folded his legs under him and squatted down as if it was something he did all the time. He slanted a wary glance their way to see if they were still looking at him.

Maeve's eyes narrowed. "Brody?"

"Oh, for Light's sake!" Nevis shouted as he clenched his

fists. "Would you please stop calling every animal you see Brody?"

Maeve shot him an annoyed look. "I have good reason to be suspicious. Brody has taken the form of a pelican before."

With a snort, Nevis motioned toward the pelican. "That's the scroungiest-looking bird I've ever seen. Brody would never look that bad. And did you see its eyes? It obviously has the intelligence of a flea."

Brody aimed a glare at Nevis, then flapped his wings to take off.

"I think you hurt his feelings." Maeve's voice could barely be heard as he flew toward the island.

"It didn't understand me!" Nevis yelled. "It's a bloody bird!"

Back in the cottage, Brody shifted into a dog. What should he do? He paced back and forth, considering his options. Soon, Maeve and Nevis would be taking a rowboat to the Isle of Mist. Should he meet them in human form? But which human—Brody or the Seer?

If he met them as Brody, they would be happy to see him. He paused in his pacing to marvel once again that Maeve had been so worried about him, she'd come all this way in hopes of finding him.

He'd always thought that she didn't care for him. After all, she kept insulting him by calling him Julia.

But he certainly cared about her. From the minute he'd first seen her, he'd known she was special. He'd known that she would grow up to be beautiful. And she had. He'd known that just the sound of her voice and laughter would attract men in droves. And it had. She had a long line of suitors at Ebton Palace.

He hated it. He wanted to growl at all of them and chase them away. It was laughable. Pathetic. A dog who wanted the most beautiful woman in the world for himself?

So he had decided to avoid her. Remain aloof. The only

time he allowed himself to enjoy her company was once a month when he could disguise himself as a seal or river otter.

He would need to disguise himself once again. This time, as the Seer. He could tell her that Brody was alive and well. And that, as the Seer, he had envisioned her future. She was supposed to go back to Ebton Palace, where she would be safe.

His heart ached at the thought of deceiving her, but what else could he do? If she had any feelings for him, he had to put a stop to them. He didn't know if he would ever get rid of this damned curse, and he could never ask her to share his accursed life. Maeve was too special, too sweet to be stuck with a man who could be a husband for only two hours a day.

And there was another reason for his impersonating the Seer. He didn't want to tell anyone that the Seer had died. If the news spread that the Seer was gone, then Cahira might not send that boat, and he'd lose his chance to capture one of the last members of the Circle of Five. He had to get rid of the Circle to protect the Seer's reputation.

But could he pull it off? He'd never masqueraded as another person before. Nevis was a close friend, and Maeve—well, she had guessed who he was while in pelican form. Would he be able to fool them both?

Chapter 4

Maeve scanned the beach as Nevis rowed their small boat toward the Isle of Mist. There was no one there. "I suppose we'll have to wander about until we find the Seer's house?"

"Actually, he will find us." Nevis glanced over his shoulder. "You see the bluff just above the beach? There's a pole up there with a red flag."

She shaded her eyes with a hand so she could see through the glare of the afternoon sun. The wind had died down momentarily, so the red flag was hanging limply along the pole. "Oh, right. I see it."

"That's how we knew which beach to come to. And I heard there's a bell at the base of the pole. If we ring it, the Seer will come."

"How do you know all this?"

Nevis exhaled as he heaved on the oars. "I asked around the docks at Luna and found the sailors who bring the Seer his supplies every month. They told me what to do."

"I see." Maeve checked the basket on her lap, making sure the linen cloth was tucked in. Mother Ginessa and the sisters at the convent had helped her put together this last-minute gift for the Seer. Underneath the cloth, there was a loaf of freshly baked bread, a crock of strawberry jam, cheese, and a bottle of wine.

The rowboat thudded to a stop when the bottom hit sand. "Careful." Nevis reached for Maeve as she stood up.

"I'm fine." She gripped the basket handle with one hand and lifted the skirt of her cream-colored convent gown with the other. Stepping into the shallow bay, she winced as the cool water came up to her calves and seeped into her thin leather shoes. Quickly, she waded toward the shore, while Nevis jumped out and hauled the boat up onto the beach.

"There." She pointed to a path that wound up to the bluff.

"I'll carry the basket," he offered, and she handed it to him.

Her shoes made squishing noises with each step and were soon coated, inside and out, with sand. She glanced with envy at Nevis's knee-high boots. Maybe she should take a lesson from her sister Sorcha and start dressing like a man. Climbing this steep path would certainly be easier without a long gown that was made heavier by its sodden hem.

Halfway up, she paused to catch her breath.

Nevis stopped beside her. "I hope we have better luck with the Seer than I did with the queen."

"Why? Did your meeting not go well?"

"It didn't go at all." He shifted the basket from one hand to the other. "I took the gifts to the waiting room and requested a meeting. The secretary took the gifts inside, then came back to tell me that the queen was busy. I said I would wait, and so I did for over two hours. Finally, I had to leave because we had this trip already planned."

"I wonder why she's reluctant to see you."

Nevis shrugged. "I thought she must be unfriendly, but then I learned at the docks that she's the one paying for most of the Seer's supplies."

Maeve nodded. "She was always very generous with the convent, too."

"Have you ever met her?"

"No." Maeve frowned. "Now that I think about it, I never heard of her ever leaving the castle. Even for celebrations."

Nevis grunted. "Maybe she's old. Or sick." He headed up the path. "Come on."

After a few more minutes of climbing, they reached the top of the bluff, then followed the worn path to the pole. Nevis set the basket down next to a wooden box that contained a large bell.

"I guess this keeps the bell from clanging in the wind." Nevis grabbed the bell, and it immediately made a loud clatter.

Maeve touched his sleeve. "You can stop." She motioned to where a man was standing across a grassy meadow on the summit of a low hill.

He seemed to be watching them, although his face was not visible. The voluminous hood of his cloak had been pulled forward till only a narrow gash of black could be seen. A breeze caught the hem of his brown cloak and fluttered it around long legs encased in brown breeches.

Was this really the Seer? Maeve had always heard that he was very old, but something about this man seemed young, healthy, and strong. Was it the way he was standing? His back was straight, his broad shoulders squared. With one hand, he gripped a long staff, but he didn't appear to be leaning on it for support.

But as quickly as she noticed these things, they disappeared. The man hunched over, and with a shaky arm, he planted the staff on the path in front of him, then shuffled slowly toward it. Staff, step, step. Staff, step, step.

With a groan, Nevis set the bell back into the box. "At the speed he's going, we'll meet him in a week."

"Aye. The bread will have grown mold," Maeve muttered, causing Nevis to snort.

"Let's go." He handed her the basket, then strode across the meadow, calling out, "Greetings, Great Seer, we have come to—"

"Why are you in such a hurry?" the Seer replied with a deep, grumbly voice. "Colonel Harden."

Nevis halted with a jerk. "You know who I am?"

The old man shrugged his shoulders. "I am the Seer." He continued his slow journey down the hillside. "You are Nevis, son of General Harden, best friend to King Leofric of Eberon."

Nevis gulped audibly, then whispered to Maeve, "By the Light, he's good."

Maeve curtsied. "It is an honor to finally meet you, Great Seer. I have brought you a gift from the Convent of—"

"The Two Moons," the Seer finished her sentence. "Where you grew up with your four sisters, who are now queens."

"Whoa," Nevis whispered. "He *does* know everything."

Maeve winced. He knew who she was, but only because of her sisters.

The Seer reached the base of the hill and paused. "You are Maeve. The most beautiful of the five sisters."

Her mouth dropped open.

The Seer walked slowly toward her. "You are special. A selkie. And a siren. When you sing, men will cross oceans to hear the sound of your voice. When you laugh, they will lose their hearts to you."

Maeve was so stunned she was speechless for a moment. "I—surely you are exaggerating, Great Seer." She turned to Nevis. "Would you cross an ocean to hear my voice?"

He shook his head. "No. Though I might if you made a cherry pie."

She snorted. Nevis and his priorities.

"You have a long line of suitors at Ebton Palace," the Seer continued in his grumbly voice. "That is where you should be."

Her back stiffened. Here was yet another person who was trying to order her about. And get her married off. "Begging your pardon, Great Seer, but I did not come to have my future told. I came—"

"Because you are looking for Brody," the Seer muttered. "And the Embraced army."

Her mouth fell open again, while Nevis cursed under his breath.

The Seer picked up his staff and planted it hard on the ground between them. "What you seek is dangerous. You must go home to Ebton. I have seen your future, and that is where you belong."

She swallowed hard. "I appreciate your concern, but I prefer to make my own decisions." A chill ran down her spine as she felt the Seer glowering at her through the dark gash of his hood. "Do you know where the Embraced army is hiding?"

"Would I be foolish enough to tell you that?"

She winced inwardly. She'd always heard that the Seer was a kindly old man, but this person was decidedly unfriendly. And overbearing. "Will you at least tell me where Brody is?"

The Seer's bony hand tightened around the staff until his knuckles turned white. "He is fine. There is no need for you to be concerned—"

"I *will* be concerned until I can see for myself that he is safe." She took a deep breath to steady her nerves. "I have reason to believe he was here on the Isle of Mist."

The Seer tilted his head. "Why do you think that?"

"I—" She shifted her weight. "I saw him in a dream. He was burying someone on a bluff overlooking the ocean."

The Seer flinched. He turned away for a moment, his hand flexing around the staff. When he finally spoke, it sounded as if his teeth were gritted together. "You are mistaken. There is no one here but me."

"I told you it was just a dream," Nevis whispered to her.

Maeve groaned. This meeting was going nowhere. Frustration pricked her, and as her gaze drifted about, it caught on something moving stealthily through the long grass. Orange-striped fur and a pair of golden eyes. "Oh, you have a cat."

"Trouble," the Seer muttered as the animal stalked closer to them.

"He causes trouble?" Maeve set the basket on the ground as she hunkered down and beckoned to the cat. "But he looks so cute."

"He is Trouble. That's his name." The Seer turned toward the cat, his brown cloak swinging around his long legs.

Maeve reached toward the cat to pet him, but he suddenly arched his back and hissed at the Seer. "Oh, my." She jerked her hand back.

The cat growled at the Seer, then darted away, disappearing over the hill.

How odd, Maeve thought as she straightened. The cat didn't seem to like his owner. "Is your house far away? We would be happy to carry this basket—"

"No need," the Seer replied, his voice sounding like a rusty hinge. "I thank you for the gift, but I can manage on my own."

"We will take our leave then." Nevis set the basket close to the Seer's feet. "Thank you for seeing us."

"But I need to know where Brody is," Maeve insisted.

"Maeve." Nevis leaned close to whisper in her ear. "I think we've overstayed our welcome."

Damn, but this was too frustrating. "You know everything, don't you?" she asked the Seer. "So you must know where Brody is. Please help me. I can't go home until I see him."

"Why?" The Seer's voice sounded strained. "Do you really care that much?"

"Yes. I do."

The Seer turned away, his head bowed as if he were in pain. "You must cast those feelings aside. It is a waste of your time."

She bristled. "How can you say that? I'm beginning to wonder if you even know Brody. Because if you did, you would know how wonderful he is. He's smart, loyal, courageous—"

"*Stop!* He cannot be the man you wish him to be." The Seer turned to her, pushing back the hood from his head. "You must believe me."

She quickly noted the Seer's wrinkled face and long silver hair, but what drew her attention were his eyes. A white film clouded his pupils, but she could still spot a glint of blue. A familiar blue. And there had been something odd about his voice when he'd shouted. The grumbly tone had disappeared, leaving his voice with a much sharper sound.

"Go home," the Seer snarled.

"Maeve." Nevis took hold of her arm.

Her eyes burned with hot tears. "I will not give up on Brody."

The Seer stabbed angrily at the ground with his staff. "You must! The man is cursed. He will not allow anyone to share his miserable life. Especially you. Go home where you belong."

She gritted her teeth. "I will remain at the convent. If you see Brody, tell him to meet me there. I will not return to Ebton Palace until I have seen him."

The Seer leaned on his staff, closing his eyes briefly. "Then wait till tomorrow night. When the moons are full, you will have your answers."

Her heart leaped up her throat. "Brody will come see me?"

The Seer gave her a sad look. "You will have your answers, but they will not be what you want to hear. Farewell to you both. Do not come here again." He leaned over to grab the basket, then started slowly up the hill.

"Farewell, Great Seer." Nevis bowed his head.

"Take care." Maeve watched as the old man trudged slowly back up the hill.

"Let's go," Nevis said as the Seer disappeared from view.

"Just a moment." Maeve waited a while, then started up the hill.

"What are you doing?" Nevis whispered as he followed her. "We were told to leave."

She reached the summit and noted the Seer in the distance. He had walked much farther than she had expected. In fact, he was moving rather quickly now. His back was straight again, his stride young and purposeful.

"That's odd," Nevis grumbled.

"I know." Maeve narrowed her eyes as she watched the Seer. Why was he walking so differently now? Why had his own cat hissed at him? And why had the blue in his eyes reminded her of Brody? She turned in place, scanning the island from the summit of the hill.

Her breath caught. There, far to the east, was a cairn marking a grave. A pile of stones on a grassy bluff, just as she had seen in her dream. Brody had been here. She was sure of it.

"Can we go now?" Nevis asked impatiently.

"Aye." Deep in thought, she followed Nevis down to the beach. Tomorrow night she would have her answers? She hoped that meant that when she shifted into a seal, Brody would come see her. She needed some answers. For this trip to the Isle of Mist had only left her with more questions.

Damn, damn, damn! Brody cursed with each step he took toward the cottage. He never should have agreed to meet Maeve again. But at the same time, his heart was racing at the thought of spending time alone with her.

You, fool! Now she would know that he was the one who had played with her every month in the guise of a seal or otter. If she discovered how much he cared for her, he would never convince her to forget about him. But at the same time, a secret corner of his heart thrilled at the idea that Maeve would finally know his true feelings. His beautiful, sweet Maeve.

But damn, he'd never realized before how stubborn she could be. The woman had refused to leave until he'd agreed to see her. A startling thought made him stumble to a stop. How well did he really know Maeve? Whenever he was in human form, he had avoided her. And the times he'd visited her as a seal or otter had merely been spent playing chase in the water. Hell, this was the longest conversation he'd ever had with her, and she hadn't even known it was he.

With a sigh, he started toward the cottage once more, his steps going faster and faster. His allotted time as a human must be almost over, since it had taken him so long to bury the Seer this morning. That was why he had tried to get rid of Nevis and Maeve as quickly as possible. It would have been awful if he'd been forced to shift in front of them. They would have realized the trick he'd played on them. And that he was capable of impersonating people. Just like that bastard Chameleon.

He dashed into the cottage and quickly unloaded the basket on the table. Good goddesses, fresh bread. It had been two months since he'd last eaten any. He tore off a hunk and spread strawberry jam on it. Oh damn, that was melt-in-his-mouth good.

Worried that at any minute he would have to shift and lose the ability to use his hands, he quickly sliced up the cheese and opened the bottle of wine. Meanwhile, the cat snuck into the house and began rubbing against his legs.

"Oh, now you want to be friends?" He tossed some left-over chicken into a bowl. "I see your attitude has changed now that you're hungry."

He took off the brown cloak and hung it on the peg by the door. As he returned to the table, his gaze caught sight of the journal on his bed. Even though he could read while in dog form, turning the pages would be difficult. He'd better get some reading done while he still could.

With a plate full of food and a glass full of wine, he settled at the table and opened the journal to the first entry.

Late summer, Year 624.
This morning I buried my father.

Brody sighed, then took a sip of wine. It was year 700 now, and he'd just done the same thing.

> My father was the Seer. My grandfather was the Seer. And now I am the Seer.
>
> My name is Burien of Aerland, the last full-blooded male of an ancient race of sorcerers. I came here to the Isle of Mist two years ago to take care of my ailing father.
>
> For the first twenty-three years of my life, I lived with my mother on the Isle of Moon, while my father lived here alone. We visited him occasionally, but he always claimed that the visions were clearer when there was no one else around, no other noise or distractions to clog up his mind. It was the fate of the Seer to endure a life of loneliness.
>
> That is now my fate.
>
> I am prepared. I have started this journal as my father instructed, so I can record my visions. My father was ninety-three when he passed away. I am twenty-five. The thought of living here alone until I die is daunting.
>
> But this is now my fate.
>
> Right after my father exhaled his last breath, I felt an odd tingling sensation in my head as his gift was transferred to me.

Brody stopped reading to take a bite of cheese. Had the Seer's gift been transferred to his daughter last night? When would she be arriving here? He slathered more jam on a piece of bread so he could eat while he continued reading.

> Tonight, in my sleep, I may experience my first vision. According to my father, it will come to me in my sleep as a dream.

A dream. Brody finished his slice of bread, then licked the jam off his fingers. A dream? Something needled his thoughts, something just beyond his reach. Dammit, what was it?

He took a long drink of wine. *"I saw him in a dream. He was burying someone on a bluff overlooking the ocean."*

He choked and sputtered wine onto the table. Good goddesses, when Maeve had said that, it had sent a chill down his spine. How the hell had she known? He hadn't been able to believe it, and so he had dismissed it. Ignored it and gone on with his attempt to get rid of her and Nevis as quickly as possible.

But had Maeve actually dreamed of him burying the Seer?

With a jolt, Brody leaped to his feet, causing his chair to topple over with a clatter. The cat sprang into the air, then hissed at him and ran out the front door.

"Maeve." The cottage swirled around him, and Brody stumbled, catching onto the edge of the table to keep from falling. The Seer had claimed that his daughter was coming, and the only female to arrive so far . . . "Maeve."

She'd come to the island. She'd had a dream that had come true. And she'd grown up not knowing who her parents were.

"Goddesses, no." Brody shook his head. If Maeve's father was the Seer, then her mother was Cahira. Her parents would be the first two members of the Circle of Five.

"Oh, shit, no." He dragged a hand down his face and was surprised by the large number of wrinkles he felt. Oh right, he was still in the guise of the Seer. But dammit, if the old man was her father, then did that make Maeve the Seer now?

"Oh, hell, no." He paced about the cottage. No, dammit, he didn't want that kind of future for Maeve. He'd known the Seer for fifteen years. He knew too well how heavy the Seer's gift had weighed on him.

And how would Maeve feel if she ever found out that both her parents had been in the Circle of Five? As far as Brody could tell, this Cahira had been the one to pervert the Seer's idea and turn it into an evil plan to take over the world. Cahira was the one he needed to get rid of in order to protect the Seer's reputation.

Oh, dear goddesses, how could he kill Maeve's mother? He winced. That would certainly put an end to any feelings she might have for him. But how devastating it would be if Maeve learned what her parents had done.

He couldn't tell her. If what he suspected was true, it would tear Maeve's heart in two. It would destroy any chance she had for a happy life.

Hadn't he promised the Seer that he would look after his daughter? So obviously, he had to keep Maeve from becoming embroiled in this mess. It would be too dangerous for her. Too painful.

Tomorrow night, he would convince her to go home. Then he would take care of Cahira himself. And the Chameleon. The Circle of Five would be no more. The world would be safe. The Seer's reputation would be safe. And Maeve would be free to live her life without the burden of knowing the truth.

Brody took a deep breath. He could do this. For now, he needed all the information he could gather on Cahira. As far as he could tell, she was not a nice woman. She'd used the Seer to promote her own evil plan. And she'd abandoned Maeve as a wee babe. Hell, she'd even told the Seer that his daughter was dead.

If Brody was going to succeed in this masquerade, he needed to know everything the Seer had known. He set the chair back on its legs and sat down to read.

For the next fifty pages or so, the journal described the Seer's daily life and the visions he had several times a week. Always bad. War. Destruction. Plague. Despair.

Brody finished the bottle of wine and kept reading. When

the light began to dim, he lit the lantern and built up the fire in the hearth. And that was when it struck him.

He was still human. Still the Seer.

His heart raced. Was he cured? He attempted to change back to his own body, but instead, he ended up as a dog.

Trouble, who had come inside earlier, hissed at him.

Brody trotted outside and lifted a hindleg to relieve himself against the garden wall. How had he managed to stay human for so long?

He thought back, remembering that horrific day. The sound of the witch's voice would be forever imprinted on his mind, but what had been her exact words?

He'd been so frantic and terrified at the time. The ship had suddenly cracked in two. Sailors had screamed and scrambled to latch on to anything in order to keep from falling into the ocean. As the ship began to sink, there were more screams. Brody's father had desperately tried to protect his two sons. Unlike the other sailors, Brody and his brother had known how to swim, and they had stayed close to their father, hanging on to broken boards. But drowning sailors had kept grabbing at them, pulling them under.

It was during one of these times, when Brody had been yanked far underwater, that his Embraced gift had suddenly been activated for the first time. He'd shifted into a seal. Able to wriggle free from the grasping hands, he had surfaced, only to find his father floating lifeless among the wreckage.

Desperate, he'd dived back into the water, trying to locate his brother. But by the time he found him, it was too late. His brother was gone. All the sailors were gone.

Devastated, he'd let himself sink. And that was when he'd heard her voice, laughing at him through the depths of the ocean. Taunting him.

"You think you can escape my wrath, boy? I could kill you in an instant, but instead I will make you suffer. From now

on, you are doomed to live with a curse. You will be able to maintain your true form for no more than two hours a day."

True form? Brody paced about the garden. He'd always interpreted that as being able to hold a human form. But the Seer was not his true form.

He snorted. So he could be human for longer than two hours as long as he wasn't himself. He'd never realized it before because he'd never masqueraded as another person before.

In a way, it stank. He still couldn't be himself for very long. But it was also a good thing. Whenever Cahira came to pick up the Seer, he would be able to hold that form for as long as needed.

He shifted back into the Seer, then strode into the cottage to continue reading the journal. When Cahira's ship arrived for him, he would be ready.

He would do everything in his power to safeguard the Seer's reputation. And protect Maeve.

Chapter 5

That evening at the convent, Maeve continued to investigate her theory that other islands might have survived the destruction of Aerland. Mother Ginessa and a few of the older nuns had heard of the legend, and they agreed with her that the existence of another island was quite possible.

In the library, she discovered a map of decaying yellow parchment that showed the ancient continent. When she placed it side by side with a modern map, she could tell that the landmass had extended far to the south and west. The Isles of Moon and Mist had been on the northeastern edge of the continent.

She stayed up late into the night, skimming through the library's aged tomes until her eyes were burning with fatigue. For all her work, she learned very little new information.

The civilization had been quite advanced, with paved roads and elegant stone villas with pools overlooking the sea. Members of the ancient race had been capable of different kinds of sorcery—shifting into animals and sea creatures, telepathy, telekinetic abilities, the gift of foresight, and even mind control. Not surprisingly, the most powerful sorcerers belonged to the nobility, and so the continent experienced a turbulent and violent history as the different noble families constantly battled one another for the throne.

How sad, Maeve thought, that people so powerful hadn't been able to live more peacefully among themselves. In today's world, only the Embraced had similar powers. Perhaps the goddesses, in their wisdom, had decided it was better if such gifts were rare.

Even though she was exhausted, when Maeve finally collapsed on her bed she found herself unable to sleep. The old bedchamber that she had shared with her sisters seemed so empty now. Who would have believed back then that the four eldest girls would become queens?

And what did the future hold for her? Maeve wondered. According to the Seer, she would have answers tomorrow night. Would she see Brody? Would he finally admit that he'd been seeking her company in disguise every month for the past four years? Anticipation coursed through her, making sleep impossible.

Shortly before sunrise, she dragged herself to join the nuns at morning mass, where they said farewell to the moon goddesses, Luna and Lessa, and asked for their protection until they returned that evening. Afterward, the sisters headed to the dining hall to break their fast, and Nevis arrived in time to eat.

"Did you sleep onboard the ship last night?" Maeve asked as they loaded their plates with eggs, bacon, bread, butter, and strawberry jam.

Nevis shook his head. "I can't stand the thought of admitting failure to Leo, so I went back to Lessa Castle to request another meeting with Queen Esther."

"Did you see her?"

With a sigh, Nevis set his plate on a table and collapsed into a chair. "No, even though I waited several hours. By the time I gave up, all the rowboats had returned to the ship. So I took a room in an inn by the docks."

Maeve sat across from him. "I wonder why she's being so unfriendly." When Mother Ginessa sat next to her, she asked, "Have you seen the queen lately?"

"Not for a long time." Mother Ginessa tilted her head, thinking. "It must be nigh on fifteen years."

"Are you sure she's alive?" Nevis muttered, and Maeve shot him an annoyed look.

Mother Ginessa smiled. "Aye, I'm sure. She sends me a note every month with a generous donation."

"So you exchange letters with her?" Maeve asked.

Mother Ginessa nodded. "She always asks us to remember her husband and two sons in our prayers."

"Oh, that's right." Maeve recalled that during every mass, the nuns would beseech the goddesses to watch over a long list of people, and that list had always included King Rudgar and his sons. Growing up at the convent, she'd heard all the names recited several times a day, year after year. Eventually, she had ceased to pay much attention to them.

"What happened to them?" Nevis asked.

"They were lost at sea." Mother Ginessa made the sign of the moons. "May the goddesses keep them in a loving embrace."

Maeve joined her in making the sign of the moons. "I remember now. I was only about five years old when the news arrived that the king and his sons had died. People all over the island were in mourning."

"Aye, 'twas terribly sad." Mother Ginessa blinked away tears. "Poor Esther. Her heart was so broken, she closed herself off in the castle and has ne'er come out since."

Nevis narrowed his eyes. "Then who's running the country?"

Mother Ginessa gave him a wry look. "She may be heartbroken, but she's still responsible and attends to her duties. The Isle of Moon is not that large, so there isn't a great deal for her to do."

"What about her daughter?" Maeve asked. "Maybe Nevis would have better luck seeking an audience with her."

"Princess Elinor?" Mother Ginessa shrugged. "I'm not sure

that would work. From Esther's letters, it appears that the princess has very little interest in politics. She's an artist."

Nevis snorted. "Who does she think is going to run the place after her mother is gone?" He winced when Maeve kicked him under the table. "What?"

She smiled. "I thought we could spend the morning down at the docks, asking the sailors if they've ever seen or heard about islands to the south of here."

Nevis grunted as he spread butter and jam on his bread. "If you say so."

An hour later they were wandering about the docks, asking anyone they could find. Unfortunately, all the fishermen had gone out to sea before dawn. Only a few had returned, their boats filled with fish, but they were too busy unloading their haul to pay any attention to Maeve's questions.

"Please, this is important," she begged a fishing boat captain.

He gave her an impatient look. "Lass, there are things ye should not ask."

"Why not?"

"Because there are places ye should not go. Places whence a boat may ne'er return."

"Where?" she asked.

He huffed. "Did ye not listen to what I said?"

"Is it to the southwest?"

He gave Nevis a pointed look. "Take her away from here afore she gets herself in trouble."

"Aye, Captain." Nevis took hold of her elbow to lead her away.

"But he knows more," Maeve protested.

"Maybe." Nevis shrugged. "Maybe not. Men who sail the sea always have stories they pass about. It doesn't mean any of their tales are true."

"Even a rumor or superstition could be based on fact," Maeve insisted.

They walked along the docks till Nevis motioned to a nearby tavern. "I ate there last night. They have good fried fish. Let's go inside."

Maeve snorted. He was hungry again? Still, it wasn't a bad idea. "While you eat, I'll question the customers."

Nevis groaned. "Don't you realize some of them will be drunkards? They would tell you anything for a drink."

"I'm not giving up," Maeve argued. "Someone is going to know about another island."

"Would ye be talking now about the Isle of Secrets?" an old man called to them from the bench in front of the tavern. He was barefoot and dressed in rags, cradling a bottle to his chest.

Maeve's breath caught, and she rushed toward him. "Is that what the island is called?"

The old man's eyes twinkled with humor. "Now how can I tell ye, lassie, when 'tis a secret?"

Nevis gave him a wry look. "Will it still be a secret if I buy you a drink?"

"Och, then I might find it in me heart to tell this pretty lass all about it," the old man said with a grin that was missing a few teeth.

"Right." Nevis trudged inside the tavern.

"My name is Maeve." She took a seat on the bench next to the old man. "And you are?"

His grin faded as he nervously plucked at his torn breeches. "Me mates used to call me Lobby 'cause the sun could cook me as red as a lobster."

Maeve winced. "That sounds painful."

He looked up at her, his ruddy face etched with wrinkles and regret. "I appreciate the offer of a drink, lass, but I should not tell ye more. 'Tis an evil place. A place where boats and sailors disappear."

"Why?" Maeve asked. "Are the currents treacherous?"

He shook his head.

"The reefs are dangerous?"

"Nay." He lowered his voice. "She is dangerous."

"She?"

He closed his eyes briefly with a pained look. "I was the only one to make it back home." He lifted his bottle to take a sip, then realized it was empty and held it tightly against his chest as he rocked back and forth. "They all died. All me mates." His eyes filled with tears. "I can't go back to sea. She's looking for me, I know it. She wants to kill me."

"Who is she?"

Lobby looked to the right, then left, and lowered his voice to the barest of whispers. "The Sea Witch."

"A witch?"

"Shh!" He hushed her and looked around once more. "She kills anyone who finds her island. Breaks yer ship in two and laughs while ye all drown."

Nevis walked out the door, holding two pewter mugs of beer, and the old man grabbed one and guzzled it down.

"Well?" Nevis asked.

Maeve shrugged, uncertain how much she could believe of the man's fanciful tale. "He says there's an island that belongs to a sea witch."

"Don't say her name out loud!" Lobby nabbed Nevis's second mug. "If she finds out I survived, she'll come after me."

"Right." Nevis eyed the man dubiously. "And where exactly is this . . . unmentionable lady?"

"On the Isle of Secrets, of course." Lobby took a long drink.

It sounded like a perfect place to hide the Embraced army, Maeve thought. "How do we get there?"

Lobby choked, then wiped his mouth with a grimy hand. "Ye cannot go there! She'll kill you, for sure."

"I'm just curious," Maeve assured him. "Is it south from here?"

"Mostly south," Lobby replied. "A little west. But don't ye dare try it. Boats that go there ne'er come back."

That was similar to what the fishing boat captain had said. Maeve was tempted to believe there could be a kernel of truth behind these tales. She stood and smiled at the old man. "Thank you for telling me."

"Och, I shouldn't have." He set his mug on the bench with a regretful look. "Promise me, lass, that ye'll not attempt to go there."

That was a promise she couldn't make. "Lobby, do you know where the Convent of the Two Moons is?" When he nodded, she continued, "If you go there, the nuns will give you a hot meal, a bath, and some clean clothes. If you're willing to work, they can help you find employment."

His face crumpled, and a tear ran down a wrinkled cheek. "Ah, lass, I've been lost without me mates. I don't know why I was the one to survive. They were better men than I."

"I'm sure it's been difficult for you." She touched his shoulder. "But the goddesses spared your life, so you should do your best with it, don't you think? Wouldn't that be the best way to honor your friends?"

He nodded, another tear rolling down his face. "I think ye're right, lass."

As she walked back to the convent with Nevis, she glanced over her shoulder a few times to see if Lobby was following them. But he wasn't.

"You did what you could," Nevis told her. "He has to make the choice himself. And he might choose liquor over life."

Maeve sighed, knowing that was true. "Have you ever heard of a sea witch?"

"No."

"It seems to me that the Isle of Secrets would be a good place to hide the Embraced army."

Nevis snorted. "If such a place actually exists."

Should she ask Captain Shaw to help her find the island? She winced, wondering if the mysterious Sea Witch might actually destroy the captain's ship and drown his crew. Perhaps they would be safer if she looked for the island herself as a seal. But she had never attempted a long journey before. How far could she swim before exhaustion set in? What if she couldn't find land?

She shook her head. It was too dangerous to go alone. Perhaps she could convince some of her seal friends to accompany her? Or Brody? Her heart leaped up her throat. Of course! Brody could go with her. He could even take eagle form occasionally to search for the island from above.

And if this mysterious Sea Witch actually existed, she would not think it odd if a seal or eagle arrived on her island. Then Maeve wouldn't have to worry about Captain Shaw losing his ship or his crew.

After they arrived back at the convent, Nevis stayed to have the midday meal with them. Then he left to try once more to see Queen Esther at Lessa Castle. Maeve went back to her room, and since she hadn't slept much the night before, she soon fell into a deep sleep.

On the Isle of Mist, Brody woke and was relieved to discover he was still in the form of the Seer. After staying up most of the night to read the Seer's journal, he'd finally fallen asleep around dawn. The orange tabby demanded to be fed before Brody did anything else, so he gave Trouble the last of the chicken. After washing up, he started a fire in the hearth. The last of the bread from the convent had grown stale, so he toasted it with some cheese over the fire. Then he sat at the table to eat while he resumed his reading of the journal.

He'd skimmed through more than fifty years of entries the night before. Sadly, they had all been too similar—visions of war, destruction, plague, and starvation. It was a wonder the Seer hadn't lost his mind after being forced to witness so much violence and despair. But then, about twenty-three years ago, he had experienced a different kind of vision, one that had left him so thrilled, his handwriting had become messy in his haste to record all the details.

Brody had marked the entry with an old ribbon, and this afternoon, he returned to the passage to read it once again.

> Early spring, Year 677.
>
> Today, my heart is light and full of a hope that I haven't felt in decades. Indeed, I find myself so excited, I can barely contain my joyful spirit long enough to write this entry.
>
> My dream last night started off much like my other visions. I was floating across the ocean on my way to the mainland. But when I arrived, I didn't see what I normally do.
>
> I flew over the kingdom of Tourin, and to my amazement, I saw happy people. Well-fed and healthy, they bustled about the markets, they labored in fields ripe with grain and vegetables, they herded fat sheep and cows, they played with children and sang songs in the taverns. Before I could offer a prayer of thanksgiving to the goddesses, a strong wind came out of the capital of Lourdon and swept me quickly south.
>
> In the kingdom of Eberon, I saw more people enjoying peace and prosperity. No battles. No disease. No starvation. But I was startled when, suddenly, a bolt of lightning shot from Ebton Palace and speared the clouds. I realized, though, that the lightning had not been intended to cause me any harm. It was the lightning that kept the people of Eberon protected. They, too, were safe and happy.

Suddenly, a dragon appeared and snatched me out of the sky. Normally, I might have felt fear, but in my dream, I understood that I was in no danger. The dragon flew toward the country of Norveshka, and as we soared over his country, I could feel his pride as he showed me how happy and safe his people were.

The dragon veered south, taking me into Woodwyn, the land of the elves. More peace. More prosperity. When the dragon released me, I fell, tumbling toward the earth. I remember growing quite agitated in my sleep, believing that I would crash into the ground far below. But then my body hit a soft cushion of leaves, and as I slipped through a leafy canopy, a large oak tree wrapped its branches around me, cradling me until I was gently set on the ground.

And that was when I awoke. I am not certain what all the details meant, but one thing is certain: The era of war and destruction will soon come to an end. And then a time of peace and prosperity will follow. For now I, Burien of Aerland, will pray to the goddesses—please let peace come quickly!

Brody took a bite of his toast and cheese as he considered the entry. In hindsight, the details that had confused the Seer now made perfect sense to Brody. The peace that had come to Tourin had been brought about when Ulfrid and Brigitta had become the rulers there. The wind that had blown the Seer south was a reference to Ulfrid, also known as the infamous pirate Rupert who could control the wind.

The lightning shooting out of Ebton Palace had to signify Leo, for he possessed the power of lightning. Eberon was now at peace because Leo and Luciana had become king and queen.

The dragon had to be King Silas, the dragon shifter who ruled Norveshka with his wife, Gwennore. And the oak tree that had cushioned the Seer's fall was a symbol of King Brennan, the elfin king also known as the Woodsman. With Brennan and Sorcha in power there, the country of Woodwyn was now also at peace.

It was the adopted sisters from the Isle of Moon who, along with their husbands, were bringing a new era of peace to Aerthlan. But twenty-three years ago, the Seer had not known how the peace would come about.

Brody skimmed through another year's worth of entries, and to his dismay, the Seer's visions had reverted to their usual doom and gloom. Each time the Seer experienced another bad vision, his feelings of despair grew.

Late autumn, Year 677.
Another vision of war and death. What happened to the peace I thought was coming? Each month my hope dwindles, my spirit dies a little more.
Goddesses, why have you forsaken me?

Early spring, Year 678.
Finally! After a year, I was blessed with another good vision. Peace and prosperity, happy and healthy people all over the mainland of Aerthlan. My relief is great . . . and yet, I am afraid that another year will pass before I see another good vision. How can I bear to see more death and violence when I know it is possible to have peace? Surely the good visions are not sent to me for the sole purpose of tormenting me. Dear goddesses, what is the purpose of the good dreams? What must I do to usher in this era of peace?

Unfortunately, the bad visions returned, and the Seer became more and more desperate. Brody winced when he read the entry in which the Seer's thoughts took a wrong turn . . .

Late autumn, Year 678.

At last, after six months, I had a third good vision. But instead of relief, I feel agitated to the point that I cannot eat or sleep. For I know in my heart that I cannot bear any more bad visions. I will not! Not when I know peace and prosperity are possible. Why did the goddesses give me those good visions if I am not to act upon them? Surely that must be their intent. They are calling me to change the world for the better.

It has taken me a long time to realize this, for I have always believed it was my place to dwell in the shadows, doing nothing more than warning the people of Aerthlan whenever devastation was around the corner. But I have been doing that for fifty-five years, and in that time, the world has remained a dark and violent place.

No more! I, Burien of Aerland, now believe the visions are telling me to step out of the shadows and do whatever I can to make sure the era of peace and prosperity begins as soon as possible.

Early spring, 679.

I am now convinced that I am right, that the goddesses have called me to action. For they have sent someone who will help me. Her name is Cahira.

She arrived this morning in the guise of a dolphin. When I saw that she had beached herself, I hurried to help her, believing her to be a dolphin in trouble. But when I reached her, she shifted into human form. The most beautiful woman I have ever seen. Granted, I have lived alone most of my life, so I have not seen many women, but I feel quite confident in insisting that she is the most beautiful woman on Aerthlan. She is quite powerful, too, for as she shifted, she manifested herself a lovely gown of shimmering sea-green cloth that matched the color of her eyes.

To my amazement, she claimed to be the last living female of the ancient race of sorcerers from the lost continent of Aerland. She had sought me out, sensing that I was the last male of our race. We immediately felt a closeness, a connection, not just through our shared blood, but through our shared dreams. She, too, wants to dedicate herself to making the world a place of peace.

Brody sighed as he continued to read. Over the next few months, the Seer had become completely enthralled with Cahira. He'd believed her, trusted her, fallen in love with her. And all the time, Cahira had manipulated him, using his ideas to form the Circle of Five, so she and her evil cohorts could take over the world.

As much as he hated reading about Cahira, he carefully studied all the passages, for he needed to know everything in order to fool the woman into believing he was actually the Seer.

He groaned when he read about the Seer's joy when Cahira told him she was with child. If his theory was correct, that babe was Maeve. The timing was right. Cahira would have given birth in the year 680, and now it was the year 700, when Maeve would turn twenty years old. Maeve even had sea-green eyes like Cahira did.

Dammit, he had promised to give Maeve the answers she wanted tonight. But this was something he could never let her know. How could he tell her that her mother had used her father in an attempt to take over the world?

He would have to convince her, somehow, to return to Ebton Palace. There she would be safe from danger. And safe from the truth.

* * *

Once again, Maeve found herself floating across a dark blue ocean, headed for an island. Not the Isle of Mist, she thought, for the sky was clear, the air warm, and the island lush with vegetation. As she moved over the isle, she spotted thick forests, sparkling lakes, and then finally signs of civilization. Some farmland. A few people.

A castle. Built of weathered gray stone, it dominated the highest bluff on the island. As Maeve approached, she noted an unusual garden, where dense bushes had been clipped into the shapes of fish, seals, and dolphins. Hedges, shaped to look like the waves of an ocean, led her to two adjoining ponds. How odd. The water in one pond was blue, but green in the other. Where the two ponds joined, a statue of a dolphin shot a spray of water into the air.

A breeze from the nearby ocean caught Maeve and sent her flying toward the castle and the long balcony that overlooked the ponds and garden. Whoosh, she was swept through an open door, suspended in the air as long purple curtains rippled around her in the breeze.

She landed on a smooth floor of polished green marble, and to her surprise, she discovered she was now wearing a beautiful gown and slippers of shimmering gold satin. The castle seemed empty, she thought, as she wandered down the hallway. To her right, purple curtains billowed in the air from the open doorways that led onto the balcony. To her left, the wall held a number of portraits, their frames decorated with golden shells.

At the end of the hallway, she found a set of golden doors, open as if to invite her inside. She eased through the doors and stopped, her mouth dropping open. The room was huge. Enormous pillars of green marble soared up to an arched ceiling painted to look like the sky. In the middle of the ceiling, a circular glass dome let the afternoon sun shine in.

The floor was even more amazing. Tiny shards of stone in shades of blue and green had been put together in a mosaic to look like the waves of an ocean. As rays of sunshine filtered through the glass ceiling, they struck the floor and made the waves look as if they were moving.

Enthralled, she walked slowly across the floor, noting that the mosaic included a fish every now and then, made of red or orange bits of shiny glass. Directly beneath the glass-domed ceiling, there was a circle of dolphins, swimming around a purple octopus. Its eight tentacles wound through the greenish waves, each tip crushing a fish in a death grip.

Maeve winced at the violence marring such a beautiful work of art. She glanced up and noted the dais at the end of the room. The bright colors drew her closer, and she was surprised to find all the decorations were made of glass. The floor of the dais was scattered with giant clams in vibrant green and purple glass. More glass was shaped and curled to look like coral and flowing seaweed. It was as if the entire dais was under the sea.

In the middle of the dais sat a large chair, solid gold, its back in the shape of the body of an octopus. Eight golden tentacles, four on each side, curled and twisted around the chair. A purple velvet cushion rested on the seat, and the armrests were shaped like seals.

This is a throne room, Maeve thought. The most amazing throne room she'd ever seen. But who was the ruler of this island?

"Ah, there you are." A woman's voice spoke behind her, and Maeve whirled about. The woman was standing outside the golden doors, in the shadows where Maeve couldn't see her face.

Still, a word slipped from her mouth. "Mother."

With a jolt, Maeve woke and sat up in bed. Good goddesses! *Mother?* Why on Aerthlan had she said that? She breathed heavily for a moment, her gaze flitting about the room. She was still at the convent. Still in her old room.

Thank the goddesses. But what a bizarre dream! *Mother?*

After living twenty years without a mother, why would she dream of one now?

She eased onto her feet, annoyed that her legs were shaking. Why was she having such strange dreams lately? Did the island in her dream actually exist? Could it be the one she was looking for, the Isle of Secrets?

Calm yourself. She took a deep breath. No doubt her dream was nothing more than wishful thinking. She was so eager to discover another island that her imagination had cooked one up for her. And her dream had included the colors purple and green because the memory of the Telling Stones had been on her mind. That had to be it. Her Embraced gift was seal-shifting, not seeing the unknown.

But why had her imagination placed her mother on the island? And in such a strange castle?

She wandered over to the window and peered out at the familiar courtyard, the same courtyard she'd seen every day of her childhood. Just a dream, she reminded herself. She needed to shake it off and focus on reality.

The sun was nearing the horizon; soon the two full moons would be rising. Hopefully, that meant that soon she would be seeing Brody. He would probably arrive as a seal, but she would need to talk to him in human form so she could convince him to help her search for the Isle of Secrets. That meant she would need clothes for him. And food. Brody was always hungry whenever he became human.

She rushed to the dining hall to pack a basket of food. Then she hurried to the storeroom where the sisters kept a variety of clothing for their charity work. As she picked out a pair of linen breeches and a shirt for Brody, she wondered if the old sailor, Lobby, had come for clothes. Back in her room, she wrapped up a towel and the men's clothing in a blanket.

The sisters didn't expect her to attend the moonrise mass or midnight mass, since they all knew she had to shift into a seal on the night of the full moons. So none of them would think twice about her spending the entire night at the nearby beach.

Her heart raced as she carried the bundled blanket and basket of food to the secluded beach. Even though she'd frolicked with Brody before in the ocean and the Ebe River, she'd always been in seal form, and he had always been a seal or river otter. Naturally, there had been no talking. They'd simply taken turns chasing each other or catching fish. He didn't even realize that she knew it was he.

But tonight would be different. Tonight, she would confront him as a human. And for the first time ever, she would be alone with the human Brody.

Chapter 6

The sun had set and the full moons were rising over the horizon by the time Brody winged his way to the Isle of Moon. He always arrived late whenever he came to play with Maeve, so she could have privacy while she shifted into a seal.

Of course, as far as she knew, he was just another seal or an otter, so she wouldn't think twice about disrobing and shifting in front of him. But damn, he'd spent too much of his life as an animal. He couldn't trust himself to turn away during those few seconds when she was naked. Not when he knew she would be beautiful. Not when he longed to touch her. Hold her. Kiss—

Stop! He put a screeching halt to those thoughts. She could never be his, not as long as he was cursed.

So tonight, he had to remain aloof. No matter what she said or did, he had to remember that his sole purpose for this visit was to convince her to go back to Ebton. And that meant he would have to talk to her. As a human.

Shit. She was going to know his secret now, that he had been the one coming to see her every month. And then she might rightly assume that he had feelings for her.

He would have to convince her otherwise. Hell, he might even have to be rude. He had to do whatever it took to make her leave. Even if he ended up hurting her feelings. *Dammit.*

He flew over the Isle of Moon, then began his descent toward the southern coast. The weathered stone buildings of the convent came into view. Beyond it, sharp cliffs gave way to a dark ocean dappled with silver sparkles from the rising twin moons. Just west of the convent lay Seal Cove and the secluded beach where Maeve had shifted for the first time at the age of sixteen.

It had been painful for her, that first time. In seal form, he had waited behind a rocky outcropping, out of sight but not out of hearing. Her cries had nearly broken his heart. Even her sisters, who had accompanied her, had started crying. Her seal friends, gathered on a flat rock in the small bay, had barked their encouragement to her.

Finally, the noise had faded away, and Brody had peeked around the rocks. Gwennore and Sorcha were alone on the beach, watching the ocean. With a splash, the seals dove into the water. Were they greeting Maeve? Had she completed her shift?

He had swum toward them, wending his way through the crowd of seals until he saw her, beautiful, black, and sleek. He'd known instantly it was Maeve. He had circled around her, and she'd joined in, gliding closer and closer to him until their slick skins had brushed against each other.

And with that one touch, he had known that his heart was lost. There could be no woman for him other than Maeve. But there could be no happy ending, either. Not with this curse. So he had resigned himself to the fate of enduring a lifelong unrequited love for her. At the same time, he couldn't allow her to fall for him and suffer the same fate. So he had settled for seeing her once a month in disguise. That way, she would never know it was he. Never know how he truly felt.

The noise of barking seals jerked him back to the present, and as he flew over Seal Cove, he spotted her, already in seal form, lounging on the flat rock with her friends. It looked like a happy reunion, with all the seals trying to talk to her at once.

He landed on a nearby cliff and waited while their conversation went on and on. Whatever she was asking was certainly garnering some lengthy replies.

Enough. Wasn't he the one she was anxious to see?

He took off and flew around the bend. Then he folded his wings and dove toward the water. Just before he hit the surface, he shifted into a seal.

Splash. He swam into the cove and surfaced a few yards from the rock. The annoying seals were still talking to Maeve, monopolizing her time. *It's me she wants to see!* But they didn't hear him or notice him. He slapped the water's surface with his fore-flipper, and while the water splashed around him, he gave a loud bark.

Instantly, Maeve turned toward him. After giving a quick yip, she plunged into the water. His heart began to pound. She was hurrying to see him! She recognized him! *You fool, she only recognizes the seal she used to play with. Not you.*

He sank into the water to watch her approach. Ah, Maeve. Even the way she moved was beautiful. Graceful. And sensual, as if she enjoyed the undulating motion of her body and the caress of water against her skin. She circled around him, and he rotated in the water, admiring the view as she came closer and closer. Close enough he could reach out a flipper to touch her.

But he resisted. He wasn't here to flirt with her. He was here to get rid of her.

Then, to his surprise, she lunged toward him and pressed her nose against his.

Was that a seal kiss? He gasped, a stupid thing to do underwater. Sputtering, he surfaced and gulped down some air.

She surfaced beside him, her eyes glimmering with amusement in the moonlight. With a quick bark, she dove back underwater.

Ah, she wants to play chase. He could do that. For a little while, until he had to seriously chase her off. He followed her

as she swam around the flat-topped rock. Thank the goddesses, the other seals were staying put and not getting in the
way. Of course, she might have asked them to do that. The
thought made his heart squeeze. Did she want to be alone
with him?

Putting on a burst of speed, he gained on her. Just as he
was about to catch up, she dove straight down, knocking
him in the snout with her hind-flippers.

Ouch. Well, two could play this game. He zoomed after
her, diving at an angle so he could intercept her. He pulled in
front, causing her to halt abruptly as she bumped into his
side. He twisted, planning to press his nose against hers.

With a fore-flipper, she slapped him.

What the hell? He watched her swim toward the shore.
Why would she kiss him, then seconds later, slap him? And
why the hell was he even trying to kiss her? That was not the
plan. He was supposed to be sending her back home.

He shook himself mentally. That was the problem when
dealing with a siren. With just one look, she could make him
forget his plans. Forget all reason and wish for the impossible.

Get a grip. He had to be strong. Resolute. Nerves of steel.
A heart of stone.

Oh, hell, she was shifting! Her hind-flippers morphed into
feet, then her body split to form two beautiful long legs. His
nerves of steel melted; his heart of stone crumbled. As the
shift swept up her body, he had a glimpse of a sweetly curved
bottom, rounded hips, narrow waist—

He shot to the surface and, gasping for air, turned away
from her. *You fool.* He'd been so obsessed with the dreaded
revelation of his secret that he hadn't realized how difficult it
would be to talk to her once she returned to her human form.
So close to him. And so naked.

Distance, that's what he needed. With a push from his
hind-flippers, he moved slowly away from her.

"Brody, I know it's you."

He spun around. *What?*

She was fully human and standing with the water up to her shoulders, her long black hair slicked back from her beautiful face. "I've always known it was you. Every month you came to see me, either as a seal or an otter."

She knew? In his shock, he forgot to tread water and promptly sank. Sputtering, he resurfaced and shifted. His feet found the sandy bottom, and he straightened to his full height, the water just below his shoulders.

She knew his secret. He shoved his wet hair back, giving her a wary look. "How did you know?"

Her mouth twitched. "It's simple. I can mentally communicate with seals. But with you, I couldn't."

He winced. Why hadn't he realized that? *You didn't want to. You didn't want a reason to stop seeing her.*

"And whenever you shifted into a river otter, you were far too large," she continued with a grin. "You were as big as a sea otter—"

"All right," he gritted out. So he hadn't fooled her for a minute. All this time, he'd been the fool, dammit. "You should've told me months ago."

Her smile vanished. "I couldn't. I was afraid you would stop coming."

He clenched his fists underwater. She was right. He would've stopped. He had never wanted her to know how much he cared.

She stepped toward him. "You've been missing for two months. Are you all right?"

"Yes." He reminded himself to be firm. "You're wasting my time for idle chitchat?"

Her expression flashed from concern to irritation. "Do you have any idea how worried everyone was? Where have you been?"

He shrugged. "I was doing my job. Everyone understands that." He gave her a pointed look. "Except you."

She huffed. "You came to see me every month for four years, then disappeared all of a sudden, and you didn't expect me to be concerned?"

"No, I didn't. I certainly didn't expect you to come looking for me. Or bother the Seer because of me. I'm not your lost pet, Maeve. You want steady companionship, get a real dog." He winced inwardly when she flinched, but forced himself to continue. "My welfare is none of your business. So go back to your own life—"

"Brody!" Her brow creased with exasperation. "I was worried sick about you."

"Not my problem."

Her mouth fell open. She glanced around for a moment as if searching for answers. "I was so excited about seeing you tonight. And when I did see you, I was so happy that I kissed you. But then I slapped you because you made me worry so much—"

"Not my problem," he repeated firmly, even though the injured look on her face was ripping at his heart. He lifted his chin. "I have things I need to do, and you're interfering. So go home—"

"Why are you acting like this?" When he merely shrugged, she huffed angrily. "Fine! I'll go." She dove underwater, headed for the shore, and he let out a sigh of relief.

Suddenly, she resurfaced and faced him. With a start, he realized the water only reached her waist now, and he could see the contours of her breasts, partially hidden beneath locks of long wet hair. *Dammit!* He spun around, putting his back to her. What the hell was she doing? Was she trying to seduce him?

"We could at least talk a little before I go." Her siren voice softened his heart. And hardened his groin. He didn't know which was more dangerous.

"I brought some food. And some clothes," she continued. "Aren't you hungry?"

Goddesses, yes. Just knowing that she was standing there, her breasts exposed, made him want to grab on to her and never let go. He tightened his fists. "You should get dressed."

She made an impatient, dismissive noise. "We're shifters. Occasional nudity is simply part of the process."

Did she not realize how seductive she was? *Don't give in,* he warned himself. "I didn't come for conversation. I want you to go home. The Seer told me your future lies at Ebton Palace."

"I don't care what the Seer says. He's rude and overbearing."

Brody winced. Apparently, he'd overdone his autocratic Seer persona, and it had backfired. "But you clearly belong at Ebton. You have family there. You have suitors. You'll have a happy life—"

"I don't want those suitors. I have someone else in mind."

A pang shot through his heart. *No, Maeve, not me.* "I have work to do. I don't have time for this."

"Ah." Her voice sounded closer. "So you know I was referring to you."

Yes! His heart celebrated. But as he turned toward her, his mind flailed with one last feeble attempt to reject her. She had moved toward him, deeper into the water, although he could still see the upper curves of her breasts. "Maeve, I'm not the one for you. I never will be."

She halted, a pained look crossing her face. "We'll discuss that later. Right now, I have something else I need to—"

"My thoughts will not change. Go home, where you will be safe."

"I am not a child."

"I know that." *All too well.* He struggled to keep his gaze on her face and not on the curves of her breasts. "But you're not a soldier, either. So go home and be safe. Please. That's all I have to say. Good-bye." He turned and walked away.

"I'll be safe if you come with me."

He glanced back at her. "What?"

"The seals have confirmed my suspicions. There is an island southwest of here. The Isle of Secrets. A perfect place to hide the Embraced army, don't you think?" She motioned to the blanket stretched out on the beach. "So we should eat the food I brought, then start our journey. We'll swim as seals, and you can even shift into an eagle to spot—"

"No!" He stepped toward her. "I won't let you get involved in something so dangerous."

She scoffed. "You won't *let* me? I don't recall that you have any authority over—"

"Dammit, Maeve." He moved closer. "You will not go looking for an army. They'll outnumber you. They'll have powers. They'll want to hurt you." He slapped a hand on the water's surface. "It is not happening!"

Her eyes narrowed. "And I'm supposed to believe you don't care for me?"

He hissed in a breath. "Look. I have my own plan for finding the army and dealing with the last of the Circle of Five, and—"

"What is your plan?"

"None of your damned business!" He glared at her. "I can't carry out my plan if you're interfering and making me worry about you. So go home!"

"Why don't *you* go home? Then I can go about *my* plan without having to worry about you!"

He scoffed. Had she always been this stubborn? Once again, he wondered how well he actually knew her.

She took a deep breath. "I can see you're going to be stubborn about this."

"*I'm* stubborn?"

"Yes." When he continued to give her an incredulous look, she shrugged. "All right, we're both stubborn. So you should go ahead and pursue your plan, and I'll pursue mine. I can ask the seals to go with me. Good luck to you." She sank underwater and shifted into a seal.

"Maeve!" She swam by him, but he leaped on top of her, grabbing hold of her to stop her from leaving.

She wiggled, trying to break loose, but he held on tight, lifting her head above water so she would be able to breathe.

"Listen to me," he begged her. "Don't do this!"

She shifted back into human form, her hair dangling in wet locks down her face. "Let me go!" She shoved at his chest.

He pulled her closer, then froze when her naked body collided with his own. *Holy goddesses.*

She gasped, and the quick intake of air pressed her breasts against his chest. "Brody?" Between strands of hair, she peered up at him.

"Yes." He gently swept her hair back so she could see.

"Let me go," she whispered.

"I did."

"Oh." She glanced at his chest, where her hands were still resting. With another gasp, she lifted her hands and stepped back, putting a few inches between them.

When her gaze met his, the last remnant of his resistance wavered. *Don't touch her. Don't—To hell with it!* He leaned forward and pressed his lips against hers.

She made a small sound, halfway between a sigh and a groan, but it roared through him, destroying the last of his resolve. He pulled her into his arms and claimed her mouth. *Maeve. My beautiful Maeve.*

And she was kissing him back! She wrapped her arms around his neck as her body melted against his.

Maeve. His kiss became more desperate. More ravaging. He'd wanted her for over four years. He'd admired her— hell, he had worshipped her from afar as she'd grown into a beautiful woman. And here she was, opening her mouth to him, letting him inside. Letting his hands roam down her back, over the contours of her narrow waist and the flare of her hips.

Heat rushed to his groin, making him grow hard against her flat belly. *Damn!* He grabbed her hips and pushed her away as he stiffened with an erection.

"What . . . ?" She gave him a dazed look, her lips pink and swollen from his kiss.

He groaned inwardly. How could he explain his predicament to sweet, innocent Maeve? She really would think he was an animal. "I-I shouldn't have—"

"Don't." She stepped back, raising her palms in a stopping motion. "That was my first real kiss. Don't ruin it for me."

He winced. But he had ruined it. He shouldn't have kissed her, not when he couldn't have a future with her. "Maeve—"

"Don't you dare act like you regret it!" Tears glimmered in her sea-green eyes, and the sight wrenched at his heart.

He took a deep breath. Maybe it would be better if he changed the subject. "Will you go home as I asked?"

She closed her eyes briefly with a pained look. "Were you trying to coerce me? Is that why you kissed—"

"No!" Shit, he'd just made things worse. Now she must think he was a monster. "There was no ulterior motive involved. It was nothing more than . . . lust." And longing.

Her eyes widened. "You feel lust for me?"

"Well, yes. A little." He waved a dismissive hand. "At the moment. Any man would. You're naked. And you're the most beautiful woman in all of Aerthlan."

She gave him a dubious look. "I've never heard anyone else make that claim."

"Believe me, the men are thinking it," he growled. "They all want you, I'm sure of it." *The bastards.* "So don't you dare shift in front of anyone else. Understand?"

A corner of her mouth curled up.

Why the hell did she look so amused? "This is not a jest, Maeve. You may think that getting naked is simply part of the shifting process, but to any man it's going to be damned seductive. So be careful. All right?"

She bit her lip as if she was trying not to grin.

Dammit, she still wasn't taking him seriously. "You don't understand the power you wield as a siren. When you sing, men will cross oceans to hear the sound of your voice. When you laugh, they will lose their hearts to you."

Her smile faded as a wary look crossed her face.

He crossed his arms over his chest. "I feel that I do need to apologize for getting carried away. Are you all right now?"

She groaned. "I'm fine. And you shouldn't apologize. As far as first kisses go, I thought it was rather nice."

"Nice?" Hell, he'd never gone stiff so quickly in his life.

"I would say glorious, but then I have nothing to compare it to."

His groin sprang back to attention, urging him to give her a full range of samples for her comparative analysis. *Control yourself, you dog.* "So, will you go home?"

"No. Will you tell me your plan so I can help you?"

"No." He couldn't let her find out that her parents had started the Circle of Five.

She sighed. "We seem to have reached an impasse." When she folded her arms across her chest, the movement lifted her breasts a little bit.

He gulped and looked away.

"You fussed at me that I would be no match for an Embraced army," she muttered. "But neither are you. It's too dangerous for you to take this on by yourself. What if they capture you? How will we know where to find you?"

He didn't want to explain that he would be safe as long as he was disguised as the Seer. But still, she had a point. As soon as he discovered the whereabouts of the Embraced army, he needed to let Leo and the other kings know. If Maeve was correct, and the army was hidden on another island, he could fly to the Isle of Moon quickly enough that no one would miss him. "All right. You can help me."

Her eyes lit up. "How?"

"Remain here at the convent. If all goes well, I'll come tell you the location of the Embraced army. Then you can have Nevis take the news back to Leo."

Her shoulders slumped. "That's it?"

"I'm counting on you. It would take too long for me to fly all the way to Eberon."

She nodded slowly. "When do you think you'll come?"

"I'm not sure. Sometime in the next few days. I'll probably have to sneak over here in the middle of the night."

She sighed. "Very well."

"Thank you." He stepped back, memorizing every curve and angle of her beautiful face, her sea-green eyes shimmering in the light of the full moons, her creamy pale skin and midnight-black hair. "Please stay safe."

She gave him a wry look. "Careful, or I might think that you care."

He winced inwardly. "I'm only thinking about myself. I don't want any distractions while I'm working."

Her mouth curled up. "Right."

Was that a hint of sarcasm? He'd better get the hell out of here. "Good-bye." He turned, and as he shifted into a seal, he heard her sweet voice calling out to him.

"Be safe, Brody."

He swam around the bend and slid up onto a rocky shore. Then he shifted into an eagle and flew away. As he passed over the convent, he heard her singing. Her siren voice was so beautiful, so alluring, it made his heart ache. It was the same song she had sung the first day he had met her.

"My true love lies in the ocean blue. My true love sleeps in the sea. Whenever the moons shine over you, please remember me. My lonesome heart is torn in two. My grief runs deep as the sea.

Whenever the waves roll over you, please remember me. Please remember me."

Ah, Maeve. How could he ever forget her?

How could she ever forget that kiss? Maeve lay back on the blanket, looking up at the stars while she let the memory sweep over her once again. Brody had actually kissed her! And with so much passion. Heat flooded her face and she pressed her hands against her cheeks.

It had been glorious. That was, until he apologized. Dammit! She sat up. Did he really regret it? Just the thought made her angry. And why had he purposefully been so rude? She hadn't expected that. He may have ignored her in the past, but he'd never been rude. She'd been so sure that he would go with her to the Isle of Secrets that she'd even left a note in her room to inform the sisters of her upcoming trip.

But the meeting had not gone at all as she had hoped it would. After Brody had left, she'd wandered onto the beach. Missing him already, she'd sung the Song of Mourning while she'd put on her gown. The basket of food and men's clothing sat there unused. He'd refused to eat with her.

But he'd kissed her!

He'd refused to travel with her.

But he'd kissed her!

He'd refused to share his plan with her.

But he'd kissed her! With a groan, she'd plopped down onto the blanket and reached for the basket.

Now, an hour later, she'd finished most of the food and half a bottle of wine, but she was still confused. Brody had kissed her with passion as if he truly cared for her. He'd begged her to stay safe as if he truly worried about her.

But he'd been rude to her, too. Rude and overbearing just like the Seer.

She shook her head. That meeting with the Seer still had

her perplexed. He'd moved like an old man who could barely walk, but then, when he'd thought he was out of sight, he'd hurried toward his cottage with the stride of a healthy young man.

Then there was the fresh grave, just like the one she'd seen in her dream. Whom had Brody buried? As far as she knew, there was only one inhabitant on the Isle of Mist.

Her breath caught, and a chill crept down her spine. If the Seer was dead, then who . . . ?

No, not possible. Brody wasn't capable of taking on a human shape.

Or was he? There had been a moment when the Seer's eyes had reminded her of Brody's. And then something Brody had said: *"When you sing, men will cross oceans to hear the sound of your voice. When you laugh, they will lose their hearts to you."* Hadn't the Seer said the same thing?

She jammed the cork back into the bottle of wine. She'd drunk too much. Her mind was cooking up some strange ideas.

With a sigh, she stashed the bottle back in the basket. In a few nights, she would have to camp out at this beach all night to see if Brody returned with information. Dammit, she'd wanted to do more than just pass on information to Nevis.

How did Brody know that Nevis was here? The Seer must have told him. Or if he was the Seer . . .

"Aargh." She lowered her head and pressed her palms against her temples. This was too frustrating. How could she wait here doing nothing? Knowing nothing?

But Brody was counting on her being here when he returned in a few days.

A few days . . .

She sat up, her mind suddenly clear. In a few days, she could find the Isle of Secrets herself and come back here.

Her heart raced as she rose to her feet. Did she dare do it?

Brody's last plea that she keep herself safe echoed in her

mind. No matter how hard he'd tried to push her away with his harsh words, she didn't want to believe him. If actions spoke louder than words, then his kiss had been the true portrayal of his feelings. He did care for her. That's why he wanted her to be safe.

But as long as she remained in seal form surrounded by her seal friends, wouldn't she be safe? If the Sea Witch or an Embraced soldier spotted her, they would simply think she was one seal out of many.

She could do this! She didn't have to follow orders from Brody. Or the Seer. Or her sisters. She could make her own decisions, dammit. And pursue her own destiny.

My darling dears! she called mentally to her friends as she pulled off her gown. *Will you come with me to the Isle of Secrets?*

They yipped in agreement, then slid off the flat rock as she strode into the water.

In just a few seconds, she'd shifted. *Let's go!*

Chapter 7

"What do you mean she's missing?" Nevis asked the next morning when he arrived at the convent for breakfast. "We're on an island. Where could she go?"

"Out to sea." Mother Ginessa handed him a folded note. "We found this in her room this morning."

Nevis opened the scrap of paper.

I'm taking a long swim with my seal friends. Don't worry. I'll be back soon. Maeve

"What the hell—oh, no offense, my lady." He read the note again while the nun waved a dismissive hand. "A long swim? Does she do this sort of thing often?"

Mother Ginessa shook her head. "No. That's why we're worried."

Dammit to hell. He had one job, watch over Maeve, and he'd completely screwed it—no, he had two jobs. He was supposed to meet Queen Esther, too. But now he'd failed miserably on both counts. "I take it she swims well?" Surely, she would be safe.

Mother Ginessa sighed. "I suppose she does, but . . ."

But if she'd left last night, she could have been swimming for hours, Nevis thought. How long could she last before exhaustion set in? And what about sea creatures like sharks? And where the hell was she going?

He stiffened as the most probable answer popped into his head. The Isle of Secrets. Oh hell, no. That was not a long swim; it was a damned voyage. Into the unknown. Surely she wasn't attempting something that dangerous.

Mother Ginessa motioned toward the dining hall. "We can discuss the matter over breakfast, if you like."

"No, thank you. Please go ahead." How could he eat now? Dammit, Maeve's sisters were going to kill him if anything happened to her. All the kings on the mainland would kill him, too. Hell, he'd kill himself if . . . "Do you mind if I check her room? And where does she go to shift?"

"Her room is there." Mother Ginessa pointed to a door that was halfway open. "And she probably left from Seal Cove. It's just west of here."

"Thank you." He bowed his head, then dashed into Maeve's bedchamber. There wasn't much inside. Two large beds, made up and unslept in. The trunk containing Maeve's clothing and the book she'd brought from the Ebton library.

On the table, he spotted a candlestick, a stack of paper, and an inkwell. He thumbed through the stack and discovered two maps. One was a new map of Aerthlan with the Isles of Moon and Mist in the Great Western Ocean. The other map, drawn on a yellowed piece of parchment, showed the large island continent of Aerland. Dammit, had she really gone off in search of the Isle of Secrets?

He ran to Seal Cove and found the path leading down to the beach. "Maeve! Are you here?" he shouted as he darted down the path. "Dammit, you had better be here!"

No answer. No seals in sight. Had they all gone with Maeve? On the beach, he discovered a blanket, a basket with empty bowls, and a bottle of wine, half-gone. Next to the basket was a stack of neatly folded clothes. A man's shirt and breeches.

Nevis straightened with a jerk. Had Brody come here? He scanned the sky and nearby cliffs. No sign of an eagle.

Something caught his attention on the cliff to the west. A glimpse of cream color and a braid of long black hair. A woman? But the morning sun shone too brightly for Nevis to identify her.

"Hey!" he shouted as the figure disappeared from view. "Maeve, is that you? Wait!"

He sprinted to the end of the beach, then scrambled up the rocky incline to the top of the bluff. Holding a hand above his eyes to block the bright sun, he pivoted around, searching for her.

There. Climbing a hill close to the shoreline, a slender young woman with a braid of long black hair. She disappeared over the crest of the hill.

"Hey!" He ran after her and soon reached the hilltop. There she was. Sitting in a grassy meadow close to a cliff overlooking the ocean. There was a large basket next to her and something in her lap that claimed all of her attention. A flat board with paper on top? She seemed to be drawing something. Was Maeve drawing another map? Why the hell was she making everyone worry about her?

"Hey, you!" He started down the hill, and she glanced up at him with a startled look.

Shit. He halted with a jerk. He'd been shouting at a complete stranger. A beautiful stranger. Damn, but she must think he was a rude oaf.

Other than her long black hair, she looked nothing like Maeve. Her face was more heart-shaped and her eyes were a brilliant blue. Her gown was a light blue, topped with a cream-colored apron that was stained with different colors of paint. She had a slender stick of charcoal in her hand that she was using to sketch something.

He bowed his head slightly. "Begging your pardon, Miss, but have you seen another woman hereabouts? Or a bunch of seals? Or an eagle? Or a pelican, perhaps?" He winced as her eyes narrowed. She probably thought he'd ask about a hedgehog next. Damn, but she must think he was an idiot.

"Are ye fond of birds and animals, then?" Her voice was soft with the musical lilt of the island accent.

"No. I mean, yes." Damn, now she probably thought he killed baby bunnies to pass the time. "I mean, actually I'm looking for a woman."

The young woman gave him a wary look.

Damn, now she must think he was a womanizer. "She's missing." He descended the hill. "She's young with long black hair. And she would be wearing a cream-colored convent gown."

The woman's eyes widened. "Ye're . . . friends with a nun?"

"No!" Damn, now she must think he consorted with nuns. "I mean, we are friends, but she's not a nun. She's a selkie."

The woman blinked. "*What?*"

"I-I'm not crazy." Damn, but he was making a complete mess of this. Why did this young woman have him so flustered? And why did her eyes look so familiar? He could swear he'd never met her before. Definitely not. He would remember this woman. "She really is a selkie. So if you see any seals . . ."

"Usually, there are some in Seal Cove, but they weren't there this morning."

With a groan, he dragged a hand through his hair. "I'm afraid she's gone off with them. Out to sea . . ." By the Light, he was going crazy. How would he ever find her in the middle of the ocean? "I can only hope that she's with Brody—" He stopped when the piece of charcoal in the woman's hand snapped in two.

"Who?" She scrambled to her feet, letting the flat board and paper tumble to the ground.

"Brody." Nevis hesitated, not sure what to make of the stunned look on this young woman's face. "Do you know him?"

"Ye believe he is with the missing woman?" she asked.

"Perhaps. Her name is Maeve."

"The youngest sister of the queens on the mainland?"
Nevis's mouth fell open. "You—you know Maeve?"

"I know of her." The young woman kneeled on the ground
to stuff her board and paper into the large basket. "We must
alert the queen. She can—"

"Ha!" Nevis scoffed. "Good luck with that. The old biddy
refuses to see anybody."

The young woman glanced up at him. "Excuse me?"

Oh, he probably shouldn't have insulted this woman's
queen. "No offense, Miss, but I've already tried to see Queen
Esther. Three times. And she always refuses. She's the most
unfriendly monarch I've ever—"

"She'll see me." The young woman grabbed the basket's
handle and started across the meadow.

Nevis snorted. "Why would she see you when she refuses
to see me? I'm an official envoy from King Leo of Eberon."

Apparently, the young woman wasn't impressed. She didn't
even bother to look back at him. "The queen has no interest in
what is happening on the mainland."

Nevis jogged to catch up with the woman. "How would
you know? Has Her Royal Unfriendliness ever deigned to
meet you?"

"Aye. Ye may accompany me if ye wish to see her."

He rolled his eyes. "You sound awfully sure that she'll
see you."

"Aye." The young woman slanted him a wry look. "The
old biddy is my mother. I am Princess Elinor."

Nevis tripped and nearly fell on his face.

"Look! A bunch of seals!"

Still groggy with sleep, Maeve cracked open her eyes at the
sound of a young male voice. He was speaking Eberoni, but
with an accent she'd never heard before.

It had been an extremely long swim, broken by a few rest

stops on tiny uninhabited islands that the seals had known about. Shortly after dawn, they had finally reached the northern coast of what she believed was the Isle of Secrets. Utterly exhausted, she hadn't bothered to even look at the island or shift into human form. Her seal friends had shown her a secluded cove, and there they had scooted onto two flat rocks for much-needed sleep.

"Quentin," a female voice replied to the boy. "Leave them be. They look tired."

"But won't it be easier to kill one of them if they're asleep?"

Maeve jerked completely awake.

"The queen loves sealskin," the boy continued. "If we bring her a dead seal, she might give us less work to do."

The queen? Lobby hadn't mentioned a queen, only a sea witch. Maeve lifted her head to look at the newcomers. Two people, one a young woman and the other a boy who looked about nine or ten, were on the western edge of the cove. They were descending a path down a grassy sand dune to the beach.

The woman was dressed in a plain, unbleached linen shift with a ragged hem a few inches above her bare feet. Around her shoulders, she had knotted a linen shawl, and in her hands, she carried a large basket. The boy, dressed in shorts and a ragged shirt, was also barefoot. When he reached the beach, he ran toward the water, lifting a primitive, makeshift spear.

Damn! He actually meant to attack them. Maeve slipped into the water and shifted. As she straightened so the water came to her shoulders, the young woman and boy flinched, dropping the basket and spear.

"What the . . . ?" Quentin retreated a step.

"Please don't hurt the seals," Maeve told them. "They're my friends." At the sound of her voice, the seals woke up and started barking at one another. *Calm down*, Maeve told them. *I'll make sure you're not harmed.*

"How did you . . . how can you look . . . ?" The young woman glanced at the other seals, who had quieted down. "Are they like you?"

"No," Maeve replied as she took a step toward the shore. "I'm a selkie. It's my gift as one of the Embraced."

The young woman stiffened with shock. "N-no. That can't be true."

Quentin pointed at her. "She's lying! We're the only ones who are Embraced."

Maeve looked them over. With their ragged clothes and bare feet, they didn't appear to be part of an army. "Are the two of you Embraced?"

The young woman moved closer, eyeing Maeve with suspicion. "There are many Embraced on this island. We were told we're the only ones."

"That's right!" Quentin glared at Maeve. "So you're a liar. And a fraud, pretending to be the queen! I'm going to tell!" He darted back up the grassy sand dune.

"Quentin, no!" the young woman shouted, but the boy disappeared over the crest.

Pretending to be the queen? What on Aerthlan did the boy mean by that? Maeve waded toward the shore, anxious to get some answers.

The young woman approached her. "I don't know where you came from or how you found us, but you had better leave now." She motioned to the seals. "And you should take them with you."

"I will." Maeve joined her on the beach. "I just have a few questions first, if you don't mind."

The young woman gave her a wary look. "I have questions, too." She unknotted her shawl and handed it to Maeve. "Here. You must be cold."

"Thank you." Maeve tied the shawl around her hips. Her long hair was covering her breasts.

"We must hurry." The young woman glanced nervously to where Quentin had disappeared.

"Why? Is there an Embraced army hereabouts?"

The young woman gasped. "How . . . ?" She stepped back with a frightened look. "How can you know about us? Where did you come from?"

"The Isle of Moon." Maeve assumed this young woman was one of the babes confiscated by Lord Morris. "You came from Eberon, right?"

"I—I don't think so." The young woman shook her head. "I've lived here as long as I can remember."

"Do you have parents here?"

The young woman frowned. "Wh-what are those?"

Maeve winced. "There was no one to raise you, take care of you—"

"Oh, you mean the queen's servants."

Another mention of a queen. Maeve recalled the dream she'd had of a castle with a beautifully strange throne room. And she'd called a woman *Mother.* Oh, good goddesses, that couldn't be here, could it?

"We were told we're the only Embraced on Aerthlan," the young woman said, interrupting Maeve's thoughts. "They said all the others were killed. How is it that you survived?"

Maeve took a deep breath to chase away all thoughts of her last dream. "It was always safe for our kind on the Isle of Moon. I grew up there with my four adopted sisters. We're all Embraced."

The young woman's face grew pale. "How . . . how can that be?"

"My eldest sister, Luciana, is now the queen of Eberon," Maeve explained quickly. "Her husband, King Leo, is Embraced, too, so it's completely safe there now. You could go back and find your family, if you like."

The young woman stumbled back a step. "What? I . . ."

"How many Embraced are here?" Maeve asked. "How big is the army?"

"I-I don't think I should say . . ." When the young woman smoothed back some strands of hair that had escaped her braid, her hand trembled. "Either you're lying, or they . . ." Her eyes glimmered with tears. "This cannot be."

Maeve winced. She'd been in such a hurry to gather information she hadn't realized how confusing and upsetting this meeting had to be for the young woman. "I'm sorry. I-I'll go now." She stepped toward the water, then turned back. "Will you be all right?"

The young woman blinked away her tears. "I don't know. Have I been lied to my entire life?"

Maeve didn't have the heart to confirm it. "My name is Maeve. And you are?"

"Bettina."

"Oh! I've always loved that name." Maeve smiled at the young woman, recalling how she'd almost named Brody that when she'd first met him as a dog. "I'm going to be twenty at the next Autumn Embrace."

"Me, too." Bettina gave her a wobbly smile that quickly vanished. "You'd better go. Your presence alone is proof that we've been lied to. You won't be safe here."

Maeve hesitated, not sure she could make the trip back on an empty stomach. The seals were happy with raw fish, but the only time she'd tried to swallow a fish whole, she'd felt like she was choking. "You don't happen to have any food with you?" She glanced at the fallen basket, but there was only wet seaweed inside.

"I could bring you some food, but for now, you had better hide." Bettina motioned to the east. "If you follow the coast, you'll find a cave—"

"There she is!" Quentin yelled from the top of the sand dune as he pointed at Maeve.

"Go!" Bettina shoved Maeve toward the water.

Maeve ran, but a sudden blast of air knocked her off her feet. *Umph*. She slammed hard onto the beach. Wincing, she looked back. Bettina had also fallen over, and her basket was rolling along the shore, seaweed tumbling out. Where had such a fierce wind come?

"Don't move!" a male voice shouted at her.

She glanced toward the western edge of the cove. Two young men were now standing at the top of the sand dune. Their linen shorts and shirts were dyed green and not ragged like the ones worn by Quentin, who was now sliding down the dune with a big grin.

The men were soldiers, Maeve thought, even though they didn't look any older than she. Their arms and legs were tanned and muscular, their hair cut short. Over their chests, they wore leather breastplates. Their forearms were banded with leather, their feet encased in leather sandals, and their calves covered with leather shin guards. They had to be members of the Embraced army, but neither of them had any weapons that she could see.

With a start, she realized they didn't need swords or spears. One of them had shot a gust of wind at her that was strong enough to knock her down. The same Embraced power that Rupert had! Good goddesses, she needed to get back to warn her sisters and their husbands.

She scrambled to her feet and made another dash for the ocean.

A bolt of lightning blasted into the ground a few feet away, kicking up sand and knocking her back onto her rear. She sat, stunned for a moment, while the air around her crackled with energy.

"Alfred, no!" Bettina cried. "Don't hurt her!"

Maeve glanced at the two soldiers. One of them still had his hand extended toward her. Alfred. He had the same power as Leo!

Hurry! Her seal friends called to her as they plunged into the water. *We need to go! Now!*

Maeve eased to her feet, keeping an eye on Alfred.

"The next bolt will strike the water," he yelled at her. "And it will fry your companions."

"Awesome!" Quentin pranced along the shore.

"Stop that," Bettina hissed at him.

A cold shiver slid down Maeve's spine. She was caught. Hooked like a fish. If she went into the water to shift, she would cause her friends to die. She would die with them. Brody had been right. She was no match for an Embraced army.

Alfred motioned to her with his hand. "Come with us."

Hot tears burned her eyes. *Go,* she told her seal friends.

We don't want to leave without you.

I know. A tear ran down her face. *But you have to. There is a sea cave east of here. Rest there and eat. I will join you as soon as I can.*

As her seal friends swam away, Maeve squared her shoulders and steeled her nerves. *I will escape,* she told herself. The kings on the mainland had to be warned.

Soon they would face an army with the same powers they had.

Chapter 8

"Your Majesty." Nevis bowed low as Queen Esther rose to her feet behind her desk. "I bring greetings from King Leo and Queen Luciana of Eberon."

The queen gave him a regal nod. "Please extend my gratitude to them for the lovely presents."

"Mother, we need to talk." Princess Elinor led the queen into an alcove behind the desk.

Nevis craned his neck, trying to hear their conversation, but he could catch only a word here and there. *Maeve.* More whispers. *Brody.* The queen's reaction to Brody's name was surprising. She gasped and reached out a trembling hand to steady herself against the stone wall.

They were in the queen's privy chamber in the castle, which overlooked the port town of Luna. Nevis was still amazed that he was even here. What a huge difference it had made when he'd entered the Great Hall with Princess Elinor. The guards who had barred him from going any farther the last few days now stepped back and bowed.

And what a shock to realize he'd met the princess. He was still cringing inside at the way he had addressed her and talked about her mother. *Hey, you? Old biddy?* Damn, he was lucky he was here in the queen's privy chamber and not wasting away in a dungeon.

He glanced around the room. The study may have belonged to the late King Rudgar at one time, but it was clearly a woman's room now. The windows were open and white curtains billowed in the breeze that swept up from the harbor. Bookcases lined the bottom portion of the stone walls, but above them, beautiful tapestries and paintings filled the room with color. Most of the paintings were seascapes. Nevis edged closer to one to peer at the name in the corner.

Elinor. Damn, but she was talented. The painting looked so real he could almost hear the waves crashing on the sand. He glanced at her. She was beautiful, too. Smart. Decisive. After hearing the news about Maeve, she'd taken immediate action. And she wasn't pretentious in any way. Her blue linen gown was simple and functional. Her lovely black hair was pulled back in a braid without any ornamentation. As someone who had grown up in the army, he found himself admiring her decisive and practical nature.

And from the great number of paintings on the wall, she was obviously a hard worker. Not at all what he had expected. So beautiful. So perfect.

What the hell? He put a screeching halt to his thoughts. *She's a princess, you idiot. Completely beyond your reach.* Besides, she probably thought he was a rude oaf. With good reason. He'd tried to apologize several times while they were walking to the castle, but she'd ignored his attempts. No doubt she had no personal interest in him whatsoever.

But it was odd how much she and her mother were interested in Brody. Nevis studied the two women. Both had long black hair, although the queen had some gray in hers. They both had brilliant blue eyes. Much like Brody.

By the Light, were they related? He recalled Brody telling him once that he had a mother and sister.

No. Nevis shook his head. This couldn't be right. Mother Ginessa had been clear that the queen had lost her husband and both sons at sea.

The queen walked back to her desk and, gripping the back of her chair, she gave Nevis an assessing look. "My daughter has explained the situation to me. Ye believe Maeve and perhaps Brody have gone south in search of an island."

"Yes, the Isle of Secrets." Nevis had told the princess everything on the way to Lessa Castle, including Maeve's theory that there could be an Embraced army on the island.

"I suggest ye return to Eberon so ye can alert the king and queen," Esther announced. "I will dispatch a ship to search for the island and missing persons."

Nevis winced inwardly. "I will gladly send Captain Shaw back to Eberon with the news. However, with Your Majesty's permission, I would appreciate it if you would allow me to travel with your ship. Maeve's well-being is my responsibility, and I cannot shirk that duty."

Queen Esther's eyebrows rose. "Are ye sure ye wish to go? Rumors have been rampant for years that any ship approaching the Isle of Secrets will be destroyed."

Nevis swallowed hard. So the queen knew about the gossip on the docks. "I still need to go. I have to bring Maeve safely home."

The queen nodded with an approving glint in her eyes. "I see ye are a man of honor. I will grant you permission, then, and if ye don't mind, I would charge you with another duty to fulfill."

"It would be my pleasure to be of service, Your Majesty." Nevis bowed his head. "The king and queen of Eberon would be delighted if you consider us an ally."

Queen Esther's knuckles turned white as her hands tightened their grip on the back of her chair. "Then I will ask, nay, I beg of you—-bring Brody back safely."

Brody again. What was the relationship here? Nevis cleared his throat. "You seem to be well acquainted with him."

The queen lowered her head as a pained look crossed her face. Princess Elinor gave her mother a comforting pat on the shoulder, then turned to Nevis. When she gave him a brief smile, the sight was so beautiful he almost fell over.

"This is Brody's home," the princess said.

The queen raised her head, her eyes shimmering with tears. " 'Tis been almost a year since I last saw him. Bring him home to me. Please."

"Then he—" Nevis dragged a hand through his hair. "No offense, Your Majesty, but I heard at the convent that you lost both your sons."

"I did." A tear ran down the queen's face. "I lost my husband and eldest son to the sea. As for Prince Brodgar, I lost him to a curse."

Brody had tossed and turned most of the night, his sleep haunted by memories of a naked Maeve in his arms. Good goddesses, he was tempted to go back. She had confessed that he was the one she wanted, so what was stopping him?

The curse, dammit. He couldn't be a husband when he was himself only two hours a day. Neither could he be a king when he spent most of his time as a dog. The people on the Isle of Moon deserved better. Maeve deserved better.

But at least he had convinced her to stay at the convent. Knowing that she was safe, he had finally been able to curl up in dog form to sleep.

It was almost noon when he woke. After shifting into the Seer's form, he fed the cat, then settled down at the table with a cup of tea and the Seer's journal. He thumbed through the pages to where he had stopped the day before.

> Spring, Year 680.
> I am thrilled beyond the moons! Today, when Cahira came to see me, she had the most glorious news! She is with child!
> Surely I am the most blessed man in all of Aerthlan. I have the love of the most beautiful woman, and together, we will have a child. We are both thrilled

and saddened, knowing that this precious child will be the last full-blooded descendant of our race.

Once again, I asked Cahira to marry me, but once again, she declined. I cannot blame her. She has an island to rule, the last remnant of the great kingdom of Aerland. Why would she want to share my lonely existence here? Besides, she is working diligently to find us allies on the mainland, so I can bring peace and prosperity to the world. I am so happy at the thought that our child could grow up in a world of peace.

The next day, Spring, Year 680.

Last night I had a dream of our child. I saw her growing up, looking much like her mother with long black hair and sea-green eyes. But to my amazement, the vision revealed that she would become even more beautiful than Cahira. And more powerful. She will surpass us in every way. My heart is so full of love and pride for her! I can hardly wait to tell Cahira!

Mid-Summer, Year 680.

Finally, Cahira returned for a visit, and I was thrilled to see her belly swollen with our child. She admitted that she has felt poorly the last few months, and she's been unable to shift or swim. For the first time, she came by ship to see me.

And for the first time, I am afraid I have seen her true nature.

I told her of my dream, expecting her to be as excited and proud as I am. But she recoiled in horror. She insisted no one could be more beautiful or powerful than she.

Stunned, I questioned how she could speak so grudgingly of our beloved child. She shrugged and told me not to think twice about the matter, since she tended to be a bit grumpy these days due to the pregnancy.

But I have doubts now. I saw the horror on her face. I heard the rage in her voice. I am afraid I have been deceived. She may not be the loving person I thought she was.

Early Autumn, Year 680.

Cahira has not returned, although I occasionally receive a short message by carrier pigeon. She claims she cannot travel because of the pregnancy. I am anxiously awaiting news of our daughter's birth. I know the child will be born healthy, for I have continued to see her in visions.

Late Autumn, Year 680.

Cahira has lied to me. She sent a note that our daughter died in childbirth. I know this cannot be true, for I have seen the child grow up in my dreams.

Cahira assured me she would continue to work on my behalf to make sure I will rule all of Aerthlan someday. My interest in being a ruler has waned. I wish to see my daughter. I wish not to live here alone for the rest of my life.

Brody groaned when he read those words. The Seer never did meet his daughter. But he hadn't had to live alone. Five years later, he'd discovered Brody washed up on the island. And then he'd raised him like a son. Brody took a deep breath and continued to read.

I no longer trust Cahira. She has used me and my visions. She is working only for herself. So selfish and vain that she rejected her own child.

I have seen my daughter growing up in a convent, safe and loved by the sisters there. Did Cahira abandon her because of the dream I had? At least I know the child is safe. Happy and loved. Perhaps it is for the best that Cahira abandoned her.

As for me, Burien of Aerland, my heart is broken. But I must remain strong. I will continue to play along with Cahira's schemes, so I will know what she is doing. Hopefully, someday, I will be able to put a stop to her evil plans.

With a sigh, Brody closed the journal. Poor Seer. It was a shame he had never met Maeve. But he'd been right. Maeve had been better off raised in the convent. Better off not knowing a mother who could abandon her for fear of being surpassed.

"I will watch over your daughter as promised," Brody whispered. "So rest in peace, old man."

Still in the guise of the Seer, Brody wandered into the garden to search for some vegetables to eat. The cat, Trouble, pretended to help him, digging little holes here and there.

A sudden clanging startled him. Good goddesses! Had the ship arrived to take him to Cahira's island?

He pulled off the Seer's clothes, then shifted into an eagle so he could fly to the cove where Nevis and Maeve had arrived two days ago. A small ship had dropped anchor, and he soared around it for a closer look. The flag on the mainsail was one he'd never seen before. A green background with a purple octopus in the middle.

A rowboat had been pulled ashore. Up on the bluff, a young man was waiting. Muscular arms and legs. Leather breastplate and armbands. Most probably a soldier. Was he a member of the Embraced army?

Brody flew back to the garden and shifted into the Seer again. After throwing on the old man's clothes, he dashed into the cottage. What did he need? Not the journal. He couldn't risk Cahira or one of her minions finding it. He stuffed it behind some books in the bookcase.

The Seer possessed only a few clothes, so they were easily stuffed into a linen bag. He donned the Seer's hooded robe, hitched the bag over a shoulder, grabbed the old man's staff, and headed out the door.

At the gate, he glanced back. Would he ever see this cottage again? His heart squeezed when he recalled all the tears and frustration he'd endured while adjusting to the loss of his family and his new life as an accursed shifter. But there had been good moments, too. Moments when he'd known that the Seer loved him.

The cat meowed and rubbed against his legs. *The cat.*

Brody winced. He couldn't leave it behind. "You'll have to come with me."

The cat meowed again as if he understood, and when Brody opened the gate, Trouble darted through, then trailed alongside him as he strode toward the cove.

He would have to slow his steps, Brody reminded himself, once he was in sight of the soldier. He would have to fool everyone into believing he was a hundred-year-old man at death's door.

The real test would be deceiving Cahira. And then somehow getting rid of her and the Chameleon so the Circle of Five would be gone for good. But could he do it?

Could he actually kill Maeve's mother?

After leaving Lessa Castle, Nevis hurried down to the port to explain the situation to Captain Shaw, who was enjoying an ale at the local tavern where Nevis had rented his room.

The captain shook his head, frowning. "How can I return to Ebton Palace without Maeve? We should search for her ourselves."

"I'm going with the queen's ship to find her," Nevis assured him. "You need to warn King Leo that the Embraced army may be on the Isle of Secrets. If it is, we must defeat it before the Chameleon can bring war and destruction to the mainland. Leo and the other kings need to rally their forces immediately."

"All right." The captain tossed a few coins on the table as he rose to his feet. "Send confirmation of the army's location as soon as you can."

"I will." Nevis headed upstairs to his room and stuffed all his clothes into his knapsack. Then he wrote a quick note to Mother Ginessa. Back downstairs, he settled his bill and asked that a boy deliver the note to the convent.

He strode down the pier, looking for the queen's ship. That had to be it with the blue-and-white flag. He halted with a wince. The damned thing was barely any bigger than a fishing boat.

Two men in uniform hurried down the plank onto the pier.

"The Isle of Secrets?" one of them yelled. "Is she trying to get us killed?"

"The queen can't pay me enough to go there!" the other one added as they strode down the pier.

They were deserting? "Wait!" Nevis called after them. "You can't just leave. Aren't you in Her Majesty's navy?"

"Not anymore!" The first man tossed his hat onto the pier. "Even our first officer has refused to go."

The two men stalked off, grumbling.

Damn. Was there no one left onboard? Nevis dragged his hand through his hair. He was a soldier, not a sailor. He couldn't sail the boat by himself.

"Sir?"

Nevis turned and discovered an older man, barefoot and dressed in ill-fitting clothes. His ruddy face was wrinkled and worried, and in his hands, he clutched a floppy hat.

"Is it true?" the old man asked. "Ye're going to search for the young lady who was nice to me?"

Nevis blinked. "Lobby?"

"Aye, 'tis me." He jammed the hat on his head. "I went to the convent this morning like the young lady told me to. They gave me these clothes and a haircut and a nice breakfast. But they were all talking about how she's missing."

Nevis nodded. "Maeve has gone in search of the Isle of Secrets."

"Och, I told her not to do that." Lobby made the sign of the moons with trembling hands.

The man was trying to withdraw from his dependence on liquor, Nevis thought. He rested a hand on the man's shoulder. "Don't worry, Lobby. I'm going to find her. Stay strong."

Lobby's chin wobbled. "But no one will sail with you. Everyone's afraid."

Nevis squeezed his shoulder. "I'm not afraid. I'll find her."

Lobby's face crumpled. "I've always wondered why I was spared. Why all me mates died, and I didn't." He drew in a shaky breath, then lifted his chin. "I know the way. I will take you."

Nevis's mouth fell open. "Are you sure?"

"Aye." Lobby tightened his trembling hands into fists. "This must be why I'm still alive. I have to help that poor lass."

"Thank you. Are you ready to go? Do you need to pack anything?"

Lobby shook his head. "I don't own anything."

"Then let's go." Nevis crossed the plank with Lobby close behind.

The ship was empty except for one lone figure behind the wheel. He stood with his back to them, a hand resting on the sword against his hip. His linen shirt and breeches were blue, along with the long, droopy feather that decorated his wide-brimmed hat.

Was this the captain? Nevis wondered. If so, he was rather small. Could he even use that sword?

Nevis cleared his throat. "Will there be any more seamen joining us?"

The small man turned around, and Nevis stumbled back, his knapsack tumbling to the deck. *Holy crap!* "You-Your Highness?"

She removed her hat, and her long braid of hair fell down her back.

"Yer Highness." Lobby doffed his hat and bowed.

What the hell? Nevis glared at the princess. "What are you doing here? Do you have any idea how dangerous this voyage could be? There's a reason why all the seamen deserted."

Princess Elinor gave him a wry look. "Are ye worried about me?"

"Hell, yes! I mean—" He dragged a hand through his hair. "You're the heir to the throne. You shouldn't take any risks."

She plopped the hat back on her head. "As far as I'm concerned, Brody is the heir. Are ye saying I shouldn't even look for my own brother?"

"You—you should let the men do it," Nevis argued.

She shrugged. "The men are too afraid. I am not."

Damn. She *was* brave. And beautiful. Nevis tried to keep his gaze from dropping to her breeches. For a petite woman, she had long legs. "D-did your mother give you permission to do this?"

"Aye, she did. And ye may address me as captain."

Nevis snorted. "On a cold day in hell."

She raised an eyebrow, then turned to Lobby. "Ye have sailing experience, do ye not?"

"Aye, my lady." He bowed again. "Lobby is the name."

"Thank you, Lobby. Ye'll be my first officer."

Nevis huffed. "Excuse me, Your Highness. I would be the obvious choice. I am a colonel, you know. In fact, that actually outranks a captain."

"Not at sea." Elinor looked him over. "But I am glad ye're

here. All those muscles ye have will come in handy when hauling up the sails."

Nevis blinked. By the Light, she saw his muscles? His heart expanded, but his mind blared in alarm. *Don't you dare fall for her, you fool!* He crossed his arms over his chest. "Do you even know how to sail this decrepit old tub?"

She narrowed her eyes. "Do ye doubt me?"

"She's the princess, sir," Lobby whispered. "She's been sailing all her life. This is her boat."

Nevis groaned inwardly. He certainly didn't have to worry about his unfortunate attraction. The princess must think he was the rudest oaf in all of Aerthlan. He gritted his teeth. "I'm quite certain this lovely boat will be sufficient for our needs."

"Exactly." Elinor nodded. "A larger ship would draw attention and perhaps come under attack. With my boat, I believe we can sneak in unnoticed."

Lobby nodded. "An excellent idea, Captain. The Sea Witch's castle is on the northwestern edge of the island, so, to be safe, we should steer toward the opposite end."

"Thank you, Lobby," she replied with a smile. "Will ye untie the mooring ropes, please, so we can be on our way?"

"Aye, Captain!" Lobby scurried off.

Nevis started to follow.

"Colonel." Elinor stopped him with a raised hand. "Ye may take your belongings belowdecks. You and Lobby will share the spare cabin with the cook."

"As you wish." Nevis picked up his knapsack. "Anything else . . . Captain?"

Her mouth twitched. "It must be getting colder."

"I must be in hell," he muttered, then trudged down the stairs at the sound of her laughter.

Chapter 9

A s Maeve approached the soldiers, she cringed inwardly at how intently the young men were staring at her. Brody had been right, blast him. She was no match for an Embraced army. And she shouldn't have shifted in front of other people. At least the soldiers seemed to be more focused on her face than the rest of her half-naked body.

"She looks so much like—" the wind-wielding soldier began.

"Shh." The other soldier, Alfred, hushed him.

"Will you carry this for me?" Bettina shoved her large basket into Maeve's arms.

Why? Maeve glanced down at the seaweed in the basket, then realized that the basket was shielding her breasts from view much better than her hair could do. She gave Bettina a grateful look. "Thank you."

"I can come with you as far as the village," Bettina whispered as she walked alongside her.

"Thank you," Maeve whispered back.

"Quiet," Alfred ordered. "And hurry it up."

"You're in big trouble now, shifter!" Quentin raced in front of the women as they slowly climbed the dune.

Maeve took a deep breath to calm her nerves and racing thoughts. How could she escape? Or would it be better not to escape? If she remained here, she might learn a great deal of useful information. Or she might end up locked in a dungeon.

In any case, there was nothing she could do now but play along. She couldn't fight or run away—these Embraced soldiers could strike her down or kill her with a wave of a hand. Could she talk her way out of being a prisoner? Brody had claimed she was a beauty, a siren who could make men cross the sea for her. She'd never believed it, but it wouldn't hurt to see how effective her so-called charm could be.

When she reached the top of the dune, she gave the soldiers a friendly smile. "My name is Maeve. It's a pleasure to meet you, Alfred and . . . ?" She glanced at the wind-wielding soldier. He looked a year or two younger than she was.

"Darroc, Miss." He bowed his head.

Maeve widened her smile. "Your gift is very impressive, Darroc."

He blushed. "Thank you."

"Are there many more like you here?" Maeve asked.

"Yes, about—"

"Shut up!" Alfred elbowed Darroc in the ribs, then glared at Maeve. "You're our prisoner. We'll ask the questions."

Obviously, her charm didn't work on everyone. Even so, Maeve figured it would be better to behave more like a guest than a captive. "I would be happy to answer your questions, Alfred."

His glare grew wary. "You would? You're not here to spy on us?"

Maeve scoffed. "Goodness, no. Are you taking me to the queen? I would be delighted to meet her."

Alfred smirked. "As if you have any choice."

Maeve forced a smile. "May I ask her name?"

"Cahira," Darroc answered when Alfred remained silent.

"She lives in the big castle over there." Quentin pointed west.

Now that she was at the top of the dune, Maeve could make out the towers in the distance. Was this the castle she'd seen in her dream? Would she meet her mother there?

"The queen might throw you in the dungeon," Quentin added, then bit his lip with a look of regret.

Maeve groaned inwardly. Her "guest" approach wasn't working well, either.

"No more talking." Alfred motioned to a path that wound down the hill. "This way." He took the lead, followed by Quentin, Bettina, and Maeve.

She realized Darroc was staying close behind her. Probably so she couldn't attempt a mad dash back to the ocean.

Once they reached the bottom of the hill, the path led them along a valley for a short distance. The sand gave way to grass that felt much cooler beneath Maeve's bare feet. When they climbed another hill, she stopped at the top with a gasp.

The wide, shallow valley was filled with a farming village. Several wooden cottages stood in the center, made of roughly hewn logs and thatched roofs. Surrounding the homes were vegetable gardens and, farther out, fields of grain and a pasture of cows and sheep. It looked much like any other farming village Maeve had ever seen, but what made her stop and stare were the laborers.

Children.

Some of them appeared to be under the age of ten. Were these the Embraced children Lord Morris had taken from their families?

"Keep moving," Darroc grumbled behind her, and she followed the others down the hill. After passing through a field of grain, they reached a garden where a few children were digging up root vegetables.

Maeve winced at their dirty feet, ragged clothes, and resigned, weary expressions. Did the queen know what was going on here? Did she actually condone it? "Are these the Embraced children?" she whispered.

Bettina nodded. "They live here until their Embraced gift shows itself. Then Queen Cahira and Kendric decide if the gift is powerful enough for the army."

"Who is Kendric?"

"The general," Bettina whispered. "If the gift is deemed . . . undesirable, the child remains here."

"As a slave?" Maeve muttered, and Bettina winced.

"Quiet!" Alfred glanced back at them, scowling.

They reached the outskirts of the village, where a young girl of about five was hanging seaweed on a rack to dry.

She ran up to Bettina. "Am I doing it right?"

"Yes." Bettina gave the girl a hug. "Thank you, Sarah. I'll bring you more seaweed in a minute." She leaned down to whisper, "And a honey cake."

Sarah grinned, then ran back to the rack.

"We use the seaweed for soup or to enrich the soil in the garden," Bettina explained.

"Do the children go to school or have time to play?" Maeve asked.

"If you don't work, you don't eat," Darroc said behind her. "That goes for you, too, Quentin. Back to work."

"Yes, sir." Quentin's skipping gait came to an abrupt halt, and he trudged into one of the buildings.

The boy looked so sad, Maeve felt guilty for disliking him earlier. As they passed the blacksmith's shop, she saw Quentin inside the three-walled building, working hard at the bellows in the searing heat. An old gray-haired man was hammering a sword.

He glanced up at Alfred. "Colonel, I have more coins for the castle."

So Alfred was a colonel in the Embraced army? And someone named Kendric was the general. Maeve watched as Alfred examined a small basket of plain iron coins.

"I'll send a servant for these, Thomas," Alfred told the old man, then pointed at Maeve. "You. Follow me." He turned and marched away.

"I have a name," Maeve muttered.

"Shouldn't she be properly dressed before she goes to the castle?" Bettina asked. "You wouldn't want to offend the queen."

Alfred stopped and glanced back.

"I could loan her a gown," Bettina offered. "It would take only a moment."

With a frown, Alfred crossed his arms. "Very well, but be quick about it."

"This way." Bettina led Maeve inside a wooden cottage and closed the door.

"Is this your home?" Maeve asked as she looked about. About a quarter of the room was taken up by a large loom. The young woman working it glanced up, her eyes widening in shock. Maeve smiled at her. "Hello."

"Who . . . ?" The young woman rose to her feet. "She looks so much like . . ."

"I know." Bettina motioned to the young woman. "This is Catriona. And Olana is there at the spinning wheel. We live here, along with Sarah and the other girls."

Olana's jaw dropped as she stared at Maeve.

"Hello. My name is Maeve." She smiled at Olana, who appeared to be about twelve years of age.

Catriona slowly approached her. "How did you get here?"

"Or more importantly—why?" Bettina gave Maeve a frustrated look. "There is nothing here for you but danger."

"And constant labor," Olana muttered.

"Let me find you a gown." Bettina took the basket from Maeve's arms and set it on the wooden floor.

Olana gasped. "She's naked!"

"I'm a selkie," Maeve explained. "I swam here, so I arrived without clothes."

Olana stepped toward her. "Then you're a shifter?"

Before Maeve could answer, Catriona grabbed her by the arm.

"You must swim away," Catriona insisted. "Now."

"She can't." Bettina selected a folded gown from a stack on a shelf. "Alfred and Darroc have taken her prisoner."

With a gasp, Catriona released her. "Oh, no."

Olana backed away, crossing her arms over her chest. "Are they taking her to the dungeon like they did Gabby?"

Maeve stiffened. There was a girl in the dungeon?

A banging on the door made them all jump.

"Hurry up!" Alfred shouted.

"That ass," Catriona muttered.

Maeve winced. "I have to agree."

Catriona leaned close. "He thinks he's superior to everyone because he's the only one with lightning power."

"But actually, he . . ." Maeve hesitated, unsure whether she should let anyone on this island know that Leo had the same power.

"Here. You can wear this." Bettina slipped a plain linen shift over Maeve's head.

"But that's your best gown," Olana said.

As the blue linen gown fell to Maeve's calves, she pulled the shawl off her hips and handed it to Bettina. "I shouldn't take your best—"

"You'll be meeting the queen." Bettina looped the shawl around Maeve's shoulders. "You must be careful."

"Why?" Maeve asked, but before anyone could reply, Alfred banged on the door again.

"Come out now!" he ordered.

The three females gave Maeve a worried look as she turned toward the door.

"Good luck," Bettina whispered.

* * *

As Maeve walked toward the castle with the two soldiers, she eyed it carefully to see if it matched the one from her dream. It was hard to tell, though, since in her dream she had floated toward the castle from the north, where it faced the sea. Now, they were arriving from the back.

The garden looked eerily familiar, though, with its hedges clipped to resemble rolling waves and larger plants trimmed into the shapes of dolphins and other sea creatures.

This had to be the castle, she thought. What other garden in all of Aerthlan would look like this? But why were her dreams coming true? Did this mean she would meet her mother inside?

As they approached the back of the castle, she noted a wide staircase leading up to the main floor that had a large balcony overlooking the garden. But instead of heading up the stairs, Alfred and Darroc led her to a plain door on the ground level that looked like the servants' entrance.

Apprehension crept into her bones as they entered and she noted the gray, unadorned stone walls. Was she on her way to the dungeon? The stone floor was cool beneath her bare feet, but felt dusty. The soldiers' leather sandals made clopping noises that echoed off the walls. *Clunk. Clunk.* The repetitive sound grated on her nerves, reminding her of the slow drumbeat that announced a doomed criminal arriving at the gallows.

Soon they entered a vast cellar room, its low arched ceiling supported by numerous stone pillars. No windows, so the air was stale and musty. Light from a few torches flickered, but most of the room remained in shadow. Across the wide room, beside one torch, she spotted iron bars. A row of prison cells.

At the end of the row, a gasp came from the shadows. Then a crash.

"What is going on?" Darroc pulled a torch from its wall bracket and walked toward the noise.

In the light, Maeve could see a girl behind the bars staring at her. In front of the bars, an older woman was hunched down, hastily collecting wooden bowls and utensils off the floor and depositing them on a wooden tray.

"What are you doing here, Ruth?" Alfred demanded.

"I came to pick up Gabby's breakfast tray," Ruth mumbled, her head bowed.

The girl behind bars was Gabby? Maeve thought she looked only about sixteen or so. Hardly more than a child. Why on Aerthlan was she locked up?

Alfred scoffed. "Well, you certainly made a mess of it."

"I'm sorry, Colonel." Ruth straightened, holding the tray. "I didn't mean to drop it. We were just shocked when we saw the young woman—"

"Right," Gabby agreed. "She looks so much like—"

"Enough!" Alfred snarled. "Get back to work, both of you. And Gabby, there will be more coins arriving this afternoon."

Gabby's shoulders slumped as she retreated into her cell.

Maeve gritted her teeth. "This is outrageous. Why is that girl imprisoned?"

Alfred scoffed, then pointed at the next cell. "You could end up there, so keep your mouth shut."

"Bully," Gabby muttered, and Alfred shot her a vicious look.

Maeve lifted her chin. "Take me to Queen Cahira immediately. I need to have a word with her."

Gabby ran to the bars and grabbed on to them. "Ask her about Gavin. I haven't seen him in—"

"Enough!" Alfred shouted. "Ruth, do you know where the queen is?"

Ruth slanted Maeve a worried look, then replied with her head bowed. "She's in the tank, taking her morning swim."

"This way." Alfred motioned for Maeve to follow him.

Darroc slid the torch back into place, then caught up with Maeve.

"Why is Gabby behind bars?" Maeve whispered.

"She refused to work," he mumbled.

Maeve sighed. The more she saw of this island, the more it angered her. What kind of queen could be so cruel to children? Even though Maeve knew she ought to be planning her escape so she could send a warning to her sisters and their husbands, the situation here was pressing on her mind and conscience. How could she leave these children without trying to help them?

Of course, if she wasn't careful, she could end up in the prison cell next to Gabby.

After walking through a maze of narrow stone corridors, they finally stopped in front of a closed door.

"Darroc, stand guard here in case she tries to escape," Alfred ordered.

"Aye, Colonel."

Alfred opened the door and shoved Maeve inside. She stumbled a few steps, then halted in shock.

Was she underwater? No, she was perfectly dry and standing on a solid stone floor, but surrounding her was water. And fish.

"What is this place?" She moved to her right and pressed a hand against clear glass.

"This is the tank room." Alfred closed the door behind them.

"I've never seen such a huge window." She peered into the tank and saw fish, sea plants and coral. "It looks like the sea."

"The tank has a tunnel that leads into the ocean, so sometimes fish find their way inside." Alfred snorted. "They rarely make it back out."

"They can't find their way out again?" She glanced at Alfred, and he smirked.

"No, they're dinner."

She stepped back from the tank and looked around. At the end of the narrow room, there was a staircase she assumed went to the top of the tank. Across from the giant glass window, the wall was covered with mirrors that reflected the water and fish, making the entire room appear to be under the sea.

A sudden movement in a mirror drew her attention, and she turned back to peer into the glass. A long sleek body shot up to the surface, then dove back down. A seal.

Maeve planted her hands on the glass. *Can you hear me? Are you all right? Are you trapped?*

The seal zoomed around the perimeter of the tank. *Who are you that you can speak to me?*

I'm a selkie.

The seal came to a stop close to Maeve and peered at her with glistening black eyes. *You.*

Yes. Are you trapped in there? Don't worry. There is a way out.

Without answering her, the seal curled under and swam away, back into the murky depths of the tank.

Maeve leaned against the glass, trying to see where the seal had gone. A sudden flash of light made her turn her head and close her eyes.

As soon as she opened her eyes, a huge purple mass slammed against the glass. She jumped back with a gasp. Thick tentacles slithered like snakes across the glass, the suction cups gripping the smooth surface to propel the large, quivering body closer to Maeve.

It was an octopus, the biggest one Maeve had ever seen, possessing a body or mantle as large as an adult human and tentacles as long and thick as a man's legs. The mantle undulated, turning until the creature's head pressed against the glass and one huge eye focused on Maeve.

She swallowed hard. Still, the octopus remained, its eye watching her intently. Should she try communicating with it? *Why are you staring at me?*

No answer. She glanced at Alfred. "When is the queen going to arrive?"

With a snort, he leaned against the door and crossed his arms.

"I thought she was taking a morning swim. Will she be safe in there with this giant—" Maeve stopped when the octopus suddenly pushed away from the glass and disappeared into the murky depths.

Another flash of light brightened the room for a few seconds. Maeve stepped closer to the tank, but couldn't see anything inside but a few fish, darting about as they tried to find the way out.

"It won't be long now," Alfred said softly.

Maeve's stomach rumbled, a reminder that she was hungry. She glanced at the mirror across from her and winced as she caught sight of her tangled hair and tired features. But she couldn't let hunger and exhaustion beat her down. She squared her shoulders. After answering the queen's questions, she would have to find a way to help the children.

A slight swishing sound drew her attention to the staircase. It was the rustling of silk. A figure came into view, a woman dressed in a purple, hooded robe. She was tall and slim, but the voluminous hood was hiding her face so that all Maeve could see was her chin and mouth.

Alfred bowed, so Maeve sank into a curtsy. This had to be Queen Cahira.

The woman came to a stop at the base of the stairs. "Where did you come from?"

She had a pleasant, melodious voice, Maeve thought. "The Isle of Moon, Your Majesty. I grew up in the convent there."

Queen Cahira's hands curled into fists. "Did you now? And how old are you?"

"I'll be twenty on the next Autumn Embrace."

The queen stiffened. "And what name did they give you at the convent?"

"Maeve, Your Majesty." When the queen was silent for a moment, Maeve continued. "I had a good childhood there, filled with laughter and love. Quite the opposite of the way the children here—"

"Enough." Queen Cahira waved a dismissive hand. "You're a selkie who can talk to seals and other sea creatures."

"Yes, Your Majesty."

"Can you shift into other creatures?"

"No, Your Majesty."

She scoffed lightly, turning her head away. "And he said you would be more powerful than I."

"Excuse me?"

Cahira didn't reply, but walked slowly toward her. Maeve could feel the woman's intense gaze boring into her.

"Why have you come here?"

Maeve winced inwardly at the sharp tone the queen had suddenly adopted. "I . . . was curious."

"Why?"

"I read about an old legend that claimed there was once an ancient continent here called Aerland. I wanted to see for myself if any of it remained."

Cahira's hand shot out and gripped Maeve by the chin. "Were you drawn to the legend? Did it speak to you?"

Maeve attempted to pull away, but the queen's fingers tightened, digging into her skin.

"Answer me," she hissed.

Maeve recalled how she had lost an entire afternoon while immersed in the old book, how she had understood the ancient language and felt the terror of the catastrophic end. "Yes. It drew me in . . . as if I was there."

With a slight smile, the queen released her. "Good. It's in your blood."

"My—" Maeve began, but was interrupted by Alfred.

"I don't think she's being entirely truthful," he muttered. "She failed to mention that she was asking about the Embraced army."

Cahira stepped back. "She did?" Her voice rose in anger.

"Did you come here to spy on me? Are you working for those evil queens on the mainland?"

Maeve shot Alfred an annoyed look, then faced Cahira. "Those queens are my adopted sisters. I love—"

"No! They are nothing to you! They are beneath you," Cahira hissed, then pointed at Maeve. "You are the last descendant of the ancient race of Aerland. You have the blood of noble sorcerers in your veins."

Maeve gritted her teeth, fighting to remain calm. "How would you know anything about me?"

Cahira scoffed. "I know more about you than you do, you silly child. Do you actually believe you were born on the Autumn Embrace?"

Maeve stiffened. "Of course I was. Being able to shift is my Embraced gift."

"You're not Embraced."

Maeve jolted and stumbled back a step. "Th-that's not true. My sisters and I are all Embraced." It was the one thing they had always known for sure. They hadn't known if they had family. They hadn't known why they'd been abandoned. But they had always agreed that they were all Embraced. "It's not true."

Cahira waved a hand impatiently. "It is. You were born a month before the Autumn Embrace."

"No!" Tears burned Maeve's eyes. This one belief had been the bedrock of her childhood, the only fact that she could count on. "It's not true! How else would I be able to shift?"

"You inherited the gift from me." Cahira shoved her hood back, and Maeve gasped.

The queen looked like an older version of herself.

Cahira smirked. "I can shift into any sea creature I desire."

"Then . . ." Maeve gave the tank a wary glance. "You were the seal? And the octopus?"

Cahira nodded, her mouth still twisted with a smirk. "Apparently, you inherited only a small portion of my ability." She grasped Maeve by the shoulders and turned her toward a mirror. "And a small portion of my beauty."

A shiver crept down Maeve's spine. Good goddesses, no. Not this woman. "You're my . . ." Goddesses help her, she couldn't even bring herself to say it.

"Yes." Cahira released her with an irritated look. "I'm your mother."

Chapter 10

The sea was so close, yet so far away, Maeve thought as she peered out the window of her new bedchamber on the third floor of the castle. She glanced back at the open door, where Alfred was standing in the hallway, giving instructions to an armed guard.

Was she a prisoner here? she wondered as Alfred marched away. If she was, then her cell was a beautiful one, not anything like the dungeon where Gabby was being held. Maeve could hardly remember the walk from the tank room to this room, for she had been too stunned by the things she'd heard from her mother.

Her *mother*. Good goddesses. It would have been shocking enough to simply find her mother, but no—her mother was hiding the Embraced army! If Lord Morris had sent the Embraced children here to her mother's island, then she must have been in league with him. How involved was she with the Circle of Five?

This was terrible, Maeve thought with a groan. Now she knew how Gwennore must have felt when she'd learned that her mother had been allied with the Circle of Five.

"Welcome to Aerie Castle," a servant said as she walked into the bedchamber, carrying a large tray filled with plates and a pitcher. "I expect you must be hungry from your long journey."

It was the same old woman who had brought a tray to

Gabby in the dungeon. How ironic, Maeve thought, that she was receiving a warmer welcome from this servant than she had from her mother.

After her mother had announced who she was, she'd turned to Alfred and told him, "Take her to the blue bedchamber and post a guard." Then she'd sauntered from the tank room without saying another word to Maeve. Without even glancing at her.

But Maeve could hardly be surprised by her mother's cold behavior. After all, the woman had abandoned her as a babe on the Isle of Moon. Like Gwennore, Maeve could only be grateful that she had been abandoned. Growing up with her sisters at the convent had been a blessing.

She hurried toward the older woman. "That must be heavy. Let me help you."

"Don't worry. I'm used to it." The servant smiled as she set the tray onto a round wooden table in front of a carved wooden chair.

"Your name is Ruth?"

"Aye, Your Highness." Ruth bowed her head.

Maeve winced at the title—not only unfamiliar, but unwelcome if it meant ruling over an island where children were forced into labor.

"If you desire more food or anything else, simply pull the cord over there." Ruth pointed to a bell pull next to the large bed.

"Thank you." Maeve selected a piece of bacon off a plate and bit into it. "I am starving."

Ruth's eyes softened as she regarded Maeve fondly. "It is such a relief to see you alive and well."

Maeve tilted her head, not sure how to interpret these words. "Why would I not be alive and well?"

Ruth glanced at the open door where the guard was standing in the hallway, then lowered her voice. "I was with the queen when you were born."

"Really?"

Ruth nodded, and her eyes glimmered with tears. "You were such a sweet baby. I took care of you for nine months, but then you were sent away."

"Why?"

"I don't know. Nearly broke my heart, it did." A tear rolled down Ruth's face, and she quickly wiped it away. "The queen said you had died."

Maeve flinched. Apparently her mother had disliked her for a long time.

"I'm so sorry, lass," Ruth whispered.

"It . . . it was a long time ago," Maeve murmured. Instead of lamenting the past, she needed to plan for the future. And it would be a great help if there was someone here in the castle whom she could trust. Ruth appeared to be her best choice. Still, it would be hard to talk to the servant with the guard so close by.

She glanced around the bedchamber as she finished the piece of bacon. The walls were painted a creamy pale yellow, but decorated with paintings of a deep blue sea. The curtains at the window were blue, as well as the curtains surrounding the four-poster bed. The coverlet was blue velvet, matching the pillows on the chairs and window seat. No wonder this was called the blue room. "Is there a privy or a dressing room?"

"Aye. I'll show it to you." Ruth walked across the room. "Her Majesty will have some appropriate clothing delivered to you." She lowered her voice once more. "Old gowns and shoes she has outgrown."

Maeve snorted, thinking about all the lovely gowns her sister Luciana was always having made for her. When Ruth opened a door, Maeve stepped inside and looked around. There was a dressing table and shelves for clothing, and toward the back of the room, a chamber pot and empty bathtub.

"Is it possible for me to have a bath?" Maeve walked farther into the room and motioned for Ruth to follow her.

"Of course. I'll have some hot water delivered to you."

Maeve stepped close to the servant and whispered, "Am I a prisoner here?"

Ruth winced. "You are free to move about the castle as long as a guard accompanies you."

"And leaving the castle?"

Ruth shook her head. "You would be stopped. Alfred is convinced you are a spy."

Maeve sighed. Alfred was right. She needed to alert her sisters and their husbands that she had located the Embraced army, but she couldn't get to the sea to shift. How could she escape to the Isle of Moon?

She wandered over to the tub and ran her fingers along the brass rim. How to get to the ocean?

She froze. The tank room. It was here in the castle and it had some sort of access tunnel to the ocean.

Her heart raced. Yes, that would be her escape plan! But before she could leave, she needed to help the children. "Why is Gabby in the dungeon?"

"She has a very special Embraced gift," Ruth whispered. "She can turn iron into gold."

Maeve's mouth dropped open. That explained why the smithy was making iron coins. "Gabby is a goldmine?"

Ruth nodded. "The queen spent most of her gold bribing a few people on the mainland to join forces with her. Just as she was going broke, Gabby's gift appeared, so you can imagine how thrilled Her Majesty was. But Gabby refused to help the queen further her evil plans."

"So the queen locked her up," Maeve muttered.

"More than that." Ruth bowed her head with a defeated expression. "She took Gabby's twin brother away. We don't know where Gavin is. Gabby will never see him again unless she makes all the gold the queen wants."

"Oh, this is terrible." Maeve recalled Gabby asking about Gavin. If the boy's life was in danger, Maeve had to do something.

She touched Ruth's hand. "Thank you for telling me so much. It's a great relief to know you are here."

Ruth smiled and gave Maeve's hand a squeeze. "I'm not the only servant who is happy to have you back home. Let me know if you need anything."

"Thank you." Maeve wandered back into the bedchamber and spotted the guard, still standing in the hallway, frowning at them. She raised her voice. "Thank you for showing me how everything works."

"My pleasure, Your Highness." Ruth bowed. "I'll have the hot water brought up for you right away." She rushed out of the room. "Her Highness will need privacy in order to bathe," she told the guard, then shut the door.

Thank the goddesses she had Ruth on her side. Or at least she thought she did. Maeve winced at the possibility that Ruth could be rushing off right now to report their conversation to the queen. *Aargh.* She needed to get away from this place as soon as possible.

She pivoted, looking around the bedchamber. Was that another door? She dashed toward it. No luck. It was locked.

With a sigh, she trudged back to the table, then sat down to eat. How could she escape? How could she help Gabby and the other children? Did she have any power here as the princess and heir to the throne? Or was she simply a prisoner and suspected spy?

Would she have more success if she pretended to play along with her mother's plans? Clearly, Cahira was working with the remaining members of the Circle of Five. If Maeve allied herself with her mother, she might learn the identity of those members.

As she poured some apple cider into her cup, her hand

trembled. Could she actually do this? Befriend her mother in order to betray her?

And what was Brody doing? He'd said he had a plan to find the army and last Circle members. Did that mean he was coming here?

Maeve jumped in her chair when a knock suddenly pounded on her door. "Yes?"

The door swung open and a line of servants marched in. The first five servants were carrying buckets of hot water, and the last five had their arms full of clothing.

"I'll get the door." Maeve dashed over to the dressing room and opened the door.

As the servants filed past her, a flash of gold caught Maeve's eye. "Wait." She stopped the woman who was carrying a stack of four gowns. On top was a beautiful gown of shimmering gold satin.

The same gown Maeve had worn in her dream.

She stumbled back a step and leaned against a wall.

"Is there a problem, Your Highness?" the servant asked.

Maeve shook her head and motioned for the woman to proceed. The servants finished their work, then headed back out the door. The guard peered in at her, then shut the door.

Maeve's knees gave out, and she slid down the wall to sit on the floor. It was all too much. She'd found her mother. She'd found the Embraced army. She'd learned she wasn't Embraced.

And now, she'd seen the gold satin gown from her dream. Why was this happening? First, she'd seen the burial cairn and Brody on the Isle of Mist. Then, she'd seen this castle on the Isle of Secrets. In her dream, she'd even addressed her mother by name.

Holy goddesses, she could no longer deny the truth. Some-how, even though she wasn't Embraced, she had acquired a new magical gift.

She was able to see the future.

* * *

"I have good news and bad news," Nevis said as he carried two tankards onto the main deck. He handed one of the tankards to Princess Elinor.

She sipped some apple cider and smiled. "Thank you. 'Tis cool and sweet."

"Aye, that's the good news." Nevis drank some cider, trying not to think about how adorable the princess looked in her breeches and floppy hat.

"Then what's the bad news?" she asked.

"Cider is all we have. The cook has drunk all the wine."

Elinor's eyes widened. "There was a whole barrel."

Nevis nodded. "He's currently passed out on the floor of the galley."

Elinor winced.

"He's afraid we're all going to die," Lobby grumbled as he stood at the wheel.

"We're not dying!" Nevis growled.

"Definitely not." The princess sat on a trunk and calmly sipped her cider.

How could she be so incredibly brave? And so perfect? Nevis wondered, then slapped himself mentally. She was a princess, dammit. Far beyond his reach. And she was Brody's sister. Brody would probably kill him if he even attempted to court her.

"Have a seat, Colonel." Princess Elinor patted the spot next to her on the trunk. "I want to hear all about my brother. What has he been doing the past six years?"

Nevis perched on the edge of the trunk in order to leave some space between himself the princess. "Did Brody never visit you in all that time?"

She sighed. "Only a few times. Mostly, he just sent us notes that he was alive and well. How did ye meet him?"

Nevis told the story of how Brody had appeared in the army camp as a bedraggled dog and how Leo had hired him as a spy. "He would be gone for a month or so at a time, gathering information; then he'd return to camp. I kept his clothes in my tent, so he could go there to shift."

"So ye were roommates?"

"I suppose you could say that. I made a pallet for him out of old blankets. The other soldiers thought he was my pet."

Princess Elinor gave Nevis a beaming smile that nearly made him fall off the trunk. "Thank you for being his friend. I'm so glad he wasn't alone."

"I-I'm not sure if I was that good a friend. I used to get mad at him when he wolfed down all my food. Or when he infested my tent with fleas."

The princess wrinkled her nose. "Fleas?"

Nevis nodded. "I hate fleas."

She gave him a wry look. "I doubt Brody liked them much, either."

"Well, I suppose that's true."

Her eyes twinkled with amusement. "Ye're blushing."

"I am not." He stiffened. "Soldiers don't blush."

Her mouth twitched. "I see."

He cleared his throat, searching his mind for a way to change the subject. "Is there a reason why your mother is reluctant to ally herself with the kings on the mainland?"

"Well, ye must know that we worship the moon goddesses." When Nevis nodded, she continued. "For centuries, the kings on the mainland persecuted and killed anyone who worshipped Luna and Lessa. So we learned it was safer to have as little contact with the mainland as possible."

"But it's completely different now," he insisted. "All four of the mainland queens grew up on the Isle of Moon. The worship of the twin moons is totally accepted."

Princess Elinor nodded. "I am aware of that, but others on the isle are not. Old traditions can be slow to change."

"Is Brody going to be king of the isle one day?" Nevis asked.

She frowned. "He should be, but he refuses to come home

until he gets rid of the curse. He doesn't think the islanders could accept a king who's a dog most of the time."

Nevis shrugged. "There could be some advantages to being a dog king. If someone made him angry, he could bite them."

Her frown disappeared as a twinkle returned to her eyes. "There are a few courtiers who would deserve that."

"And they couldn't expect him to listen to their complaints for hours on end," Nevis added. "Since Brody wouldn't be able to talk very much."

"That would be an advantage for someone who tends to put his foot in his mouth," she said with a pointed look.

With a wince, he shifted his weight on the edge of the trunk. "I—I am really sorry for the way I addressed you and your mother."

" 'Hey, you'? 'Old biddy'?"

"It was a . . . a mistake."

"Ye're blushing again."

"Am not." He gulped down more cider.

"I told my mother what ye called her."

He choked, then swallowed quickly, his eyes watering. "What? How could . . . ? Dammit! I mean, pardon my language, but the queen must really hate me now."

"No." Princess Elinor grinned at him. "It made her laugh. And I haven't heard my mother laugh in ages. Thank you so much, Colonel." She touched his arm.

He fell *splat* onto his rump on the deck. *Dammit!* He jumped to his feet and acted as if nothing had happened, even though the princess was biting her lip to keep from laughing.

"So." Nevis propped an elbow on the ship's railing as he leaned nonchalantly against it. "Brody told me once that he had a mother and sister, but of course, I never imagined that you would be royalty."

She twisted on the trunk to face Nevis. "Brody mentioned us?"

"Aye, and he said he'd sought out many witches to undo the curse, but he'd learned that the only one who could lift it was the witch who had put the curse on him to begin with."

"Oh." Her shoulders slumped. "All I know is that the curse began when my father's ship was destroyed at sea. My father and eldest brother died, along with the crew. Brody only survived because he was able to shift."

"It had to be the Sea Witch," Lobby muttered.

The princess sat up. "Are ye sure?"

The old man nodded. "She's the only one powerful enough to blow up a ship. That's what she did to the ship I was on. When I lost all me mates."

"And you say this Sea Witch lives on the Isle of Secrets?" Nevis asked.

Lobby's hands trembled and he grasped the wheel tighter. "Aye, she's there. If she sees us, she'll destroy our ship. She'll try to kill us."

"Don't worry," Princess Elinor assured him. "She won't see us."

How could she be so confident? Nevis wondered.

"This is excellent news," she added. "If we find the Sea Witch, then we can make her lift the curse and Brody will go back to normal."

Lobby shook his head. "She'll kill us first."

"Nay." The princess waved a dismissive hand. "We'll be fine, believe me."

Was the island really that dangerous? Nevis wondered. "I hope Maeve is all right."

"Aye," Lobby agreed. "We need to find the lass and get her out of there."

"If Brody is with Maeve, we can rescue them both." Princess Elinor finished her cider, then turned toward Nevis.

"Do ye think something is going on between my brother and Maeve?"

"I-I'm not sure." Nevis turned his gaze to the sea. "I know she cares a great deal for him, but as long as he's cursed, I don't think Brody will pursue her."

"Then he is a fool," the princess muttered. "If a man falls in love, he should be bold in the pursuit of his lady's heart."

Nevis slanted a quick glance her direction. "Even if one of them is royalty?"

"Ye mean because Brody is a prince?" Princess Elinor set her tankard on the deck by the trunk. "It shouldn't matter. Not if he loves her."

Nevis's hand tightened its grip on his tankard. Should he pursue the princess, then? How could he? She and her mother both considered him a fool who made them laugh.

"Land ahoy!" Lobby announced, pointing at a strip of land barely visible in the distance.

"Wonderful!" Princess Elinor jumped to her feet to watch.

"I'm bringing us up on the eastern coast," Lobby said. "Far enough away from the Sea Witch's castle that hopefully she won't see us."

"She won't see us." Princess Elinor rummaged through a bag and withdrew a stack of papers. "I came prepared."

"What is that?" Nevis set his empty tankard on the deck and approached her. The paper on top was a painting of the ocean.

She dropped the painting on deck, then scattered more paintings around them. The deck shimmered, then suddenly, there was ocean all around them.

"What the hell?" Nevis collapsed onto the trunk and held on. The trunk was still there. The deck was still there, but all he could see was ocean.

"Holy goddesses!" Lobby wrapped his arms around the wheel. "Are we all going to drown?"

"Don't worry." The princess crossed the now invisible deck and touched Lobby on the shoulder. "'Tis only an illusion. If anyone looks our way, all they will see is ocean."

"Your . . . your paintings did that?" Nevis gave her an incredulous look.

She nodded. "Brody isn't the only Embraced one in our family."

He gaped at her. "You . . . you're amazing."

She smiled. "Thank you."

"If you painted a cherry pie, could you make it become real?"

She laughed. "Yes, but ye wouldn't want to eat it. It would still taste like paper." She turned to Lobby. "We should find a place along the coast to hide the ship. This illusion will only last about an hour."

Nevis continued to gawk at her as she walked toward him and sat beside him on the trunk.

"Colonel?" She peered up at him from below the brim of her floppy hat. "Ye're staring at me."

"Yes," he croaked.

Her mouth twitched. "Ye look quite stunned."

"I am." *Dammit.* She was the most amazing woman he'd ever met. He cleared his throat. "Your Highness?"

"Aye?"

"You . . . If you don't mind, you could call me Nevis."

She blinked. "Then ye would need to call me Elinor."

He gulped. "I can?"

She nodded. "It's better than 'hey, you,' don't ye think?"

"Ah . . . yes."

She leaned close to him. "Ye're blushing again."

"Am not."

"Holy goddesses," Lobby muttered as he made the sign of the moons. "Why are they flirting when we're all going to die?"

"We are not," Elinor insisted.

"We're not flirting?" Nevis asked.

She gave him a wry look. "We're not going to die."

Then they *were* flirting. Nevis smiled to himself. "Don't worry, Elinor." He gripped the handle of his sword. "I won't let any harm come to you."

"Thank you, Nevis."

His heart stilled at the sound of her saying his name. The Light help him, he was completely, irreversibly smitten. Brody was going to kill him.

Chapter 11

Maeve sat up in bed when a knock sounded on her door. "Yes?"

Ruth slipped inside. "Oh, I'm sorry to wake you."

"It's all right." Maeve climbed out of bed. "I was awake." After eating and taking a bath, she'd slipped on a nightgown so she could rest. But she'd been too anxious about having another dream to let herself actually sleep.

"Her Majesty wishes you to attend her in the throne room," Ruth said. "She said to wear the golden gown."

Maeve swallowed hard. Her dream was coming true. She followed Ruth into the dressing room. "Do you know why Her Majesty wants to see me?"

"She didn't say, but I've heard someone important is coming to the island."

Who could it be? Maeve wondered while Ruth helped her into the gold satin gown and matching slippers. Once her hair was brushed and pulled back from her face with a pair of golden combs, Maeve was pronounced ready.

"The guard will show you the way." Ruth busied herself with some metal knobs close to the tub. "This is how you make the water drain from the tub to a gutter outside."

Maeve stepped closer to study the ingenious plumbing. "That's very clever."

Ruth nodded. "It dates back hundreds of years. But you

should be on your way. You don't want to keep the queen waiting."

"All right." Maeve hurried out the door.

As the guard led her down a passageway, she attempted to befriend him, but he ignored her. Finally, they reached the corridor she had seen in her dreams.

"The Great Hall is down there." He gestured to the end of the passageway.

She already knew that but kept her mouth shut. As she walked along the corridor, a chill skittered down her spine. The hall was exactly the way it had appeared in her dream: long and at least two stories high.

To her right, glass-paned doors opened onto the balcony that overlooked a garden of wave-like clipped hedges and bushes in the shapes of seals and dolphins. Just beyond the garden lay a small harbor and the ocean.

Long purple curtains rippled in the breeze that fluttered through the open doors. Her slippers were silent on the green marble floor, but the guard's boots clunked heavily as he trailed behind her at a distance.

To her left, the wall was covered with portraits. Were these her ancestors? Had they all been sorcerers? Had some of them been able to foresee the future?

Finally, she reached the open golden doors, and her heart stilled for a moment as the grandeur of the throne room swept over her. It was just as she had dreamed, with the mosaic floor designed to look like the sea. Green marble pillars supported a ceiling that had to be three stories high. The glass dome in the center allowed rays of sunlight to dance and shimmer along the mosaic floor, making it appear like a sun-dappled ocean. At the end of the room, the dais was covered with purple and green glass ornaments in the shapes of giant clams. More glass spiraled up from the pretend seabed as if it was coral or underwater plants. In the center of the dais sat the golden octopus-shaped throne.

Hanging over the throne was an enormous flag, suspended from the high ceiling. A purple octopus on a sea-green background. Purple and green, the colors of the Telling Stones that she'd accidentally picked.

Her steps came to a stop as she reached the octopus pictured in the mosaic floor, its giant tentacles stretched out to capture fish. It all made sense now. The octopus represented her—

"Ah, there you are."

Maeve stiffened as the exact words of her dream were repeated. She turned slowly, spotting the figure in the shadow beyond the golden doors. Her mother.

She opened her mouth to greet her and fulfill the final moment of her dream, but the word caught in her throat. This was the woman who had abandoned her as a babe, who was forcing children to labor in the fields, who was imprisoning Gabby and hiding the Embraced army.

Still, if Maeve was going to survive here, if she was going to help the children and defeat the army, she had no choice but to play along. If she didn't, she could end up in the cell next to Gabby, unable to accomplish anything.

"Mother." She forced the word out.

Queen Cahira sauntered through the doors, wearing a gown of purple satin and a gold crown designed to look like coral and seashells. "What do you think of my throne room?"

"It is magnificent," Maeve answered, relieved that for a few seconds she could be perfectly honest. "I have seen the throne rooms of all four mainland kingdoms, and this is by far the most beautiful."

A corner of the queen's mouth lifted with a satisfied smirk. "Of course it is. Our civilization was flourishing back when they were still living in caves and straw huts."

Maeve bowed her head to appear in agreement.

"The gown becomes you." Cahira stopped in front of her and eyed her carefully. "Since it was the legend of Aerland that spoke to you and drew you back to the place of your birth, I am considering the possibility that you were fated to return. In that case, you may be worthy of my acceptance."

Maeve fought to keep her hands from curling into fists as indignation twisted her gut. Instead she gripped her skirt and sank into a curtsy. "Thank you, Mother."

"I cannot deny you are of superior blood." The queen stepped closer. "But I'm not convinced you can be trusted."

"All my life, I have wondered who I am and whence I came. My trip here has been a dream come true." Maeve winced inwardly. That last sentence was too close for comfort.

Queen Cahira sighed as she strolled toward the dais. "When I sent you to the convent, I meant for your life to be uneventful. I never imagined that you would grow up with four girls who would all become queens." She whirled around, her purple satin skirts swishing around her ankles. "So, are you loyal to those false sisters? Or to me, your real mother?"

How to sound convincing? Maeve wondered. Perhaps if she included a sliver of emotional truth. "I have to admit that I grew up loving my sisters. But after they became queens, everything changed. They confer with themselves and completely leave me out, as if I'm no longer good enough for them."

Cahira snorted. "Ridiculous. They have no idea how special you are."

If I'm so special, why did you abandon me? Maeve suspected her bitterness might be apparent on her face, so she used it to her advantage. "Actually, I was glad to leave my sisters. I never really fit in with them."

"Of course you didn't." The queen stepped up onto the dais. "You're far superior to them, the last full-blooded descendant of our ancient race. Your father, you see, is the last full-blooded male. That is why I selected him."

Her father? Maeve blinked. "Is . . . is my father here?"

"He's on his way." Cahira settled on the golden octopus throne. "Burien and I always made an excellent team. He was the one who came up with the Grand Idea, while I was the one to implement it."

"The Grand Idea?"

Cahira nodded. "The Circle of Five, of course."

Maeve flinched and stumbled back a step. Her parents had begun the Circle of Five?

Cahira smirked. "You look surprised."

More than surprised, Maeve thought. Appalled. Sickened. She struggled to keep her emotions from showing. Luckily, her mother was no longer looking at her, but gazing up at the glass dome in the ceiling.

"It was an excellent idea, but unfortunately, it has proven difficult to bring to fruition." The queen made a fist and tapped it against the seal-shaped armrest. "The problem was we had to ally ourselves with inferior beings on the mainland. I spent a bloody fortune on Lord Morris to ensure his loyalty and acquire a network of spies, but in the end, the fool ended up killing himself."

Maeve's mind was still swirling as she cringingly accepted this new reality. So her parents were the first two members of the Circle of Five. Lord Morris must have been the third. "I-I wouldn't call Lord Morris a complete failure. Wasn't he the one who sent the Embraced children here for your army?"

Cahira scoffed. "And the bastard went around taking credit for it." She sat forward, her sea-green eyes glittering. "Do you want to hear how it came about? It's quite an interesting story."

Before waiting for a reply, the queen continued. "You see, about twenty-seven years ago, King Frederic of Eberon sired a bastard son on a chambermaid. Kendric was his name, born on the Spring Embrace. Normally, Frederic had all Embraced babies killed, but he found himself somewhat reluctant when it came to his own son."

"Understandable," Maeve muttered with a wry tone, but her mother was so caught up in the story that she missed it.

"So Frederic asked Lord Morris to hide the child somewhere far away." Cahira motioned to herself. "At that point, I stepped in and offered to take the baby, so Morris would be indebted to me. Kendric grew up here, and by the age of seven, his powers were already apparent. Amazing powers, really. That's when I realized how useful these Embraced children could be. So I told Morris to start sending them all here."

"Then the Embraced army was your idea?"

Cahira smiled. "Of course." Her smile suddenly faded and her eyes widened. "Oh! I just had another fabulous idea!"

Maeve forced an excited look onto her face. "Really?"

"Yes!" Cahira rose to her feet. "I just realized how you can prove your loyalty to me." She clapped her hands together. "And the timing is perfect! Kendric should be here in the next day or two."

Maeve steeled her nerves. Whatever her mother was planning, it was bound to be awful.

Cahira pointed a finger at Maeve. "You will marry Kendric."

Maeve flinched. *No.* Brody was the only one she could ever marry. "I . . . how . . . how can I marry someone I don't know?"

"He's of royal blood. Young, handsome, intelligent, and powerful. What else could you want?"

A bloodcurdling burst of panic erupted inside Maeve, demanding that she flee immediately. If she could make it to the shore, she could shift and swim away. But could she do it? Wouldn't there be guards to stop her? Hell, her own mother might shift and come after her, wrapping her tentacles around her to capture her. Imprison her.

Cahira stepped off the dais and approached Maeve. "I can

see you are shocked, but if you wish to prove your loyalty, you will do as I say." She scoffed. "It's not as if I'm asking for much. Kendric is an amazing man."

Who was this Kendric? Maeve had heard the name before. Oh, right. Bettina had called him the general of the Embraced army.

"Since you're a shifter, yourself, you should find him very attractive," Cahira added. "He's the second most powerful shifter in the world." With a smirk, she motioned to herself. "I am the first one, of course."

Second most powerful shifter? Wouldn't that be Brody? Unless . . . with a gasp, Maeve stepped back. No, it couldn't be . . .

"I'm sure you've heard of him before." Cahira crossed her arms as she pondered. "Ah. I know what the problem is. The silly people on the mainland don't know his real name. So the fools call him the Chameleon."

As the boat approached the Isle of Secrets, Nevis moved to the prow to search for a good place to hide the small vessel. He spotted a rocky area on the northeastern edge of the island where huge boulders, as large as three-story buildings, were sitting along the coast as if they were guarding it. "Can we go over there?"

"Aye." Elinor turned the wheel while Lobby made adjustments to the mainsail.

The boat skimmed along the coast, and Elinor gave the wheel to Lobby so she could join Nevis by the railing.

"This is perfect!" she announced as they passed the first boulder. The huge, craggy rocks outlined a small bay. "Come to starboard," she ordered Lobby, then turned to Nevis. "We'll lower the sail and drop the anchor."

Soon, they were safely hidden inside the boulder-lined bay and, to their surprise, they spotted a sea cave on the coast. A barking sound drew their attention to a flat rock where a few seals were watching them. The seals plunged into the water to approach their boat, and a few more seals emerged from the cave.

"I think they're from the Isle of Moon," Elinor said as she leaned over the railing to get a closer look at them.

"How can you be sure?" Nevis asked.

"I've been sailing around the isle for years. These seals recognize me." She waved at the seals, who barked back.

"They sure are loud," Nevis muttered. "If Maeve was here, she'd be able to talk to—wait, these must be the seals she was traveling with."

Elinor craned her neck, looking around. "I don't see her. Or Brody."

"They're probably hiding inside the cave." Lobby took off his hat, squeezing it tight in his fists. "That's where I would be. Hoping that the Sea Witch didn't find me."

"I'll take the rowboat ashore and look," Nevis announced.

"I'll go with you." Elinor turned to Lobby. "Did ye want to stay here?"

The old man twisted his hat in his hands. "I-I think I should go with you. Ye're our princess, so 'tis me duty to protect you. And I need to help that poor lass Maeve."

Elinor touched his sleeve. "Thank you, Lobby. Yer bravery is commendable."

Lobby blushed.

"Then I'll drag the cook up here to stand guard," Nevis muttered as he headed down the stairs to the galley.

Soon they had the bleary-eyed cook sitting on deck, while the others clambered into the small skiff that was tethered at the back of the boat. Nevis and Lobby rowed while Elinor held a lit lantern and her canvas bag full of paper. When they hit land, everyone jumped out and Nevis dragged the rowboat onto the pebbly beach.

He took the lantern from Elinor. "Wait here while I investigate the cave."

She hitched her bag over her shoulder. "I'll go inside with you."

Nevis frowned at her. "No, you won't."

She frowned back. "Are ye giving me orders now? Have ye forgotten I'm the captain?"

"Have you forgotten I'm a colonel? We're on land now, so I outrank you."

She scoffed. "Have ye forgotten I'm a princess? I still outrank you."

He winced inwardly. Dammit, did she have to remind him how far out of reach she was? He gritted his teeth. "Then, as the princess, you shouldn't do anything dangerous. We don't know what could be inside the cave. There might be some sort of hideous creature."

Her mouth twitched. "Then I'll draw an even more hideous creature so it can protect us."

With a snort, he grabbed the handle of his sword. "There's no need for that. I'm fully capable of protecting us."

"Good. Then ye won't mind if I tag along." She smiled up at him, and his heart skipped a beat.

Damn, but this woman knew just how to get her way with him. He cleared his throat. "Very well, then. Stay behind me, so you'll be safe." He held up the lantern and ventured inside the cave. There was a narrow pathway along a black, glistening wall, but most of the cave was filled with water. He eyed the water with suspicion. Something could be lurking in there.

"Maeve?" His voice echoed around them. "Maeve, are you here?"

There was a fluttering sound, then a giant whoosh as a black cloud swept toward them.

Bats! Nevis turned and pulled Elinor against his chest with

his head bent over hers. He winced at the stirring of air against his neck and scalp.

Soon the swarm of bats had passed them by.

"Are you all right?" Nevis asked, and Elinor's head nodded against his chest. "I hate bats."

She nodded again. "Me, too."

With a start, he realized he was hugging her. He released her and jumped back. "My apologies, Your Highness."

"There's no need to apologize. Ye were protecting me. Thank you."

He held up the lantern, hoping to see the expression on her face, but she had turned back toward the entrance. "I don't think Maeve or Brody were here."

"No." He followed her out. "But the seals are here, so she should be somewhere close by."

"Did ye find the lass?" Lobby asked as they approached him on the pebbly beach.

"No." Nevis blew out the lantern's flame and set it on the ground. "You two wait here. I'll go search for her."

"I'll come with you," Elinor said once again.

"No, you won't," Nevis growled. "Do you know how dangerous it could be? The Embraced army might be here."

"And the Sea Witch, too," Lobby muttered, wringing his hat in his hands.

Elinor gave both men an annoyed look. "I didn't come all this way to wait behind." She started down the beach, headed west.

Dammit, the woman was too fearless. Nevis caught up with her.

"That's the way to the Sea Witch's castle," Lobby whined as he stumbled along behind them. "Holy goddesses, we're going to end up dead."

When they reached the boulder-lined edge of the bay, Elinor slipped between two pedestal rocks, splashing through

the shallow water in her boots. "Watch out for the crabs."
She pointed at the water.

Nevis winced as he stepped through. "I hate crabs."

Elinor glanced back at him with a smile. "Why would ye
hate them?"

"They look strange. And they try to pinch you."

"They're tasty."

He made a face, and she laughed.

"Then what do ye eat?" she asked.

"Real food. Cows and pigs."

She scoffed. "I take it ye never lived on an island. Or along
a coast."

"No." He walked beside her while Lobby followed behind
them, muttering about the Sea Witch. The beach was now
white and sandy, the sky blue, and the sea a pretty turquoise
color. "I've spent most of my life moving up and down the
border of Woodwyn and Norveshka."

She gave him a curious look. "Ye didn't have a home?"

"I did. My tent."

Her expression turned sad.

Damn, he didn't want her feeling sorry for him. "I've had
a good life with the army. Well, the battles are awful, but—"

"Have ye ever been wounded?"

He waved a dismissive hand. "A cut or scrape here and
there. But nothing important. I'm a fully functional male—"
He halted with a wince. Holy crap, had he just said that?

Obviously, he'd spent too much of his life surrounded by
soldiers who said whatever they wanted to. He ventured a
glance at the princess and discovered she was grinning.
Great. He'd proven once again that he was an idiot. "Of
course, there may be some doubt that my brain is fully functional."

She laughed and touched his arm. "Thank you. Ye know
exactly how to ease my worries."

"I do?"

She nodded, then gave him a teasing look. "I'm quite positive yer brain is working as well as the rest of you. Though yer mouth tends to work more than it should."

He winced. "True."

"Ye're blushing again."

He smiled. "Am not."

"Holy goddesses," Lobby muttered behind them. "We're going to die, and they're flirting again."

Nevis slanted a look at Elinor, just as she glanced at him. She grinned, and his heart flipped over in his chest. Holy Light, maybe he had a chance with the princess, after all.

How could she marry the Chameleon? Cahira had demanded an answer, but Maeve couldn't wrench the word "yes" out of her throat. She didn't want to refuse, either, and appear disloyal. So, she did the only thing she could think of: She begged for time.

"Please," she pleaded with tears in her eyes. "I'm afraid to marry a stranger. Could you let me get to know him first? Could you give me two weeks?"

Cahira studied her with narrowed eyes. "Well, it will take some time to prepare for the wedding, so I will give you one week. No more."

One week. Could she escape before then? Maeve sank into a curtsy. "Thank you, Mother."

Cahira shrugged. "I'll send my seamstress to you in the morning. You'll need a wedding gown."

"Thank you." As Maeve straightened, she gathered her courage. "May I ask for another small favor?"

"Must you?" Cahira frowned at her, then huffed. "Very well, what is it?"

"Could you remove Gabby from the dunge—"

"Absolutely not!" Cahira stepped closer, her eyes flashing

with anger. "How do you know about her? You are spying on me, aren't you?"

"No!" Maeve stepped back, shaking her head. "I just happened to see her in the dungeon because Alfred and Darroc brought me into the castle that way. Believe me, I never would have asked to see the dungeon. It was an accident that I even saw Gabby."

"Hmm." Cahira crossed her arms, eyeing Maeve with suspicion. "I'll have to question them about this."

"Please do. I would never want to anger you, Mother."

She scoffed. "And yet you ask me to move Gabby, when I need the gold that she makes."

"It occurred to me that if you treat her nicely, she might be more willing to work," Maeve argued. "In fact, she could probably increase her production if she had a more comfortable room and more nutritious food."

Cahira arched a brow. "You think so?"

"And if she knew her brother was all right, she would probably work with a grateful heart."

Cahira waved a dismissive hand. "Of course the boy is all right. What do you take me for?"

Maeve carefully schooled her features not to show what she really thought. "It's a sign of true nobility to be magnanimous."

Her mother snorted. "Very well. I'll move her to a servant's room. But if her production goes down, she's going right back to the dungeon!"

"I understand." Maeve bowed her head. "Thank you, Mother."

With a prolonged sigh, Cahira turned away. "Your demands are tiresome." She waved a hand. "Go back to your room while I question Alfred. I'll send for you when your father arrives."

She'd been dismissed like a child, but Maeve didn't object. She was happy to get away for a little while.

Back in her bedchamber, she paced from one end to the other. Trapped, that was how she felt. No, disgusted was more like it. For the past few years, everyone she cared about had been fighting against the Circle of Five. And now, she had learned that the founders of that evil group were her parents.

She drew to a stop. *There is nothing you can do to change what happened in the past. You can only deal with it the best you can.* She rubbed her brow where her head was beginning to throb. Overloaded. Overburdened. Mentally and emotionally attacked. That was how she felt. She'd been assaulted too quickly with too much information.

Not only had she learned about her parents, but she now knew who the Chameleon was. How on Aerthlan could she marry him?

A sudden thought jumped into her mind. If the Chameleon was the bastard son of King Frederic . . .

She struggled to breathe as the full horror crashed over her. The Chameleon had killed his own father! And when he'd killed Prince Tedric, Frederic's legitimate heir, he'd murdered his own half-brother. He'd attempted to take Tedric's place so he could be king, and when that hadn't worked, he'd gone after his father.

How could she marry such a monster?

She stumbled toward a window and opened it to take in big gulps of fresh air. Goddesses help her, she had to escape. The ocean was there, taunting her, so close but impossible to reach. She couldn't go to the tank room when there was a guard at her door.

Leaning farther out the window, she examined the walls of the castle to see if she dared to escape that way. Beneath the window of her dressing room, she spotted the gutter that took away the bathwater. Could she climb down it without breaking her neck? On the ground below, guards were marching around the perimeter of the castle. Even if she made it safely to the ground, they would probably spot her and capture her.

She scanned the sky, searching for an eagle. "Brody, I hope you're on your way," she whispered. "I really need you right now."

But the sky was clear. No sign of Brody.

Far to the west, the sun was lowering in the sky. Thank the goddesses. She'd endured enough for one day.

But the day wasn't over yet. Out at sea, a small ship was approaching the harbor. Was this the arrival of her so-called father?

An idea popped into her mind. What if she was able to befriend her father and convince him to call off her wedding?

The idea faded quickly. How could she possibly befriend her father? He was the first member of the Circle of Five. Whoever he was, he had to be as power hungry as Cahira. So it was highly doubtful he would take her side. Hadn't he abandoned her, too?

A knock sounded on her door, and the guard peered inside. "Her Majesty is requesting your presence on the balcony."

"I understand." Maeve followed him back to the corridor that led to the Great Hall. But this time, she was escorted through one of the glass-paned doors onto the balcony.

Queen Cahira motioned for her to join her by the stone parapet. "Your father is arriving."

As Maeve approached the parapet, she spotted the twin ponds just below them. One green and the other blue, they were joined by a dolphin-shaped fountain that spewed water into the air. Farther out, the garden stretched down to the harbor. And there, a small ship had been tied off at the dock. On the pier, four male servants waited by a litter, made by lashing two long poles to a chair.

Were they intending to carry her father to the castle? Was he unable to walk?

Maeve narrowed her eyes as she spotted a lone figure hobbling at a snail's pace down the gangplank. He wore a brown robe with the hood drawn over his head. In one hand, he gripped a long staff, and cradled against his chest, he held a cat.

Good goddesses! She jolted with recognition. It was the Seer!

Beside her, her mother gave her a curious look. "What is this? Have you met your father before?"

Maeve's thoughts raced. She wasn't supposed to know the Seer. "I . . . I'm just surprised. He seems rather . . . old and feeble."

"Ah." Cahira nodded. "No doubt you're wondering why I was attracted to him. But as I said, Burien is the last full-blooded male of our race. And he has a powerful gift." Her eyes gleamed with pride. "He's known around the world as the Seer."

Maeve let her mouth drop open as she feigned surprise. Not hard to do since she was still in shock. "My father is the Seer?"

"Yes." Cahira's expression became even more smug. "What a thrill it must be for you to discover you have such powerful parents."

Maeve nodded. "Yes." Was this why her dreams were coming true? Had she inherited a bit of her father's gift? But why had the gift waited almost twenty years before manifesting itself?

Cahira sighed. "Unfortunately, Burien is quite ill. I brought him here because I couldn't bear the thought of him dying all alone on that isle of his."

"You care about him."

"Of course." Her mouth twisted with an annoyed look. "But I wish he hadn't brought along that silly cat."

When the Seer finally reached the pier, the cat scrambled out of his hold and leaped to the ground. The Seer reached for him but was too slow. The cat, Trouble, darted off, dashing across the garden in an orange blur.

With a snort, Cahira muttered under her breath, "Another problem to deal with."

Meanwhile, the Seer settled into the cushioned chair, and the servants grabbed the poles to heft it up to their shoulders.

Cahira rubbed her hands together as anticipation glinted in her sea-green eyes. "Burien will be so excited to meet you."

But he'd already met her, Maeve thought. If the Seer truly knew everything, then he must have known that she was his daughter when she'd visited him on the Isle of Mist. Why had he been so rude to her, then? Was it because she had asked about the Embraced army? As the founding member of the Circle of Five, he must have been angered by her questions.

Good goddesses! Was he going to tattle on her? Would he tell Cahira that she had questioned him about the whereabouts of the Embraced army? This was terrible. Her mother would be more convinced than ever that she was a spy.

But did this even make sense? How could the Seer have started the Circle of Five? Wouldn't he have foreseen the damage that the Circle would cause?

Could she even be sure that this was the Seer? If he was, then whom had Brody buried on the Isle of Mist under the cairn of stones? Feeling increasingly confused and tense, she tightened her fingers on the stone balustrade.

As the guards carried the Seer toward the castle, his hood turned from side to side. Maeve figured he was looking at the garden. Then his head stopped, and she could feel his gaze locked on her and her mother.

Suddenly, he pressed a hand to his chest. Then he doubled over, as if he were in great pain.

"Oh dear," Cahira murmured. "I fear he will not live to see your wedding."

Chapter 12

Damn, damn, damn! Brody remained hunched over. What the hell was Maeve doing here? By the goddesses, he ought to wring her neck! Hadn't she agreed to remain on the Isle of Moon? After all his attempts to keep her safe, the stubborn girl had landed herself right in the middle of danger.

"Are you all right, sir?" one of the servants asked.

He shook his head. Thank the goddesses he was pretending to be the Seer. No one would question the hissing sound he made as he breathed through gritted teeth. No one would wonder why his fists were tightly gripping his staff. It would all be interpreted as an old man suffering from a sudden onslaught of pain.

The sad truth was it *had* been painful when he'd first spotted Maeve. The shock had hit him like a donkey kick to the chest, knocking all the air from his lungs. Luckily, his hood kept his face hidden so no one had seen his stunned expression.

How had she gotten here? She must have swum all the way with her seal friends. And now, she was at Cahira's castle. Voluntarily or not, he didn't know. The older woman standing next to Maeve had to be her mother, Cahira. They resembled each other too much. In appearance only, for sweet Maeve had a kind and loving heart, while Cahira was a power-hungry liar and manipulator.

Oh, dear goddesses, how much had Maeve learned? Did she know that her mother was the driving force behind the Circle of Five? Did she know her parents had started the Circle? If so, she had to be devastated.

The heat of his anger melted away as he realized she must be hurting. He had to help her. Protect her.

He sat up and took a deep breath. The servants had carried him across most of the strange garden and were now skirting the two differently colored ponds. He was close enough now to see the faces of mother and daughter. Maeve looked tense, while Cahira's expression was full of concern and sympathy. The woman must actually care about the Seer.

You are *the Seer*, he reminded himself. He would have to act as if he and Cahira were old friends, even if it curdled his stomach. And he would have to act shocked and delighted to be finally meeting his daughter.

Should he let Maeve know who he was?

Cahira waved at him, and he gave her a weak wave back. The servants who were carrying him arrived at the base of the stairs and lowered the litter to the ground. Apparently, this staircase was too steep for them to carry him up. He made a show of slowly rising from the chair and hobbling toward the stairs.

"Do you need help, sir?" one of the servants asked.

"I can manage," he grumbled as he planted his staff on the first stairstep, then grasped the stone balustrade and ascended one step.

"My dear Burien." Cahira sauntered to the top of the stairs. "Welcome to Aerie Castle."

He froze with his foot on the next step. That voice . . .

"I have a wonderful surprise for you." Cahira pulled Maeve forward. "Our daughter is here!"

Brody collapsed to his knees as the world swirled around him and the dreaded memory slammed back into his head.

He was in the middle of the ocean, screams of terror assaulting his ears, grasping hands pulling him under. He squeezed his eyes shut, but still he could see the lifeless bodies of his father and brother. The memory dragged him down, forcing him to relive the moment he had sunk into the water, overwhelmed with so much despair he wanted to die.

But his body, still hungry for life, had shifted. The sudden onslaught of physical pain had wracked him, and yet he had welcomed it as a diversion from the mental anguish of grief. And finally, as a seal, he had heard the Sea Witch's voice. Taunting him. Cursing him.

It had been an odd voice. Strangely compelling. A siren's voice, but chilling, unlike Maeve's voice, which had always felt warm and comforting. He'd always believed he would recognize the Sea Witch's voice if he heard it again.

And he had.

Cahira. She was the one who had cursed him. The one who had killed his father and brother and all the rest of the crew. After years of searching, he'd finally found her. With a moan, he dropped his staff and lowered his head into his hands. Why the hell did she have to be Maeve's mother?

Hands grasped at his arms as the servants tried to help him back onto his feet.

"Burien, let them help you," Cahira said with concern in her voice.

Bitch. Brody felt as if he could burst into fire from the sudden surge of hot rage pulsing through his veins. *Die.* The woman needed to die. He was tempted to run up the stairs and strangle her. *Not now. Not in front of Maeve.* Still, it took him a few minutes to tamp down the fury swirling inside him.

Patience. He forced his hands to relax. *You will have your revenge.* But for now, he needed to control his thoughts and emotions. It would be a terrible mistake to kill the witch right away. First, he had to force her to lift his curse. Then, he could have a normal life. He could even court Maeve.

Fool. How could Maeve have any desire for him if he killed her mother? And how would his own mother and sister react once they learned that Maeve's mother was the murderer who'd destroyed their family? Shit, his relationship with Maeve was more doomed than ever.

Persevere, he told himself. He'd survived until now, and he would continue to do so. Shaking off the servants' hands, he lifted his gaze to the two women. "Is it true?" he asked in a shaky voice. "This young woman is my daughter?"

"Yes." Cahira sighed. "I guess I should have waited before telling you. It was too much of a shock for you."

Brody closed his eyes briefly. Let the bitch think that was the reason he had collapsed. Once again, he was grateful for the camouflage of being the Seer. He lifted a trembling hand in Maeve's direction. "My daughter?"

Maeve gave him a wary look. "Yes."

She was undoubtedly afraid that he would mention having met her before on the Isle of Mist. "My dear child, will you help me up the stairs?"

"Go." Cahira gave her a small push, then motioned to the servants. "Bring the chair up here."

While the servants hauled the litter up the steep staircase, Maeve made her way to Brody.

He reached for her and felt her stiffen as he pulled her into an embrace. "Thank the goddesses!" he cried in a loud voice, then whispered in her ear. "Don't be afraid. I'm on your side."

She pulled back, her eyes wide as she tried to see his face inside the hood.

"Come now, let me lean on you." He grabbed the balustrade with one hand and looped his arm across her shoulders. "Will you bring my staff?" When she reached for it, he added, "What is your name, my dear?"

She straightened, the staff in one hand and her other hand lifting her skirt a few inches so they could slowly climb the stairs. "I am Maeve."

"A lovely name. And where have you been all these years?"

She slanted a confused look his direction. "I grew up on the Isle of Moon. In the convent there."

"I see. What a shame I didn't know." Was she recalling how on the Isle of Mist, he'd already known all about her? *Figure it out, Maeve.* "What a delight to finally meet you. For years, I feared that you were dead."

She blinked. "Why would you think that?"

"Well." He glanced at Cahira, and the temptation to poke at her was too much. "Didn't you tell me our daughter had died?"

Cahira winced, then waved a dismissive hand. "It's a long story. We can talk about it later. Right now, I think we had better take you straight to your bedchamber so you can rest."

"I am quite tired." He reached the top of the stairs and took Maeve's hand in his own. "I always prayed that you had survived. For I knew from my visions that you would become the most beautiful woman in all of Aerthlan."

Cahira scoffed.

"Oh, not that I have forgotten you, my dear." Brody turned toward the witch. "But we can't stay young forever, can we?" He celebrated inwardly when she gritted her teeth. "It is always a joy to see you. Thank you for bringing me here." He reached a hand toward her.

"Of course, Burien." Cahira stepped forward to clasp his hand, but he avoided contact by suddenly lifting his hand to push back his hood. He'd tried to make his face appear even more gray and thin, and apparently it had worked, for Cahira reeled back in shock.

"Oh, my dear Burien. We must get you to bed immediately." She latched onto his arm and hustled him into the chair. "Take him to the silver room," she told the servants.

While the servants hoisted him up, Brody groaned as if he were in pain. "Now that I have finally met my daughter, I cannot bear to be separated from her. May I have a bedchamber next to hers so I can see her often?"

Cahira frowned. "That is not what I had planned."

Brody let his shoulders slump. "Will you not grant a dying man his last wish?"

Cahira hissed in a breath. "Of course, Burien." She turned to the servants and snarled, "Take him to the green room."

"Thank you, my dear." As the servants carried him down a hallway, Brody recalled how badly the Seer had wanted to meet his daughter. The poor old man. He let his eyes fill with tears. "Now I will die a happy man."

"Oh, Burien." Cahira grabbed his hand and kissed it.

He struggled to keep the disgust off his face. "Oh, I feel nauseous." He pulled his hand away to rub his stomach.

Cahira gave him a sympathetic look. "You're not used to traveling on the ocean, are you?"

He shook his head. "I was on the Isle of Mist for seventy-five years."

"You'll feel better once you're in bed." As Cahira walked beside the litter, she launched into a long lecture about Aerie Castle—how ancient it was, and how it had been built when those on the mainland still lived in mud huts. "But then, you already know that we're from a superior race."

He grunted in reply. Before the witch could start bragging again, he turned to Maeve. She was on the other side of the litter, still holding his staff. "How long have you been here, my dear?"

She gave him a quick glance. "I arrived this morning."

"By boat?" he asked.

Maeve shook her head, but before she could reply, Cahira butted in.

"She swam here. She's a selkie, which means she inherited a small portion of *my* power." Cahira motioned to herself. "While our daughter is limited to the form of a seal, I can shift into any sea creature I like."

"Like a pufferfish?" he muttered under his breath.

"Excuse me?" Cahira stepped closer to the litter.

"I'm worried about Trouble," Brody said, raising his voice.

"Oh." Cahira scoffed. "There will be no trouble here. I'm completely in charge."

"I meant the cat you gave me two years ago." Brody had learned about it from the Seer's journal. "I named him Trouble. He ran away, and I'm worried—"

"He'll be fine," Cahira insisted, then muttered under her breath, "He definitely is Trouble."

So the cat had annoyed her, and that was why she'd foisted it on the Seer? Strange, Brody thought, wondering what the cat had done. And something else was strange . . . "I'm curious, my dear. How can it be that one of the ponds is green, while the other is blue?"

"I was wondering that myself," Maeve murmured.

Cahira gave them a smug look. "It has to do with tiny creatures who are living in the water and how they reflect the sunlight." She chuckled. "But of course the islanders think it is a magical spell I put on the water."

"There are other people here?" Brody asked.

"Of course." Cahira waved a dismissive hand. "Servants, guards, and the Embraced children brought here by Lord Morris. You remember him, don't you? He was the third person to join our Circle."

Brody's hands tightened on the arms of his chair. So Maeve knew the truth about her parents now. And she had been correct about the Embraced army being here. He tried to recall how much the Seer had actually known about the Circle or the army. Not much, really, for Cahira had kept him in the dark about her more nefarious plans. If the witch suspected he was not the real Seer, she might be fishing right now. "Did we talk about that?" He gave her a confused look. "I'm afraid my memory is not what it used to be."

She nodded. "I'll explain everything after you've had some rest. And I'll have some hot porridge brought to you, too."

Porridge? He winced inwardly. What he needed was some real food. While the servants carried him up a shallow staircase to the next floor, he came up with a plan. "Could you have a tray of food delivered for Maeve? I would like to dine with her and hear all about her life."

Cahira huffed. "How exciting could that be? She grew up in a convent."

"Perhaps, but I want to hear her siren voice. I find it quite soothing."

Cahira's mouth twisted in annoyance as she climbed the stairs beside the litter. "I'm a siren, too. Where do you think she got it from?"

Brody ignored that. "No doubt, if my daughter sang, men would cross the ocean to hear her voice. If she laughed, they would lose their hearts to her."

Maeve stumbled on a step, her face growing pale and her knuckles turning white as she gripped his staff hard.

"Is that why you lost your heart to me?" Cahira asked with a smug look.

"Quite so, my dear." Brody smiled at her. The servants reached the next floor and carried him down a hallway. He glanced back to make sure Maeve was following them.

"Could you bring our daughter two trays of food? She barely made it up the stairs. Have you not been feeding her?"

Cahira gritted her teeth. "She is not going hungry."

He might be overdoing the pettiness, Brody thought. So he gave Cahira a tearful smile. "I can't thank you enough, my dear. Being here is such a blessing. Please forgive me if I'm out of sorts. I've been in too much pain lately."

Cahira's face softened. "I understand, Burien." She stopped beside a door and opened it. "Here we are. The green room."

The servants lowered the litter, and Brody eased shakily onto his feet.

As Cahira led him into the bedchamber, she told the servants, "Take the chair away, and tell the kitchen staff to bring plenty of food and wine here, along with a bowl of hot porridge."

"Yes, Your Majesty." They bowed and carried the litter away.

Maeve slipped inside the room and rested his staff against the wall. Her gaze wandered about the bedchamber.

Brody gave the room a quick glance. The walls were a creamy yellow and covered with paintings of the garden. Against one wall sat a large four-poster bed with a dark green coverlet. There were matching curtains at the windows. One door close to the windows, then another door back in a recessed sitting area. He spotted a key in the door. "Is my daughter's room through there?"

"Yes." Cahira smirked. "If you grow tired of her, send her to her room and lock the door."

Maeve rolled her eyes, but Cahira didn't see it since she was busy turning down the covers on the bed.

"Come and rest now." Cahira drew him toward the bed. "Later tonight, I'm planning a small party for you."

Brody collapsed onto the bed. "Oh, but I'm far too exhausted. Would you mind if we have the party tomorrow? I really need to sleep now."

Cahira sighed. "Very well."

Brody yawned. "After the food arrives, I would like to be left undisturbed till morning."

"Are you sure?" Cahira frowned. "You're quite ill, Burien. I don't mind checking on you."

"I'll be fine." He reached a trembling hand for Maeve. "I'll have my daughter here to nurse me."

Maeve hurried toward him and took his hand. "I would be grateful for this time with my father, so I can get to know him."

Still frowning, Cahira muttered, "Very well. I'll see you in the morning, Burien."

"Good night, my dear." Brody waited for the witch to leave the room.

As soon as the door shut, Maeve dropped his hand and stepped back, scowling at him.

Was she angry? She couldn't be as angry as he was.

He sat up, listening for the witch's footsteps to fade away. Then he slipped out of bed and rushed toward the door.

"You're moving much faster now," Maeve muttered.

He held a finger to his lips to warn her to be quiet, then he cracked open the door to peer outside. No guard outside his door, but he spotted one down the hallway at the next door. Was Maeve a prisoner?

Quietly, he closed the door, then dashed over to the entrance to Maeve's bedchamber. It was indeed locked. He retrieved the key and headed back to his door. Yes! The key worked. He could talk to Maeve now. And vent his anger.

He turned toward her and cleared the white film from his pupils so he could see her better.

Her eyes widened.

He stalked toward her. "What the hell are you doing here, Maeve?"

Her eyes flashed with anger. "What the hell are you do-ing, Bro—"

He stopped her with a finger on her lips. "You should avoid saying my name here in the castle."

She shoved his hand away. "Fine. What are you doing here, *Julia*?"

"Get down." Nevis pulled Elinor to her knees as he ducked behind a sand dune. "There's a woman on the beach."

"The Sea Witch?" Lobby whispered as he cowered behind them.

"I don't know." Nevis peered over the top of the sand dune. The woman was alone and appeared to be gathering seaweed into a basket. Beyond her, the sun was lowering to-ward the horizon, painting the sky pink and gold while caus-ing the ocean to sparkle.

"She looks fairly young," Elinor whispered.

Nevis hissed in a breath when he realized the princess was also peering over the dune. "I told you to get down."

Elinor ignored him and glanced back at Lobby. "When was yer boat destroyed?"

"Six years ago."

"Then I don't think this could be the Sea Witch," Elinor told Lobby. "She looks about my age."

"Quiet," Nevis warned them as he watched the lone woman. It was possible that she might have seen Maeve. A fluttering of wings sounded overhead, and he glanced up as a flock of sea-gulls flew over them. The birds began squawking as they landed on the beach next to the young woman.

She turned toward the birds, then suddenly her gaze lifted straight to the dune where Nevis and his companions were hiding.

"Damn." Nevis ducked down, pulling Elinor with him.

"We could try talking to her," Elinor whispered.

"No." Lobby shook his head. "She might report us to the Sea Witch."

"I know you're there," the woman called to them.

"You two stay hidden. I'll take care of this." Nevis rose to his feet. "Good evening. I'm Colonel Nevis Harden from—"

"And I'm Elinor from the Isle of Moon."

Dammit. The princess was standing right next to him. "Do you never follow orders?"

Elinor smiled at him, then the young woman. "May we ask yer name?"

The young woman set down her basket and glanced around the beach nervously. "I'm Bettina."

"We're delighted to meet you, Bettina." Elinor climbed to the top of the dune. "Can ye help us? We're looking for a young woman who may have arrived here this morning—"

"You mean Maeve?" Bettina asked.

"Yes!" Nevis charged down the dune, his feet sliding in the sand. "Do you know where she is?"

Before Bettina could reply, Elinor slid down the dune behind him. "Was there a man with her? He might have been in the form of an eagle or a dog."

Bettina's eyes widened. "There was no one like that."

"Where is Maeve?" Nevis repeated.

With a grimace, Bettina glanced over her shoulder. "You shouldn't have come here. It's not safe."

"I keep telling them that," Lobby muttered as he slowly descended the dune. "But they don't listen."

"We won't stay long," Nevis assured the old man. "We'll just grab Maeve and leave."

Bettina shook her head. "You can't do that. She was captured—"

"What?" Nevis stepped closer. "Who has her?"

"She was taken to the castle." Bettina motioned toward the west. "But you mustn't—"

"Goddesses have mercy," Lobby cried. "The Sea Witch has her!"

Bettina blinked. "A sea witch?"

Lobby nodded. "She can destroy whole ships. And change into horrible sea creatures."

"Oh." Bettina winced. "You mean our queen. Cahira."

Their queen was a witch and a shifter? Nevis took a deep breath. Rescuing Maeve was not going to be easy. "What can you tell us about this castle?"

Bettina gasped. "You can't be planning to go there! It's too dangerous!"

"She's right," Lobby whined. "The Sea Witch will kill us!"

"You don't have to go, Lobby. You can stay on the boat with Elinor." Nevis gripped the handle of his sword. "As for me, I am not leaving this island without Maeve."

"I will go, too," Elinor said, and he glared at her.

"Neither one of you can go," Bettina insisted. "You'll be terribly outnumbered. The queen has guards—"

"How many?" Nevis asked.

"Thirty," Bettina replied. "But then there's Alfred and Darroc and the others with their powers—"

"What kind of powers?" Nevis's grip tightened on his sword.

"Embraced powers," Bettina explained. "Alfred has the power of lightning, and Darroc can control the wind—"

"What?" Nevis stepped back as a shiver of horror crept down his spine. "Lightning and wind?"

Bettina nodded with a sad look. "They're the ones who captured Maeve."

"The Embraced army," Elinor whispered, exchanging a worried glance with Nevis.

He swallowed hard. Maeve had been right. The Embraced army was here. And two of them had the same powers as Leo and Rupert. *Damn.* He needed to warn Leo immediately.

Captain Shaw would be arriving at Ebton Palace by sunset, but all he would be able to tell Leo was the possibility that the Embraced army was here.

Nevis needed to confirm it, so Leo and the other kings could rally their troops and head this way. The Embraced army had to be defeated here, before they could wage war and destruction on the mainland. But how could he leave now to warn Leo? That would mean abandoning Maeve.

Nevis glanced at the setting sun. Which should he choose? The safety of the entire world, or the safety of one woman?

Chapter 13

"Don't call me Julia," Brody growled at her.

It was perverse of her, Maeve knew, but she was so angry, she felt satisfaction when her barb hit home. "What should I call you, then? *Liar?*"

With his teeth gritted, he pointed at her. "*You're* the one who lied. You said you would wait on the Isle of Moon for me to return. Do you have any idea how furious I am?"

"It could be only half of what I'm feeling."

He scoffed. "There's no reason for you to be angry."

"Are you jesting?" She gave him an incredulous look. "I'm hearing your voice, but it's coming out of a stranger's mouth. Do you have any idea how creepy that is?"

"Fine." His gray, wrinkled face began to shimmer.

Maeve's breath caught as Brody shifted right in front of her. His shoulders and chest grew broader, filling the Seer's brown woolen robe. His familiar face replaced the old wrinkled one, while his hair changed from silver to black. His beautiful blue eyes sparkled like icy shards as he glowered at her. His gorgeous mouth—how could she look at his lips without remembering his kiss?

He was so damned handsome, blast him. In the four years that she'd known him, he'd matured, becoming more attractive every time she saw him. She'd admired him from afar. Longed for him to pay her some attention while he was in human form. But now, she had to wonder if she even knew him. How many more secrets was he hiding?

"You should have stayed put on the Isle of Moon," he fussed at her. "Now you're in danger—"

"It was my choice. I'll deal with it."

"Dammit, Maeve. Have you always been so stubborn?"

"Have you always been so secretive? Did you ever tell anyone that you can shift into a person? What am I to think? Are you just like the Chameleon?"

He hissed in a breath. "Don't you dare compare me to that bastard."

She had to admit he was right to take insult. The Chameleon was a mass murderer, while Brody always helped others. But still, it hurt that he'd hidden his true nature from her. It hurt badly enough that angry tears gathered in her eyes. "Am I the only one who didn't know? Or did you keep it a secret from everyone? Do any of us even know who you really are?"

He groaned. "You're making too much of this."

"I don't think so." She motioned to his face. "Is this how you actually look?"

"Of course it is." He gave her a frustrated look. "I've never taken on a person's form before. I only did it now because the Seer begged me to."

"My . . . father asked you to do this? How can that be? Isn't he allied with my mother?"

"He only pretended to be, so he could find out what she was doing. Your father was a good man."

She blinked. "Was?"

Brody nodded. "He passed away. I'm sorry."

A twinge of regret lodged in her heart. She would never know her father. But apparently, she had inherited his power of foresight. Her vision of Brody burying someone on the Isle of Mist had been correct. "How well did you know him?"

When Brody hesitated a moment, she wondered if he was

deciding which secrets to hide and which to reveal. The annoying man.

Finally, he replied, "After I was cursed, I washed up on the Isle of Mist. The Seer found me and raised me. He was like a father to me."

That was obviously true, for she could see the pain of mourning in Brody's eyes. "How long have you known that my father started the Circle of Five?"

"I found out the afternoon before he died. At first, I was horrified. But then I read his journal and understood what had happened. I'll give you his journal someday, so you can see for yourself. His only crime was a mistaken belief that he could bring peace to the world. It was Cahira who twisted his idea into something evil."

Maeve winced. "So masquerading as the Seer was the plan you wouldn't tell me about?" When he nodded, she narrowed her eyes. "Was it you who was so rude to me on the Isle of Mist?"

"I was trying to pro—"

"It *was* you!" Her anger flared. "Did you enjoy deceiving me?"

"No, I didn't," he ground out. "But I did what was necessary to protect you."

"You told me my future was back at Ebton Palace. You lied to me!"

"I was trying to keep you safe, dammit, but you—"

"You don't have the right!" Hot tears burned her eyes. "You told me we could never have a future together, but then you tried to control my future? How dare you!"

"Maeve—"

"How long have you known who my mother is?" A tear ran down her face. "Were you intending to keep that a secret, too?"

He took a deep breath and glanced around the room as if he were trying to figure out what to say.

Her heart constricted in her chest. "You weren't going to tell me, were you?"

He closed his eyes briefly. "I knew the truth would be devastating for you."

"So you were never going to tell me? You were going to deceive me for the rest of my life?" She balled her hand into a fist and punched lightly at his chest. "How could you do that to me?"

He grabbed her by the wrist. "I would do it again. I would go to hell and back if it kept you from feeling pain."

She ripped her hand away. "Then why did you reject me? Nothing is more painful than that!"

His face turned pale.

She turned and walked away a few steps. As she wiped more tears from her face, she realized her anger was fading away. All that was left was a horrible fear that her feelings for Brody would continue to be rejected.

"I can't deny that I care about you," he said softly behind her.

Her heart squeezed in her chest. She'd always hoped to hear him confess his feelings for her, but she'd always thought it would be a joyous occasion. Not like this. She curled her hands into fists. Dammit, why did she have to accept this? "I know you can be yourself for only two hours a day, but I'd rather have two hours than nothing."

"That wouldn't be fair—"

"Since when is life fair?" She whirled around to face him. "I *am* stubborn, Brody. I'm not giving up on you."

His eyes flared with an intensity that stole her breath away. He did want her—she could feel it. She took a step toward him.

A knock sounded at the door; then the latch moved and caught on the lock.

"We have your food," a voice called from the hallway. "And clothing."

Brody ran and jumped into bed. Maeve approached the door, waiting to be sure Brody had shifted back into the Seer before she turned the key and opened it.

Ruth and two more servants came inside carrying trays loaded down with food, goblets, and pitchers of wine. They placed the trays on the round table in the sitting area. More servants brought in the Seer's bundle of clothes as well as some new garments. They took them to the dressing room.

"This is medicine to relieve pain." Ruth showed Maeve a small green bottle. "In case your father needs it."

"Thank you," Maeve told her.

"Are you all right?" Ruth whispered. "You look like you've been crying."

"I—I fear I will lose my father soon."

Ruth clucked her tongue in sympathy. "I'm so sorry, lass." She motioned to the trays. "We'll come back for these later."

"No need," Maeve assured her. "I'll put them in the hall. I don't want anything to disturb my father's rest."

Ruth glanced at the false Seer, who was moaning in bed. "Very well. But if you need me, just tug on the bell pull."

"I will. Thank you, Ruth."

She and the other servants curtsied, then filed out of the room. Maeve quickly locked the door.

Brody leaped out of bed, shifting back to his true form. "I'm starving." He dashed toward the table.

Now this was the Brody she knew. Maeve sat across from him. "How are we going to stop my mother? Do you have a plan?"

He bit into a chicken leg. "I'm flying back to the Isle of Moon tonight, so I can have a message sent to Leo. Are Nevis and Captain Shaw still there?"

"I suppose they are." Maeve poured two goblets full of wine.

"Thanks." Brody took a sip from one, then went back to eating. "Tell me what you've learned so far."

She described everything that had happened that morning. Brody's eyes widened when she described Alfred's and Darroc's powers.

He wiped his mouth with a napkin. "Lightning and wind power? That won't be easy to beat. How many soldiers are there in the Embraced army?"

"I don't know." Maeve fiddled with her food, wondering if she should tell Brody about her upcoming wedding. If she did, he might try to kill the evil shifter. He could end up injured or dead. Also, his disguise as the Seer would be exposed, and then Cahira would have the Embraced army attack him. If Maeve wanted to protect Brody, she had better keep her mouth shut.

"Anything else I should know?" Brody asked.

She winced. Now she understood why Brody had withheld information from her. She was doing the same thing. But he did need to know what she had learned about the Chameleon. "The general of the Embraced army is the Chameleon."

Brody sat forward. "Is he here?"

"He's supposed to arrive soon." Maeve explained who he was.

Brody's mouth dropped open. "He killed his own father? And half-brother? Damn." He stood and paced across the floor. "No wonder he tried to take Eberon first. We have to tell Leo about him. You say his name is Kendric?"

Maeve nodded and suppressed a shudder at the thought of being forced to marry the monster. She couldn't do it. Somehow she had to stop it. Without telling Brody. He hated the evil shifter with a passion. And from what she'd heard, the hatred was mutual. Had the Chameleon sensed that Brody had the same powers he had? That would explain why the evil shifter hated Brody so much.

She couldn't risk a fight between the two of them. There had to be another solution . . .

While she was thinking, Brody opened a window to peer

outside. "The sun is setting. I'll leave as soon as it gets dark."
He glanced back at her and narrowed his eyes. "Is something
bothering you? You're pale. And you hardly touched your
food."

She crushed her napkin in her fists. "It's nothing."

He gave her a wry look as he walked toward her. "I guess
I'm not the only one with secrets."

"I-I'll tell you later."

"All right." He picked up his goblet. "I'll hold you to that.
Make sure no one comes in while I'm gone."

"I will."

"Good." He took a long drink.

She tossed her napkin on the table. "When you come back,
I want to lose my virginity."

He sputtered wine down his robe. "What?"

"I believe you heard me."

"*What?*"

Surely the Chameleon would reject her if she told him that
she'd already bedded his archenemy, Brody. Besides, Brody
was the only man she could ever take as a mate. She rose to
her feet. "It has to be you."

He set his goblet down with a clunk. "Isn't this a bit sudden?"

"You are capable, are you not?"

He arched an eyebrow. "Are you trying to insult me into
bedding you?"

"If that's what it takes."

He scoffed. "Maeve—"

She stepped up to him and placed her hands on his chest.
"You do want me, don't you?"

He gulped. "What has come over you?"

"Lust. Pure unbridled lust." She smoothed her hands up to
his shoulders.

"Wait a minute." He grabbed her wrists. "You . . . you

must have experienced too much of a shock today. You should lie down and rest while I'm gone."

"I'll be sure to be well rested." She pressed her body against his. "And I'll be ready for you when you return."

He frowned at her. "I'm going to be really tired."

"Then I'll do all the work."

He gave her an incredulous look. "How would you know what to do?"

"I'll figure it out." She glanced down to where she could feel a growing bulge beneath his robe. "How hard can it be?"

"A lot harder." He grabbed her by the shoulders to move her back a few inches. "I'm not sure what this is all about, but we'll talk when I get back. Turn around while I shift."

"Must I? I'd rather watch you undress."

"Maeve." He scowled at her.

"Fine." She turned her back. Why was he acting so damned noble all of a sudden? "I know you want me. So when you come back, it will be you and me. You agree, don't you?"

She turned toward him, but he was already in eagle form, his hooded robe and small clothes discarded on the floor. He swooped through the window and out into the darkening twilight.

"You'll be safe after the sun has set," Bettina told Nevis and his companions. "The soldiers come to the village during the day to harass us and make sure we're working, but they never come at night."

"Are you sure?" Nevis asked.

Bettina gave him with a wry look. "They're not worried about any of us escaping. Where would we go?"

Nevis nodded. "We'll stay for a while, then." If he learned more information, he might figure out a plan to rescue Maeve. But at the same time, he needed to send a message to Leo. Somehow, he would manage to do both.

"We should remain hidden till the sun goes down," Bettina told them, and they followed her over a big sand dune. After she set her basket down, they sat in the sandy valley to wait for sunset.

"What can you tell us about the island?" Nevis asked.

"What can you do for us here?" Bettina countered.

"What do ye need?" Elinor asked.

Bettina sighed. "It's hard to explain. We were raised here, so this is the only home, the only life, we have ever known. But from what Maeve told me, I believe we were taken away from our families in Eberon."

Nevis nodded. "That is true."

"There are young children in the village and two toddlers in the castle nursery," Bettina said sadly. "If they could be returned to their homes, I would greatly appreciate it."

"We can certainly do that," Nevis told her. "But we'll need to defeat your queen and her cohorts first. For now, I need all the information I can get."

"The Sea Witch is going to kill us all," Lobby muttered.

"We're not going to die," Nevis growled. "We just need to increase our number. Once I get a message to Leo, all the kings on the mainland will come here with their forces."

Bettina's eyes widened. "You mean there will be a battle?" When Nevis nodded, she asked, "Can you take the young ones to safety before that happens?"

"Of course," Nevis assured her. "So Cahira lives in the castle with thirty guards. What else can you tell us?"

"The guards have their headquarters at the south end of the garden. There's also a dormitory there for the Embraced army, along with some practice fields."

"Ye mentioned a village?" Elinor asked.

"That's where I live with the other Embraced children," Bettina replied. "Once the little ones in the castle nursery reach the age of five, they're moved to the village so they can work."

Elinor gasped. "Children that young are forced to work?"

Bettina nodded. "The Embraced children live at the village until their powers are manifested. Then Cahira and Kendric decide if their power is good enough for the army." She ducked her head, blushing. "There are older ones in the village like me. Our powers were deemed worthless."

"What is yer power?" Elinor asked gently.

Bettina grimaced. "I can communicate with birds."

"Ah." Nevis recalled the flock of seagulls on the beach. "That's how you knew we were here. The birds told you?"

Bettina nodded.

Elinor huffed. "That is not a worthless power."

"It's an excellent one," Nevis agreed. "You have access to a huge network of spies. Cahira was foolish not to realize how valuable you are."

"Oh." Bettina's eyes widened.

"How many soldiers are there in the Embraced army?" Nevis asked.

"Seven," Bettina replied.

Nevis blinked. "That's all?"

Elinor gave him a wry look. "Ye wanted more?"

"I feared there would be many more," Nevis admitted.

Elinor shrugged. "Perhaps there weren't very many children born in Eberon on the nights the moons embraced. Or it could be that most parents simply lied about the time of their baby's birth so their babe wouldn't be taken away from them. I know I would certainly lie in order to keep my child."

Nevis nodded. "I would, too." He glanced at Bettina. "So there are only seven."

Bettina frowned at him. "Seven may not sound like many to you, but with the powers they have, I fear they could destroy a much larger army. And then, there is their general, which brings their number up to eight. But Kendric is rarely on the island."

"Who is this Kendric?" Nevis asked.

"He's a powerful shifter," Bettina replied. "He can take the form of any animal, bird, or person."

Nevis sat back. *The Chameleon.* "Is he here now?"

Bettina shook her head, then rose to her feet and picked up her basket. "The sun is almost gone. I can take you to the village now."

As they followed her, Elinor sidled up close to Nevis. "Can we take the children to my boat? We need to get them away from here as soon as possible."

Nevis considered. "We should wait a few days. If we do it now, their disappearance will alert the army and they'll come after us. We won't be able to help anyone if we're captured." He gave her a pointed look. "Speaking of which, I would feel a hell of a lot better if *you* got away from here. You can take the boat back tonight with Lobby."

She shook her head. "I'm staying."

He groaned. "It's not just for your safety. You need to go back so we can send a warning to Leo."

She bit her lip. "I'll think about it."

By now, the last of the twilight was fading away, and Nevis was grateful Bettina knew where she was going. He never would have found the village in the dark.

At the summit of a hill, he spotted the village. A half dozen torches illuminated a few wooden huts. They headed downhill, then traversed a field of wheat and a vegetable garden.

"That's the house where the smith lives with the boys." Bettina motioned to the different buildings. "This is the smithy. And over there is the house where I live with the other girls."

"Bettina, is that you?" An elderly man stepped out of the smithy, along with two boys and a young woman. "Catriona was just telling me that ye were missing."

"Bettina!" The young woman ran toward her. "We were worried about you."

"I'm fine." Bettina motioned to Nevis and his companions. "I was waiting until it was dark to bring our guests."

"Who are these strangers?" the younger boy demanded.

"Mind yer manners, Quentin," the elderly man grumbled. "Ye're still in trouble for the way ye snitched on that poor woman earlier."

Quentin winced and shuffled his bare feet in the dirt. "I said I was sorry."

Nevis assumed the elderly man was the smith. "Good evening, I'm Nevis."

"Tommy?" Lobby whispered. "Is that you?"

The smith gasped. "Lobby?"

"Holy goddesses!" Lobby lurched toward the smith. "Ye're alive!"

"Lobby!" Tommy grabbed him in a tight embrace. "I thought ye were dead."

Tears streamed down Lobby's old weathered face. "I thought ye were dead, too. I thought all me mates were gone."

"I did, too." Tommy leaned back to look at his old friend. "After the shipwreck, I washed up here on this accursed island. What happened to you?"

"I hung on to a broken mast for two days; then some fishermen found me and took me back to the Isle of Moon." Lobby grinned at Nevis and Elinor. "I found one of me mates!"

Nevis nodded, smiling. "We gathered that."

The young boy, Quentin, pranced around the two old men, grinning.

"I'm delighted to meet you." Elinor shook Tommy's hand. "We'll be happy to take you back home."

"She's the princess," Lobby whispered in a loud voice.

"Princess Elinor? Good goddesses!" Tommy quickly bowed.

Bettina's eyes widened. "You're a princess?"

"She's a princess?" Quentin gawked at her.

She nodded. "Please call me Elinor. And yer names?"

"I'm Quentin!"

"A pleasure to meet you, Quentin." Elinor ruffled his hair, and the boy grinned up at her.

"Elam." The young man sketched an awkward bow.

"I'm Catriona." The young woman sidled up close to Bettina. "Where did you find these people?"

"They found me. Come this way." Bettina led them all to the girls' cottage. After leaving her basket by the front door, she ushered them inside.

Elam agreed to stand watch outside. Inside, Nevis noted five girls of various ages, all eating bowls of soup as they sat on the wooden floor at one end of the cottage.

Quentin sat beside them and whispered loudly as he pointed at Elinor. "She's a princess!"

The girls all stared.

"I'm afraid we have only two chairs." Bettina motioned to a chair in front of a large loom and another by a spinning wheel. "If Your Highness would like—"

"I'll be quite comfortable here." Elinor sat on the floor next to the girls. She smiled at them. "Hello. I'm Elinor."

They all nodded, their eyes wide.

Nevis smiled to himself. He loved how the princess never put on airs.

Catriona sat next to Quentin. "We never get any visitors here, so they're a bit stunned."

Nevis settled on the floor on the other side of Elinor while Lobby and Tommy sat by the door, whispering to each other.

Bettina brought two wooden cups to Nevis and Elinor. "I'm afraid we're out of soup. All we can offer you is water."

"Thank you." Nevis downed his cup.

"Ye're very kind." Elinor took a sip, then set her cup on the floor so she could rummage through her canvas bag. "Ah, here it is. I brought this in case we needed it." She opened a linen-wrapped bundle, revealing seven honey cakes topped with cherries.

The young girls gasped.

Elinor passed the bundle to Bettina. "Please enjoy these. Nevis and I are quite full, so we don't need them." She gave him a pointed look. "Isn't that so?"

He winced inwardly. He hadn't eaten in hours. "Exactly. We're stuffed." His stomach growled, and he cleared his throat to cover up the noise.

With a smile, Elinor gave his hand a squeeze, and he suddenly felt full to the brim.

"This is wonderful. Thank you." Bettina handed out the seven cakes to Catriona, Quentin, and the other five girls.

"The other boys don't know what they're missing!" Quentin laughed, then gobbled down his cake.

"What about you?" Catriona asked Bettina.

She waved a dismissive hand. "I'm fine."

The youngest girl rose to her feet and hesitantly approached Bettina. She tore off a piece of her cake and offered it to her.

With tears in her eyes, Bettina knelt down and gave the girl a hug. "Thank you, Sarah. You're very sweet."

Nevis took a deep breath. Damn, but Elinor looked like she was about to cry, too. He needed to get back to business. While the girls in the room happily nibbled on honey cakes, he turned to the older men. "Lobby, can you and Tommy take the boat back to the Isle of Moon tonight?"

The two men exchanged a glance, then nodded.

"I can't stay away for very long," Tommy said. "The soldiers will know I'm missing."

"We could tell them you're ill," Bettina suggested.

Tommy nodded. "That could buy us a day or two."

"Good." Nevis turned to Elinor. "You have paper and pen with you, right?" When she nodded, he continued. "I need you to write down as much information as you can. Then Lobby and Tommy will take it to your mother, and she can have it sent on to King Leo of Eberon."

"A king?" Quentin whispered, then turned to Bettina. "What's going on?"

"Hope," she whispered back. "Freedom and a better future for all of you."

Quentin's eyes widened. "A better future?"

Elinor took out her stack of paper, then opened a bottle of ink and readied her pen.

"Now let's start with a list of your names and ages," Nevis began.

As the girls introduced themselves, Elinor wrote down their information. Then Quentin told her the names of the boys.

Elinor paused in her writing. "Yer names seem to be in alphabetical order."

"They are," Catriona agreed. "The queen named us that way so she could keep us straight. Alfred and Bettina are the oldest, followed by Darroc and myself."

Nevis glanced at the list. "Is this everyone who isn't in the army?"

"There are two four-year-olds in the castle nursery." Bettina winced. "And there are the twins, Gabby and Gavin. They're seventeen years old. We . . . we don't know where Gavin is."

"He's missing?" Nevis asked.

"The queen insists he's still alive, but we don't know what happened to him," Tommy grumbled. "No one has seen him for two years."

"That evil Sea Witch," Lobby muttered, and his friend agreed with a mumbled curse.

"Gabby's in the dungeon," Olana whispered, and the other girls shuddered.

"She can turn iron into gold," Bettina explained. "But she didn't want to help the queen, so Cahira took away her brother and locked her in the dungeon."

Elinor shook her head. "This is terrible."

"That's why I spend most of my time making iron coins," Tommy mumbled.

Catriona sighed. "I hope Maeve isn't in the dungeon."

Nevis winced. He hoped not, too. "So the youngest Embraced children are four years old?"

"Aye." Bettina shrugged. "We don't know why the babies stopped coming."

Nevis thought back to when Leo had taken over Eberon. That had been about four years ago, so that was when Lord Morris had lost his position as chief counsel and head of the Eberoni Church of Enlightenment. "Lord Morris fell out of power, so he was unable to send any more children. Shall we talk about the Embraced army now?"

Elinor readied a new sheet of paper.

"First we have the general," Nevis began. "We call him the Chameleon on the mainland."

"You know about Kendric?" Bettina asked.

Nevis nodded. "Who else is in the army?"

Bettina described them all while Elinor took notes.

Nevis looked over the finished list. There were a total of eight, including the Chameleon. Five males, three females.

"They're so powerful," Catriona muttered. "I don't know how anyone could defeat them."

Her concern was echoed by Quentin and the other girls as they talked amongst themselves.

"The kings from the mainland will help us," Nevis assured them all. "They're very powerful. You all have Embraced gifts, too, don't you?"

Catriona winced. "Our powers aren't any good."

Elinor scoffed. "Says who? We think Bettina's is excellent."

Nevis nodded as an idea formed in his head. With the right strategy, he might be able to turn these rejected Embraced children into a formidable force. "What is your gift, Catriona?"

Sarah opened her arms wide. "She blows things up!"

Nevis and Elinor gasped, while Catriona winced.

"That's a fantastic power!" Nevis exclaimed while Elinor quickly wrote it down.

"But it's quite limited," Catriona mumbled, her face turning pink. "I can blow up only one thing."

"Castles?" Nevis asked. "Mountains?"

Catriona bit her lip. "Fish."

Nevis blinked. "Fish?"

Catriona looked away, her face bright pink.

"That's why she stays here, working the loom," Bettina said quietly. "If she goes to the beach, too many fish die."

Catriona nodded. "And I'm not allowed anywhere near the castle, because I make the queen's fish dinner explode."

Nevis bit his lip to keep from smiling. "I see. What other gifts do you have?"

"Elam can make people trip!" Quentin boasted.

"That's a good power." Nevis imagined making an entire army of soldiers fall flat on their faces.

"Only one person at a time," Bettina added.

Sixteen-year-old Hannah raised her hand. "I can make it rain."

"That's a wonderful power," Nevis told her and she blushed.

"But I can do only a small area," she mumbled.

"We're very grateful for your gift," Bettina told her. "We're able to water the vegetable garden every day while leaving the wheat field dry."

"And then there's Kurt," Catriona said. "He can shift into a rabbit."

"A human-sized rabbit?" Nevis hoped. "With huge, chomping teeth?"

"He's a cute little bunny." Eight-year-old Rose grinned. "I like to feed him carrots."

Bettina sighed. "We have a hard time keeping him out of the vegetable garden."

Nevis glanced at the list. It was going to be a challenge to turn these outcasts into an army. "Anyone else?"

Bettina shook her head. "The others are so young, their powers have yet to be revealed."

"I want to make honey cakes appear!" Sarah said.

"I want to make our chores disappear," Quentin muttered.

"So Kurt is a shifter." Elinor finished writing her notes. "Has anyone seen my brother around here? He's a shifter, too. Usually in the form of a dog."

The children shrank back with frightened looks.

"The only dog on the island belongs to the guards," Bettina explained. "They use the dog to scare the young ones into working."

Elinor grimaced. "This is terrible."

A flurry of scratching noises sounded at the door.

"Oh!" Elinor sat up. "That could be Brody!"

Nevis jumped to his feet, silently beseeching the Light that it would be his old friend.

Chapter 14

It wasn't Brody.

As soon as Tommy had cracked open the door, an orange blur shot into the cottage.

Elam followed it in, exclaiming, "I think it's Gavin!"

The cat leaped into the circle of girls and looked around. Then he let out a desperate cry.

Nevis narrowed his eyes. This orange tabby looked just like the Seer's cat.

"Gavin, is that you?" Bettina asked, and the cat meowed.

"He must be looking for Gabby," Catriona added.

"She's not here." Olana shuddered. "Poor Gabby is in the dung—"

Hannah elbowed the younger girl. "She's in the castle."

"Wait a minute." Elinor lifted her pen in the air. "Are ye saying Gabby's brother is a *cat*?"

"Why not?" Catriona gave her a wry look. "Your brother is a dog."

Elinor tilted her head. "All right." She added a few words to her notes.

Nevis sat back down. "I saw this cat a few days ago. He was on the Isle of Mist with the Seer."

The cat nodded his head and made a yipping sound.

"The Isle of Mist?" Bettina reached a hand toward the cat. "Gavin, is that where you've been the last two years?"

The cat butted against her hand and meowed.

"Wait a minute." Nevis motioned to the cat. "How did he get here?"

"Good question," Elinor murmured. "Can he shift back to human form to tell us what happened?"

Catriona shook her head. "The queen was so mad at Gabby that she put a curse on Gavin. He's unable to shift back."

Gavin let out a pitiful howl.

"Poor kitty." Bettina rubbed the cat's head.

Elinor's grip on her pen tightened until her knuckles turned white. "Queen Cahira has that kind of power?"

"She's a bloody sea witch," Tommy muttered. "She can make things explode and put curses on people."

Lobby nodded. "She blew up our boat."

Nevis sat back. Gavin's curse sounded a lot like the curse that afflicted Brody.

Elinor drew in a sharp breath, then turned to Nevis. "Are ye thinking what I'm thinking?"

"Brody?"

Elinor nodded with tears gathering in her eyes.

Nevis touched her shoulder. "I know it's upsetting to you, but this is actually good news. Once we capture the queen, we could make her lift the curses on Brody and Gavin."

Elinor dropped her pen and fisted her hands. "We can't stop there. We have to kill her."

Nevis blinked. He hadn't expected this streak of vengeance in the princess. "I agree she's made Brody suffer. Gavin, too, but—"

"The witch who cursed Brody was the same one who killed my father and eldest brother," Elinor hissed. "She destroyed their ship and left them all to drown."

A number of gasps echoed around the room.

Nevis was shocked, too. Brody had mentioned the curse, but he'd never talked about his family getting killed. "Cahira murdered the king of the Isle of Moon?"

Elinor nodded. "My brother, too. Prince Edgar." A tear rolled down her cheek. "I have to avenge them."

"She'll get what she deserves." Nevis squeezed her hand. "You have my word on that." While Elinor wiped the tears from her face, he gathered up the notes she'd written and passed them on to Lobby. "Can you and Tommy leave now? Tell the guards at Lessa Castle that you have news from the princess, then pass these papers on to Queen Esther. Ask her to send them to King Leo as quickly as possible."

"Aye, Colonel." Lobby saluted and took the papers.

"Here." Elinor wrote a quick note, signed it, then jumped to her feet to hand it to Lobby. "This will get you an audience with my mother right away."

"Aye, Yer Highness." Lobby gave her a worried look. "Be careful here."

Elinor nodded as the two men hurried out the door.

"It's time for the young ones to sleep now." Bettina pulled some blankets off the shelves and gave them to the youngest girls. "Are you tired? The princess can bunk with us, and Nevis can go with Elam and Quentin to the boys' cabin."

Nevis glanced at Elinor, who still looked pale and drawn from the recent revelation of who had killed her father and brother. "I think the princess should rest. I would like to get a closer look at the guards' headquarters. The castle, too, if possible."

"I'll take you," Quentin offered, his eyes lit with excitement. "I can be really sneaky."

"I'll go, too," Elinor said quietly.

"Are you sure?" Nevis asked her.

She nodded. "I need to stay busy. If I don't, I'll think about . . ." Her eyes glistened with tears.

Nevis touched her shoulder. "I'm sorry."

She took a deep breath. "I'll be all right. 'Tis better this way, knowing the truth."

"Aye," Nevis agreed. "And now Brody has a chance to get his life back."

She nodded, then touched his hand. "Thank you for being here with me."

He folded his fingers around hers. When her gaze met his, he was tempted to pull her into his arms. Unfortunately, there was a room full of people watching their every move. He released Elinor's hand just as a knock sounded on the door.

An older woman opened the door and peeked inside.

"Ruth," Bettina greeted her. "Come in." She glanced back at Nevis. "Ruth is the servant who raised us in the nursery. We can trust her."

The woman entered, casting a curious glance at Nevis and Elinor.

"I'm Colonel Nevis Harden from Eberon, and this is Princess Elinor from the Isle of Moon."

Ruth gasped. "Oh, no! You must take the princess away from here. Queen Cahira hates her family with a passion."

Elinor hissed in a breath. "She's the one who killed my father and brother, isn't she?"

Ruth nodded. "I'm so sorry, Your Highness. Cahira believes the Isles of Moon and Mist should be part of her domain."

Elinor lifted her chin. "I'm not leaving. Not until justice is served."

Ruth sighed. "So many new people here today. Maeve arrived earlier, and then the Seer."

"The Seer is here?" Nevis asked. "No wonder his cat showed up."

Ruth noticed the cat for the first time and gasped. "Gavin, is that you?"

The cat trotted up to her and meowed.

Ruth leaned over. "Don't worry. Gabby is fine. She's been moved to a servant's room, the one next to mine."

"Oh, thank the goddesses," Catriona said, while everyone in the room let out a sigh of relief.

"We have Maeve to thank for it," Ruth explained. "She talked the queen into moving Gabby out of the dungeon."

Gavin meowed again and reared up on his hind legs.

"Do you want to see her?" Ruth asked, and Gavin leaped into her arms.

"How did Maeve manage to convince the queen?" Nevis asked. "Isn't she a prisoner?"

"Well, yes, she is," Ruth conceded. "She's being guarded night and day, because the queen doesn't trust her. But she's being treated well. After all, she's the queen's daughter."

Everyone in the cottage gasped. Elinor stiffened.

"Good goddesses." Bettina pressed a hand to her chest. "I suppose I shouldn't be surprised. Maeve looks so much like her."

Elinor turned to Nevis with a stricken look. "Maeve is the Sea Witch's daughter?"

Nevis grimaced. For years now, he'd suspected that Brody was smitten with Maeve. But dammit to hell, that meant the poor sod was in love with his worst enemy's daughter.

"I have more news," Ruth declared, and Nevis prepared himself for something even worse.

After making sure the doors were securely locked, Maeve sat at the table and forced herself to eat. After all, she needed to keep her strength up if she was going to seduce Brody when he came back. Her heart raced at the prospect, but the more she thought about it, the more she felt a heavy sense of regret.

This was not how it should be.

She'd grown up hearing Brigitta weave her overly dramatic stories of true love. It simply wouldn't be romantic if she coerced Brody against his will. Oh, she had no doubt he wanted her. She'd seen desire flash in his eyes, and he'd admitted to lusting for her. He'd also confessed to caring for her.

But according to Brigitta's stories, he should want her with a passion that could not be denied. So far, he'd been quite successful at denying it, blast him. Did that mean he didn't want her badly enough?

With a groan, she gave up on eating. What choice did she have but to seduce Brody? This was the only thing she could think of that would cause the Chameleon to reject her.

She wandered over to Brody's bed and imagined him kissing her the way he had the night before. It had certainly seemed passionate. Surely, it could happen again. And thank the goddesses, with the doors locked, they would have privacy.

Or would they? She glanced at the door with the key in the lock. What if Cahira or one of the servants had another key?

Quickly, she arranged the pillows on the bed so it would look as if someone was sleeping there. Then, she drew the curtains shut around the bed.

Should she ask for more food? When Brody returned, he might be hungry. And he might want to bathe.

She grabbed the key, unlocked the door to her bedchamber, then locked the door from the other side. After giving the bell pull a tug, she paced the floor, waiting. Soon, there was a knock on the door, and she asked the servant to bring hot water and a tray of food.

Once everything had arrived, she poured one bucket into her bathtub for a quick bath, then put on a nightgown.

She unlocked the door to Brody's bedchamber, then deposited the tray on his table. Quickly, she brought in the remaining buckets of water, then locked the door. She set the buckets in Brody's dressing room, next to his bathtub.

Done. Everything was ready for him.

She paced back and forth, wondering how long it would take. A few hours, most probably.

A cool breeze swept through the open window, chilling her

in her thin nightgown. But she had to keep the window open, so Brody could fly back inside.

Shivering, she slipped into his bed and under the covers. As she snuggled up against the pile of pillows, her eyes slowly closed and her thoughts drifted.

Could she seduce him? The answer filtered into her drowsy mind. No matter how hard she tried, her success would ultimately depend on one thing: Brody had to be willing.

As Brody flew over the harbor of his hometown, Luna, he couldn't spot any Eberoni vessels in port. Captain Shaw must have left. Had Nevis gone with him?

If Nevis was still here, where would he be? Brody landed close to the local tavern, then shifted into a pelican. He hopped up onto the windowsill and peered inside. This late at night, only a few patrons were gathered around the fireplace, drinking from their pewter tankards. No Nevis in sight. He must have hurried back to Ebton Palace to report Maeve was missing.

Maeve. Why had she suddenly asked him to bed her? He could only think that she had suffered too many shocks during the day and was in desperate need of some comforting.

But a simple hug would be comforting. Maeve had said she was determined to lose her virginity, and that could actually be painful for her. He would try to be as gentle as possible.

What? With a squawk, he fell off the narrow windowsill and landed with a splat. Was he actually planning to bed her? *Hell, yes,* a greedy inner voice growled. He'd wanted her for four years now. The fact that she wanted him, as well, was too tempting, too miraculous to ignore.

But it's not honorable, his conscience warned him. He wasn't sure yet if he could get rid of his curse. And once he attempted to capture Cahira and force her to lift the curse, Maeve would know the truth about her mother. If he bedded

Maeve now, she would feel hurt and betrayed later on when she realized how much he'd hidden from her.

So before taking her to bed, he needed to tell her everything. Tell her who he really was and what her mother had done to his family. How would she react? Would she still want him? Would she be so devastated that she might reject him?

The thought of losing her hit him like a bludgeon to the chest. Now that there was an actual chance to rid himself of the curse, he realized how fiercely he wanted that chance. A normal life, living with Maeve as her husband? Good goddesses, he craved that more than anything. More than revenge.

Damn. He couldn't bear to lose her. Not Maeve. Anything but Maeve.

There was no point in denying it any longer.

He loved her.

For the past four years, he'd told himself that he was merely attracted to her, that he simply admired her, respected her, cared about her. He'd used every word but *love.*

How could he admit to loving her, when he'd feared he would be cursed for the rest of his life and never worthy of her? But in spite of his fear, he loved her with a passion that never failed to take his breath away.

Did she love him? He believed so, but how much could love endure? Would she still be able to trust and love him, knowing what her mother had done to him and his family?

As for him, once Brody had recovered from the revelation, he had realized his feelings for Maeve remained constant. She had nothing to do with her mother's villainy. Maeve was going to be sickened and appalled when she learned the truth.

She was nothing like her mother. He preferred to think of her as the Seer's daughter. She had inherited his gentle and loving soul. Yes, she was stubborn, but now that Brody thought about it, the Seer had definitely had a stubborn streak, too. That made him smile to himself. Stubbornness could be a strength, after all. It might help her endure whatever would happen over the upcoming days. And it might help her feelings for him to survive.

For now, he needed to figure out what to do on the Isle of Moon. With Nevis and Captain Shaw gone, he would have to ask his mother to send a message to Leo. With an inward groan, he took flight and headed for Lessa Castle.

It had been almost a year since his last visit. He knew he should see his mother more often, but holy goddesses, he was so tired of the same old blandishments. *"Ye've been gone far too long. Ye've even lost yer island accent. When are ye coming back home? When are ye going to take yer rightful place as king?"*

It was so damned frustrating when his answers were always the same. No, he hadn't found the witch. No, he didn't know how long it would take. No, he couldn't be king as long as he was cursed.

This time his answers could be different, but he wasn't sure he should get his mother's hopes up.

He landed on the balcony to his bedchamber and shifted into human form. His mother always kept this entrance unlocked, so he opened the glass-paned door and stepped inside. She also kept his bedchamber clean and ready for him. He glanced at the large four-poster bed and, for a second, imagined Maeve naked and waiting for him under the covers.

Not now. He pushed those thoughts aside and hurriedly pulled on some breeches and a shirt made of fine linen with the family crest embroidered on the shirt pocket. Then he headed down the hallway to Queen Esther's suite of rooms. There was a guard stationed outside the door to the royal privy chamber, so she had to be still at work, even though it was after midnight.

He saluted the sleepy guard, who jumped to attention and saluted back.

"Yer Highness." The guard bowed. "Are ye here to see Her Majesty?"

"Yes." Brody knocked on the door, then cracked it open. "Mother?"

She whirled around at the sound of his voice. "Brody! Come in, come in." She dashed toward him and pulled him into an embrace. "Och, it's been too long."

"You're up late." He looked her over. There were circles under her eyes, and now tears were making her blue irises shimmer.

"Are ye all right?" She laid a palm on his cheek. "Ye seem too thin."

"You always say that."

"Because I'm always right." She rushed to the door and addressed the guard, "Vernon, could ye ask a servant to bring up a tray of food? Make that two trays."

"Aye, Yer Majesty." The guard bowed and hurried away.

With a small smile, Queen Esther strode back to Brody. "I just remembered I forgot to eat dinner."

"Is something worrying you?"

"Aye." Her smile faded away. "I thought yer sister would be back by now."

"Elinor? Where did she go?"

"She took her boat in search of the Isle of Secrets."

"*What?*" Brody's heart lurched up his throat. "Do you have any idea how dangerous it is there?"

Esther gripped her hands together. "She should be safe. She has powers of her own. And I sent that nice colonel with her."

"*Nevis?*"

"There's no need to shout, dear." His mother strode to the window and glanced out at the harbor. "The colonel seemed quite capable to me."

"*Nevis?*"

She gave Brody a curious look. "Ye must know him, then?"

"Aye. You sent Elinor off with him?"

"And the rest of her crew," Esther said, glancing out the window again. "Although I thought they would be back by now. Nevis believed that ye might have gone to the Isle of Secrets with Maeve. He was quite determined to find you both."

"Maeve did go there."

"Really?" His mother narrowed her eyes. "Now that I think about it, this is all yer fault."

"*What?*"

She nodded. "If ye came here more often and kept me informed, I would have known Maeve was there."

Brody sighed. "I didn't know she was there until I got there this afternoon. When I go back, I'll find Nevis and tell him to bring Ellie back home."

"Ye should come back, too. Ye're twenty-five years old now. 'Tis time for you to assume yer royal duties."

"Mother—"

"I know, I know." She waved a dismissive hand. "Ye're going to give me yer usual excuses, but no one here cares if ye have to be a dog most of the time."

He scoffed. "A canine king?"

"Better than no king." She gave him a pointed look.

"Actually . . ." He shifted his weight, wondering how much he should say.

"Ye have news?" His mother stepped toward him, her eyes growing wide. "Did ye find the witch who cursed you?"

"Yes."

"Oh, praise the goddesses!" Esther clapped her hands together. "Then ye can make her lift the curse!"

"Hopefully." Brody frowned. "But we can't be sure how this will play out. Cahira is very powerful."

His mother grew pale. "Is she the one who . . . ?"

Brody nodded. "She destroyed our ship."

Esther pressed a hand to her chest. "Ye mean she . . . she murdered my husband."

"Aye."

Tears glistened in his mother's eyes. "She murdered my son."

"Aye. And all the crew."

Esther drew in a shaky breath. "So at last we know." She closed her eyes briefly, and Brody reached out to grab her arm, fearing she was going to faint. "Is the witch on the Isle of Secrets? Where Elinor is?"

"Aye. Cahira is the queen. That's why it's so dangerous for Elinor to be there. As soon as I get back, I'll tell Nevis to bring Ellie home."

"Good." Esther squared her shoulders and lifted her chin. "I will notify the admiral immediately. He can have our navy ready to leave in two hours. We will capture this witch—"

"Mother, we can't manage this on our own. Cahira can destroy ships, and she has the Embraced army there with their magical powers—"

"Then what can we do?" His mother gripped her hands together. "We must have justice!"

"The kings on the mainland also have magical powers. I know them well, and I'm positive they'll want to help us. After all, Cahira is planning to use the Embraced army to take over all of Aerthlan, so my mainland friends have a stake in this. It's much better for them to defeat Cahira on the Isle of Secrets, rather than risk a war in their own countries."

Esther nodded slowly. "All right. I'll have Captain Chapman ready his ship right away. It's small and fast. With a good wind, he can make it to the mainland by morning."

"Excellent. With a small ship, he should be able to sail up the Ebe River to Ebton Palace." Brody strode over to his mother's desk and sat down. "I'll write down everything I know, then Captain Chapman can pass it on to King Leo."

He located a blank sheet of paper and dipped a pen into the inkwell. As he wrote, he heard his mother giving instructions to her guard. He'd just started a second page when he heard her let out a long sigh. "What?" He glanced up at her.

She was watching him with tears in her eyes. "That is where ye belong. At yer father's desk."

Brody swallowed hard and resumed his writing. This was never supposed to have been his place. His elder brother should have been the next king. Eddy had always been so quick at his studies and so brave at sword practice.

A knock sounded at the door, and servants brought in two trays of food. While the ink dried on his report, Brody sat at the table to eat with his mother. But she was so nervous about Elinor and the upcoming events, she hardly ate.

She set down her knife and fork. "I've ordered the admiral to have our ships ready. Are ye sure the kings from the mainland will help us?"

"Aye, they will." Brody cut off a piece of roast beef and stuffed it in his mouth. "The kings of Eberon and Tourin have numerous ships. And we'll get help from King Silas and the Norveshki war dragons. Also, Sorcha and her husband, the king of Woodwyn."

Esther's eyes widened. "Ye know all of them?"

"I've been busy." Brody gave her a wry smile. "Working like a dog."

His mother winced, obviously not finding his jest amusing. She tapped the table nervously with her fingertips. "Finally. After all these years, we will have justice for yer father and brother."

"I'll take care of Cahira. Don't worry about that."

"But ye must make sure she lifts yer curse first. That is most important." Tears shimmered in Esther's eyes. "I cannot bring Rudgar or Edgar back to life, but I can have you back."

"It'll work out. Trust me." Brody reached across the table

to squeeze his mother's hand. How would she react, he wondered, if he told her he was in love with Cahira's daughter? Would she be able to accept Maeve? After all, she knew all about the five Embraced girls who had grown up at the local convent.

Another knock sounded, and Vernon cracked open the door. "Yer Majesty, there are two men here with news from Princess Elinor."

Esther jumped to her feet. "Bring them in."

Two older men shuffled into the room, wringing their hats in their wrinkled hands. They bowed, and then their eyes widened as they noticed Brody.

"Och, ye're here!" the sunburned one exclaimed. "We went to the Isle of Secrets to look for you and the young lass, Maeve."

Brody stood. "You traveled there with Princess Elinor and Colonel Harden?"

"I did. Lobby is me name." He motioned to the other man. "I found me mate, Tommy, there on the Isle of Secrets."

"Aye." Tommy nodded. "The Sea Witch blew up our ship six years ago. I washed ashore on the witch's island."

"Where is Elinor now?" Esther asked. "Is she all right?"

"She's fine, Yer Majesty," Lobby replied. "She and Nevis are in the village." He withdrew a parcel of papers from his jacket. "She wrote all these notes for ye to send on to the kings on the mainland."

Esther opened the notes, and Brody looked over her shoulder to read the first page.

Embraced children in the village
on the Isle of Secrets

Bettina, 19 (Spring Embrace) Can communicate with birds

Catriona, 19 (Fall Embrace) Can blow up fish

Elam, 18 Can trip people one at a time
Hannah, 16 Can make it rain in small areas
Kurt, 15 Can shift into a small rabbit
Powers of the following children are not yet
    revealed:
Naomi, 12
Olana, 11
Peter, 10
Quentin, 9
Rose, 8
Sarah, 6
Terrance, 5
In the castle:
Two toddlers, Uma and Victor, age 4, in the nursery
Gabby, 17, a prisoner, can turn iron into gold
Gabby's twin brother, Gavin, can shift into an
    orange tabby cat. Cursed by Cahira, he cannot
    shift back into human form. He spent the last two
    years with the Seer.

Brody jolted with surprise. Trouble was a young man? A
shifter? No wonder he'd run off the minute they'd landed on
the island. He must have gone searching for his sister.

Esther set the first page on her desk and studied the second
page. Brody read over her shoulder.

The Embraced Army on the Isle of Secrets
General Kendric (Chameleon)
Colonel Alfred, 19 (Spring Embrace) Lightning
    power
Darroc, 19 (Fall Embrace) Wind power
Farah, 17 Fire power
Irene, 16 Power to make things grow
Jared, 15 Power to make rocks explode
Logan, 14 Power of speed (for running)

Mikayla, 13 Power of flight

Brody counted a total of eight soldiers, including the Chameleon. Some were very young and most probably inexperienced in using their powers during battle. "We can offset their lightning and wind power with Leo and Rupert. They have the same powers."

"It all sounds dangerous." Esther's hand trembled as she set the second page on her desk. "I'll make a copy of these, so I can send them with yer report to King Leo." She turned to Lobby and Tommy. "Thank ye so much for yer assistance. Ye should rest a bit afore returning to the Isle of Secrets. I'll have a room and meals prepared for you."

"Thank you, Yer Majesty." Lobby bowed.

She ushered the two old men out the door and gave instructions to the guard there. Then, she strode back to her desk. "What of you, Brody? Will ye rest here afore flying back?"

"I wish I could, but I need to be back before dawn. And I have to see Nevis and Elinor first."

Esther sat down and readied a piece of paper to copy Elinor's notes. "I'm going to be beside myself with worry. Both my children on the same island with that murderous witch."

"It won't take long before help arrives," Brody told her. "Once the kings have gathered their forces onto ships, Rupert can blow them here in a few hours."

"Our naval forces will be ready to join them." Esther lifted her chin with determination. "Together with our allies, we will be sending an armada to the Isle of Secrets."

Brody nodded. "And then the war will begin."

Chapter 15

The twin moons were nearing the horizon by the time Brody spotted the village on the Isle of Secrets. He was exhausted from flying so much in one night, but before he could return to the Sea Witch's castle, he needed to talk to Nevis. After landing next to what looked like a blacksmith's shop, he shifted into a dog and went sniffing about. There were only two other cottages. He trotted over to the one filled with the scent of males, then scratched on the door and barked.

Voices murmured inside; then a young man cracked open the door.

He looked Brody over, and turned back to his companions to say, "It's a black-and-white dog. I've never seen it before."

"That has to be Brody," Nevis said. "Elam, do you have a pair of breeches you can spare?"

After a short while, Nevis emerged from the cottage and gave Brody a frustrated look. "Now you show up? Where the hell have you been?" He tossed the breeches at him.

Brody shifted and caught the breeches in one hand. "What the hell are you doing here with my sister?"

"She's fine." Nevis pointed at the other cottage. "She's sleeping with the other girls. You'd better hurry up and get dressed before any of them see you." He crossed his arms, frowning. "You never mentioned that you're a damned prince. Does Leo know about this?"

Brody shook his head as he buttoned the breeches, which only reached his calves.

"You should have told us," Nevis grumbled. "All these years, I've been treating you like a dog."

"I was a dog." Brody shrugged. "Don't let it bother you. Whenever I felt annoyed, I chewed up your boots."

Nevis grimaced. "I'm on my fifth pair now."

"Exactly."

Nevis snorted. "Well, at least you're all right. You had everyone worried. Where have you been for the last two months?"

"Searching for the Embraced army and the last members of the Circle of Five. That's my job. It's definitely not Elinor's concern. I want you take her home as soon as Lobby and Tommy return with the boat."

Nevis's eyes widened. "You know about them?"

"Aye, I've just returned from the Isle of Moon. I was seeing my mother when they arrived. Thank you for all the information, by the way. My mother is sending it to Leo, and he should have it by morning."

"That's a relief." Nevis took a deep breath. "We're going to need everyone's help."

"Everyone but Elinor. Send her back home today."

Nevis scoffed. "Do you think I haven't tried? I begged her to go back with Lobby. She keeps refusing."

"Make her go. Aren't you used to giving orders?"

"She outranks me!" Nevis raked a hand through his hair. "The stubborn wench thinks she should be ordering *me* around."

"Did you just call my sister a wench?"

Nevis winced. "No offense. Honestly, she's really amazing."

Brody narrowed his eyes. "Are you saying you admire her?"

Nevis gritted his teeth. "What are you doing here? Do you want to hide out here with me?"

"What are your plans?" Brody asked.

"I'm going to have Lobby and Tommy take the younger

children to safety. As for the older ones with rejected powers, I'm going to turn them into my own Embraced army. With the right strategy, I think they could be quite effective. Do you want to help me?"

Brody shook his head. "I have my own plans, but I'll coordinate them with yours. And with Leo's, once he and the others arrive. If you can incapacitate the guards, that will leave the mainland kings to deal with the Embraced army."

"I can do that. What will you be doing?"

"I'll handle the queen."

Nevis winced. "You . . . know she's Maeve's mother?"

Brody waved a dismissive hand. "Maeve has nothing to do with her."

"Well, perhaps, but still . . ." Nevis shifted his weight. "Aren't you attracted to Maeve?"

"I'm in love with her."

"And you're planning to kill her mother? You don't see a problem with that?"

Yes, he did, but he didn't want to think about it. "I have to capture Cahira first, so I can make her release me from this curse."

"True." Nevis nodded. "I tell you what—once I take care of the guards, I'll be able to infiltrate the castle. Why don't you let me deal with Cahira?"

So his old friend was trying to save his relationship with Maeve. "I appreciate that, but it's my responsibility." Brody clenched his fists. "Cahira is the one who killed my father and brother."

Nevis sighed. "I know. And Elinor knows. A servant from the castle came by. Ruth was her name, and she told us quite a bit. She said Cahira hates your family with a passion. She thinks your kingdom should belong to her. Oh, and she said something else . . ."

"What?" Brody asked when Nevis gave him a nervous look.

"The Chameleon is supposed to arrive soon."

Brody nodded. "I'll take care of him." He glanced at the sky. The sun would be rising soon, and he needed to be in the Seer's bed before Cahira or one of the servants came to see him. "I should get back to the castle now."

"You're in the castle?" Nevis asked. "How? Are you disguised as a dog?"

Brody hesitated, then admitted, "The Seer."

Nevis blinked. "What?"

"I'm impersonating the Seer."

Nevis stepped back with a gasp. "*Bloody hell!* Are you telling me you can shift into other people?"

"Not so loud." Brody looked around, and sure enough, the door to the girls' cottage cracked open and several faces peered out.

Nevis lowered his voice and hissed, "You have the exact same powers as the Chameleon?"

"Don't . . ." Brody gritted his teeth. "Don't compare me to that bastard."

"How can I not when—" Nevis stopped when Elinor ran from the girls' cottage.

"Brody!" She threw her arms around him. "Are ye all right? Where have ye been? How did ye find us?"

"You can ask a ton of questions, but don't expect any answers," Nevis muttered and Brody shot him an annoyed look before turning back to his sister.

"Ellie, as soon as Lobby and Tommy return, I want you to take your ship back home."

Elinor frowned at her brother. "I believe I'm needed here. Nevis has a plan to use everyone's Embraced powers, and my gift would come in handy. Don't ye think so, Nevis?"

"Well . . ." Nevis dragged a hand through his hair.

Brody snorted. Nevis, one of the toughest soldiers on the battlefield, couldn't stand up to his sister at all. The wimp. "Ellie, I'm serious. An armada will be coming from the mainland, along with our navy from the Isle of Moon. A war is about to break out here."

"Then I have to help!" she declared.

"Elinor!" Brody glowered at her.

"I told you she doesn't follow orders," Nevis grumbled.

Elinor scoffed. "Don't tell me ye two have been making decisions for me."

Brody sighed. "We're just trying to keep you safe."

"Aye, because we care," Nevis added, and Brody shot him an incredulous look.

"Since when do you care about my sister?" Brody asked and Nevis's face turned pink.

"Brody." Elinor touched his shoulder. "Do ye know that it was Cahira who killed our father and brother?"

"Aye, I know. And she will pay for her crimes, I assure you."

Elinor planted her hands on her hips. "No need to assure me. I have every right to avenge them, too. That's why I refuse to leave." Before Brody could object, she continued. "Do ye know Maeve is Cahira's daughter?"

Brody nodded. "Yes, I know."

Elinor's eyes softened with sympathy. "Do ye know that Cahira is probably the one who cursed you?"

"She is definitely the one who cursed me," Brody muttered, then added, "I hope you won't blame Maeve for the crimes of her mother. She's innocent in all this."

"I understand that." Elinor waved a dismissive hand. "Do ye know that the Seer has arrived?"

Nevis snorted. "He definitely knows that."

"Well." Elinor huffed. "Do ye know when the mainland forces will arrive?"

Brody winced. She had him there. "I'm not sure. Mother is sending the news to Leo, and he should have all the information at some point in the morning. Then he has to send messages to the other kings and so forth. Once they're all on ships, Rupert can blow them here in a few hours."

"Two to three days at the most, I would say," Nevis concluded.

"That's a relief." Elinor heaved a big sigh. "Since we need to defeat Cahira within a week."

"Why a week?" Brody asked.

Nevis sidled up close to Elinor and whispered, "I don't think we should mention that right now."

"But he should know," Elinor whispered back. "So it won't come as a shock later on."

"Know what?" Brody demanded.

Nevis suddenly slapped Elinor on the back, and she gave him a startled look.

Brody stiffened. "You just hit my sister?"

"There was a mosquito about to bite her." Nevis bowed his head to Elinor. "I apologize. I hate mosquitos."

"Me, too." Elinor smiled at him. "Thank you for protecting me."

Nevis blushed.

Was there something going on between these two? Brody wasn't sure whether Nevis was flirting with his sister or trying to change the subject. Maybe both, damn him. "Ellie, you were about to tell me what's going on?"

She nodded. "Yes."

"Wait." Nevis lifted his hands in a calming gesture. "Brody, you might find the news a bit alarming, but don't let it upset you. You know how important timing is, so we have to remain patient. We mustn't attack anyone until Leo and the others have arrived."

Brody narrowed his eyes. Why was Nevis acting as if he might go berserk? "Just tell me," he growled.

Elinor took a deep breath. "Cahira doesn't trust Maeve, so she's making her prove her loyalty. In a week, Maeve has to get married."

Brody jerked back a step. *What?* Maeve was being forced to marry? He shook his head. "No. It won't . . . I won't let it happen." A chill skittered down his spine. "Who? Who is she supposed to marry?"

Elinor winced. "The Chameleon."

Damn, damn, damn! Brody cursed with each flap of his wings as he sped toward the castle. He was going to kill that damned Chameleon! As soon as that bastard arrived at the castle, he had to die. Nevis could preach patience all he wanted, but . . .

But you know he's right, Brody admonished himself. He couldn't screw up everyone's plans just because he wanted to kill the Chameleon the minute he saw him.

Dammit, Maeve should have told him. Why would she keep something this huge a secret? *Because she knows you'll try to kill the bastard.* Was she worried he wouldn't win the battle? He scoffed. She should have more trust in him than that. Of course he would win.

Wouldn't he? As far as their shifting powers went, he and the Chameleon were evenly matched. Brody suspected he was better with a sword. But when it came to being ruthless, the Chameleon was the clear winner. The bastard had killed his own father and half-brother. Maeve was right to be worried. *Dammit.*

He flew through the open window into the Seer's bedchamber, landed on the floor, and shifted into human form. The light of one candlestick flickered, illuminating the dark room enough that he could see.

"Maeve?" he whispered, but there was no reply. She must have gone to sleep in her own bedchamber. Good. He was too exhausted to have a difficult conversation with her now. And too upset that she'd kept her upcoming wedding a secret. Besides, after talking to his mother and Nevis, he'd used

up most of his allotted two hours to be himself. He probably
had less than thirty minutes left.

He glanced about the room, noting that the curtains
around the bed had been drawn shut. All was quiet. Good.
No one had realized that he'd been gone all night.

He wandered over to the sitting area, where a candlestick
sat on the round table with a fresh tray of food. That was
thoughtful of Maeve. Even though he'd eaten his fill on the
Isle of Moon, the long flight back had made him hungry
again. He stuffed some ham and cheese into a small loaf of
bread, then ate while he headed into the dressing room.

There were two buckets of water next to the tub. Maeve
had been considerate again. He set down his sandwich and
quickly washed up. After drying off, he wrapped the towel
around his waist and resumed eating his sandwich as he
headed toward his bed.

He drew back the curtains and nearly choked on the food
in his mouth. What the hell? Maeve was in his bed!

Damn. His first instinct was to tear off his towel and climb
into bed with her. After all, it was what she wanted, wasn't it?

No, he argued with himself. He'd already decided to be honest with her. He needed to bare his soul first. Then, if she could
accept him, if she could still love him, he would claim her.

For now, she needed to go. He couldn't risk Cahira or any
of the servants seeing her in his bed.

"Maeve?" he whispered.

With a small groan, she snuggled closer to the pile of pillows that was supposed to be him. Damn but that made him
ache with longing. She should be snuggling up to him. She
should be sleeping through the night with his arms around
her. But with the curse, that could never be.

He strode to the door leading to her bedchamber, unlocked it, and left it wide open. After dropping the last few
bites of his sandwich on the table, he returned to the bed.

"Maeve." He pulled back the covers and winced at the way the thin nightgown accentuated her curves. It was bunched up around her hips, leaving her long legs bare, and for a second, he imagined them wrapped around him in the throes of passion.

He pushed that thought aside, but his body still reacted, his groin tightening.

"Maeve, you need to sleep in your own bed."

She rolled onto her back. "Mmm."

He groaned. She was so beautiful, her dark lashes framing her closed eyes, her pink mouth slightly open, her long black hair strewn against the white pillowcase.

Mine. The thought hit him hard. He'd realized earlier that he loved her. But now, he realized he couldn't live without her. He couldn't possibly send her back to Ebton to marry one of her suitors there. He had to be the one. Even she had said earlier that he had to be the one.

No doubt she was desperate to avoid marrying the Chameleon. Was that why she'd suddenly insisted on losing her virginity? She'd called it unbridled lust, but what if it was simply a strategy to avoid her upcoming wedding?

Damn. That possibility deflated his ego. And the bulge beneath his towel.

Gritting his teeth, he slipped his arms beneath her and lifted her up.

"Brody?" she mumbled, her eyes still closed.

"No need to wake up," he muttered as he carried her into her bedchamber. It was dark in there, so he was forced to slow down. And forced to think about how good she felt in his arms. When his eyes adjusted, he spotted her four-poster bed and headed straight for it.

Her eyes blinked open. "You're back."

"Aye."

She touched his bare chest. "Are you going to make love to me now?"

He jerked to a stop. *Yes.* "No. We're out of time. The sun will be rising soon."

"How much time does it take?"

He hurried over to the bed and dropped her on top. "I've flown all the way to the Isle of Moon and back. I'm too exhausted."

She sat up. "That's all right. As long as you're willing, I can do all the work."

Work? Was that how she saw it? Dammit, she really was doing this just to avoid an unwanted marriage. "It's not happening. We need to have a long talk first. And I'm almost out of time to be myself."

"Then we'll do it really fast."

He scoffed. "You're not doing this out of love for me, are you? You're just trying to avoid the wedding."

She gasped. "You know about that?"

"Hell, yes. You should have told me! I had to find out from Nevis and Elinor."

"What? How would they know?"

"They're here on the island. Hiding in the village. They came looking for you."

She tilted her head, thinking. "I can understand Nevis coming here, but why on Aerthlan would Princess Elinor come? It's too dangerous for her here."

"That's what I said, but she's refusing to leave." Brody hesitated, wondering if he should go ahead and admit to being Elinor's brother and a prince. "Maeve, I—"

"So you know I'm being forced to marry the Chameleon." Her shoulders slumped. "I can't do it. I really can't—"

"Don't worry. I won't let it happen."

She sat back up. "Then you agree to take my virginity?"

"No!"

With an angry huff, she jumped out of bed. "Why are you being so stubborn? Is it such a chore for you?"

"It's not a chore. But this is the wrong time—"

"I don't have time! The wedding is in a week!"

He gritted his teeth. "The wedding won't happen. I will kill the Chameleon."

She scoffed. "You'd rather kill someone than bed me? Am I that undesirable?"

"I do want you, Maeve. I've wanted you for years. But I don't want that bastard being the reason I bed you."

"So you'd rather risk your life? I don't want that! My idea is much better, so let's get started." She reached for his towel.

He jumped back, but his towel slipped loose. "Dammit." He grabbed the towel, making sure his crotch was covered. "Maeve . . ." He paused when he saw her gaze was focused on his hands. Damn, but he could feel himself starting to swell. He'd better change the subject fast. "The mainland kings will be coming here soon. As soon as they arrive, we will be at war."

She blinked, and her gaze lifted to his face. "All of our friends will be in danger? Surely there is another way . . ."

"The Circle of Five and the Embraced army must be defeated. Honestly, Maeve, even if there was no wedding, I would still have to fight the Chameleon. I'm the only one who can do it. The final battle between us has been destined for years. The time has come, and there's no avoiding it."

Her eyes glistened with tears. "I don't want you to get hurt. If we could force them to surrender—"

"The Chameleon murdered his own father in pursuit of power. He's not going to surrender. I will have to kill him."

She winced. "And my mother? Will you have to kill her, too?"

He tightened his grip on the towel. This was the perfect time to tell Maeve that her mother had killed his father and brother. He opened his mouth, but the words refused to come out.

"Are you afraid I will blame you?" A tear rolled down Maeve's cheek. "I love you, Brody. No matter what happens, I will always love you."

His heart expanded. "I love you, too, Maeve."

Another tear fell down her face, and she wiped her cheeks dry. "Then what are we waiting for?"

"I want it to be good for you, but I don't have much time left as myself. Maybe about twenty minutes."

"Then we have no time to lose." She turned her back to him and whisked her nightgown over her head.

His eyes widened at the sight of her bare back and buttocks, her skin pale in the dim light. Her nightgown fell to the floor as she climbed into bed and pulled the covers up to her breasts.

"Maeve." There were still things he needed to say. He hadn't admitted who he was or what her mother had done to his family. "I'm still cursed. I have only two hours a day—"

"And I'll be grateful for them." She reached a hand toward him. "Because I love you."

His beautiful, stubborn Maeve. He could only hope her love for him would endure the hardships to come. Letting his towel drop to the floor, he strode toward the bed.

Chapter 16

It was happening! Maeve's heart raced as Brody slipped into bed beside her, his naked body brushing up against hers. No more excuses about the curse. He was truly hers, and she would never give him up.

With tears in her eyes, she laid a hand on his cheek. "Brody."

"Mmm." He gave her a brief kiss. "Will you promise me one thing?"

"Anything." She wrapped her arms around his neck.

He brushed her hair away from her brow. "Never call me Julia again."

She winced. "It was a mistake at first because you make such a pretty dog."

"But after you knew it was me, you kept doing it."

"Because you kept ignoring me."

His eyes widened. "You were purposely trying to annoy me?"

"You were purposely ignoring me." She frowned at him. "It hurt my feelings."

He smoothed a finger over her pouting bottom lip. "What else could I do, Maeve? I wanted you from the first time I saw you and heard you singing on the beach. Your beauty astonished me; your voice captivated me. I knew there would never be anyone else for me—"

"Then why did you avoid me?"

"You were only sixteen. I knew I had to wait."

"But you wouldn't even dance with me."

"I didn't trust myself." He nuzzled her neck and kissed her beneath her ear. "I wanted you too much."

His voice sent a shiver down her arms. "I wanted you, too." She felt something hard pressing against her hip. It must be his manhood. She'd caught a glimpse of it when he'd approached the bed, and she'd been surprised by its size. But good heavens, it seemed even bigger now. And harder.

Too big. This was going to hurt. But she was determined to complete her deflowering mission tonight. Steeling her nerves, she rose up on one elbow and pushed Brody onto his back.

The first light of dawn crept through the window, chasing away enough darkness to allow her to see the surprised look on his face.

She smoothed her hand over his muscular chest. "I know you're exhausted, so just lie there and rest. Tell me what to do, and I'll get right to it."

His mouth twitched. "Are you going to follow my orders for once?"

She narrowed her eyes. Was he planning on abusing his authority? "I'll do whatever you say as long as it makes sense."

"Ah." His blue eyes twinkled with mischief.

She sat up. "You are knowledgeable in this sort of thing, aren't you?"

He nodded. "Somewhat. Though I'm terribly out of practice."

"Why?"

He gave her a wry look. "First, I'm only human two hours a day. Secondly, most women do not find my situation appealing. Thirdly, and most importantly, I've been waiting the last four years because I wanted you."

So he'd been faithful to her? "Oh, Brody." She leaned toward him and gasped when her bare breasts brushed against his chest. "Quickly now, tell me what to do."

"Kiss me."

She pressed her lips against his. "Now what?"

He frowned at her. "I meant a real kiss. A long one that makes us—"

"We're short on time. We need to move on to the next step."

"You said you would follow my orders."

"If they make sense—" Her breath caught when he suddenly pushed her onto her back and planted his mouth against hers.

His lips melded against hers as he kissed her slowly and thoroughly. Her thoughts scattered and all her determination to rush through the ordeal melted away. This was far too pleasurable to do in a hurry. Her hands delved into his hair to pull him closer, and when his tongue entered her mouth, she welcomed it with a stroke of her own tongue. A warm, languid feeling slid down her body, and soon, she was rubbing her legs against his.

He broke the kiss and whispered, "Does it make sense now?"

"Yes." She pulled his head down for another kiss. His taste, his scent, the feel of his body against hers, they were all so pleasurable. Intoxicating. *Brody.* She tangled her tongue with his. How long had she waited for this moment?

The insistent pressure of his manhood no longer frightened her. Quite the opposite. Now she welcomed it as a sign of his passion. She wanted it. She wanted it so badly that her own groin started to ache for him.

"Brody." She trailed kisses across his handsome face. "What do we do next?"

"This." He cupped her breast, then dragged a thumb across her nipple.

She hissed in a breath. "Th-that's very nice, but do we have time for—" She halted when he dipped his head down and sucked her nipple into his mouth. Oh, dear goddesses, this was heaven. "I suppose a few minutes wouldn't hurt."

The aching emptiness between her legs flared with heat.

After a final tease with his tongue, he glanced up at her. "Did that make sense?"

"Well . . . only if you do both."

He nodded. "Very sensible." He latched onto her other nipple while he teased the first one with his fingers.

As the needy feeling grew, she squeezed her thighs together, relishing the sharp friction, the insistent feeling that she was spiraling toward something tremendous. "Brody, what . . . what's next?"

"This." He smoothed his fingers lightly down her torso, and her skin prickled with gooseflesh.

"Yes—" Her breath caught when he rested his hand on the black curls guarding her womanhood.

"Open your legs," he whispered. "Let me touch you."

She blinked. "Is that done?"

His blue eyes glimmered with heat. "Yes. But only by me."

Slowly, she opened her legs. She gasped at the touch of his fingers caressing her most intimate flesh. The shock quickly faded as the most glorious pleasure made her melt. "Oh. Oh, Brody."

"You're so beautifully wet." He sat up and tilted his head so he could look at her. "So pretty and swollen."

She slammed her thighs together, pinning his hand between them. "Why are you looking at me?"

His mouth curled up. "Because I want to."

"Is that done?"

"Yes, but only by me."

"Oh." She relaxed her thighs. Now that she thought about it, it made perfect sense for him to see her. After all, she could see him. His manhood was thick and stiff with black curls at its base. Since he was touching her, shouldn't she be allowed to touch him?

She reached toward him, then jolted when he inserted a finger inside her. Oh, dear goddesses. Whatever he was doing was glorious. Just when she thought it couldn't possibly get any better, his thumb brushed over a special place. She saw stars for a second, then moaned when he rubbed against her briskly.

"Oh." She shook her head. This was far too pleasurable. How could she endure this?

"You're so wet, I want to taste you." He moved between her legs, and grasping her by the hips, he lowered his head.

"What?" She attempted to sit up. "Is that done?"

"Yes, but only by me." He pushed her back down.

"What?" She jerked when she felt his tongue stroke her swollen and slick skin. Oh, this was truly the most pleasurable thing yet. With a groan, she lifted her legs, resting her feet on his shoulders.

He lapped. Thrust. Suckled.

She panted, writhing beneath him, soaring higher and higher until she teetered, breathless, on an edge. The sound of him growling pushed her over, and with a jolt, she shattered.

For a moment, she could hardly see. But as the throbbing sensations faded away, she realized he'd moved away from her to the edge of the bed. "Brody?"

"I'm sorry. I—" His body began to shimmer. "I'm out of time." He collapsed onto the floor.

"Brody!" She sat up and peered over the edge.

His human form blurred, and then suddenly, he snapped into the familiar form of a black-and-white dog. He looked at her with his beautiful blue eyes.

"Oh, Brody." She slipped out of bed.

With a whining sound, he hung his head.

"It's all right." She fondled the ruff of fur around his neck. "After midnight tonight, we'll have two more hours."

A sudden knock on her door startled her.

"Are you awake, Your Highness?" Ruth's voice called as she cracked open the door.

Maeve glanced at the window, where early morning sun-light was pouring into her room. "Oh, no."

Brody had immediately crouched down to remain hidden. He jabbed at her nightgown with a front paw and slid it across the floor within her reach.

She pulled the nightgown over her head, then peered over the bed. "I'm awake."

"Oh, good." Ruth swung the door wide open, and another servant marched inside, carrying a breakfast tray. "What are you doing on the floor?"

"Oh, I—I dropped something." Maeve sat on the edge of the bed. Oh, dear goddesses, how would she explain the presence of a dog in her room? She slanted a frantic look at Brody. The door to the Seer's bedchamber was wide open, but he couldn't make a mad dash for it with two servants nearby.

"What is the meaning of this?" Cahira's voice shouted from the hallway. "Burien's door is locked!"

"It's all right, Your Majesty," Ruth told her. "You can enter from this room."

Oh, no! Maeve gritted her teeth. If her mother went into the Seer's bedchamber, she'd find an empty bed.

"How am I supposed to check on Burien?" Cahira stopped at Maeve's doorway and glared at her. "How dare you lock me out?"

Maeve jumped to her feet. "Please forgive me. Father had a difficult night, and he just now fell asleep. I wanted him to be able to rest undisturbed."

"Silly child, I can check on him without waking him." Cahira stepped into the room, glancing at the open door. "You took care of him during the night?"

"Yes, Your Majesty."

"Hmm." Cahira shrugged, looking a little less annoyed. "I suppose you can be useful. Hurry up and eat. My seamstress will be here soon to take your measure—what?" She jumped back when an orange blur shot past her. "How did that damned cat get in the castle?"

The orange tabby zoomed around the bed and stopped short when it spotted Brody.

The Seer's cat? What was it doing here? Maeve wondered as the cat jabbed a paw at canine Brody.

"My apologies, Your Majesty." Ruth curtsied. "I figured Gavin was looking for his sister, so I brought him inside the castle last night to see Gabby."

Cahira glowered at her. "You overstepped yourself."

Ruth bowed her head. "Gabby was so happy to see him, she promised to work twice as hard for you."

"Really?" Cahira tilted her head, considering that. "I suppose it's all right, then."

"Excuse me?" Maeve lifted a hand. "Are you saying Gabby's brother is this *cat*?"

Cahira waved a dismissive hand. "It's a long story."

Maeve glanced down at the floor and blinked. Now there were two orange tabbies! Brody must have shifted into one.

One cat dashed through the door into the Seer's bedchamber, while the other one slipped underneath Maeve's bed.

"That damn cat," Cahira grumbled as she walked toward the open door. "He must have missed the Seer."

"The cat knows my father?" Maeve asked, playing for more time so Brody would have a chance to shift.

Cahira stopped and glanced back. "I sent the cat to Burien two years ago, so he wouldn't be so lonely."

"Oh, that was nice of you." *Not really*, Maeve thought, if the cat was actually Gabby's brother. She followed Cahira into the Seer's bedchamber.

"Burien?" Cahira asked softly as she drew back the curtains surrounding the Seer's bed.

Maeve heaved a sigh of relief when she spotted the fake Seer lying in bed, pretending to be fast asleep. It was a bit of a jolt, though, to see Brody looking so old and frail. His shoulders were so thin, his skin like gray parchment. Only moments ago, he'd been in her bed with a young, healthy, muscular body.

"Why is he not dressed?" Cahira demanded.

"He . . . he took off his clothes," Maeve said. "He said it was too hot."

Cahira snorted. "Of course it's too hot. You closed the bed curtains." She jerked them open. "Go fetch one of his shirts from the dressing room."

"Yes, Mother." Maeve ran into the dressing room, noting the tub still filled with water. Brody had used the buckets of water she'd left him. She brought a shirt of fine white linen back to the bed.

"Burien." Cahira touched his shoulder.

He shook his head. "I'm fine," he mumbled. "I just want to sleep."

"Very well." Cahira drew the covers up to his chin and left the shirt on a pillow next to him. "I'll check on you later." She strode toward the adjoining bedchamber, pausing by the Seer's table, where Maeve had left a tray of food the night before. "He seems to be eating well."

"Yes, Mother."

"Good." Cahira walked into Maeve's room. "If Kendric arrives today, I'll arrange for a small party this evening. Hopefully, Burien will be rested enough to attend."

"Yes, Mother." Maeve groaned inwardly. She had no desire ever to meet the Chameleon, though it might be interesting to see what he actually looked like. The real problem would be Brody. Could he meet his archenemy without trying to kill him?

"Are you hungry?" Maeve tore up a piece of her bacon and set it on the table next to her tray.

She was alone in her bedchamber, eating breakfast, when

the orange tabby crawled out from beneath her bed and approached her.

"Thank you for coming to the rescue," she told the cat.

With a yip, the tabby jumped onto the chair next to her and nibbled at the bacon pieces.

"So you lived with the Seer for the last two years?"

The cat nodded and continued to eat.

Maeve added a spoonful of scrambled eggs to the cat's breakfast. "And you're Gabby's brother, Gavin?"

The cat nodded again.

So he was a shifter, Maeve thought. Why wasn't he shifting back to his human form so he could talk to her? "I know you're trying to help Brody and me, but please be careful. All right?"

Gavin studied her a moment with intelligent eyes, then resumed eating his bacon and eggs.

After a few minutes, Ruth returned for the breakfast tray.

"Oh, there you are," she greeted Gavin. "Are you ready to go back to your sister now?"

The cat purred in agreement.

Maeve sidled up close to Ruth and whispered, "Is he unable to shift back into his real self?"

With a sigh, Ruth nodded. "Her Majesty did this to him. She told Gabby her brother would never be normal again if she didn't turn the iron coins into gold."

"How awful." Maeve cast a sympathetic look at the orange tabby. "But how could my mother make Gavin unable to shift?"

Ruth winced. "She cursed him. It's one of her abilities as a witch."

A trickle of unease slithered down Maeve's spine. "My mother is a witch?"

"Aye." Ruth nodded. "Some call her the Sea Witch."

Maeve stepped back. Wasn't that what Lobby had talked

about? A sea witch who was powerful enough to destroy his boat and drown all his friends.

Ruth picked up the tray. "I'll be going now. The seamstress will be here soon." She strolled out the door with Gavin following her.

The guard glanced in at Maeve, then slammed the door shut.

Slowly, Maeve turned and walked into the Seer's room. Brody was sound asleep, exhausted from all his flying the night before.

The unease inside her grew as her thoughts raced. Her mother was more than a powerful shifter. She was a witch. The Sea Witch. Able to destroy ships. If Leo and Rupert came here to do battle, would she destroy their ships? Would she drown all their soldiers?

Her mother had also cursed Gavin, making him unable to shift back into human form. Good goddesses, this sounded too familiar.

As Maeve watched Brody sleeping in the form of the Seer, tears gathered in her eyes. Apparently, he could impersonate the Seer or another human for hours. It was only his own form that he couldn't hold for more than two hours.

Cursed by a witch. She'd heard in the past that the curse could only be lifted if he found the same witch who had originally cursed him. But he'd never been able to find her.

Until now?

Maeve pressed a hand to her mouth to stifle a cry. Brody's curse and all his years of suffering—was the one responsible for it her own mother?

Chapter 17

In the kingdom of Eberon, King Leofric was standing by his desk in the privy chamber of Ebton Palace. He finished reading the latest report from Captain Shaw, then passed it on to his wife.

Luciana sat on a settee between her adopted sisters, Brigitta and Gwennore, and all three of them read the report together. Gwen's husband, Silas, was anxiously pacing across the room.

"Any confirmation yet on the Embraced army?" Silas asked.

"No." Leo shook his head. "Shaw was reporting from Ebport. Our navy will be ready to leave in an hour. General Harden has arrived with five troops of soldiers, one for each of our five ships."

"Excellent." Silas continued to pace.

Leo wandered to the window that overlooked the Ebe River. The royal barge was tied off at the pier, ready to take him and the dragon shifters, Silas and Dimitri, downriver to Ebport. Silas had offered to fly there, giving Leo a ride on his back, but Leo had thought it best to decline. If he accidentally gave Silas a lightning shock while in flight, he might severely injure the dragon and cause him to crash.

On the front lawn, Dimitri was playing chase with Leo's twins, Eric and Eviana, and Brigitta's son, Reynfrid. Leo smiled to himself, relieved to see that Eviana was comfortable with the dragon shifter. Eric looked back to see how close Dimitri was and tripped, falling onto his face.

Dimitri swooped him up and tossed him in the air. When Dimitri set him on the ground, Eric was laughing and Eviana was demanding her turn.

Silas glanced out the window and snorted. "Dimitri must be practicing. His wife is expecting."

Leo nodded as the familiar twinge of regret jabbed at his heart. How easy it was for someone else to play with his children. They were four years old, but because of his lightning power, he'd never been able to touch them.

He flexed his gloved hands. He'd realized while the twins were mere babies that all the regret in the world would not change his situation. But still, it hurt.

To keep Luciana from being distressed, he tried to hide the pain, but deep down, he knew she understood. She was expecting again, and he loved resting his hand on her belly so he could feel the babe moving inside. He cherished those moments, for it was as close as he would ever get to the child.

There's no point in dwelling on it. He turned away from the window and focused his mind once again on business.

Yesterday, late in the afternoon, Captain Shaw had arrived from the Isle of Moon with a message from Nevis. Maeve had disappeared, and Nevis suspected she'd gone to a mysterious island to the south to see if the Embraced army was hiding there. Leo suspected Maeve was right, since all four mainland kings had scoured their countries and not found the army anywhere on the continent.

Of course, Luciana had been alarmed by the news that her youngest sister could be in danger. She'd insisted on sending the navy right away to search for Maeve and rescue her, but Leo had convinced his wife that they needed to be prepared in case Maeve was correct and the Embraced army was, indeed, stationed on the Isle of Secrets. And so, they had immediately sent messages by carrier pigeon to Tourin and Norveshka, urging the kings there to prepare for a possible sea battle.

Brigitta had arrived late last night with her son and a small troop of Tourinian soldiers. Her husband, King Ulfrid, whom she preferred to call Rupert, was busy preparing the Tourinian navy. They were leaving Rupert's general and old friend, Stefan, in charge of the country while they were gone.

Once Silas had received his message in Norveshka, he'd used his telepathic powers to communicate with his dragon friend, Aleksi, in Woodwyn. Aleksi had passed on the news to Sorcha and her husband, King Brennan of Woodwyn. They had headed south down the Wyn River to Wynport, where the elfin navy was being made ready to sail. Six ships, fully manned with soldiers, Aleksi had reported.

Silas and Dimitri had flown in this morning in dragon form with Gwennore riding on Silas's back. They had left Annika in charge of Norveshka. She'd wanted to come and fight, but Silas and her husband, Dimitri, had convinced her to stay at home.

Annika wasn't the only woman who had wanted to go. After Luciana, Brigitta, and Gwennore were reunited, the three sisters had announced their intention of traveling with the naval forces. Leo and Silas had objected, of course. All three women were expecting, and it was simply too dangerous for a country to risk the lives of both its king and queen. Besides, none of the three queens were trained to fight. Nor were their Embraced powers of any use during battle.

Leo winced, recalling the hurt look on his wife's face when he'd said that last part. But he'd been determined to keep her safe. Finally, they had reached an agreement.

The three queens would wait here at Ebton Palace, and as soon as their husbands were successful in defeating the Embraced army, Rupert would come take them to Maeve. With his wind power, the Tourinian king could deliver them in just a few hours.

The plans were ready, Leo thought. They just needed to know where the Embraced army was hiding.

Some shouts on the front lawn drew his attention, and he

turned back to the window. Luciana's father, Lucas Vintello, the Duke of Vindalyn, had arrived and was happily hugging his grandchildren, Reynfrid included. Since all the queens considered themselves sisters, Lucas had declared himself the grandfather of all their babies.

"The duke has arrived," Leo said as he watched Dimitri, Lucas, and the children climb the stairs to the palace entrance. Down on the lawn, servants were taking the duke's horse to the stables and his guards to the kitchen.

Last night, Luciana had sent a message to her father, urging him to come to the palace as quickly as possible. Lucas must have traveled all night to arrive before noon. As they climbed the steps, Dimitri was talking and gesturing with his hands. No doubt he was explaining what was going on.

Luciana joined Leo at the window. "Papa made it here faster than I thought."

Leo took her hand, and she gave him a smile. He thanked the Light every day for bringing her into his life. Hell, he even thanked Luna and Lessa, the moon goddesses. And every star in the heavens. According to his wise cousin, Tedric, they were all made by what he called the Great Creator.

It was a shame, Leo thought, that he couldn't make Tedric his chief counsel. Unfortunately, though, Tedric was a ghost, murdered over four years ago by the Chameleon. It was only because of Luciana's Embraced gift that Leo was able to communicate with his late cousin.

"Let's go see your father." Leo led her into the Great Hall.

Silas, Gwen, and Brigitta followed them just as the front doors opened and the children dashed inside.

"Grandpa's here!" They pulled the duke through the doorway.

"Your Majesty." Lucas sketched a quick bow to Leo, then embraced his daughter. "I came as quickly as I could. Dimitri tells me you might know our enemies' location?"

"Maeve may have found them," Luciana said.

Leo nodded. "We'll leave as soon as we have confirmation."

"I want to go, too!" Eric announced, and the other children joined in.

"Right now, you're going to the kitchens for lunch," Luciana told them as she motioned to a servant. "Aren't you hungry?"

Eric rubbed his tummy. "I am."

Eviana huffed. "He's always hungry."

"I am, too," Reynfrid added.

"Can you eat with us, Gwennie?" Eviana tugged at Gwennore's skirt.

"I'll be along in a little while." Gwennore touched the little girl's cheek. "Save some food for me."

"We will!" Eviana followed the boys and the servant through the door that led to the kitchens.

Gwennore sighed. "They think we've come here for a fun family reunion."

"Aye," Luciana agreed. "But I'd rather they not hear about their fathers going to war."

Lucas winced. "I wish I had known about this. I could have brought you several troops of soldiers from Vindalyn."

"We have enough soldiers." Luciana took his hand. "What we need is you."

Her father nodded. "I'll gladly fight. And the guards who came with me."

"We need you here at the palace," Leo told him. "There's no one we trust more than you."

"What?" Lucas gave his daughter an incredulous look. "Don't tell me you're going!"

"I wanted to," Luciana grumbled.

"We all did," Brigitta muttered.

Gwen nodded. "I still think my healing powers would come in handy."

"I need to know that you're safe," Silas said quietly, reaching for Gwen's hand.

"It's too dangerous—" Lucas began.

"We know." Luciana interrupted with gritted teeth. "So we're going to stay here and worry ourselves to death."

"We'll be fine," Leo assured her, giving her hand a squeeze.

Lucas regarded his daughter with a stern look. "You must be strong, Luciana. It is your duty to rule Eberon while your husband is away."

"I know, Papa. But I'll feel better having you here."

Leo stepped close to his father-in-law. "I wanted you here, too. If the worst happens and we're defeated, the Embraced army will head straight to the mainland to conquer the countries here while their kings are gone. You will have to lead our army to defend Eberon."

Luciana gasped. "You just said you would be fine!"

"We will be," Leo insisted. "We just have to be prepared in case . . ." He stopped when he saw tears forming in her eyes.

"Shouldn't General Harden be in charge of the army?" Lucas asked.

"He's coming with us," Leo said.

With a frown, Lucas nodded. "I will do as you ask. But if the worst happens and the women and children are in danger—"

"I've made arrangements," Silas told them. "A few war dragons will take them to a hidden place in the Norveshki mountains. They will be safe there."

Lucas took a deep breath. "I will pray that it never comes to that."

"We all will," Leo agreed.

"A ship is approaching!" Dimitri called from the open doorway.

They all filed out the door onto the stair landing.

"The flag looks like two white circles on a bright blue background," Dimitri said.

Luciana lifted a hand to shield her eyes from the bright sun. "That's the flag of the Isle of Moon."

It must be an envoy from Queen Esther, Leo thought as he and the others headed down the stairs. By the time they crossed the front lawn, his servants had helped the small ship tie off next to the Eberoni royal barge.

"Welcome to Eberon!" Leo shouted as he stepped onto the pier.

"I'm Captain Chapman of the Isle of Moon," a tall man with a flamboyant hat called from the ship's deck while his crew set a gangplank in place. "I have urgent news for King Leofric of Eberon."

"I am the king." As Leo approached, he quickly identified his companions.

Captain Chapman strode across the gangplank, whipped his hat off, and bowed. "Yer Majesties. Queen Esther has bid me deliver these messages." He handed Leo a leather parcel.

While Leo quickly untied the leather thongs around the parcel, Silas stepped closer to the captain.

"What can you tell us?" Silas asked. "Is the Embraced army on the Isle of Secrets?"

"Is Maeve all right?" Luciana asked.

"The army is, indeed, there," Captain Chapman confirmed, and everyone exchanged looks.

"We will be leaving right away, then," Leo said as he opened the leather parcel and removed some folded papers.

"I saw yer navy when we passed by Ebport," the captain said. "They stopped us, and General Harden questioned me. He asked me to assure you that they would be ready by the time ye arrive."

"Has the Tourinian navy arrived?" Brigitta asked.

The captain shook his head. "There were five ships there, all flying the Eberoni flag. If ye don't mind, I'll take my ship back with you. Our Queen is readying her navy—"

"You're joining us in battle?" Leo asked.

"Aye. We have five ships, including mine." Captain Chapman bowed his head. "We thank you for assisting us."

Leo nodded. "We'll head to the Isle of Moon first so your ships can join ours."

"Queen Esther will be delighted to meet you," the captain said with another bow.

"After we arrive at the Isle of Moon, I'll shift and fly south to locate the elfin navy," Silas offered.

The captain blinked. "Ye'll . . .fly?"

"He's a dragon," Dimitri explained. "So am I."

The captain stepped back, his eyes widening.

Meanwhile, Leo had unfolded the papers, and he began reading the first page. To his surprise, it was a letter from Brody.

> *Leo,*
>
> *You and the other kings must prepare immediately for war. We have discovered the last members of the Circle of Five and their Embraced army on the Isle of Secrets, located southwest of the Isle of Moon.*
>
> *Attack them while they are still on the island. Beware of their leader, Cahira, a powerful sea witch, who can destroy ships. The leader of the Embraced army is the Chameleon. One of their soldiers has lightning power like you, and another has wind power like Rupert.*
>
> *Queen Esther of the Isle of Moon is preparing her naval forces to join yours. I will be on the Isle of Secrets with Maeve and Nevis, where we will coordinate our attacks with yours.*
>
> *Brody*

"A letter from Brody." Leo passed the first page to Silas, who held it up so Brigitta and Gwennore could also read it.

Then Leo started reading the second page, which was a list of Embraced children living in a village on the Isle of Secrets.

"But what about Maeve?" Luciana asked. "Is she all right?"

Captain Chapman nodded. "Yes. According to the prince, she's fine."

Luciana blinked. "Prince? What prince?"

"Queen Esther's son," the captain explained. "And heir to the throne."

Leo paused in his reading. "I thought her daughter was heir to the throne."

"So did I." Luciana frowned. "I know the queen had two sons, but they both drowned at sea with their father. I remember the whole island being upset . . ."

"One of the sons survived," Captain Chapman admitted. "But Prince Brodgar rarely comes to the island. He suffers—"

"Prince *Brodgar*?" Luciana asked.

"Aye." The captain nodded. "He suffers from a curse that keeps him from taking his human form—"

"*Brody?*" All three queens screeched so loudly, the captain jumped back a step and nearly fell off the pier.

Leo exchanged a shocked look with his wife, then turned to the captain. "Brody is your prince?"

"Aye." The captain stepped away from the dock's edge and adjusted his hat, which had listed to the side. "Only friends and family call him Brody. Ye must know him?"

Luciana nodded, her eyes still wide with shock. "Aye, we do. Quite well."

"Not well enough," Leo muttered. "I can't believe that rascally dog is a prince."

Gwen huffed. "I can't believe he never told us."

"I always knew he had some secrets," Brigitta added. "But I never guessed he could be a prince."

Luciana gasped. "And Maeve is smitten with him!"

Brigitta grinned, clapping her hands together. "This is better than one of my stories! Maeve found herself a secret prince!"

"But the two of them are in danger," Gwennore reminded them quietly.

"Yes." Luciana winced. "We'll have to hope their story doesn't turn into a tragedy."

Brigitta tilted her head, her eyes narrowed. "I wonder if he's told her yet."

Silas held up a hand. "I just got a message from Aleksi. The elfin navy has set sail. I told him they need to head toward the Isle of Secrets."

"Good." Leo turned his attention back to the papers he was holding. The third page listed the Embraced army and their powers. Only eight soldiers, including the Chameleon, whose real name appeared to be Kendric. Odd that he possessed a royal Eberoni name. Some of the soldiers were very young. Leo felt a twinge of guilt at the thought of fighting children.

He passed the third page on to Silas, then read the fourth and final page. Another note from Brody. Or Prince Brodgar, he corrected himself with a snort.

> Leo,
> You should know the truth about the Chameleon. He's Kendric, an illegitimate son of your uncle, King Frederic. He was born Embraced, but Frederic was reluctant to have his own son killed. He passed the babe on to Lord Morris, who made arrangements for Kendric to be raised by Cahira on the Isle of Secrets. In his attempt to take over Eberon, Kendric killed his own father and half-brother, Tedric.

Leo stiffened with shock. His grip on the letter slipped, and the paper fell to the ground.

"What's wrong?" Luciana grabbed the paper.

He motioned to the paper, and everyone gathered around Luciana to read it over her shoulders. Her gasp was echoed by the others.

Leo took a deep breath and flexed his gloved hands. The Chameleon was his cousin. And if Brody didn't kill him, Leo would.

Chapter 18

Impersonating the Seer, Brody hobbled down the hallway alongside Maeve. In one hand, he gripped the Seer's staff. His other arm was looped around Maeve's shoulders as he pretended to need her assistance. He slowed his steps to a mere crawl to allow more distance between them and the guard who was leading them to the Great Hall.

After sleeping most of the day, he'd been awakened at sunset by Maeve, who had given him some bad news. They were both required to attend a dinner party this evening, a party to celebrate the return of Kendric. As if that murderous bastard deserved a celebration.

Maeve had helped him dress in the fancy new clothes that Cahira had given the Seer. Now they were headed down the hallway with glass doors that opened onto the long balcony. He recognized it as the balcony where he had first spotted Cahira and Maeve when he'd arrived at the castle.

A cool breeze swept through the open doorways, fluttering the purple silk curtains. He peered at the sky, noting the darkening of twilight. Tonight, after everyone was abed, he needed to sneak off in eagle form for another meeting with Nevis.

He glanced at the guard, who was now far enough away that he could safely whisper to Maeve.

He leaned close to her ear. "Is something wrong?"

She shook her head.

There was definitely something wrong. She was frowning. And she'd hardly said a word all evening. "Did you enjoy last night?"

Her cheeks turned pink. "We shouldn't talk about that right now."

"You didn't enjoy it?"

She gave him an exasperated look. "Of course I did. It was glorious."

He smiled to himself. He'd loved it, too. Until he'd run out of time while still sporting a painful erection. After shifting into a dog, he'd wanted to howl with frustration. Ten minutes more, hell, only five minutes would have been enough. After watching his beautiful Maeve shatter in his arms, he'd been so close to a climax. "Were you upset that I wasn't able to finish?"

"It's not your fault . . ." With a wince, she looked away.

"We'll do better tonight." He noticed she was still frowning. "Are you worried I'll attack the Chameleon? You shouldn't be. I'll behave myself."

She nodded. "I know."

"You must be worried about the wedding."

She made a face. "I was measured for my wedding gown today."

He squeezed her shoulder. "It won't happen. I won't let it."

She bit her lip. "I-I have something I need to tell you. Later. When we're alone."

His heart stilled. Was she having second thoughts about being stuck with a lover who could be himself for only two hours a day? He should tell her that it was now possible for him to get the curse lifted. But then he would have to admit that it was her mother who had done this to him.

He swallowed hard. "We'll talk tonight." *Don't give up on me, Maeve.*

The guard reached the golden doors to the Great Hall and waited for them, so they walked the rest of the way in awkward silence. Brody paused at the entrance, astounded by the size and beauty of the throne room.

"It is amazing, isn't it?" Maeve whispered.

"Indeed," he answered in the grumbly voice of the Seer. After quickly scanning the room, his gaze landed in the center, where a long table had been set up.

Servants bustled around it, setting down platters of food and filling glass goblets with wine. To the side stood a group of youths, both male and female. They were dressed in army uniforms and chatting with one another. *The Embraced army*, Brody thought. At the far end of the table, he spotted Cahira talking to a man who had his back to them.

The Chameleon? Brody's hand tightened on his staff, and he breathed deeply through his nose. Yes, through all the smells of food on the table, he could still detect the scent of the Chameleon. The bastard was here, and apparently in his true form. But all Brody could see was shoulder-length, reddish-blond hair.

"Oh, Burien!" Cahira spotted him and smiled. "You made it."

The Chameleon turned around, and Brody stiffened. Next to him, Maeve gasped.

The bastard looked very much like Leo. He had the same build, the same color hair, and very similar green eyes, although there was an odd glint of silver in the Chameleon's. *Of course he looks like Leo*, Brody thought. He was Leo's cousin. It would feel strange fighting someone who was almost identical to one of his best friends.

"Burien, you look so much better. What a relief!" Cahira sauntered toward them, followed by the Chameleon. "Come in, come in. I want you and Maeve to meet Kendric."

Brody and Maeve moved slowly forward.

Kendric gave them an assessing look as he approached. "So this is the Seer and your daughter?"

"Yes." Cahira latched onto Brody's arm and pulled him

away from Maeve. "Burien was the one who came up with the brilliant idea of the Circle of Five."

"Now, now, my dear." Brody gave the evil witch a strained smile. "You did all the work."

Cahira beamed up at him. "It's sweet of you to say so."

Kendric's nostrils flared, and his expression grew wary. "I smell another shifter."

Brody tensed, his fingers digging into his staff. If the Chameleon figured out who he was, the final battle would begin now.

Cahira laughed. "Of course you do, Kendric. The castle is full of shifters. You, me, Maeve." An orange blur shot into the room. "And that damned cat! Who let that cat in?"

Several servants chased after Gavin, but he weaved around the chairs of the dining table.

Kendric watched the cat with narrowed eyes. "He's a shifter?"

"Yes, yes." Cahira waved a dismissive hand. "But don't worry about him. He won't cause any—"

"Trouble," Brody finished her sentence. "That is what I named him."

Cahira laughed. "And a very suitable name, I must say."

Brody suppressed a spurt of anger. How could this witch find it amusing that she'd forced a boy to live two years as a cat? "I always thought he was a real cat."

Kendric snorted. "You don't see very well for a Seer."

Brody gritted his teeth. "I merely assumed that my dear Cahira had actually given me a pet." He glanced at her. "It never occurred to me that you were torturing a young man."

Cahira gasped. "Burien, how can you say that? I never harmed Gavin. He was happy with you. Weren't you happy with him?"

Maeve gave Brody's shirt a slight tug in the back, a reminder that he needed to play nice, so he nodded.

"I was very happy," he grumbled. "Thank you, my dear."

Cahira grinned, clasping her hands together. "Good. Then that's all settled. And you'll never feel lonely again, now that you're here with me."

Brody forced a smile. "Quite so."

Cahira glanced at the servants. "Can one of you please get that cat out of here, so we can start our dinner?"

Gavin dashed across the room, and one of the older Embraced soldiers lifted a hand in his direction.

"No!" Maeve cried out as a zap of lightning shot across the room toward the cat.

With a screech, Gavin jumped behind a green marble pillar.

Cahira huffed. "Alfred! Are you trying to destroy my throne room?"

So that was Alfred, who had the power of lightning. Brody studied him and the other soldiers. They were hardly more than children, eager to use their powers, but not mature enough to know when they shouldn't.

Alfred shrugged. "I was just trying to scare him into leaving."

One of the female soldiers frowned at him. "We grew up with Gavin. You shouldn't be so mean to him."

Alfred snorted. "Can I help it if he's a pest?"

"I'll take care of him," Maeve offered and darted toward the pillar. "Gavin, come with me."

The cat leaped into Maeve's arms, and she carried him back to the golden doors.

Ruth met her there. "I'll take him back to Gabby."

"Thank you." Maeve transferred the cat to Ruth's arms, then gave Gavin a pat on the head.

"Enough of that." Cahira motioned to Maeve. "I want you and Burien to meet our soldiers. Alfred is the oldest—"

"And the most reckless." Kendric slapped Alfred on the back. "How many times have I told you to save your energy for what's truly important?"

Alfred nodded with a sheepish look. "My apologies, General. It won't happen again." He extended a hand toward Brody. "It is an honor to meet you, Great Seer."

Brody eyed the young man's hand. If anyone other than Luciana touched Leo, they were fried to death. But the Chameleon had touched Alfred's shirt without hesitation.

"Don't let his power frighten you." Cahira grasped Alfred's hand. "See? It doesn't hurt."

Brody shook Alfred's hand and didn't feel any heat at all.

"Hello, Alfred," Maeve muttered in a wry tone. "We meet again."

Alfred winced, then bowed low. "Your Highness."

She poked at his arm with a finger. "How is it possible to touch him without dying?"

"I cast a spell on him," Cahira explained. "So he's perfectly safe when he wants to be."

"That's . . . amazing." Maeve exchanged a look with Brody. No doubt she was hoping Leo could be helped in the same way.

"Well, yes, I am amazing." Cahira motioned to the next soldier. "This is Darroc. He can control the wind."

Hopefully not as well as Rupert, Brody thought as he shook Darroc's hand.

Darroc bowed to Maeve. "Your Highness."

"I'm Farah," said the young woman who had fussed earlier at Alfred. "My power is fire." She snapped her fingers and a flame appeared at her fingertips.

"Incredible." *And just like Sorcha*, Brody thought as Farah blew out the fire.

"I'm Irene," another young woman said, shyly ducking her head. "I can make things grow."

"Excellent," Brody told her. The girl seemed too gentle to be in an army and better suited for the village where they were doing the farming.

"I can blow up rocks!" a young man announced with a grin. "I'm Jared."

"You could destroy a castle?" Maeve asked, and the young man winced.

"No," he mumbled. "It has to be a lone rock."

"Still very impressive." Brody shook the boy's hand. From the list Nevis had given him, he knew Jared was only fifteen.

"I'm Logan," the next boy said. "I can run really fast."

"Just don't run away," Alfred muttered, and the boy blushed.

The youngest of the group came forward, and Cahira wrapped an arm around her.

"This is Mikayla," Cahira said with a proud smile. "She can fly!"

Mikayla blushed. "I'm still learning."

Brody knew from experience that learning to fly meant some rough landings that really hurt. And this girl was only thirteen, dammit. He was tempted to slap the smirk off Cahira's face. How dare she force children into an army? Did she expect them to kill for her?

He took Mikayla's hand. "My dear child, you have your whole life before you, so be careful with your lessons. Don't attempt anything until you feel comfortable doing it."

Tears glimmered in Mikayla's eyes. "Thank you."

"No need to coddle them." Cahira marched to the head of the table. "Let's eat! Burien, please sit on my right. Kendric, you may sit on my left. Maeve, sit next to him."

Brody grabbed onto Maeve's arm. "I need her next to me, in case I feel faint."

Cahira frowned as she took her seat. "Very well."

It was a relief she actually cared about the Seer, Brody thought. As far as he knew, he was the only one in the castle who could make her change an order.

After everyone sat at the table, the servants circulated with the platters of food. Brody feigned weakness, so Maeve helped him by putting food on his plate.

"Thank you, my dear," he told Maeve. "I don't know what I would do without you."

"I'm just happy to be here with you," Maeve murmured.

Cahira stabbed a shrimp with her fork. "Thank the goddesses you will have me to take care of you, Burien. After Maeve is married in a week, she'll have to live with her husband."

Brody tightened his grip on his fork and knife. "I had to wait twenty years to finally meet my daughter. Surely there is no need to marry her off so quickly."

Cahira ate a few bites in silence. "Perhaps we can wait another few weeks, but sooner or later, Maeve will have to marry and have a child. We cannot allow our superior race to die off."

Brody chewed slowly, then helped himself to a sip of wine. "I am not opposed to her getting married as long as she is able to choose the groom herself."

Cahira sat back with a huff. "Are you jesting? We can't leave an important decision like that to her! I have already chosen the best suitor possible."

Kendric gave Maeve a passing glance, then turned to Cahira. "Whom did you choose?"

With a short laugh, Cahira touched Kendric's sleeve. "Why, you, of course."

Kendric sat back with a jolt. His fork fell from his hand with a clatter.

"It's a brilliant idea, don't you think?" Cahira continued with a smile. "Maeve will be able to prove her loyalty to me and the Circle of Five. And you will have a bride who is the last full-blooded descendant of an ancient and noble race of sorcerers."

Brody opened his mouth to object, but the Chameleon beat him to it.

"I'm not marrying your daughter," he hissed, his eyes

glimmering with an odd silver tint. "I've told you before that I want Brigitta."

Cahira waved a dismissive hand. "That silly girl is already taken."

Kendric slammed his hands on the table and rose to his feet. His face turned a mottled red. "I *will* have Brigitta! Once I take over the mainland, I will claim her."

"*You* will take over the mainland?" Cahira scoffed. "You mean Burien and I will. Don't forget that you and the rest of the Embraced army are fighting for me."

Kendric gritted his teeth. "Why should you get the mainland when you've been sitting here on this stupid island doing nothing? I've done all the work, and it's nearly cost me my life more than once!"

Cahira leaped to her feet. "I raised you when no one else wanted you! Don't forget that!"

While the two glared at each other, Brody glanced down the table. Alfred seemed to be enjoying the spat, but the others were cowering in their chairs. They were simply children, being forced into something they wanted no part of. He would have to make sure none of them were actually harmed in the upcoming war.

"I have killed three kings, including my own father," Kendric growled at Cahira. "I will not allow anything or anyone to stop me."

"You're not the only one who's killed a king," she countered. "I destroyed King Rudgar and his sons."

Brody stiffened, and beside him, Maeve gasped.

"Then take the islands," Kendric said. "But the mainland will be mine."

Cahira scoffed. "The islands are already mine. I just need to kill that old woman on the throne and her daughter."

Brody dug his fingers into his thighs to keep from throttling Cahira. The damned witch had admitted to killing his father and brother, and now she was threatening the rest of his family?

"Are . . . are you referring to Queen Esther?" Maeve asked.

"I wouldn't call her a queen," Cahira muttered as she sat back down. "The Isles of Moon and Mist were once part of Aerland, so naturally they belong to me." She took a sip from her goblet, then set it down with a thud. "All of Aerthlan will be mine."

"No, it won't," Kendric argued. "King Frederic was my father, so Eberon will be mine. And once I marry Brigitta, Tourin will also be mine."

Cahira watched him with narrowed eyes. "Do you really think you can defy me? I could curse you like I did Gavin, and leave you as a cat for the rest of your life. Or perhaps a *mouse*."

Kendric leaned over the table to glare at Cahira. "Try it, Sea Witch. You'll be dead before the words leave your mouth."

Cahira waved her hand, and the Chameleon's glass goblet exploded, splashing wine all over his white linen shirt. "Remember this, Kendric. No one at this table is more powerful than I."

With a smirk, Kendric sat down. "Then try taking over the mainland without me. You need me, Sea Witch."

Cahira sighed. "Very well. Help me and I'll make sure you get Eberon. And Brigitta." She waved at the servants. "Clean up this mess and bring him more wine."

Maeve dabbed at her mouth with her napkin, then set it beside her plate. "I'm wondering, Mother, if you have ever cursed anyone besides Gavin?"

Brody slanted Maeve a quick look. Did she suspect that her mother was the one who had cursed him?

Cahira scowled at Maeve. "Are you planning to defy me, too?"

Dammit, Maeve was getting herself in trouble. Brody leaned over and feigned a fit of coughing.

"Burien!" Cahira turned toward him. "Are you all right?"

He shook his head and wheezed, "I—I need to go back to my room and lie down."

Maeve jumped to her feet. "I'll take him."

"Very well. I'll have a tray sent to his room." Cahira motioned to the servants. "You can serve dessert now. I feel like having something sweet."

As Brody hobbled toward the door, he glanced back at the Sea Witch. The woman had to be insane. Cruel and insane. The Chameleon wasn't much better. The two of them ruling the world would be a disaster. But the fact that they were snarling at each other was a good sign. Getting them to turn on each other would be the best strategy.

He would have to tell Nevis about this dinner party from hell. But first, it was time to tell Maeve the truth about himself. Unfortunately, that also meant she would learn the truth about her mother.

As they passed through the golden doors into the hallway, he slanted a quick look at Maeve. She was frowning again as she had earlier. How much had she already figured out?

Would she still be able to accept him once she knew the truth?

Chapter 19

M aeve was about to scream with frustration. It was taking forever to get back to the Seer's bedchamber. But as long as there was a guard accompanying them, Brody had to keep up his pretense and move at a snail's pace.

There was so much she needed to know, so much that he was still keeping secret. Finally, they arrived, and the guard stationed himself once again in front of her bedchamber. As she entered the Seer's room, she looked around to make sure no servants were about. They had obviously been here earlier, for the bed was turned down, a fire had been started in the hearth, and several candles had been lit.

But the room was empty now. She shut the door and locked it.

Brody raised his arms and stretched. "Oh, I get so tired of being hunched over."

Maeve winced at the sound of his voice. This was too strange. He sounded just like Brody, but he still looked like the Seer.

"Wait a minute." She dashed to the dressing room and peered inside. No servants there. Then she looked in her room to make sure it was empty, too. On her way back, she locked the adjoining door.

She found Brody peering out an open window.

Moonlight filtered into the room, along with the sound of seagulls.

"The birds are very active tonight," he murmured.

"Brody, we need to talk."

"I know." He closed the window and turned toward her, still wearing the Seer's face.

Maeve looked away, biting her lip. "When can you shift back to Brody?"

"Midnight." He tilted his head. "Are you uncomfortable with how I look? I could take on another face. Or I could see Nevis first and come back later."

"No, I . . . I've waited too long. I want to hear everything."

A knock sounded at the door, and a servant called out, "I have a tray of food for the Seer!"

"Just a minute." Maeve hurried to the door to unlock it as Brody collapsed on the window seat.

A servant came inside to deposit a tray of food on the table in the sitting area. After lighting the candle there, she bobbed a curtsy and left.

Maeve locked the door once again as an idea popped into her mind. "I know what to do." She dashed about, blowing out all the candles, then closed the curtains to keep the moonlight from shining in.

As she retreated across the room to the table in the now-dark sitting area, she noted with satisfaction that only a small portion of the room was visible, due to the fire in the hearth. Brody was on the other side of it, a dark form in the shadows.

She sat at the table. "Now we can talk."

He heaved a sigh. "It's me, Maeve. It's only me."

"I know. But when you look like someone else, it feels too strange to reassure you that I love you—"

"Maeve." He stood up.

"Don't . . ."

His form remained still for a moment; then he sat back

down on the window seat. "I love you, too. I love you enough that I can let you go if you find it too difficult—"

"I'm not going anywhere!"

"But I'm still cursed, and there's no guarantee that I'll ever—"

"Was it my mother?" Maeve's voice broke and she steeled her nerves to hear the truth. "Was she the one who cursed you?"

There was a pause, then a quiet reply: "Yes."

Maeve hissed in a breath. *You can handle this. You were expecting this.* "How long have you known?"

"I knew the minute I heard her voice. When she welcomed me to Aerie Castle."

"Yesterday?"

"Yes."

Maeve thought back. After Cahira had welcomed the Seer, he had stumbled on the stairs. It hadn't been an act. *Oh, Brody.* Her heart tightened in her chest. "I'm so sorry."

"Why? It's not your fault. You had nothing to do with the Sea Witch."

"I'm her daughter!"

"I don't give a shit!" He jumped to his feet. "Don't use your mother as an excuse to turn away from me. If you want to leave me, do it for yourself."

"I would never leave you!"

He paused for a moment, then asked, "Even if I have to kill her?"

Maeve drew in a shaky breath. "Even then."

"Then it's settled." He took a step toward her. "You will be mine."

Tears gathered in her eyes. She had always been his. "Is that the last of your secrets? Or is there more?"

He stood still for a short while. "There's more."

Good goddesses. In the dark, she fumbled for a goblet and poured some wine into it. "All right. Tell me."

He paced across the room. "I suppose I should start at the beginning. Twenty-five years ago, I was born on the Isle of Moon."

"Really? You don't have an island accent."

He snorted. "My mother complains about that. She says I've been gone too long."

"I heard you have a mother and sister." Maeve took a sip.

"I do. Queen Esther and Princess El—"

Maeve sputtered wine all over the table. "Wha—?"

"I'm the second son of King Rudgar and Queen Esther."

"*What?* You . . . you're a prince?"

"Aye. My older brother, Edgar, was the heir."

"You're a *prince?*"

"Aye, Prince Brodgar."

"You're Prince Brodgar?"

"Is that a problem?"

She sat back. Good goddesses, she'd heard his name a million times over the years, every time the nuns at the convent had said their prayers for the dead during mass. She'd always believed that the princes had drowned. "I . . . I'm confused."

He scoffed. "So was I when I found out you're a princess."

She winced. "Believe me, I never would have chosen my situation."

"I understand." He paced back to the window. "We can't always control what fate has in store for us."

Maeve recalled the story she'd heard as a young child. How the king and his two sons had drowned at sea, and the poor queen had requested that the nuns remember them in their prayers every day. "Everyone at the convent thinks that you're . . ."

"Dead. Yes, most people think I died with my father and brother. My mother let them believe that in order to protect me. Only a few high-ranking officers know the truth."

With a gasp, Maeve remembered her mother boasting at

the dinner party that she had destroyed King Rudgar and his sons. Dear goddesses, no! She slapped a hand over her mouth to keep from crying out. And then her mother had actually threatened to kill Queen Esther and Princess Elinor—Brody's mother and sister.

She dropped her head into her hands. This was too terrible. How could Brody accept her now? How could he even stand to look at her?

But he couldn't see her in the dark, so he kept on talking.

"When I was ten years old, Father took Edgar and myself out to sea for a sailing lesson. It was supposed to be a fun outing. We headed south from the Isle of Moon, and I guess we ventured too close to this island."

Maeve blinked back her tears. "My mother?"

"She blew up our ship."

Maeve jammed a fist against her mouth to keep from letting a sob escape.

"My father and Eddy drowned," Brody continued in a soft voice. "And all the crew. I was sinking, so filled with despair that I wanted to die, too."

"Oh, Brody." Tears ran down her cheeks. How could a ten-year-old boy cope with something so awful?

He sat on the window seat. "My gift was awakened as I struggled to survive. I shifted into a seal and swam to the surface. When I tried to swim away, I heard the Sea Witch's voice."

Maeve wiped the tears off her face. "Was that when she cursed you?"

"Aye. I've never forgotten her voice. It terrorized me in my dreams." He took a deep breath. "But your voice always brought me comfort."

That made more tears run down her face. He still loved her. He still needed her. She stood and walked slowly toward him. "Did you swim home?"

"No, I . . . I couldn't bear to return home without my father and brother. I felt so guilty for surviving when they hadn't. I swam north till I was exhausted, then washed ashore on the Isle of Mist. The Seer, your father—he found me and raised me as if I was his own son."

She sat next to Brody on the window seat. "I can't begin to tell you how sorry I am."

"I'm sorry the Seer died before you could meet him. He wanted so much to see you."

It no longer mattered what Brody looked like. Maeve wrapped her arms around him and held him tight. He held her, too, his head nestled in the crook of her neck.

She rubbed his back. "I'm so sorry."

"It's not your fault."

She thought back to what her mother had said at dinner. "Cahira targeted your ship and your family on purpose. She thinks your island should belong to her."

Brody nodded. "Aye. Now I know why the Seer always made me hide in the cave whenever anyone came to the island. He knew he had to keep my survival a secret."

"Even from Cahira?"

"Aye. When she told him you had died as a babe, he knew she was lying and he could no longer trust her. He just played along so he would know what she was doing."

Maeve took a deep breath. "Well, it's a relief to know one of my parents was good."

"True." Brody straightened. "Are you all right? I wanted to tell you all this last night, but—"

"It's better this way. Last night was perfect."

He snorted. "I wouldn't say that."

"I thought it was perfect."

"I was left as a dog with a bone."

"Excuse me?"

"We'll finish what we started tonight." He cradled her face and, using his thumbs, wiped her cheeks dry. "If you can still accept me."

She scoffed. "I'm the one who should be worried. Can you accept me after all that my mother has done?"

"She abandoned you because the Seer foresaw that you would be more powerful than she is. She doesn't even deserve to be called your mother."

Maeve blinked. "I'm going to be more powerful than Cahira?"

"That's what the Seer said."

She sat back, wondering what her father had meant. Had he been referring to her new gift of foresight?

"I should go see Nevis now." Brody stood and she heard some rustling noises.

He must be disrobing in the dark, so he could shift. She opened the curtains, then the window. "Be careful."

"I'll be back at midnight."

So he could be Brody. And make love to her. Maeve smiled to herself as an eagle swooped out the window.

"Now let me see you tie them up," Nevis told Elam and Hannah, and the two children kneeled beside Lobby and Tommy and tied their hands and feet with strips of linen.

Nevis checked their knots. "Excellent."

Elam grinned at Hannah. "We did it!"

She nodded. "This is much more exciting than making it rain."

Nevis cut loose the bindings on Tommy and Lobby, who had volunteered to play the role of unconscious guards. "How are you two doing?"

"We're fine," Tommy assured him. "All we have to do is lie here." When Lobby snored, Tommy chuckled. "He keeps dozing off."

Nevis stifled a grin. The two old men were exhausted after sailing all the way to the Isle of Moon and back last night.

This morning, while coming up with a strategy to eliminate the guards, Nevis had soon realized he couldn't kill them in front of the children. And he certainly couldn't instruct the children to kill them. So now the plan was to simply knock out the guards, then tie them up and gag them.

He'd spent most of the day with Elinor in the blacksmith shop, devising their master plan. Tommy had cleared his worktable, and Elinor had used paper and ink to draw a map of the castle grounds and location of the guardhouse. Then she'd illustrated the plan, so the children could understand what they were expected to do.

This evening after dinner, Nevis had taught the children how to properly tie up their prisoners. They were practicing now on their volunteers, Tommy and Lobby. Bettina lit some lanterns as the sky darkened, while Catriona, Naomi, and Olana were busy ripping sheets into strips. They would need enough to tie up thirty guards.

Quentin grabbed a few strips. "Is it my turn now?"

Nevis shook his head. "Tommy and Lobby will be taking everyone under the age of ten to our boat—"

"That's not fair," Quentin grumbled. "I showed you where the guards live. You can't make me leave!"

Nevis regarded the nine-year-old boy. He seemed much more eager to participate in their battle than ten-year-old Peter. "This will be dangerous. You could be hurt."

"So?" Quentin lifted his chin in defiance. "I've been working in the smithy since I was five. I know how to be careful."

"The lad is a good worker," Tommy said, giving the boy a wry look. "When he isn't running off somewhere."

Quentin hung his head. "I just get tired of being cooped up all the time." He glanced up shyly at Nevis. "I feel bad about snitching on Maeve. I want to help. Please."

Nevis gave him a stern look. "I'm in charge of our group. Do you pledge to follow my orders to the letter?"

"Aye, Colonel!" Quentin saluted. "Can I stay?"

Nevis narrowed his eyes. "Yes, you may, soldier."

"Yea!" Quentin bounced around, grinning. "This is going to be so—"

"Quiet, soldier," Nevis growled, and Quentin halted, slapping a hand over his mouth.

Elinor smiled as she set down her pen. "Shouldn't we have a name for our group?"

Catriona snorted. "Something like the Undesirables?"

"Or the Rejects?" Elam grumbled.

"No, something strong and positive." Nevis strode to the worktable, seeking inspiration from the plans Elinor had drawn. A spider crawled onto one of her pages, and he slammed a hand down so hard everyone jumped.

"What?" Lobby sputtered, waking up. "What was that?"

"Sorry," Nevis muttered. "I hate spiders."

"Spiders!" Quentin shouted.

"Yes." Nevis wiped his hand on his breeches. "I didn't want it getting on—"

"No, we can be the Spiders," Quentin said. "We'll be fast and sneaky and spin our webs to trap all the guards."

Nevis glanced at all the children, who were nodding their heads and smiling. "Is that what you want?"

While the children cheered, Elinor tapped her fingers on the worktable. "Spiders?"

Nevis stepped closer to her. "We can use something else if you don't like it."

"Nay, 'tis brilliant!" She smiled at him. "I've been struggling to come up with an idea to make the guards leave their house. I thought about drawing some sort of scary creature that could come alive, but I have no colored paints with me. Just black ink." She opened the bottle of ink. "Spiders will be perfect."

"But will they be scary enough?" Nevis asked.

Her eyes twinkled with mischief as she unfolded some large pieces of paper. "*Giant* spiders."

"Awesome!" Quentin shouted, and the children cheered. Frowning, Bettina slipped out the wide doorway.

"Is something wrong?" Elinor whispered to Catriona.

She shook her head. "She's probably trying to hear the birds."

"They do seem very noisy today," Nevis said as he followed Bettina outside.

She was standing still, gazing up at the stars. Suddenly, she turned toward Nevis. "Twelve ships have arrived at the Isle of Moon. Warships."

Nevis blinked. "Already?" Damn, Leo and Rupert had worked fast to get their navies ready.

"And six more warships are rounding the southern coast of Eberon," Bettina continued.

That had to be the elfin navy from Woodwyn, Nevis thought. They would be moving much more slowly since they didn't have Rupert with them.

An eagle swooped down and landed beside them, then shifted into a dog.

Nevis leaned through the wide opening to the blacksmith's shop. "Brody's here. Can I give him some of your breeches, Elam?"

Elam nodded, while Elinor rushed outside. She gave Brody a hug, then the dog trotted off with Nevis to the boys' cottage.

"You won't believe this," Nevis told him as he tossed Brody a pair of breeches. "The Eberoni and Tourinian navies are—" He stopped when Brody shifted into the Seer. "Damn, I don't believe this. You look just like the Seer."

"You wouldn't know." Brody pulled on the breeches. "You've never seen the Seer."

"I have, too. When Maeve and I went to the Isle of Mist, we saw—"

"Me." Brody buttoned the breeches. "You saw me."

"What?" Nevis stepped back. "You . . . you tricked us? What an asinine thing to do!"

Brody gave him a wry look. "I was trying to convince Maeve to go back to Eberon. I didn't want her doing anything dangerous or finding out that Cahira is her mother." He opened the door and strode outside.

Nevis followed him. "Does she know that her mother is the bitch who cursed you? And murdered your father and brother?" He stopped with a wince when he realized that Elinor had been waiting for them and had heard every word.

A pained look crossed her face.

"Oh, crap," Nevis muttered. "I'm sorry."

She took a deep breath and squared her shoulders. "I'm all right." She turned to Brody with a curious look. "Is that really you? Ye can impersonate people?"

"Aye." Brody touched his sister's shoulder. "Don't worry. We will have justice soon."

"Sooner than you think," Nevis said, motioning to Bettina, who was still listening to the birds. "She just heard that twelve warships have arrived at the Isle of Moon."

"That quickly?" Brody's eyes widened. "It was after midnight when my mother sent Captain Chapman. He couldn't have arrived at Ebton Palace until this morning."

Nevis nodded. "But two days ago, I sent Captain Shaw with a message for Leo and the other kings to prepare for war. They must have started preparations immediately." He turned to Elinor. "We'd better practice some more with the Spiders."

"I agree." She nodded.

"Spiders?" Brody asked.

"That's the name of our Embraced army," Elinor explained.

"I have more news." Bettina approached them. "The birds say that a dragon is flying south from the Isle of Moon."

"Headed here?" Brody asked.

Bettina shook her head. "Toward the south of Eberon."

"Silas must be looking for the elfin navy." Nevis turned to Brody. "Woodwyn is sending six ships. After sailing all night, they might catch up with the other ships by morning."

Brody nodded. "I'll fly to the Isle of Moon to see if Leo and Rupert are ready to come here."

"Dear goddesses." Elinor made the sign of the moons. "If they leave in the morning, they could be here by noon."

"And then the war would begin," Brody concluded.

Nevis took a deep breath. He would have his Spiders do some practice runs in the morning. "Do you have a plan yet for eliminating Cahira and the Chameleon?"

Brody shrugged. "I'm working on it. Obviously, I have to capture Cahira, so she won't have a chance to blow up the ships coming in."

"Does Maeve know about her mother?" Elinor asked quietly.

"I . . . I just told her."

Nevis winced. "That must have been awkward."

He nodded. "She tried not to cry, but I could hear . . ."

Elinor rubbed her brother's shoulder. "It will be all right. We'll have justice for Papa and Eddy, and ye'll be rid of the curse." She gave him a wry look. "Ye realize ye won't have any more excuses, then? Ye'll have to come home and be our king."

Nevis snorted. "Everyone gets to be a king but me. I'll have to find a deserted island somewhere and declare myself royalty."

"Why?" Elinor gave him an amused look. "There's nothing wrong with being a colonel."

His heart expanded, and he took a step closer to her. "You're all right with that?"

"Of course." Her mouth twitched, and she nudged him with an elbow. "Ye're blushing again."

"Am not."

"What the hell is going on with you two?" Brody demanded.

"Nothing." Nevis stepped back, then winced when he noticed the disappointed look on Elinor's face. *Dammit.* "I realize I'm not worthy of your sister, but—"

"No, you're not," Brody said, interrupting him.

Elinor huffed. "Nevis is the noblest man I've ever met. He's brave, loyal, dependable, generous, strong, and handsome."

Handsome? Nevis gave her a surprised look. He was a bit shorter and stockier than his royal friends, so he'd figured he could never be as appealing as they were. "You think I'm handsome?"

"Of course." Elinor smiled. "And all those muscles—"

"Enough!" Brody glared at Nevis. "Don't even think about my sister."

Nevis sighed. He was doing a great deal more than thinking. His heart had already surrendered, and there was no point in denying it. He was in love.

Chapter 20

It would happen tonight, Maeve thought as she settled into a tub of hot water. After midnight, she would lose her virginity. And not because she needed to avoid a marriage to the Chameleon, but because she and Brody loved each other. No matter what fate had thrown at them, they still loved each other.

The forced wedding no longer seemed to be a problem. The Chameleon was against it as much as she, and Brody, in disguise as the Seer, had bought her more time. Besides, she suspected the Chameleon's days were numbered. Brody would be facing off with him soon.

Please protect my darling Brody and keep him safe, she prayed to the moon goddesses. He would be all right. He was excellent with a sword. And so good with his hands. Her cheeks warmed as she recalled how he had examined every inch of her body the night before. Goodness, he'd even kissed her all over.

She scrubbed herself clean in case he wanted to do that again. Tonight would be ever better, wouldn't it? After all, they had bared their souls, shared their secrets, and confessed their fears. Her heart felt as if it would burst whenever she contemplated how his love for her had remained constant in spite of everything he'd suffered at the hands of her mother.

Would he have to kill Cahira? With a wince, Maeve grabbed the soap to lather up her hair. She knew good and well that her mother was guilty, but still, it would be horrible to witness her death. Was there a way to convince her mother to surrender and remove Brody's curse?

The beginnings of an idea trickled into Maeve's mind. Her mother was intent on getting the Isles of Moon and Mist back into her domain. What if Maeve told her she wanted to marry a prince from those islands? Then, when Prince Brodgar became king, she would be his queen, and those islands would return to Cahira's descendants without spilling any blood.

But obviously, doing things peacefully didn't matter to Cahira. When she blew up King Rudgar's ship, she thought she'd killed him and both of his sons. She must have thought Brody was just a servant when she'd cursed him. The realization that she'd actually let a prince escape might infuriate her. And if Maeve ended up queen of the Isles of Moon and Mist that might enrage Cahira even further. She wanted the power for herself, not her daughter.

There was no peaceful solution. Maeve would have to help Brody capture her mother. And then she'd endure the accusation of betrayal.

With a frustrated groan, Maeve reached for the bucket of water and rinsed her hair. She'd kept herself busy after Brody's departure. After locking his room to keep any servants from discovering he was missing, she'd gone to her room to order more food and twelve buckets of hot water. Once the food arrived, she'd arranged all the dishes on the table in Brody's sitting room. She'd eaten a little, then taken half the buckets of hot water into his dressing room.

Hurry up, midnight. She'd never been so anxious for a day to end before.

She leaned back against the tub and closed her eyes. Would he kiss her breasts again? She smoothed a hand over a breast and felt the skin pebble, the nipple harden. A pleasant sensation, but not nearly as exciting as when Brody had touched her and suckled on her. Just remembering it made her feel hot and needy between her legs. Goodness, the things he had done with his fingers and mouth.

What did it feel like for him? Curious, she slipped her hand between her legs to examine the area for herself. With a small gasp she located the nubbin that incited such incredible pleasure.

And to think that in the past she'd used her bath time to practice seal-shifting. This was something she'd never thought of doing. But still, it was much better with Brody. She never knew what to expect next with him. Alone, she just felt lazy. And sleepy . . .

"Have you started without me?"

With a jerk, she opened her eyes and sat up. "Brody! I didn't know you were back."

He was in her dressing room, wearing nothing but a smirk and a towel around his hips. His shoulder-length black hair was still wet, causing a drop of water to meander down his muscular chest. In his hands, he was holding two wine goblets. His beautiful blue eyes twinkled as his gaze shifted to her exposed breasts.

She ducked back down. "What are you doing in my dressing room?"

"It's midnight." His mouth twitched. "What exactly are *you* doing?"

Her cheeks grew warm. "I—I must have dozed off."

"Ah." He took a sip from one of the goblets. "Were you having sweet dreams?"

She bent her knees and pressed her thighs together. "I was remembering last night."

"I've been remembering it, too." He stepped closer to the tub to look inside. "I keep thinking about how soft your skin was. How sweet you tasted. How beautiful you looked when you—"

"Could you pass me a towel?"

"No. My hands are full."

She snorted. "I'll take one of those." After he handed her a goblet, she took a sip. "I suppose you found the food I left for you, and the hot water?"

"Yes, thank you. I had to eat and bathe as the Seer, waiting for midnight." He set his goblet on her dressing table and brought the stool over to the tub.

"What are you doing now?"

He sat next to the tub and rested a hand on her bent knee. "I'm going to finish what you started."

"I wasn't really—" She sucked in a breath as his hand slid down her thigh. "I mean, I was only curious—" She gasped when his fingers reached her womanhood.

"Curious?" He explored her gently. "Did you discover how beautiful you are?"

"I-I don't . . . Oh!" She jolted when he rubbed against the spot that sent shivers coursing through her.

"Did you learn how incredibly sensitive you are?"

She hissed in a breath. "I—I'm much more sensitive when you're doing it."

He snorted. "Well, it's a relief to know that I'm needed."

"Oh." She was shivering and feverish at the same time. "I definitely need you." Her hand shook, and wine spilled into the bathwater. "Oops."

"I'll take that." He set her goblet on the floor. "Now, where were we?"

"In heaven." She opened her knees wider.

"I always did enjoy playing with you in the water."

"We never did anything like this." She tilted her head back and moaned as his fingers teased and rubbed against her.

He leaned close to her and whispered in her ear. "One day I will swim with you in the ocean, and there I will make love to my siren in the deep blue sea."

And with that promise, she climaxed, throbbing against

his hand. She was still seeing stars when he picked her up and carried her to her bed.

"We'll get the sheets wet," she warned him.

"Good." He dropped her on the bed, tore off his towel, then climbed in beside her. As he pulled her closer, his hand slid down her back and over her buttocks. "I like you slick and wet."

"You're wet, too." She ran her fingers into his damp hair. When he squeezed her rump, she felt his manhood pressing into her belly. And suddenly a surge of need enveloped her. "Brody, I want you now."

"I want you, too." He kissed her, molding his mouth against hers.

With a groan, she broke the kiss. "I mean now."

He blinked. "Now?"

She reached a hand down to touch his manhood, and he hissed in a breath. "Now."

"Are you ready?" He pushed her onto her back and slid a hand between her legs.

With a moan, she pressed against his hand.

"You definitely seem ready." He caressed her lightly. "So hot and wet."

She shoved him onto his back. "Are *you* ready?"

"I've been ready for years."

She eyed his manhood, so thick and hard. "Not this ready. I think I would have noticed this." She curled a hand around the erect staff.

He groaned. "It was one of the reasons I avoided you so much."

"You've had this problem before?" She traced a vein with her finger.

"Every time I saw you. Or heard your beautiful siren voice."

She noticed a drop of fluid seeping from the top. "You're

wet, too." She touched the drop and smoothed it over the head.

He gritted his teeth. "You're torturing me."

"Good. That's what you get for avoiding me all those years."

He pushed her onto her back, and his blue eyes gleamed with intensity. "Playtime is over."

Her heart lurched into a fast rhythm. "Then take me."

He settled between her legs and pulled her knees up. "Wrap your legs around me."

She did, drawing in a shaky breath when she felt his manhood pressing against her. "I-I always thought it would be like animals with you taking me from behind."

"We'll do that, too."

"We will?"

He nodded. "We can do whatever we like." He eased himself inside a little bit. "But for now, I want to see your face when I take you."

She swallowed hard. It was beginning to hurt, but she didn't want him to stop.

He paused. "I'm causing you pain. I can see it in your eyes."

She cradled his face in her hands. "I can handle it. I can do anything as long as you love me."

Tears glimmered in his beautiful blue eyes. "I do love you. More than I can say."

"Then show me."

He reached down to fondle her sensitive spot, and when she was writhing with pleasure, he plunged inside her.

She gasped. There had been a sharp pain, but it quickly subsided as she felt a glorious sensation of fullness. He was inside her. Brody inside her. She wrapped her arms around his neck. "I love you."

When he began to move, she moaned from the intense pleasure. It was too much, and yet she wanted more. More. Soon, he was pushing deeper and faster, and she felt a fire consuming them both, making them frantic. With a hoarse cry, he pumped into her, emptying his seed, and the wonder of it all sent her over the edge.

As the throbbing slowly subsided, she clung to him, never wanting to let him go. He rolled onto his side, still holding her.

"You're mine now," he whispered.

With a sigh of satisfaction, she cuddled up against him. "Silly man, I was always yours."

"Did you just call your future husband *silly*?"

She looked up at him. "Did you just propose to me?"

"Do you really think I could ever let you go?"

She smiled. "There's no escaping from me. I've already proven that I'll cross an ocean to find you."

He smoothed a hand up and down her back. "Maeve."

"Yes."

"I don't want to leave now, but I must."

"Why?"

"Leo and Rupert have arrived at the Isle of Moon with their naval forces."

She sat up. "Already? How can you know?"

"The birds are keeping Bettina informed. The elfin navy is also on its way. The battle could happen today, so I need to preserve all the time I can for my true form."

So he would be able to fight the Chameleon and her mother. Maeve swallowed hard. "It will happen today?"

He sat up. "I think so. But first I need to fly to Luna to see Leo and Rupert, so we can coordinate our plans."

"I understand."

He touched her cheek. "Try to get some sleep while I'm gone."

She winced. "If you're up all night, you'll be too tired when the battle—"

"I'll be fine." He kissed her brow. "Sleep well."

She watched him as he opened a window, then shifted into an eagle. "Be careful," she whispered as he flew into the night sky.

In the royal cabin of his flagship, Leo was having trouble sleeping. His mind kept going over his meeting with Rupert, Queen Esther, and her admiral and naval captains, when they had discussed the upcoming battle. Since her navy was accustomed to standard warfare, they had wanted to stick to tried-and-true strategies. It had taken a while for him and Rupert to convince them that the upcoming battle would be far from normal.

Queen Esther had agreed with them, reminding her officers that the Sea Witch, Cahira, could blow up ships. Also, they would be encountering an army of eight soldiers with supernatural powers. Certainly, some of them were young, but a bolt of lightning was just as dangerous from a youngster as from a seasoned warrior. Leo knew that all too well. He'd accidentally killed his nanny at the age of six.

Another problem was that they didn't know for sure what Brody and Nevis were planning. Silas had offered to locate them, but Leo had thought it best for the dragon shifters to stay away from the Isle of Secrets for now. The dragons were too noticeable, and they couldn't afford to let Cahira or the Chameleon know that their hiding place had been discovered. The enemy would be on the alert then, and Leo and his allies would lose the element of surprise.

Some loud voices on deck caught his attention, and he got up and pulled on some breeches. As he opened his door, he heard his guard arguing with a sailor.

"That's not a man!" the sailor yelled, brandishing a sword. "He landed on deck as a bird, then turned into a dog! He's something evil, he is!"

Leo spotted the familiar black-and-white shaggy dog behind his personal guard. Thank the Light, Brody had arrived.

"Your Majesty." His guard bowed his head. "I was bringing Brody to your cabin when this—"

"I understand." Leo turned to the sailor. "Thank you for
protecting me, but this shifter is actually in my employ."

"Oh." The sailor lowered his sword, then bowed. "My
apologies, Your Majesty."

"No problem." Leo motioned for Brody to enter his cabin.
Leo's soldiers all knew who Brody was. But here on his ships,
his sailors had never encountered the shifter.

Leo stepped back as Brody trotted inside, making sure his
bare feet were several feet away from the dog. Or prince, he
corrected himself with a snort.

He shut the door. "I'm glad you're here." He located a
pair of breeches and turned to toss them at Brody. "Holy
crap!"

This wasn't Brody, but an old, frail man.

"Who . . . ?" Leo could easily kill an intruder with a bolt
of lightning, but this elderly man didn't look strong enough
to be dangerous.

"It's me." Brody's voice came from the old man's mouth.
He pulled on the breeches. "Don't zap me."

"Brody?"

"Aye." He buttoned the breeches. "You know that I can
only be myself for two hours a day, so I'm trying to preserve—"

"You can shift into other people?" Leo gave him an incredulous look.

Brody sighed. "Aye, but I never did it before—"

"You're just like the—"

"Don't say it!" Brody growled. "I'm nothing like the
Chameleon. Dammit, why do people keep saying that?"

Leo scoffed. "Because the two of you have the same
power, obviously."

"What's important is not the power, but how you use it. You know that."

Leo smiled to himself. It made sense to him now how Brody had always talked to him as if he was an equal. "So this power is another one of the secrets you kept from us, *Prince Brodgar?*"

Brody winced. "I guess you heard."

"Yes. I met your mother today. A lovely woman. She expects you to take the throne after this battle."

"I know." Brody glanced around the room. "You have something to drink around here?"

Leo strode to a table and poured some water into a wooden cup. He tended to use wooden plates and utensils so his electric energy wouldn't be transferred. "Here." He set the cup and a plate of bread and cheese in front of a chair, then sat in the chair across from it. "Tell me your plan."

Brody sat down and took a sip of water. "I have infiltrated Aerie Castle in this form. The Seer had an affair with Cahira about twenty years ago, and she's still very fond of him. She knew he was in poor health, so she wanted him to come to her castle, where she could take care of him."

"So she believes you are the Seer?" When Brody nodded, Leo continued. "You must know the Seer really well to be able to fool Cahira."

Brody tore off a piece of bread. "After I was cursed, I washed up on the Isle of Mist. The Seer was like a father to me."

"You never mentioned that before. Is the real Seer still on the Isle of Mist?"

With a sigh, Brody dropped the bread back on the plate. "Yes. I buried him there. Before he died, he begged me to impersonate him so I could stop Cahira's evil plan."

Leo nodded slowly. "Your mother told us how Cahira

blew up your father's ship and killed him and your brother. And she was the witch who cursed you."

"Aye." Brody picked up the bread again and took a bite. "Obviously, my plan is to keep Cahira busy so she can't blow up your ships. And I need to make her lift my curse."

"So Cahira and the Chameleon are two of the remaining three members of the Circle of Five." Leo leaned forward. "Who is the last one?"

Brody took another sip of water, then set his cup down. "He's dead, so there's no need to discuss him."

Leo sat back, narrowing his eyes. Brody seemed to be protecting the last member. Who would he . . . ? "By the Light, was it the Seer?"

Brody winced. "Don't tell anyone. The poor man only wanted to bring peace and prosperity to the world. His mistake was trusting Cahira enough to confide in her. She was the one who twisted his idea into her own plan for world domination. She also raised the Chameleon and financed the other members of the circle. The Embraced army was her idea."

"I understand. So you're planning to kill her after she lifts the curse?"

Brody hesitated, staring at his plate of food.

"Is there a problem?" Leo asked. "Is she too powerful?"

"She's Maeve's mother."

Leo drew in a long breath. "Crap."

"Exactly."

"And Maeve knows everything?" Leo asked. "Is she all right? Her sisters are worried sick about her."

"She's fine." Brody took a bite of cheese. "She will be fine. She's strong."

"That's good." Leo thought back to what Brody had said about the Seer having an affair with Cahira. "Then the Seer is Maeve's father?"

Brody nodded. "Aye. You saw my note about the Chameleon?"

With a grimace, Leo balled his fists. "If you don't kill him, I will. He murdered Tedric."

"And his own father," Brody added. "By the way, I saw his true form tonight. He actually looks quite a bit like you."

Leo scoffed. "That bastard."

"So I'll deal with Cahira and the Chameleon. Nevis and my sister are training the rejected Embraced children. They're going to take out the castle guards." Brody leaned forward. "Once your ships are sighted, the Embraced army will try to destroy you."

With a frown, Leo nodded. "We figured that."

"I heard you arrived with twelve ships?"

Leo nodded. "Five Eberoni ships, six Tourinian ships, and Captain Chapman's ship. There are two more from the Isle of Moon, making a total of fourteen."

"And when you add the six elfin ships, you have an armada of twenty," Brody concluded.

"You know about those?"

"Aye. One of the Embraced children, Bettina, has the gift of communicating with birds, so she's keeping us informed."

"Excellent." Leo smiled. That was one less problem to worry about.

"Are you leaving in the morning?" Brody asked.

"Midmorning," Leo clarified. "Silas is keeping Dimitri apprised of the elfin navy's progress. We believe they can make it to the Isle of Secrets by noon. So we are planning to arrive at roughly the same time."

"Then the battle will begin at noon." Brody stood. "I'll fly back and let Nevis know."

Leo rose to his feet. "Be careful." As he strode toward the door to open it, he grew increasingly worried about Brody trying to eliminate both Cahira and the Chameleon. He glanced back at Brody, but the shifter had already turned into a dog. "Brody, you should let Nevis help you. Or I could send one of the dragons to back you up."

But Leo wasn't sure Brody heard him, since the dog dashed onto the deck, then shifted into an eagle and flew away.

In a dream, Maeve found herself floating over the sea, headed toward Aerie Castle. She flew through the open doors of the balcony, then floated toward the Great Hall. This time, the castle seemed familiar to her. She noted the purple curtains fluttering in the breeze, the mosaic floor that resembled the ocean, the dais with its golden octopus throne and colorful glass decorations in the shapes of clams and underwater plants.

Suddenly, all the glass exploded, and colored shards flew about the room. Maeve screamed and covered her head.

Everything went black for a moment. When she came to, she saw her mother lying on the floor by the dais, her throat slit, her eyes glassy.

Dead? Had Brody killed her?

A surge of pain erupted inside her, doubling her over. Her knees gave way, and she collapsed on the floor. What was this awful pain? Had she been stabbed? Was she going to die?

A sudden clashing noise drew her attention, and although her vision was blurred with pain, she could see Brody and the Chameleon engaged in a swordfight. The Chameleon slashed his sword down, slicing Brody's thigh. As Brody fell to the floor, the Chameleon raised his sword to deal the fatal blow—

"No!" Maeve woke up, her heart pounding. "No." She shook her head. Brody couldn't lose the battle. He couldn't die.

Holy goddesses, were they both going to die?

She glanced at the window, where the first light of dawn was barely visible. Was Brody back? She ran into his bedchamber and found him asleep in his bed in the guise of the Seer.

"Brody," she whispered as her eyes filled with tears.

It was a bad dream, that was all. A bad dream caused by her fear of the upcoming battle.

Goddesses, please protect Brody. And myself. A tear ran down her cheek. It had to be a bad dream. For if it was foresight, the two of them might be doomed.

Chapter 21

Nevis was up at dawn to make sure the children practiced their roles in the upcoming attack on the guards. By midmorning, Ruth arrived with the two toddlers from the castle nursery. Then, Nevis, Elinor, and the two eldest Embraced girls escorted the younger children to the hidden cove by the sea cave, where Elinor's boat was anchored.

Bettina set a basket of food in the rowboat, then turned to twelve-year-old Naomi and eleven-year-old Olana. "You're in charge of the little ones now. They'll look to you when they're afraid."

Naomi nodded. "We'll be fine."

"We'll just be worrying about you and the others," Olana added with tears in her eyes.

Catriona gave her a hug. "We're the sneaky Spiders, remember? They'll never see us coming."

"We'll take good care of them," Tommy assured Nevis, then helped five-year-old Terrance into the rowboat along with Naomi.

As Tommy rowed toward the bigger boat, Sarah clung to Bettina's skirt. "When will we see you again?"

"Soon." Bettina kneeled down to give the six-year-old a hug. "Tommy and Lobby are going to take you for a short ride to the south side of the island. If all goes well, we'll see you later tonight."

After a few trips with the rowboat, all the young children

were safely aboard, and Lobby and Tommy hauled up the anchor. The chef was still there, and without any wine to drink, he'd sobered up enough to be helpful.

As the Spiders walked back to the village, Nevis noticed that Elinor was clenching her hands.

He leaned close to whisper, "If you're not comfortable doing this, you could stay in the village and—"

"Don't say that." She frowned at him. "How can I expect children to do something dangerous if I'm not willing to help?"

"You have a brave heart—I know that. But I really shouldn't let you put yourself at risk. You're a princess."

She scoffed. "All the more reason I should display good leadership. Besides, I want to do this. Brody and I have to avenge our father and brother."

He touched her fisted hand. "I can tell you're nervous."

"Of course I am." She wrapped her fingers around his. "Don't ye get nervous afore a battle?"

He nodded. "There is always some fear. That's why I had everyone practice so much. You feel better when you know exactly what you're supposed to do."

She squeezed his hand. "I'm glad ye're here."

"I'm glad I had this time with you." He entwined his fingers with hers. What would happen once the battle was over? he wondered. No doubt Elinor would want to return to Lessa Castle to be with her mother and brother.

As for himself, Nevis had already been named the next general of the Eberoni army. His father wanted to retire soon, and Leo was expecting him to take charge. That meant a life of living in army tents, something he was accustomed to, but not a proper life for a princess.

They walked in silence for a while. Bettina and Catriona were about twenty feet in front of them.

Suddenly, Bettina stopped and tilted her head as if she

were listening. "Fourteen ships have set sail from the Isle of Moon. The birds are amazed by how fast they are traveling."

"That's because the king of Tourin can control the wind," Nevis explained.

"He's just like Darroc?" Catriona asked.

"Yes. And the king of Eberon has lightning power just like Alfred," Nevis added.

Bettina and Catriona exchanged excited looks.

"Then we really would be accepted on the mainland," Catriona said.

Bettina nodded. "I'm hoping we can reunite the little ones with their families."

"Have you heard anything about the elfin navy?" Nevis asked. "Where are they?"

"They're approaching from the east," Bettina replied. "Six ships."

"So there will be twenty ships in all," Elinor concluded.

"With Rupert pushing them here, it won't take long for them to arrive." Nevis began walking at a brisk pace. "We need to get started."

As soon as they returned to the village, Nevis gave the order for the Spiders to advance. There were a total of eight in their little army, including himself and Elinor. Bettina, Catriona, Hannah, and Peter each carried a large canvas bag filled with strips of linen for tying and gagging their prisoners. Elinor's canvas bag was filled with paper, pen, and ink, along with the six spider pictures she'd drawn. She had also strapped on her sword belt.

Nevis had his usual sword at his hip and two knives in his boots. As they strode through the forest toward the castle, they passed by the hole they had dug to hide any confiscated weapons they couldn't use. They stopped at the edge of the forest, close to the guardhouse.

The thirty guards worked in two shifts—fifteen guarding

during the day and the other fifteen at night. So right now, the night-shift guards were inside the house sleeping.

"Ready, Elam? Kurt?" Nevis asked the boys and they nodded. Kurt dashed behind some trees to undress and soon a dark gray bunny came hopping out from beneath the bushes.

The three of them darted toward the guardhouse. Nevis hid around the corner, while Elam and Kurt approached the door. It was a long, rectangular building with many windows, but fortunately all the shutters were closed so the guards inside could sleep during the day.

Elam knocked on the door.

Standing close to a shutter, Nevis could hear some rustling noises inside as the guards stirred.

"Go away!" one of the guards yelled.

Elam pounded even harder on the door.

"Dammit," one of the guards growled. "Sheldon, go see who it is."

"Why me?" a whiny voice answered.

"Because I told you to!"

"Aye, Captain," Sheldon grumbled.

As the guard shuffled toward the door, Nevis moved to the building's corner and from his boot, he drew a knife that had a hard metal knob on the handle.

Sheldon opened the door and let out a big yawn. "Why the hell did you wake us up?"

"Quentin is missing!" Elam said in a frantic voice. "He didn't come to work today."

"What else is new?" The guard yawned again. "Go tell one of the day guards."

"I couldn't find any," Elam said. "Can you help us? We're worried about him."

"Go look for him!" the captain shouted.

"Who, me?" Sheldon cried.

"Yes, you!" the captain yelled. "Take care of it and make sure we're not disturbed again."

"Aye," another guard complained. "We're all exhausted. If I ever catch that cat, I'm going to wring its neck!"

That cat? Nevis wondered what Gavin had done to upset the guards.

"I'm going to wring Quentin's neck," Sheldon grumbled. "Wait here. I need to get my boots on."

While Elam waited, Nevis peeked around the corner. The door was still partially open, and Kurt slipped inside the building unnoticed by the sleepy guards.

Sheldon returned and, with a yawn, he shut the door behind him. "So where do you think Quentin could be?" He walked forward a few steps, and, with a wave of his hand, Elam tripped him.

As Sheldon landed on his face, Nevis dashed forward and clonked him on the back of the head. He hefted the unconscious man over his shoulder, and then he and Elam ran toward the edge of the woods.

When Nevis dropped the guard on the ground, Elinor and Bettina quickly tied his hands and feet while Catriona gagged him. Then the three women dragged him a bit farther into the woods.

Nevis and the others waited at the edge of the woods, and soon they heard loud voices filtering through the closed shutters.

"Ouch!" a guard shouted. "Something bit me!"

"What is it? Ouch, it just bit *me!*"

"What the hell?" the captain growled. "I can't see in the dark." He flung open some shutters.

"It's a rabbit!"

"Where? Ouch! Dammit, he bit me."

"Kill the damned thing!" the captain shouted.

"But it might be Kurt," a guard protested.

"Then chase it out of here!" the captain ordered.

"Aye, Captain." Footsteps ran to the door; then a guard flung it open.

Kurt bounded outside, headed for the forest, with two guards chasing him, shouting and waving their swords. As soon as they reached the forest, Elam tripped one and then the other. With a quick clonk to the head, Nevis knocked both guards out. Elinor and the others quickly tied and gagged them.

The captain peered out the door. There was no one in sight, so he let out a big sigh. "At last we can get some sleep."

That's what you think, Nevis thought as the captain slammed the door shut, then closed all the shutters.

Nevis threw one of the unconscious guards over his shoulder, while Elam and the women dragged the other guard. Soon they deposited the two guards next to the first one.

Quentin pranced around the three unconscious guards. "It's my turn now, right?"

"Yes." Nevis gave the young boy an encouraging slap on the back. "Good luck, soldier."

"Aye, Colonel." Quentin saluted him, then skipped through the woods.

As they headed back to the guardhouse, Nevis realized they were lucky that Quentin was so nosy. He had known the captain's greatest weakness. According to Quentin, the captain had gotten drunk one night and confessed that he was enamored of the Embraced soldier Farah.

Nevis and Elam positioned themselves at the corner of the building while Quentin sneaked up to the door, grinning. He pounded on the door.

"What the hell is it now?" the captain bellowed.

Quentin pounded again on the door.

"See who it is and get rid of him," the captain ordered.

"Aye, Captain." More footsteps shuffled toward the door, and then a guard opened it. "Oh, it's Quentin."

"Tell him to go back to work!" the captain growled.

"Did Sheldon find you?" the guard asked. "Where is he?"

"He's talking to Alfred," Quentin said in a loud voice. "And guess what I heard."

"You little snitch," the guard mumbled. "Go back to work." The door squeaked as he started to shut it.

Quentin raised his voice. "They were talking about you, Captain!"

"What?" the captain asked, and the squeaky sound of the door stopped.

"Alfred said you were fat and lazy," Quentin announced.

"*What?*" the captain roared.

"And Farah was there, and she agreed with him."

"What the hell? I've had enough of that asshole Alfred." After some rustling sounds, booted feet stomped toward the door. "I don't care what kind of power he has. I'm going to whip his ass!" The captain charged out of the guardhouse, slamming the door behind him.

Elam promptly tripped him, and Nevis clocked him. Soon, the captain was tied and gagged and lying next to his unconscious comrades.

Back at the edge of the forest, Elinor gave two of her pictures to Bettina, another two to Catriona, then kept two for herself.

Nevis made sure everyone was equipped with a sword, knife, or hammer from the smithy. "This will be the tricky part," he warned them. "There are eleven who will come running out. Elam will trip the first two, and hopefully, the rest will fall over them. We have to knock them all out quickly."

The Spiders nodded, their hands tightly gripping their weapons.

"Let's go." Nevis led half the group to huddle by one corner of the guardhouse, while Elam led the other half to the corner on the other side of the door.

The women with the pictures sneaked up to the shuttered windows at the back of the building. There was a back door, but Nevis figured that once the pictures came to life at the back of the building, all the guards would flee out the front door. That would mean the three women at the back would be safe. Still, he worried about them, so he eased to the back corner to make sure they were all right.

They had the drawings unfolded and ready to go. With a nod from Elinor, they all quickly opened the shutters and tossed the drawings in to land on the floor. Then they ran to join the groups at the front corners of the building.

"Hey! It's too bright in here," a guard yelled. "Who opened the shutters?"

"What's that? *Ack!*" a guard shrieked.

"Sp-sp-spiders! Giant spiders!"

"Run!"

The front door burst open, and the guards jostled with one another as they all tried to escape at the same time. Two squeezed out, and Elam promptly tripped one, then the other. As the others broke free from the jammed entrance, they fell over the first two.

Nevis and Elam and their groups dashed forward to clobber all the guards on the head.

Nevis had knocked three unconscious when one that Elinor had hit turned to her and said, "Ouch! What the hell are—" He slumped over when Nevis hit him.

Elinor winced. "I'm not very good at this."

Nevis smiled to himself. "You're not hitting hard enough." Another soldier that Hannah had hit sat up, and Nevis clonked him, too. Then Catriona's target sat up, and Nevis hit him.

Quentin laughed. "They're like moles sticking their heads up."

Nevis grinned as he knocked out Bettina's guard. "I'll make sure they're unconscious. You all just start tying them up and dragging them away."

"Aye, Colonel!" Quentin saluted, then helped the others tie the guards up.

As they started to drag the guards into the woods, Nevis

noticed a huge, hideous spider creeping out of the guard-house.

"Dammit." He drew his sword and sliced the spider in two. More spiders were crawling about the room, so hideous looking that he leaped into the room and hacked them to bits. Black hairy legs flew through the air. "Die, you ugly beasts!"

"What are ye doing?" Elinor asked from the doorway.

"Don't worry. It's safe now." He sheathed his sword. "I killed them all."

Her mouth twitched as she entered the room. "Ye didn't have to do that. They would have turned back to paper in an hour or so."

"That's too long." Dammit, why did she have to look so amused? "I hate spiders." He motioned to the weapons stashed at the back of the building. "And we have to hide all these weapons. We couldn't do that if the damned spiders were in the way."

She nodded, her eyes still twinkling. "That's true."

He stepped over some dead spider parts to retrieve a sword from a table in the back. "Would you like a sword? This is a good one."

"No thank you." She patted her canvas bag of art supplies. "In my case, the pen is mightier than the sword."

He smiled. "That's true." When she smiled back, his heart squeezed in his chest. He cleared his throat. "Have all the guards been dragged into the woods?"

"Yes. The children will be back soon to take the weapons away." She stepped closer. "Ye do realize that ye're their hero? Especially Quentin—he practically worships you."

Nevis scoffed. "Whenever his gift appears, he'll probably be able to kick my ass. I'll never be Embraced like they are. Or you are." To his surprise, she suddenly wrapped her arms around his neck. "Wh-what are you doing?"

"Now ye're embraced."

Damn, if he didn't suddenly feel twice as powerful.

"Oh, look!" Quentin was in the doorway with Peter and Hannah.

Nevis jumped back.

"What is it?" Bettina asked as she peered in the doorway. "Are the spiders still in there?"

"No." Quentin pointed at Nevis. "The colonel was—"

"The colonel has killed all the spiders," Elinor announced. "Ye can come in now."

As the human Spiders filed in, Nevis and Elinor handed them all the swords, knives, and spears.

"Take these to the pit we dug, then cover them up," Nevis ordered.

As they rushed outside, Quentin whispered loudly to the others, "I saw the colonel hugging the princess!"

Nevis winced. "Sorry."

"Why should ye be?" Elinor frowned at him. "I'm the one who hugged you."

"I realize that. And I'm grateful, but . . ."

Her beautiful blue eyes narrowed. "But what?"

"You're a princess—"

"And ye're a strong, brave, and handsome colonel. I don't see a problem." She folded her arms across her chest, glowering at him. "Why are ye just staring at me? Am I a mess?" She hooked a tendril of hair behind her ear.

She was a bit of a mess. Her hair was escaping her braid, and there was a smudge of dirt on her cheek, but he'd never thought her more desirable than she was now. He swallowed hard. "You're always beautiful to me."

Her gaze searched his. "Ye do like me, don't you, Nevis?"

"How can anyone not like you? I'm sure you have plenty of suitors."

"I only need one, if he's the right one."

"I'm not a nobleman."

"Who said I wanted a nobleman?" With a huff, she turned to leave.

He caught her by the arm. "Is there truly a chance for me?"

She lifted her chin. "That's up to you. Chances only happen when ye're bold enough to claim them."

"In that case . . ." He pulled her into his arms and planted his mouth on hers. And she responded, wrapping her arms around him and kissing him back. By the Light, he was in heaven, and Elinor was his angel.

"Oh, my goddesses, now they're kissing!" Quentin yelled from the doorway.

Nevis broke the kiss with a groan.

"Shh." Bettina pulled the boy away from the door.

Nevis slanted a worried look at Elinor, but she smiled back and gave him an encouraging nod.

With a smile, he took her hand and led her outside where the Spiders were waiting. "We've eliminated fifteen guards, but there are still fifteen more to go. Time for step two of the plan. Are you ready?"

The Spiders gave him a cheer, and they strode back into the woods, headed in the direction of the castle.

Chapter 22

"Are you all right?" Maeve asked when Brody woke up, still in the guise of the Seer.

He blinked, then sat up. "What time is it?"

"Midmorning." She rose from her chair at the table in his sitting room. While he'd been sleeping, she'd been tearing her sheets into strips.

Earlier, when Ruth had brought Maeve her breakfast, the servant had mentioned that Nevis and his group were planning to use linen strips to tie up the guards. With a guard still stationed outside her door, Maeve had decided to follow Nevis's lead.

She had invited Ruth to share her breakfast, and while they ate, she'd explained who the Seer really was. Once Ruth had recovered from her shock, she'd sworn to help Maeve and Brody. She was already helping Nevis, who had told her the battle would happen today. Now Maeve was even more worried about her bad dream coming true.

"You should have wakened me." Brody jumped out of bed and pulled on some breeches. "We have to get ready."

Maeve swallowed hard. "For the battle?"

"Aye." Brody buttoned his shirt. "Leo and all the ships have probably set sail by now. By noon, they plan to rendezvous with the elfin ships near the island."

A knock sounded on the door.

"Burien!" Cahira called. "Are you awake?"

"Dammit," Brody muttered and he leaped back into bed.

"Just a minute!" Maeve yelled back. She covered up her linen strips with a tablecloth, then rushed to the bed to tug the covers up to Brody's chin. "My mother came earlier this morning," she whispered. "I chased her off, saying you'd finally fallen asleep after a rough night."

Brody touched her cheek. "It was a glorious night. Are you all right?"

"Of course." Another knock sounded at the door, and she slipped his hand beneath the covers. "Behave."

She unlocked the door, and Cahira sauntered in, followed by Ruth carrying a breakfast tray.

"Oh, at last you're awake." Cahira rushed to the Seer's bedside. "I was worried about you."

"I'm fine," Brody said in a shaky voice. When he struggled to sit up, Cahira helped him. "I just needed some rest."

"Of course." Cahira grabbed the tray from Ruth and set it on his lap. "And now you need some hot porridge."

Maeve bit her lip to keep from smiling. She knew how much Brody hated porridge.

Brody gave Cahira a strained smile. "Thank you, my dear."

Cahira patted him on the shoulder. "It's a joy to take care of you, Burien. If you need me, I'll be in my workroom. Ruth can clean up your dressing room." She strode toward the door.

"I was thinking . . ." Brody started, and Cahira turned to face him with a questioning look. "Your garden is so lovely, what with the hedges clipped into different shapes and the colored ponds—"

"Of course it's lovely." Cahira preened. "I designed it myself."

Brody smiled at her. "I would love to have lunch with you on the balcony, so I could admire both you and your garden."

"Oh, what a wonderful idea!" Cahira clasped her hands together. "A luncheon party for just the two of us."

Brody slumped over and said in a weak voice, "I don't think I can make it there without my daughter."

Cahira shot Maeve an annoyed look. "Very well. But if we invite her, then I will also invite Kendric. Surely if he spends more time with Maeve, he will see that she would make a much better wife than that silly Brigitta."

Maeve gritted her teeth. Soon, she would be telling her mother exactly whom she was planning to marry.

"That would be perfect," Brody said. "We'll be there shortly before noon."

"Excellent. I'll have the servants get to work on it right away." Cahira strolled out the door.

Maeve motioned for Ruth to stay behind; then she locked the door. Noon? Obviously, Brody wanted to be on the balcony so he could see when the ships arrived.

He moved the tray aside, then jumped out of bed.

Ruth gasped. "He really is a young man."

Brody stopped in his tracks. "Oh. I can explain."

"Don't worry," Maeve assured him. "I told Ruth everything this morning. She wants to help us. She's already helping Nevis."

Ruth nodded. "It's been breaking my heart to see the babies I took care of turned into killers. And the others rejected and forced to work, even the little ones . . ." Her eyes filled with tears. "And when I think about how Gavin was cursed and you, too . . ."

"I'm glad you're on our side." Brody touched her shoulder. "Don't worry. I'll make Cahira lift the curse on Gavin."

Maeve thought back to when her mother had threatened to turn the Chameleon into a mouse. "What if she just makes it worse? If we capture her and threaten her, she might turn you into an animal permanently to be rid of you."

Ruth shook her head. "You needn't worry about that. She's already cursed Brody and Gavin. A second curse won't work unless she first removes the prior curse."

Maeve exhaled. "Oh, that's a relief."

Brody slipped on his leather shoes. "Is there anything else you can tell us?"

"Do you know what Nevis and his Spiders are planning?" Ruth asked, and Brody nodded.

"Spiders?" Maeve asked.

"That's what Nevis's army is calling themselves," Brody explained. "They plan on getting rid of most of the guards."

"Gabby wants to help, too," Ruth added. "And I think Gavin is trying to help in his own way. He escaped from their room last night and ran around the castle causing trouble. The night guards were exhausted from trying to catch him."

"Excellent." Brody smiled. "The Seer was right, naming him Trouble."

"I thought we should do our part." Maeve whisked the tablecloth off to reveal the linen strips she'd made. "How many guards can we tie up before lunch?"

Brody snorted. "We won't know until we try." He grabbed a candlestick from the table and strode into Maeve's bed-chamber. "Your guard will be first."

Maeve stuffed a few linen strips into her pockets and followed him. "How do we do this?"

"You get him to run inside, and I'll do the rest." Brody positioned himself beside the door, where he would be hidden when it opened.

Maeve took a deep breath, then screamed. The door immediately opened, and the guard peered inside.

"Help!" Maeve frantically motioned toward her dressing room. "Th-there's a man in there!"

"What?" The guard dashed into the room, and Brody clobbered him from behind.

Ruth ran over to shut the door, while Maeve tied the man's hands and feet.

Brody pulled a knife from the guard's boot, then unhooked his sword belt. "I could use these." He gagged the guard, then dragged him to Maeve's dressing room.

"Where should we go next?" Maeve asked.

"There's a guard outside Gabby's room," Ruth suggested. "I'll show you the way."

Maeve and Ruth pocketed the rest of the linen strips, while Brody pulled on the Seer's hooded robe to hide the sword belt that was now strapped around his hips.

He slid the spare knife into the belt, then grabbed the Seer's staff. "Let's go."

"Oh! Just a minute." Maeve ran into the Seer's bedchamber to grab the key, so she could lock her room as they left. She didn't want any servants coming in and discovering the guard.

The hallway was empty now, so they were able to walk quickly.

"Where are the guards?" Brody whispered to Ruth.

"There should be four circling the castle," Ruth replied. "Two more at the back door and another two at the front door."

"That's eight," Brody said. "Nevis will take care of them."

"How many are inside the castle?" Maeve asked.

"Seven," Ruth replied. "There was one stationed at your door, then there's one at Gabby's room, two at the throne room, one on the lookout tower, and two who move about patrolling the hallways."

When they reached the stairwell, they paused at the sound of booted feet climbing the stairs.

"It's one of the guards on patrol," Ruth whispered, and they ducked around the corner.

Brody whipped his knife from his belt.

"I'll distract him," Maeve offered. She eased to the head of the stairs and gasped in feigned surprise as the guard reached the landing below.

He glanced up at her, his eyes narrowed. "Your Highness. You're not in your room."

Maeve shrugged. "I thought I'd go for a swim. Can you tell me the way to the tank room?"

He scoffed. "You're not going there. It's an escape route. Where is your guard?"

Maeve let out a small squeal and ran up the stairs. With a muttered curse, the guard gave chase. He reached their floor and turned to follow Maeve up the next flight. She stopped at the landing and glanced back. Brody sneaked up behind the guard and clobbered him with the blunt end of his knife.

She hurried down the stairs to tie and gag the guard.

"Where can we stash him?" Brody asked Ruth, and she used a key to open a nearby storage room.

With the guard locked away, they proceeded down the stairs to the servants' hallway. Maeve peered around the corner and spotted the guard in front of Gabby's room. She nodded at Brody, and he immediately hunched over like the Seer. They walked slowly down the hallway with Brody leaning heavily on his staff.

The guard watched them with a suspicious look.

After what seemed like an eternity, Maeve finally arrived at Gabby's door with Brody and Ruth. "We're here to see Gabby."

The guard looked away with a sniff. "No one is allowed in except Her Majesty."

Maeve circled around him so his back would be to Brody. "Apparently, you don't know who I am. I am Princess Maeve, heir to the throne, and I command you to—"

Clonk. The guard crumpled to the floor.

Brody slid his knife back into his belt. "*Princess* Maeve?"

She gave him a wry look. "*Prince* Brodgar?"

He shrugged. "I prefer being Brody. But I'll take the title if I can be *your* prince."

She smiled. "Then I'll be your princess."

Ruth shook her head. "I can't believe they're flirting right now." She retrieved the key from the guard's pocket and unlocked the door. "Gabby?"

"Yes?" The young woman ran up to the door. "Oh, my!" She stepped aside while Brody dragged the unconscious guard into her room.

"Are you all right, Gabby?" Maeve asked as she closed the door.

"I'm fine. Thank you for getting me out of the dungeon." Gabby frowned as Brody tied and gagged the guard. "How can such an old man move so quickly?"

"He's a shifter like your brother," Ruth explained.

Brody bowed his head. "I'm Brody from the Isle of Moon."

"Prince Brodgar," Ruth whispered.

Gabby's mouth fell open.

"Do you know where Gavin is?" Maeve asked, and Gabby shook her head.

"He sneaked out last night to terrorize the guards," she confessed. "He must be hiding somewhere now, probably taking a nap."

Brody snorted. "I don't know how a little cat can terrorize anybody, but I'm grateful for his help." As he strode toward a window, Maeve noticed Ruth and Gabby exchanging an odd look.

"I wonder how much progress Nevis has made." Brody peered out the window.

Maeve joined him. "Look!" She pointed at two guards who were slowly marching around the castle.

Gabby and Ruth gathered at the second window.

"I wish we could get rid of them," Maeve muttered. "Maybe you could fly at them as an eagle—"

Suddenly, one of the guards tripped, then the second one. As they sat up, dazed, a flock of birds flew straight at them.

"Ack!" They ducked down, covering their heads as the birds pooped all over them.

Gabby laughed. "It must be Bettina! She told the birds to do that."

Nevis and his Spiders emerged from the nearby woods. They ran to the guards, knocked them out, then dragged them back into the forest.

"Excellent." Brody opened the window and waved.

After a moment, Nevis stepped from behind a tree and waved back. He showed his hands, his fingers splayed.

"Seventeen?" Maeve asked.

"That's how many guards they've taken." Brody raised his hand, displaying the number three.

Nevis responded with a thumbs-up, then disappeared once again into the woods.

"I have an idea!" Gabby darted over to her worktable and grabbed a handful of gold coins. When the next two guards came marching around the castle, she tossed a few coins out the window.

"Is that gold?" one of the guards shouted, and they both sprinted over to retrieve the coins.

"Woo-hoo!" Gabby shouted and flung more coins out the window.

The guards scrambled about on the grass, frantically picking up coins. Meanwhile, Nevis sneaked up behind them and clobbered them both on the head. As the Spiders dragged the guards into the woods, he flashed the number nineteen at Brody.

"Hell, no." Brody thumped his chest, then raised a hand to show the number five.

Nevis responded with one finger, and Brody snorted.

Maeve gave him an incredulous look. "Are you arguing over who gets credit for those two?"

"Gabby should get credit," Ruth announced.

"I agree," Maeve said.

Gabby grinned. "What do we do now?"

"We take out the guards at the throne room," Brody announced as he strode to the door.

Maeve winced, recalling the dream that had revealed Brody getting injured in the throne room. That was the last place she wanted to go.

With no more guards walking the perimeter of the castle, Nevis and his Spiders were able to dash across the garden at the back of the castle. They arrived at the base of a giant hedge clipped into the shape of a dolphin.

"Blindfold her," Nevis told Bettina, and she quickly wrapped a linen strip around Catriona's head.

He retrieved the dark canvas bag that Ruth had left for them beneath the hedge. "Let's get closer to the door."

The Spiders moved slowly toward the door that led into the castle's dungeon with Bettina leading the blindfolded Catriona. Once they were close enough, they all hid behind a hedge. Between the branches, he spotted the two guards and the dog they used to frighten the children into working.

The dog could apparently sense their presence for he started barking. Peter, Kurt, and Hannah cringed.

"It will be all right," Elinor assured them.

Kurt shuddered. "I'm afraid one day when I'm a rabbit that the dog will eat me."

Bettina sighed. "They keep the dog half-starved so he'll be mean."

Nevis patted the bag that Ruth had brought from the kitchen. "That's why our plan should work. Ready?"

Elam and Bettina nodded. After taking the canvas bag from Nevis, they slowly approached the guards. The dog growled and tugged at his leash.

"What are you doing here?" one of the guards demanded. "Go back to the village and work."

"We brought a gift for you." Bettina pulled out two large fish. "Here!" She tossed them to the guards.

The fish landed at the guards' feet, and just as they leaned over to look at them, Elinor whisked Catriona's blindfold off.

Bam! The fish exploded, knocking the guards off their feet. The dog pulled loose and charged toward Bettina and Elam. He pulled a ham bone from the bag and threw it to the side. The dog immediately changed direction and dashed to the bone. While he happily gnawed away, Bettina and Elam tied and gagged the two guards.

Nevis and his Spiders ran toward them. After retrieving the keys from one of the guards, he unlocked the door. They dragged the guards in and locked them in the dungeon.

Now that they were in the castle, Nevis was tempted to change his plan and hunt down Cahira.

"Something wrong?" Elinor asked when he hesitated.

"No." He headed for the dungeon door. "We follow the plan." First they would capture the guards at the front door, then he would help Brody deal with Cahira and the Chameleon.

After running back to the forest, he and his Spiders made their way to the front of the castle. The ocean was visible now, and he shielded his eyes from the noonday sun to scan its surface. No sign of the armada yet, but they should be here soon.

He glanced up at the highest tower of the castle. There was a lone guard up there. No doubt he would be the first to spot the invading ships. He might also see Nevis and his Spiders moving through the front garden.

"Elam will come with me," Nevis told his group. "The rest of you will remain hidden here in the woods."

"That's not fair," Quentin grumbled.

Nevis gave him a stern look. "You said you would follow orders."

Quentin quickly saluted. "Then I'll be in charge here, right?"

Hannah scoffed. "Why would you be in charge? You're the youngest."

"Elinor is in charge until we get back." Nevis pointed at the guard on the lookout tower. "Make him trip. Then we'll run for that hedge there."

"Aye, Colonel." Elam waved a hand at the guard, who promptly fell over.

Nevis and Elam dashed for the cover of a large hedge clipped to look like an ocean wave. They followed the hedge toward the front door.

"We'll do the usual trip and clobber," Nevis whispered as he spotted the two guards.

Elam nodded, gripping his knife tightly.

Suddenly, the door opened and a group of young people emerged. Nevis winced. It was the Embraced army. Seven of them, fully armed. Dammit to hell! He knew from his years of being in the military that no matter how well he executed his plans, there was always some unknown variable that would screw things up. He knew it, but it still pissed him off whenever it happened.

"Why do we have to practice now?" the youngest boy whined.

"The general ordered it," Alfred grumbled. He pointed at the balcony overhead. "The queen is having lunch up there soon, so Kendric wants us to show off our skills."

Nevis looked at Elam and shook his head. There was no way the two of them could handle the guards and the Embraced army. While the soldiers did their warm-up exercises, he and Elam sneaked back down the hedge. When Elam caused the lookout guard to trip once again, they ran back to the rest of the Spiders.

"What do we do now?" Elinor asked.

Nevis glanced at the castle. The back door was open, so he could still sneak in to help Brody. He turned his head to gaze at the ocean. Or he could stay here to help Leo.

"We wait," he told the Spiders. "And when the right opportunity comes, we seize it."

Chapter 23

Brody exhaled with relief as Ruth locked the door on a storage closet. Inside he had stashed the two guards stationed outside the throne room and the last of the patrolling guards. He assumed Nevis had eliminated the guards at the front and back doors to the castle. That meant the only guard left was the one on the lookout tower. It was best, Brody believed, to leave that guard in position so he could sound the alarm as soon as he sighted the armada. That distraction was needed if Brody was going to deal with the Sea Witch.

It was nearing noon and time for Cahira's luncheon party, so Brody and Maeve rushed toward the balcony. Ruth was expected to help in the kitchen so she headed there, while Gabby went in search of her brother.

When Brody reached the last hallway, he slowed his walk, his arm linked with Maeve's, in case Cahira or any servants saw them approaching. He noticed all the doors to the balcony were open, and a breeze from the ocean was fluttering the purple curtains.

"Green and purple," Maeve whispered.

"What?" He leaned heavily on his staff and made sure his robe was closed and his sword hidden.

"Those were the colors of my Telling Stones," she explained. "And the colors of my mother's flag and throne room."

"Those stones have a creepy way of being right," he muttered.

"Can we stay away from the throne room?"

"Why?" He noticed the glint of fear in her eyes. The Telling Stones weren't the only ones with the power to predict the future. "Did you see something in a dream?"

She gave him a worried look.

"Ah, there you are!" Cahira breezed through a doorway and smiled at the Seer. "Everything is ready, Burien."

"I've arranged for some entertainment," the Chameleon announced as he entered the hallway behind them.

Brody stopped and turned as the Chameleon strode past him. Maeve stayed by his side, holding his arm as if he needed her support to stand.

"What a delightful surprise." Cahira clasped her hands together. "What could it be?"

The Chameleon joined her as they strolled onto the balcony. "The soldiers of the Embraced army are going to display their skills." He stopped at the balustrade. "They're warming up now."

"Oh, Burien," Cahira called to him. "Come and see!"

Brody passed through the nearest doorway with Maeve at his side. When he reached the balustrade, he saw the seven members of the Embraced army below. Damn, he couldn't kill the Chameleon or capture Cahira with the soldiers so close. He would have to wait until the armada showed up to keep the army busy.

Did this also mean that the guards stationed at the front door were still there? They had to be, or the soldiers below would have noticed them missing. No doubt Nevis's plans had also been derailed by the appearance of the Embraced army.

Brody glanced at the woods in the distance. Were Nevis and his Spiders there? They were probably waiting for the armada to arrive. He moved his gaze to the ocean, squinting his eyes in the noonday sun. Was that the dim outline of a ship?

A crack of lightning drew his attention back to the Embraced soldiers below. Alfred had just split a log in two.

Cahira clapped, and Alfred bowed to her. Meanwhile, servants began carrying in trays of food and pitchers of wine.

"Shall we eat?" Cahira took a seat at the head of the table and motioned to the chair on her right. "Burien, come sit by me."

"Yes, my dear." Brody hobbled slowly toward her, pausing to let servants rush back and forth.

Suddenly, a horn blasted from above. Everyone froze for a few seconds, and then the Chameleon rushed to the balustrade.

"I think I see a ship." He shielded his eyes with his hand.

"Three ships!" the guard above them shouted. "No, six . . . Ten ships!"

Cahira dashed to the balustrade. "*Ten* ships?"

"Fourteen!" the guard yelled.

Only fourteen? Brody thought. Then the elfin ships hadn't arrived yet.

"So many?" Maeve helped Brody hobble back to the balustrade. "Could it be a merchant fleet?"

The Chameleon snorted. "I don't think so."

"Why not?" Maeve asked in an innocent voice. "I thought merchants liked to travel together for safety purposes. There's the danger of pirates or—"

"Enough!" The Chameleon slanted her an annoyed look. "It's an attack, and you know it."

Cahira gripped the stone balustrade, her knuckles turning white. "Our enemies are attacking? I don't understand. I've always destroyed any ship that came close to us. How did they know our location?"

The Chameleon scoffed. "No doubt it was your daughter—"

"What?" Cahira turned toward Maeve, her expression going quickly from shock to rage. "You. Did you betray me?"

"No!" Maeve raised her hands. "I've been under guard since I arrived. How could I—"

"There's no point in arguing about it," the Chameleon interrupted. "We just need to destroy the invaders."

Cahira shrugged. "When the ships get close enough, I'll blow them up."

The Chameleon motioned to the Embraced soldiers, who were already running to the bluff overlooking the harbor. "Let the army handle it. They need the practice."

Cahira waved a dismissive hand. "It would be so much simpler if I—"

"The general is right," Brody interrupted with a shaky voice. "Our soldiers need the practice so they will be ready to take over the mainland. I can foresee this."

Cahira sighed. "Very well, Burien."

The Chameleon gave him a thoughtful look. "What else do you see, old man?"

Brody pointed a trembling hand toward the ships. "The kings from the mainland have come to destroy us. If we defeat them now, their countries will be ours for the taking."

The Chameleon's eyes glinted with silver. "Leo of Eberon is out there? And Brigitta's husband?"

Brody nodded. "I can see them."

The Chameleon dashed down the hallway, and soon they saw him running across the garden to join the Embraced army on the bluff.

Brody exhaled with relief. Now that the Chameleon was gone for a while, he could deal with Cahira.

The Sea Witch tapped her fingers on the stone balustrade. "I suppose this is a blessing in disguise. Now that the mainland kings are attacking us, it gives us the perfect opportunity to kill them. And if the army fails to defeat them, I can still blow up the ships. Either way, we're going to win." She turned to Brody and smiled. "Shall we go ahead and eat?"

"Yes, my dear." Brody squeezed Maeve's hand as she helped him to the table. It was time for them to get started. "We have much to discuss over lunch. Maeve has decided on the man she wishes to marry."

Cahira's smile faded. "She will marry whomever I tell her to."

"No, I won't." Maeve gave her mother a defiant look. "You would never allow me to marry the man I love, because you think he's dead. You think you killed him."

Cahira rolled her eyes. "Whatever are you mumbling about?"

"You've been living with the false assumption that you killed Prince Brodgar of the Isle of Moon," Brody explained.

Cahira blinked. "Burien, what's happened to your voice?"

"I am Prince Brodgar." Brody shifted into his true self, and Cahira stumbled back with a gasp.

"What? Who?" Her eyes widened with horror. "Wh-where's my Burien?"

"Dead." Brody strode toward her. "I buried him on the Isle of Moon."

"No." Cahira stepped back again. "Not my Burien . . ."

"You murdered my father and brother and put a curse on me." Brody shoved his robe back to reveal his sword belt and gripped the hilt of his weapon. "I would gladly kill you for your crimes, but I will show mercy if you remove my curse. And Gavin's, too."

Cahira gave him a confused look. "You . . . you're the boy I cursed in the ocean? You were one of the princes?"

"Mother, please," Maeve pleaded. "Remove the curse now. Prince Brodgar is the man I want to marry."

"No!" Cahira turned to her daughter, her eyes flashing with rage. "You betrayed me, you ungrateful whelp! I will never help you or this . . . this *mistake*!" She motioned toward Brody.

"If I marry him, all the islands will be united again," Maeve argued. "Isn't that what you want? Your descendants will rule—"

"No!" Cahira screamed. "The islands are mine!" She dashed into the hallway. "Guards!" She ran toward the throne room. "Arrest my daughter! And kill that man!"

"The guards are gone," Brody shouted. "You will do as I say, Sea Witch!" As he chased after her, he heard Maeve let out a moan.

"Not the throne room."

When Kendric reached the front door, the two guards saluted him.

"What's going on, General? Have they come to attack us?"

Kendric glanced at the ocean, where all fourteen ships were now clearly visible. "My soldiers will defeat them. You two go upstairs to guard the queen."

"Aye, General." They saluted and rushed inside.

Kendric sprinted across the garden, past the two ponds and clipped hedges. His soldiers were on the bluff above the harbor, but they hadn't taken any action yet. The ships were too far away for Alfred's lightning power to reach them.

A sudden blast of wind slammed into Kendric, knocking him onto his back. Dammit, that had to be that bastard Rupert, who had stolen Brigitta from him. He scrambled to his feet and fought against the wind to join his soldiers, who were struggling just to stand up. Meanwhile the enemy ships were coming in fast.

"Push them back, Darroc!" Kendric ordered, and Darroc sent a surge of wind out to sea. His power collided with Rupert's, and with nowhere else to go, the two opposing winds were forced straight up into the air, sucking the ocean with them to form a wall of water. Now it was difficult even to see the ships on the other side.

Darroc gritted his teeth as he strained to push his hands

forward. "I-I can't blast through. Why is the wind coming at us so hard?"

"It's that damned Rupert, King Ulfrid of Tourin," Kendric growled. "He has the same power that you do."

Farah gave him a shocked look. "One of the mainland kings is Embraced?"

"I thought the people on the mainland killed all the Embraced babies," Irene shouted over the roaring noise of the wind.

"That's what I thought," Jared agreed.

Kendric waved their questions aside. "Most of them were killed. You were lucky to be sent here. You'll be the future rulers of the world. But first you have to defeat the mainland kings who have come to destroy you. You've trained hard for this, so now prove yourselves worthy!"

"Aye, General." Alfred nodded. "You can count on us. Mikayla, fly over that wall of water and report back. I want to know how many—"

"I can't fly in that wind!" Mikayla cried. "I'll fall into the ocean and drown."

"Don't question my orders," Alfred snarled.

"I never learned how to swim." Mikayla motioned to Kendric. "Why don't you go, General? You fly so much better than I."

Kendric considered going as an eagle, but he didn't want to land on Rupert's ship without any weapons.

Suddenly, a barrage of cannonballs shot through the wall of water, headed straight toward them.

With a frantic shout, Darroc stopped the wind he was directing against the ships and focused instead on intercepting the cannonballs. They halted in midair, then plunked harmlessly into the ocean.

"Oh, thank y—" Irene started, but Kendric interrupted her.

"You, fool!" he shouted at Darroc. "You let them trick you

into stopping your wind." He pointed at the ships, which were quickly advancing toward the harbor now that Rupert's power was unchallenged. Even the wall of water had crashed down. "Push back at them now!"

Darroc resumed his surge of wind against the ships, and the wall of water began to climb once again.

"But the cannonballs were coming straight at us," Jared protested.

"They never would have reached us," Kendric growled. "Their ships were out of range." Dammit, this was the problem with his soldiers: They were completely inexperienced when it came to actual battle.

"Now that they're closer, I could try striking them," Alfred offered.

"All right," Kendric agreed. "If you see a man up in a crow's nest, moving his arms, that's Rupert. Blast him. Darroc, stop your power just long enough for Alfred to take aim."

Alfred extended his hand. "Ready!"

Darroc released his power. The wall of water crashed down, and the invading ships lunged forward. Alfred shot a bolt of lightning toward the nearest manned crow's nest. With a loud crack, the mast snapped in two, and the sailor in the nest plummeted to the deck.

But the wind was still coming at them.

"That wasn't Rupert!" Kendric quickly scanned the fourteen ships that were advancing once again. Dammit, there were six that were flying the blue-and-gold Tourinian flag. He pointed at the first one. "Try that one."

Alfred shot another bolt of lightning, but this time a second bolt crashed into it, sending the lightning harmlessly into the clouds. "What? Where did that come from?"

"Bloody hell." Kendric clenched his fists. That had to be Leo, the bastard who'd stolen Eberon from him. "Darroc, put the wind back up before they get any closer!"

Darroc did as he was told, but Alfred just stood there with his mouth agape. "How did that happen? Is there someone else with lightning power?"

"Yes," Kendric growled. "Leofric of Eberon."

Farah gasped. "There's another king who's Embraced?"

Logan's shoulders slumped. "How are we supposed to win against them?"

"I'm not the only one with lightning power," Alfred muttered to himself. He raised a fist. "I have to kill him, so I'll be the only one."

"Exactly. We need Leo and Rupert dead." Kendric eyed the wall of water. It seemed to be inching slowly toward the harbor. That could only mean Rupert's power was stronger than Darroc's. That bastard. "Mikayla, fly over the wall. I want to know which ship Rupert is on."

Her face turned pale. "But I—"

"You will follow orders, soldier!" Alfred yelled.

Farah gave the young girl a sympathetic look. "You'll be all right. Fly high over the wall to avoid the winds."

"I'll give you a push," Darroc added.

Mikayla nodded, then sprinted toward the edge of the bluff. She jumped, zooming up into the air as Darroc shoved her high with his wind. She flew over the wall of water, then disappeared from view.

He needed to use the rest of his army, Kendric realized. Alfred's power was not going to work as long as Leo kept diverting it. "Farah, make a ball of fire. Then Darroc will drop the wind long enough to blow the fireball at the closest ship. We'll set their fleet ablaze."

"Aye, General." Farah snapped her fingers to start a fire, then circled her hands around to form a fireball.

"Shoot it!" Kendric ordered, and as soon as the wall of water crashed down, Darroc sent the fireball hurtling toward the closest ship.

A blast of wind stopped the fireball in midair, and it dropped into the sea.

"Wh-where's Mikayla?" Irene asked. "I don't see her!"

Kendric quickly scanned the sky. With the wall of water down, they should be able to see Mikayla. The silly girl must have crashed.

"We need to help her!" Logan cried. "You could fly over there to rescue—"

"Enough!" Kendric yelled. Shit, the younger ones looked like they were going to cry. "There are always casualties in battle—you know that. Now make more fireballs, Farah."

With trembling hands, Farah began shaping numerous small fireballs, but then a dark cloud suddenly appeared over their heads.

"What is that?" Kendric glanced up just as a deluge of rain swooshed down on his army, causing the fires to sizzle out. He peered through the heavy sheet of rain. It was only raining on them.

"It's Hannah!" Alfred wiped raindrops from his face. "She must be close by. Logan, find her and make her stop."

"Aye, Colonel." Logan took off with a blur of speed.

Kendric gritted his teeth as the rain continued to pelt them. With two soldiers gone, they were now down to six. Alfred's lightning power was useless with Leo there to stop it. Darroc was not powerful enough to defeat Rupert. As long as it was raining, Farah couldn't use her fire power.

He glanced around and hefted up a small boulder. "Darroc, can you blow this through the wall? Then Jared can make it explode."

"I'll try." When the boulder was thrown into the air, Darroc gave it a push, but halfway to the wall of water, it plummeted into the ocean.

Shit. Kendric scoured his mind to come up with another plan. He could shift into a dragon and fly over the ships, but unfortunately, he couldn't breathe fire. Could he shift into a whale and ram one of the ships? Or could he use the sea creatures that were already there?

He glanced at Irene. He'd always considered her power to be the weakest of the group. Making things grow? It was more suitable for a farm than an army. In fact, she'd only practiced her gift on plants. "Irene, how big can you make all the sea creatures?"

Her eyes widened with shock. "You . . . you want . . . ?"

"Sea monsters!" Alfred shook his fist. "Let's do it!"

Irene winced. "It will cause them a lot of pain."

Kendric nodded. "That's all right. If they're angry, they can take it out on the ships. Do it."

Irene hesitated.

"Follow orders, soldier!" Alfred yelled at her.

With a trembling hand, Irene shoved wet strands of hair away from her face. Then she stretched her arms toward the ocean. The surface frothed and churned as all the nearby sea creatures began to grow larger. And larger.

Kendric smiled to himself. This strategy was going to work.

Chapter 24

Leo scanned the wall of water as he stood on the quarter-deck of the Eberoni flagship with Captain Shaw, General Harden, and the dragon shifter Dimitri. The ship to his left was Rupert's flagship, and Leo could see him with a fellow seaman up in the crow's nest. Rupert was straining hard to push the armada forward.

The fleet had left the port of Luna two hours ago with Rupert pushing them slowly toward the Isle of Secrets while they waited for the elfin navy to join them. Unfortunately, the wind was not cooperating for the elves, and Silas had sent a telepathic message to Dimitri that they were running a little late. By then, the fourteen ships had been sighted by the Embraced army, so they'd had no choice but to start the battle.

Before leaving the Isle of Moon, Leo and all the ship captains had devised a system so they could communicate with one another and act as a unified force. They would use different colored flags to represent the different battle strategies they had planned. Leo and his advisors would decide when to enact each strategy, then use the flags to relay the orders to the other ships. Just as they had planned, the first volley of cannonballs had tricked Darroc into dropping his wind, and Rupert had taken advantage by moving the entire fleet forward.

Now the wall of water was back up, making it impossible to see what the Embraced army was doing. Even so, Leo had to stay vigilant. Alfred had already shot two lightning bolts, so Leo had to be ready to divert any more.

"I believe we're within range now for the cannons," Captain Shaw told him.

"All right. Let's do it." Leo waved a small black flag.

His man in the crow's nest saw it and waved a larger black flag. Soon, all the seamen in the crow's nests of the fourteen ships were waving a black flag, and each ship began loading their cannons. As soon as they saw an orange flag, they would open fire.

Leo was reaching for his small orange flag when General Harden grabbed his arm to stop him.

"Look!" The general pointed at the sky. A young soldier was being tossed about in the wind like a ragdoll. "What the hell is he doing up there?"

Leo winced. "That must be Mikayla, the one who can fly."

"She's not flying now," Dimitri muttered. "She's falling."

Leo recalled the information on the list he'd received. The girl was only thirteen years old. "Those bastards are using children."

"I'll get her." Dimitri pulled off his clothes and shifted into a dragon, causing the ship to dip from the added weight. He took off just as the girl plummeted into the ocean. Swooping down, he scooped her up, then circled back to drop her on the quarterdeck.

Leo took a step toward the unconscious girl, then retreated as a pool of water spread around her. Even with his boots on, he was afraid he might accidentally kill her with his lightning power.

Captain Shaw kneeled beside her as she coughed and sputtered. "Are you all right, Miss?"

Dimitri landed on the main deck and shifted back to his human form.

General Harden tossed him his clothes. "Get dressed. She's

been frightened enough. And see if you can find a blanket for her."

After Dimitri dashed belowdecks, Captain Shaw helped the girl sit up.

Mikayla looked around, terror in her eyes. She began to shake, her teeth rattling. "Am . . . am I a prisoner?"

Captain Shaw patted her shoulder. "Nay, Miss. You're a guest here."

A swooshing noise drew Leo's attention, and he turned to see the wall of water crashing down. A ball of fire had been hurled toward them, but Rupert promptly stopped it.

A now-dressed Dimitri climbed the stairs to the quarterdeck with a blanket in hand. "Here." He wrapped it around Mikayla's shoulders.

She clutched the ends together under her chin. "Thank you."

"We'll get you some hot soup in a little while," Captain Shaw assured her.

"Aye, we're a little busy now," the general grumbled, frowning at the wall of water, which was climbing once again. "Can you fly over that, Dimitri?"

"We can't send him," Leo quickly said. "Alfred would hit him with a lightning bolt." An inkling of an idea took root in his mind. "But if Dimitri gave me a ride, I could shoot back. How close are the other dragons now?"

"They're almost here," Dimitri replied. "Just a few more minutes."

The ocean surface began to churn and foam.

"Something's happening." Leo leaned over the railing to look at the water. An enormous shark leaped up, snapping its jaws at him, and he jumped back.

"What the hell?" Captain Shaw ran to the railing as the giant shark skidded down the side of the ship, causing it to shake and wobble.

"Are sharks usually that big?" Leo asked.

"No." The captain pointed at a huge swordfish that leaped from the ocean. "Look at that!" It flew at Rupert's ship and embedded its sword near a porthole.

An enormous whale, bigger than any of their ships, breeched nearby, then slammed back into the water with so much force, a large wave crashed onto the fleet of ships. Some of the smaller ones listed dangerously to the side.

Leo and all his men staggered about as their ship rolled back and forth.

"It must be Irene," Mikayla cried as she crawled toward the railing. "She made all the sea creatures grow." She screamed when a giant tentacle slithered past her.

The ship teetered as a humungous giant squid spread its tentacles across the quarterdeck and pulled it down toward the sea. The bow rose, and seamen tumbled about on deck.

"Stand back." Leo shot a bolt of lightning into a tentacle, and the squid retreated into the water.

They were safe for now, but a few of the smaller ships had come under attack from other creatures and had capsized, the men falling into the ocean. Screams filled the air as sailors were attacked by huge sharks.

The giant squid turned its attention and rage toward Rupert's ship, wrapping its tentacles around the bow and cracking the ship in two. The men scrambled for lifeboats, but Rupert remained in the crow's nest, frantically blowing the giant creatures out to sea. Unfortunately, with Rupert no longer pushing against Darroc, the whole fleet was being moved farther out to sea.

The whale returned, ramming its head into Leo's ship. The impact caused the ship to rock violently, and everyone careened along the deck. A few men screamed as they fell overboard.

Rupert managed to shove the whale out to sea, but a gaping hole had been left in the ship's side.

"To the lifeboats!" Captain Shaw ordered, then turned

back to Mikayla, who was crying and clinging to the railing. "Don't worry, child. We'll take care of you."

"Dimitri, fly her to the elfin ships," Leo yelled over the shouting voices of sailors scrambling to get on lifeboats.

Dimitri shifted, his clothes ripping, and with a gasp, Mikayla fainted. He grabbed her and flew east.

The ship was now taking on water fast.

"Get yourself to a lifeboat!" General Harden yelled at Leo.

"You go!" Leo ran to the mainmast and began to climb. He didn't dare try a lifeboat. They were all bobbing wildly, with waves splashing in. Some had capsized, dumping the men in the water. The risk of falling into the ocean was too great.

He climbed into the crow's nest, then looked below. Water was seeping onto the deck. *Crap.* There was no way out of this. The entire armada was in trouble. Some ships had broken in two. Others were so damaged that they were sinking. Rupert was still in the crow's nest of his floundering ship, using his power to push the sea creatures farther away. Soon he would be in the water.

Leo surveyed the ocean surface, where hundreds of seamen were clinging to pieces of wood. Dammit to hell. If he fell into the water, his lightning power would kill everyone. Rupert would die. Nevis's father, who had been like a father to Leo, would die. All the seamen would die.

His heart tightened as the crow's nest sank lower and lower. *Holy Light, don't make me kill these people.*

What could he do? He pulled the wooden-handled knife from his belt. If he killed himself, wouldn't his power die with him?

Then everyone else would be safe.

Brody followed Cahira as she dashed into the throne room. She spun in a circle, looking frantically about. "Guards! Where are my guards?"

"You have none." Brody pulled his sword and stalked toward her. "If you wish to live, you will remove my curse."

Cahira backed away. "No. Once I remove it, you'll kill me."

"Mother, you have my word." Maeve strode toward her. "I won't let any harm come to you."

"Why should I trust you?" Cahira sneered. "You sided with my enemy! How could you?"

"I fell in love with him long before I knew he was a prince," Maeve said. "And long before I knew you were my mother. He's suffered enough! Please remove his curse."

Cahira snorted. "I should have killed him when I had the chance."

Brody gritted his teeth. This was taking too long. He couldn't afford to run out of time in his own body. "An armada of twenty ships is arriving. Your Embraced army will be defeated. It's over for you. Your only hope of survival is to cooperate."

Cahira lifted her chin. "Never."

Brody groaned inwardly. He had no choice now but to attack the woman. And he'd have to do it right in front of Maeve.

"Have you seen Gavin?" Gabby shouted as she ran into the throne room. "I can't find him anywhere. He needs to be with us so his curse can be removed."

Maeve looked around, then gasped. "There he is!" She pointed to the throne on the dais, where an orange tabby was curled up, napping on the purple cushion. He raised his head and blinked sleepily at them.

Cahira huffed with indignation. "That bastard is on my throne!"

The cat stretched, then scratched at her pillow.

"How dare you!" Cahira waved a hand, and several glass ornaments close to the throne exploded.

"No!" Gabby screamed as the cat ducked down.

Gavin leaped off the throne, easily jumping over the broken glass on the dais. He landed, then grew larger and larger as he stalked toward the queen.

Brody blinked, not believing his eyes. Gavin could turn into a tiger? He snorted, recalling all the times he'd fed the cat on the Isle of Mist, when Gavin could definitely have taken care of himself. No wonder there was a shortage of deer on the island. And no wonder Gavin had terrorized the guards all night long.

"How . . . ?" Cahira retreated, her eyes widening with horror as the large cat advanced.

Gabby smirked. "You cursed him to be a cat for the rest of his life, but you never said what size he had to be."

Cahira backed into a green marble pillar, her gaze shifting frantically from the tiger to Brody as they both moved closer.

Brody raised his sword, the tip only a few inches from her neck. "If you undo the curse, Gavin will no longer be a tiger who wants to kill you."

"Your Majesty!" two guards shouted as they entered the throne room.

Brody glanced back. *Damn.* They must be the guards from the front door.

One of them grabbed Gabby and held a knife to her neck. "Let the queen go, or I kill her!"

"You heard him," Cahira hissed. "Let me go."

Gavin roared, and the guards jumped back, even the one holding Gabby. She reached into a pocket and pulled out some gold coins.

"Release me, and the gold is yours." She tossed the coins to the side. As soon as the guard loosened his hold, she elbowed him in the ribs and escaped.

The guards dropped their weapons and ran for the coins, but Gavin was faster. With a roar, he landed on one of the men and sank in his teeth. The guard screamed, and the second one sprinted out the door, screeching for help.

Brody turned back to Cahira. "Lift the curse now, or the tiger attacks you next."

"Stay away from me! I'll turn you both into slugs!"

Brody snorted. "Try it. But you'll have to lift the first curse before you can attempt a second one, and you'll be dead before that happens."

Cahira turned pale. "You dare to threaten me? I am superior to you all! I will cut you to shreds!" She lifted her arms and screamed.

With a horrendous blast, all the glass ornaments and windows exploded. Even the window in the ceiling shattered, raining glass down on the room.

Maeve collapsed on the floor, covering her head and crying out as several shards of flying glass cut her arms.

Brody glanced at her, wincing as a shard nicked his cheek. Thankfully, the Seer's voluminous robe kept his arms and legs protected. When he turned back to Cahira, she'd picked up a jagged piece of glass. Blood dripped from her hand as she threw it at Brody.

He sidestepped it and strode toward her. "Dammit, woman, don't make me kill you!"

Kendric smiled as he watched the enemy fleet sinking fast. Screams could be heard as a few seamen were attacked by giant sharks. He spotted Rupert, standing in a sinking crow's nest using his power to blow the sea monsters away. No doubt a few men were getting blown away with them. And as long as Rupert was focused on the sea monsters, he couldn't move their ships to shore. Darroc was slowly pushing them out to sea, where most of the men would drown.

An utter disaster. He chuckled. Even Leo was sinking. Soon the kings of Eberon and Tourin would be dead. And he,

Kendric, son of Frederic, would rule Eberon and take the Tourinian queen to be his wife. Both countries would be his. Brigitta would be his.

Even the sun had come out to shine on them. Logan must have found Hannah, for the rain had stopped.

"Good work," he told his soldiers.

Alfred grinned. "When that king with lightning power goes underwater, he'll fry everyone."

Kendric nodded. "Aye, he will." Although Alfred was clearly pleased, the others looked as if they were going to be sick. Damned fools. He wondered what would be the best way to kill them. After all, once he took over the mainland, they would no longer be needed.

Screams sounded behind him, and he turned to see a guard shouting and waving his arms on the balcony. *Boom!* A loud explosion rocked the castle and every glass window of the throne room blew apart.

"What was that?" Jared asked.

"The queen must have done it," Farah replied.

"Something's wrong." Kendric nodded at Alfred. "You're in charge here." Not that there was anything left to do, he thought as he dashed to the castle. He tore off his shirt, then shifted into an eagle, leaving his breeches behind as he flew to the balcony.

The guard was shaking in his boots as he pointed toward the throne room. "T-t-tiger!"

Tiger? What was the fool talking about? Still in eagle form, Kendric landed in the passageway. The scent of shifters wafted toward him. Cahira, Maeve, and Gavin, no doubt. But the first two could only shift into sea animals, and Gavin was a small cat.

Brody? Dammit, was he here? Kendric shifted into his human form. "Your breeches and your sword. Now!"

The guard quickly obeyed orders.

Kendric pulled on the breeches and grabbed the sword. He'd fought Brody as a tiger once before in Norveshka. Damn, but he was sick of that other shifter always getting in his way. Thankfully, the Light was on his side today. Rupert and Leo would die. And soon, Brody would, too.

Chapter 25

On a rocky bluff near the forest, Nevis watched in horror as the armada began to sink. All fourteen ships. His father was onboard. Leo, his best friend. Rupert. Soldiers that he'd known all his life. All dying and drowning right before his eyes.

Elinor took his hand and stood silently beside him.

"There has to be something we can do." He racked his brain. "Catriona! Can you blow up the sea monsters?"

"I can only do fish." She sighed. "And those are too far away."

Hannah stopped raining on the Embraced army and collapsed on the ground in tears. "We lost. We tried so hard, but we lost."

Nevis winced. Now was the time to encourage the children, but with Leo and his father about to die, he couldn't bring himself to do it.

A boy shot through the forest and skidded to a stop in front of them. "Hannah! I found you."

"Logan!" Bettina strode toward him. "What are you doing here?"

"I-I'm supposed to make Hannah stop . . ." He looked around the clearing at all the Spiders. "What are you doing here?" His eyes widened at the sight of Nevis and Elinor on the rocky bluff overlooking the ocean. "Who are you?"

Nevis glowered at him. "Come here, boy, and see how many men you have killed."

Logan gasped. "I-I didn't . . ."

"You're one of them!" Hannah cried.

"No, I . . ." Logan looked around at all the angry faces. "Kurt? Wh-where's Naomi? Is she all right?"

"She's fine," Kurt growled. "She's with the little ones."

Catriona leaned close to Nevis to explain. "Logan grew up in the nursery with Kurt, Naomi, and Mikayla."

At the sound of Mikayla's name, Logan fell to his knees. "They made her fly over the wall!" Tears ran down his face. "She's gone!"

Everyone gasped. Bettina doubled over, her face in her hands.

Dammit to hell. Nevis dragged a hand through his hair. "Those damned bastards, using children to do their dirty work."

"I'm a bastard, too," Logan cried. "Alfred always said I was only good for running away, and that's what I did. I ran away!"

Elinor walked toward him. "Dry your tears, young man. Refusing to be a villain is nothing to be ashamed of."

"She's right," Catriona said. "We know you never harmed anyone."

Logan wiped his face. "Th-then you forgive me?"

Kurt gave him a slap on the back. "Are you joining us now?"

"You can be a Spider!" Quentin jumped up and down, and the others cheered.

Nevis glanced back at the ocean and the floundering ships. It made his heart ache, but there was nothing he could do for them. However, he could still help Brody.

Boom! An explosion sounded in the distance.

"What was that?" Elinor asked.

"The castle. You all stay here." Nevis ran as fast as he could toward the castle. The Sea Witch must have caused the explosion. And that meant Brody was in danger.

In the crow's nest, Leo watched the ocean rising and could think of no other solution. The seamen and soldiers in the water were already struggling to stay alive. He couldn't kill them all.

Tears sprang to his eyes as he thought of Luciana. He'd promised her that he would return. Now he would never see Eric and Eviana grow up, never see the newborn babe. *Luciana, I love you. Forgive me.* He aimed the knife at his chest.

A sudden shriek made him look up. Dimitri? No, there were three dragons! One of them grabbed him so fiercely, the knife fell from his hand. He wasn't sure which dragon had him, but he carefully kept his hands and face from touching the one who had saved him.

He looked about. Another dragon had grabbed Rupert. The third dragon was breathing fire on the remaining sea creatures. And there to the east, Leo spotted the elfin navy.

Suddenly, the wooden ships began to rise. Higher and higher until they floated in the air just above the ocean surface.

It was the Woodsman! Leo watched in amazement as King Brennan of Woodwyn brought cracked ships back together. Broken pieces of wood in the water flew back to patch up holes. Once the ships were intact, the Woodsman lowered them into the water. He flipped capsized lifeboats back over, and seamen scrambled in to row back to their ships. Using ropes, the sailors climbed back onboard.

Cheers rang out, and Leo sent up a silent prayer of gratitude. They were saved.

Rupert started blowing the repaired ships back toward the harbor.

A bolt of lightning shot toward the third dragon, and Leo quickly struck the bolt aside. With a screech, the dragon zoomed toward the Embraced army and breathed fire, setting the grassy bluff ablaze. The soldiers retreated while Darroc used his power to blow the flames out.

Rupert sent a blast of wind at them, knocking them all back a hundred feet. The younger soldiers ran for the cover of the nearby forest, where other children were waving and calling them over. That had to be Nevis's group, Leo thought.

Only the oldest two soldiers remained.

Darroc aimed a gust of wind at the dragons, but Rupert knocked him back another hundred feet.

"Damn you!" Alfred shot a lightning bolt at Leo's dragon, but Leo managed to divert it.

His dragon breathed fire, forcing Alfred to retreat into the castle garden. The strangely clipped hedges were now aflame.

Alfred turned and shot another bolt, aimed straight at Leo. Quickly, Leo returned fire, hitting Alfred's bolt head-on. The two bolts sizzled and crackled, sparks flying where the two had collided.

Leo reached into his inner reserves, forcing all his strength into his bolt. With a loud crack, he forced Alfred's lightning back till the power of both bolts struck the young man in the chest and sent him flying.

He landed in a green-colored pond, where his body thrashed and jolted in an electric seizure. Finally, he grew still.

Leo's dragon swooped down to the ground, dropping him, then landing about twenty feet away. The dragon shifted into human form.

Silas. Leo smiled at him. "Thank you. I'd shake your hand, but . . ."

Silas snorted, then glanced at Alfred. "A shame to die so young, but he gave you no choice."

Leo nodded. The other dragon shifters joined them, both

in human form, with Dimitri dragging a frightened Darroc by the shirt collar.

"A-Alfred," Darroc whispered as he spotted the young man's dead body in the pond.

Dimitri tossed Darroc on the ground. "Aleksi and I will go back to rescue anyone still in the water."

"Thank you," Leo told them. "Where is Rupert?"

"He's blowing the ships into harbor," Aleksi replied. Then he and Dimitri shifted into dragons and flew off.

Silas strode up to Darroc, who was cowering on the ground. "Prisoner, I have a question for you."

"I-I'll tell you everything." Darroc pointed at the castle. "Kendric is in there. And Queen Cahira."

"And Brody?" Leo asked.

"I-I don't know him."

"The Seer?" Leo corrected himself.

"Oh. He's in there, too." Darroc bobbed his head nervously. "And Princess Maeve."

"Now here is my question," Silas growled.

Darroc's eyes filled with tears. "Anything, I'll tell you anything."

Silas crossed his arms over his massive chest. "Where can I find some breeches?"

Maeve froze at the sight of all the broken glass around her. Blood stained her sleeves where she'd been cut. *Oh, dear goddesses, no.* This was just like her dream! She glanced up and saw Brody advancing on her mother. Would he kill Cahira now? She recalled the look of her mother's glassy eyes.

"I thought you might be here," a voice sneered from the doorway.

Brody spun around.

Maeve winced. The Chameleon strode into the room, brandishing a sword. Would he stab Brody as he had in her dream?

The Chameleon glared at Brody. "So you have arrived. The meddlesome animal shifter, always showing up at the last minute to ruin my plans."

"Actually, I've been here for days. I was the Seer." When the Chameleon blinked, Brody snorted. "Right. You're not the only one who can shift into people."

The Chameleon smirked. "I always suspected you could but were too cowardly to try it."

"Kill him!" Cahira screamed at the Chameleon.

"Gladly." He lifted his sword. "I've been waiting for this moment for years."

Cahira laughed. "Now you will die, Prince Brodgar, still under my curse."

The Chameleon glanced at her. "You're the one who cursed him?"

"Of course." Cahira strolled over to a window. "I cursed him and Gavin. And I'm the only one who can undo the curses."

Gavin growled, and the Chameleon jolted with surprise, noticing for the first time that there was a tiger crouched behind the dead guard.

He stepped back. "That's the cat?"

"What's the matter, Kendric?" Brody taunted. "Are you afraid you can't handle us both?"

Kendric's mouth curled with a snarl. "When you're dying and crying for mercy, there will be no help from your friends. The ships have all been destroyed. Leo and Rupert are dead!"

Maeve gasped.

"You lie!" Brody ran toward the Chameleon, his sword raised. Gavin charged toward him, too.

The Chameleon shifted into a sparrow, leaving his breeches to fall to the floor as he flew over them.

"Coward!" Brody yelled at him.

Gabby grabbed a piece of glass and threw it at the bird as it circled the throne room.

Maeve suspected Kendric was stalling for time, figuring out what to do.

Brody strode toward Cahira. "He's not saving you. Undo the curse now!"

"He will save me." Cahira lifted her chin. "I raised him when no one else wanted him."

The sparrow landed beside her and quickly shifted into the Chameleon. As he straightened, he grabbed a sharp piece of glass.

"Attack them!" Cahira hissed.

Instead, he grabbed her and slit her neck.

"No!" Brody ran toward them.

With a laugh, the Chameleon stepped back and let the gasping queen slide to the floor. "Now you will be a dog for the rest of your life!"

Maeve shuddered as she watched the light dim in her mother's eyes. *No. Now Brody would be cursed forever.*

Brody stumbled, falling to his knees. "No," he whispered.

Gavin let out a mournful howl, and Gabby collapsed on the floor in tears.

The Chameleon shifted into an eagle and flew to where he'd dropped his sword. He grabbed it and charged toward Brody.

"Watch out!" Maeve screamed.

Brody spun around, lifting his sword, but the Chameleon's momentum worked in his favor, and he knocked Brody down. As Brody scrambled back, the Chameleon slashed him in the thigh.

Oh, goddesses, no! Her dream was coming true! Maeve looked around her for a weapon, but all she saw were shards of glass. And her mother's glassy eyes. Cahira was dead.

An abrupt pain shot through Maeve, and her vision blurred.

She fell to the floor, writhing as energy sizzled up her spine, then burst into her head. With a scream, she balled up, holding her head. Dear goddesses, it felt as if her head would explode!

"Maeve!" She heard Brody yelling.

She turned her head, forcing her eyes to focus despite the pain. *Don't die, Brody. Don't die.*

With a snarl, Gavin leaped at the Chameleon, but Kendric swung his sword at the tiger, cutting his back leg. In that time, Brody managed to get to his feet. Swords clashed again and again as Brody and the Chameleon fought. Blood from his wound pooled beneath Brody's feet, and he slipped to one knee.

The Chameleon lifted his sword, ready to strike the fatal blow.

Maeve gasped. This was what she'd seen in her dream. "No!"

As the Chameleon's sword swung down, Brody rolled to the side and, with an upward thrust, jabbed his sword into the Chameleon's gut.

Gavin pounced on him from behind, forcing Brody's sword in farther. With a gurgling cry, the Chameleon fell down, then disappeared.

"What?" Brody sat up.

An insect was darting toward the door, leaving a trail of blood behind it.

Just then, Nevis ran into the room, his sword raised. "Brody! Where—" He spotted the insect and stomped it with his boot. "Damn! I hate cockroaches!"

The insect shifted back into the smashed body of the Chameleon, and Nevis jumped back.

"What the hell?" Nevis took a closer look at the dead man. "He looks a lot like Leo." He glanced around the room. "Is everyone all right? Wait!" He lifted his sword. "Brody, don't move. There's a tiger beside you. I'll take care of this."

With a snort, Brody reached out a hand to pat the tiger. "He's on our side. This is Gavin."

"That's Gavin?" Nevis gave the tiger an incredulous look.

With a pitiful howl, Gavin shrank down into a tabby cat. Still crying, Gabby pulled the cat into her lap.

The pressure in Maeve's head was making her see stars. And now there was a rushing noise thundering in her ears, making it hard to hear.

"Why do you all look so sad?" Nevis's voice sounded as if it was coming from the end of a tunnel. "The Chameleon is dead. Cahira's dead."

"And we're alive," Leo announced as he and Silas strode into the room.

"Thank the Light!" Nevis grinned as he shook Silas's hand and gave Leo a thumbs-up.

Brody sighed as he remained sitting on the floor. He gave Maeve a sad look. "I know you're upset. I'm sorry."

She opened her mouth to reassure him, but couldn't manage to talk.

"What's there to be sorry about?" Nevis asked. "We won!"

Brody shook his head. "We're still cursed. Gavin will be a cat. And I will be a dog. Until we die."

As Gavin let out another howl, Maeve lost her struggle, and everything went black.

Chapter 26

B rody didn't know which was worse—the pain of having his wounded thigh cleaned and stitched or the fear that Maeve was avoiding him. Had she given up on him?

His allotted time to be himself was almost used up for the day, so where was she? The last time he'd seen her, she had fainted in the throne room. Had the shock of knowing he was cursed for the rest of his life upset her so much that she'd lost consciousness?

Nevis had helped him limp back to his bedchamber, and now Ruth was torturing him while Nevis enjoyed it. Damn him.

"You're sure you don't want more wine?" Nevis asked.

Brody shook his head and gritted his teeth as Ruth made another stitch on his thigh.

"I could knock you out." Nevis pretended to clonk him with the end of his knife. "I've had plenty of practice today."

"Where is Maeve?" Brody ground out. "Is she all right?"

"She's fine," Nevis assured him. "Silas carried her to her room."

"And I checked on her," Ruth added. "I'm sure she'll be waking soon."

Brody sighed. Poor Maeve. In a week's time she'd discovered and lost both her parents and found herself saddled with a cursed lover. At least the Chameleon was dead. The Embraced army, defeated. After Alfred had been killed, the rest of the soldiers had gladly surrendered. Nevis had spent the last ten minutes describing everything that had happened outside the castle. He was in jolly spirits after learning that Leo, Rupert, and his father had all survived.

The door swung open, and Brody lifted his head to see if it was Maeve. With a groan, he dropped back onto the pillow.

"Brody!" Elinor ran toward him. "I heard ye were injured."

He hissed in a breath as Ruth made another stitch. "This is the least of my problems. I'm still cursed—"

"We don't care!" Elinor interrupted him. "Don't ye dare use this as an excuse not to come home."

"No one wants a canine king!" Brody shouted. "Damn!" He jolted when Ruth poured more liquor on his wound.

"I wouldn't mind a dog king," Nevis said.

"No one asked you," Brody growled.

Nevis nudged Elinor. "His bark is worse than his bite."

"Sod off!" Brody yelled. "You find this is amusing? Did you hear Gavin howling? And Gabby crying? Shit, Maeve was so upset she fainted!"

"I know it's crappy!" Nevis shouted back. "That's why I'm trying to cheer you up!"

"It's not working!" Brody's heart tightened in his chest. "You think I'm upset for myself? It's Maeve I'm upset for. She's stuck with a dog for the rest of her life."

Elinor sighed. "She loves you, so she won't mind."

"She shouldn't love me." Brody fought back the tears that wanted to come. *Dammit.* "Check on her, Ellie. Please. I'm worried about her."

Nevis pointed toward the adjoining door. "Her bedchamber's right there."

"Oh." Elinor gave her brother a wry look. "That was convenient."

"Sly dog," Nevis muttered, and Brody threw a pillow at him.

Elinor gave Nevis a smile before strolling over to the door and going in.

"I saw that," Brody grumbled. "Don't even think about courting my sister."

"Don't take your foul mood out on me," Nevis told him.

Elinor rushed back in. "She's not there!"

"What?" Brody struggled to sit up, but Ruth gave his chest a push.

"You're not going anywhere," the old woman ordered. "You'll tear the stitches. Now lie still while I put a bandage on you."

With a frustrated groan, Brody lay back down. "Find her, Nevis."

"Don't worry," Nevis assured him. "She can't be far." He headed for the door.

"I'll go with you." Elinor linked her arm with his.

Shit. Brody watched as the two of them smiled at each other before sauntering out the door. What was he going to do about them? And where the hell was Maeve? Why hadn't she come to see him when she'd wakened? He was so close by. Did she not care for him anymore? Had she given up on him because he was cursed?

"Get some rest now." Ruth tied off the bandage, then picked up her supplies and left.

With a groan, he realized his two hours for the day had come to an end. As he shifted into the Seer, tears came to his eyes.

Wouldn't it be better for Maeve if she did give him up?

In the throne room, Leo's boots crunched on the broken glass as he paced to a window. He peered down at the harbor below and the fourteen damaged ships docked along the pier. Rupert and Brennan the Woodsman looked as if they were discussing repairs while the surviving seamen rested on the castle lawn. Leo made a mental note to have the servants deliver some bread and jugs of water to the men.

The elfin navy had anchored close to the harbor, and elfin

seamen and soldiers were still rowing to the pier in lifeboats. Out at sea, he spotted the three dragons circling about, searching for survivors.

Here in the castle, Leo and Nevis's father, General Harden, had taken charge until Maeve was ready to take on her duties as the next queen. The general, with help from Gabby and the Spiders, had located all the guards and locked them in the dungeons, along with Darroc. The last guard had been found cowering in the lookout tower, hoping he had been forgotten.

The younger members of the Embraced army were being detained in their dorm rooms with Eberoni soldiers guarding the doors.

Down on the pier, Leo spotted Sorcha talking to Rupert and her husband, King Brennan. After hugging Brennan, she hurried toward the castle. No doubt she wanted to see Maeve. Unfortunately, Leo had heard that Maeve was unconscious in her room. The shock of seeing her mother die and realizing Brody would never be free from his curse must have been too much for her.

Poor Brody. Leo shook his head. The man would have to learn to live with it, much as Leo endured the pain of never being able to embrace his own children.

He turned and spotted the pool of blood where a guard had been mauled to death by a tiger. Gabby had insisted her brother was harmless, and indeed, as a tabby cat, Gavin did appear that way. Still, Leo had thought it best for Gavin to stay in his room under guard for the time being. The shifter was understandably upset, but Leo didn't want Gavin to lose control and accidentally hurt someone in his highly emotional state.

General Harden had ordered his soldiers to remove the guard's body from the throne room. Cahira and the Chameleon had also been taken away, their bodies laid in a cool cellar for now. Maeve would probably want to give her mother a proper burial. As for the Chameleon, Leo felt obliged to bury him. The man was his cousin, after all. But if Brody hadn't managed to kill him, Leo would have.

He took a deep breath. So all five members of the Circle of Five were dead. The entire world of Aerthlan could now be at peace. Even so, there were still tasks to be undertaken. Months ago, he had discovered a hidden stash of documents in the library at Ebton Palace, left behind by Lord Morris. The papers listed the Embraced children he had acquired over the years, and the families he had taken them from. So it was possible that some of the children from this island could be reunited with their parents.

The sound of booted feet drew his attention to the golden doors, where General Harden was entering with two of his soldiers. They were escorting two girls equipped with brooms, pails, and baskets.

The girls spotted Leo and dropped their supplies so they could each sink into a curtsy.

"This is Farah and Irene," the general introduced them.

"From the Embraced army." Leo nodded, recalling their names from his list. "Farah has the gift of fire, and Irene can make things grow."

Farah bowed her head. "We'd like to apologize for any damage we caused. And we thank you for saving Mikayla."

Irene glanced up at him, her eyes filled with tears.

The general nodded approvingly as he crossed his arms over his chest. "They begged me to let them clean up the throne room. I thought it a good idea."

Irene suddenly fell to her knees. "I'm so sorry! I didn't want to hurt anyone." Tears ran down her face. "I know some peo-people died." She leaned over, sobbing on the floor. "I didn't want to hurt the animals. I didn't want to hurt the sailors."

Leo's heart squeezed in his chest. This sixteen-year-old girl would have to live with a terrible burden for the rest of her life. In reality, she was another victim of the Chameleon's bid for power. "Were you ordered to do it?"

She nodded, still sobbing. Next to her, Farah started to cry silently.

"Was there ever a time when you didn't follow orders?" Leo asked.

Farah nodded. "If we disobeyed Kendric or Alfred, we had to stand outside in the rain all night. On the posts along the pier."

Leo winced. If they fell off, they would land in the water.

Irene sniffled. "And we were locked in the dungeon for three days with no food."

Leo exchanged a look with General Harden. If the Chameleon or Alfred came back to life, he'd kill them all over again.

He squatted on the floor in front of the girls. "You've been through some horrific ordeals. I know you will be struggling with some guilt, but I'm telling you now that we do not blame you. We will never blame you. We consider you victims, just as much as the children who lived in the village. Do you understand?"

The girls nodded.

"All right, then." General Harden clapped his hands together. "Let's get to work."

"Aye, General." The girls rushed off. Irene began sweeping up glass by the windows, while Farah took her baskets to the broken glass on the dais.

Leo hefted himself to his feet. "General, could you have some servants take bread and water to the seamen outside?"

"Aye, will do." He motioned to his men to take care of it, and they rushed off.

Leo lowered his voice. "How is Brody doing?"

General Harden sighed. "Nevis says he's in pain and distraught."

"And Maeve?" Leo asked.

"Yes," Sorcha said as she strode into the room. "How is Maeve?"

General Harden shrugged. "The last I heard she was unconscious in her room."

"Unconscious?" Sorcha asked, her eyes widening with concern.

"I believe the shock may have been too much for her," Leo murmured.

Sorcha huffed. "That doesn't sound like Maeve. She's tougher than that." She tilted her head to look at the two girls who were cleaning. "Who are they?"

"Farah and Irene," the general replied.

Sorcha's brows rose. "Farah's the one with fire power?"

Leo nodded. "She's the one by the dais."

"Interesting." Sorcha walked over to the dais, where Farah was rummaging through the broken glass and filling different baskets. "Ye're sorting the glass by color? Why?"

Farah looked up at her, then bowed her head. "I can melt these to make new ornaments."

Sorcha gasped. "Ye use yer fire power to make glass?"

Farah nodded. "I made all the glass art here." She blinked away tears. "The queen blew it up."

"I'm so sorry." Sorcha kneeled down and picked up a piece of glass with different shades of green and gold running through it. "This is beautiful. I would have loved to have seen what it originally looked like."

Farah gave her a shy look. "I have a few finished pieces in my workroom."

"Wonderful!" Sorcha dropped the green glass into the correct basket. "I'd love to see them. And I want to see how ye do it."

"Like this." Farah snapped her fingers and a flame appeared.

Sorcha grinned. "I know how to do that much. It's the glass part I don't understand."

"You . . . you know how . . . ?"

Sorcha nodded. "I do it the same way." She snapped her fingers to make a flame.

Farah gasped.

Sorcha smiled at her. "I always thought I was alone, but here ye are."

"Who . . . may I ask who you are?"

"Sorcha, princess of Norveshka and queen of Woodwyn."

Farah's mouth fell open.

"I'm an artist, too," Sorcha added. "But my talent lies with drawing and painting."

Farah continued to gape at her.

"Ye wouldn't believe the beautiful craftsmanship in Woodwyn. We have the most fabulous wood carvers and silversmiths. The elves would love to see yer glass art."

Farah swallowed hard. "That's all I ever wanted to be. A glass artist."

Sorcha smiled at her. "Then that is what ye will be. I think we could become good friends, don't you?"

Farah nodded.

Sorcha rose to her feet, then went to talk to the other girl.

General Harden leaned close to Leo and whispered, "I have a feeling the Woodsman is going to acquire a new artist and gardener for Wyndelas Palace."

Leo nodded. A new beginning for the older Embraced children would probably be for the best.

Just then, Nevis and Princess Elinor rushed through the door. When Nevis spotted Sorcha, he waved her over. "Thank the Light you're here. Maybe Maeve will let you in."

"What?" Sorcha hurried over to them, and Nevis quickly introduced her to Brody's sister.

"I thought Maeve was in her bedchamber," Leo said.

Elinor shook her head. "She's locked herself in her mother's workroom. We're terribly worried about her. She refuses to open the door or even talk to us."

Sorcha hissed in a breath. "This is bad. I'll go see her right away." She turned to Leo. "Send Rupert to Ebton Palace to bring our sisters here."

"None of his ships are seaworthy at the moment," Leo said.

"Then he can borrow one of our ships," Sorcha insisted. "Brennan won't mind." She grabbed Elinor's arm. "Now show me where this workroom is."

Chapter 27

The next day, Nevis was standing on the balcony with Elinor, watching the scene before them. In the distance, Leo, Brennan, and the dragon shifters were repairing the ships with help from most of the seamen and soldiers. Down below in the garden, the children from the village and the Embraced army played while the older ones watched and talked.

The evening before, Nevis, Elinor, and Bettina had trekked back to the sea cave to meet the boat. After delivering the children ashore, Lobby and Tommy had listened to all the news.

"The Sea Witch is dead?" Lobby had asked. "'Tis safe now?"

"Aye, 'tis safe," Elinor reassured them. "There are now four ships from the Isle of Moon in the harbor. I'll have no trouble finding a ride back home."

"We'll take you back," Tommy offered. "After all, this is yer boat."

Elinor smiled. "I'm thinking two brave men like you deserve a reward. The boat now officially belongs to you."

Lobby and Tommy gasped.

"Y-ye're giving us yer boat?" Lobby asked, and Elinor nodded.

Tommy looked at his old friend. "We have a boat!"

"And a chef," Nevis added in a wry tone.

Tommy and Lobby laughed.

"He can stay if he wants," Lobby said.

After saying their good-byes, Nevis had headed back to the castle with Elinor, Bettina, and the children. Those who were accustomed to living in the village were surprised when Nevis told them they would be staying in the castle for a few days.

Now all the Embraced children were together again, no matter what their gift was. They had all been thrilled when Mikayla had returned safe and sound.

" 'Tis good to see them playing together," Elinor said as she stepped closer to Nevis on the balcony. She curled a hand around his arm and leaned her head on his shoulder. " 'Tis a shame everyone is happy but my brother and Maeve."

Nevis nodded. Brody was moping in his room, and Maeve was still locked in her mother's workroom. She'd even refused to let Sorcha in.

"Then you must be happy?" Nevis turned his head so his jaw brushed against Elinor's hair.

"Aye. I'm glad to be safe and sound. I'm happy the children are all right. And you, too, of course." She squeezed his arm.

He cleared his throat. "Would you consider going to Eberon? You could stay at Ebton Palace. I'm sure Luciana would love to have you visit."

Elinor straightened and looked at him. "Why would I go there?"

"Well, I . . . I work in Eberon. That way, we could become better acquainted."

"Do ye live at Ebton Palace?"

"No. I live with the army."

She gave him a wry look. "Then why would I go to Ebton Palace?"

He winced. "I would see you often. We've known each other only a few days. Don't you think we need more time together?"

She tilted her head, thinking. "No."

His heart lurched up his throat. "No?"

"I think I should take the children home with me. They know me and feel safe with me. Ruth has already agreed to come. We can take care of them while we try to locate their parents. We have schools and libraries they can go to. And if we can't find their parents in Eberon, we could find homes for them on the Isle of Moon. Why don't ye come with me and help?"

"My life is in Eberon. My father wants to retire, so I'll become the next general."

She snorted. "The entire world is at peace now. What is there for an army general to do?"

He stiffened. "There are always bandits. And pirates. I think I really should become a general."

She gave him a frustrated look. "Why?"

"It might make me a worthier suitor."

"Worthier?" She scoffed. "Ye really should show more confidence than that."

"Ha! You know good and well that you outrank me."

"Does that really bother you?"

"Yes! Elinor, I grew up in the army. Rank is extremely important."

She narrowed her eyes. "Very well. Since I outrank you, I order you to stay with me."

He huffed. "Y-you think you can order me around?"

"Yes."

"Ha!" He pounded a fist on the stone balustrade. "On a cold day in hell."

"And I order you to marry me."

He jumped back with a start. "You . . . what?"

She shrugged. "Forget I said it. Ye've already told me that I can't order you around."

"Would you marry me?"

She blinked. "Are ye asking me?"

"No, I'm begging you. I know I'm not worthy—"

"Are ye saying ye'll be an unworthy husband?"

"What? No!"

She lifted her chin. "Will ye be below average in the bedroom?"

"Hell, no!"

She lunged toward him, wrapping her arms around his neck. "Prove it."

He snorted. "Are you asking me . . . ?"

"No. I'm begging you."

He laughed. "In that case . . ." He pulled her close and planted his mouth on hers. By the Light, they hadn't known each other very long, but he knew she was perfect. A treasure he would always cherish . . .

"Ahem."

Nevis broke the kiss and glanced to the side. Brody was standing in the doorway, glowering at him. "Ah, hello, Brody. Nice weather we're having."

Brody arched a brow. "It's not the weather you appear to be enjoying."

Nevis gave him a wry look. "It's good to see you out and about, instead of moping all alone in your room."

Brody snorted. "I see you're well acquainted with my sister now. Even though I told you to stay away from her."

She smiled. "Actually, he was complaining that we're not acquainted well enough."

"You dog," Brody muttered.

"Look who's talking," Nevis replied.

Brody's mouth twitched. "True. I've been thinking about it, and I've decided it really wasn't all that bad being a dog. I mean, if I don't have any choice in the matter, I might as well enjoy it."

"Now you're talking." Nevis gave him a thumbs-up.

Brody snorted. "People used to think I was Nevis's pet."

"Really?" Elinor gave Nevis an amused look.

Nevis shrugged. "Brody needed a place to sleep and shift and change clothes, so I let him use my tent."

Brody nodded. "He was always grumbling at me for bringing in fleas."

Nevis grimaced. "I hate fleas."

Elinor grinned. "And bats, crabs, spiders, and roaches."

"So are you going back to Eberon?" Brody asked.

Nevis glanced at Elinor. "I'm not sure. Are you going to the Isle of Moon to become king?"

Brody sighed. "How can I be king when I have only two hours a day in my real form?"

"Don't worry," Elinor assured him. "Nevis and I will help you. I'm sure Maeve will, too."

Brody winced. "She'll be the queen here. I don't think she wants to be with me anymore. She still hasn't come out of her mother's workroom."

"She just needs time to adjust," Nevis insisted.

"I'm sure she'll be all right," Elinor added. "Rupert should be arriving any minute now with her sisters. They'll help her feel better."

"Help her feel better about the fact that I can never live as a human?" Brody muttered.

"Brody." Nevis clasped him on the shoulder. "You're as human as any of us. Even more so, I would say. Your time is shorter, so you value it more."

Brody closed his eyes briefly. "Actually, Nevis, I can't think of anyone I'd rather see with my sister."

He stepped back with a shocked look. "Then you'll approve if we . . ." He reached a hand toward Elinor.

With a grin, she grabbed onto his hand. "We want to get married."

Brody nodded, giving them a sad smile. "That's good." He limped down the hallway, mumbling, "At least someone will have a happy ending."

* * *

When all four of her sisters knocked on the door and begged to be let in, Maeve unlocked it.

Her sisters barged in.

"Are ye all right?"

"What have ye been doing?"

"Do ye know how worried we've been?"

Luciana grabbed her by the shoulders and looked her over. "You look like you haven't slept at all."

"I haven't." Maeve shut the door behind them and locked it.

"What the hell is going on?" Sorcha demanded. "Do ye know how terrified I was yesterday when ye wouldn't see me?"

"I'm sorry." Maeve motioned to the worn-out chairs surrounding an old table. "Have a seat and I'll try to explain."

"Ye're not giving up on Brody, are you?" Gwen asked as she took a seat.

"Ye'd better not," Brigitta added. "It would break his heart."

"Shh." Luciana hushed them as she sat down. "Let her speak."

The four sisters watched her expectantly as Maeve moved behind a worktable filled with books, pages of notes, and several lit candlesticks. She straightened a stack of papers. "I haven't given up on Brody. I'm fighting for him."

"How?" Sorcha demanded.

With a tired sigh, Maeve sat on a stool.

"You look exhausted," Luciana said softly. "Have you had anything to eat?"

Maeve motioned toward an empty bottle. "My mother had some wine stashed away in the cupboard. Would you like some?"

"No, we're fine," Gwen assured her.

Maeve took a deep breath. "Then I'll tell you what happened. About a week ago, when I was traveling to the Isle of

Moon, the Seer passed away on the Isle of Mist. That night when he died, a strange sensation came over me in my sleep. And then I had a dream. Later on, I learned that it had come true. And since then, I've had other dreams that have come to pass."

Luciana leaned forward. "Are you saying that somehow the Seer's power of foresight was transferred to you?"

"Aye." Maeve nodded. "It was. Because the Seer was my father."

Her sisters gasped.

"Yer father was the Seer?" Brigitta asked.

"And now ye have his power?" Gwen asked.

Sorcha inhaled sharply. "Ye're the new Seer."

Her sisters all exchanged shocked looks, then Luciana muttered, "I think we'll have some wine after all."

Maeve opened the cupboard and set four glasses on the table. She pulled the cork from a wine bottle and poured a little in each glass. "When my mother died in the throne room, another strange sensation hit me, although this time it was much more intense. More painful. So much power surged through me, I thought my head would explode! And that was why I fainted."

"Ah." Sorcha reached for a glass. "Now that makes more sense. All the men think ye simply fainted from shock."

Gwen snorted. "She's much tougher than that."

"Exactly," Brigitta agreed and took a sip of wine.

Maeve retrieved another glass and poured herself a drink. "When I woke up in bed, my first thought was how devastated Brody must be." She set her glass on the worktable. "And I thought about how easy it would have been for my mother to lift the curse on him and Gavin. But she refused! And it makes me so *angry*!" She waved a hand, and her wineglass exploded.

Her sisters gasped.

Maeve winced and grabbed a towel to sop up the mess. "Sorry. I'm not very good at controlling it yet."

"Controlling what?" Gwen asked.

"My power," Maeve replied. "When I woke up in bed and felt so much rage for my mother, the windows in my room cracked. I suspected then that I must have inherited my mother's power. So I rushed here to see what I could learn from her books and notes."

Luciana gulped down some wine. "And what have you learned?"

"Quite a bit." Maeve swiped the broken glass into a rubbish tin that was nearly full. "As you can see, I've been practicing. It wasn't exactly safe in here, so I didn't want anyone coming in. And I wanted to make sure I knew what I was doing before I tried anything on a person."

"So ye're a witch now?" Brigitta asked.

Maeve nodded. "And a Seer, a shifter, and a siren. My father said I would be more powerful than my mother, and he was right."

"So what happens now?" Gwen asked.

Maeve took a deep breath. "Magic."

Brody was in his bedchamber, sitting on the window seat, staring out the window. Everyone was busy around the castle. Leo had buried the Chameleon in the back garden. Rupert had returned with the three eldest sisters and their children. Maeve had allowed her sisters inside the workroom with her. Nevis and Elinor were off somewhere getting better acquainted. Brody snorted.

Everyone had something to do but him. He was supposed to be resting, actually, since he had a wounded leg, but he felt utterly useless. He wasn't even himself. He'd reverted to the guise of the Seer so he could save his allotted time as Brody in case Maeve came to see him.

But of course, she wasn't coming.

His door swung open, and for a second, he hoped it was Maeve. But no, it was Nevis. And of course, he had Elinor in tow. "What do you want?"

"You, you grumpy old man." Nevis motioned for him to come. "The queen has called everyone to the throne room."

"Queen?"

"Queen Maeve. Remember her?" Nevis waved once again. "Come on. She's ordered everyone to attend."

Brody snorted. She must be enjoying her new status. He limped toward the door, shifting into his true form.

He was exhausted and in pain by the time he hobbled into the Great Hall. The throne room was full. All the Embraced children were there with Ruth, including Gabby and her brother, Gavin, who sat by her feet. Leo and the other kings were in attendance, along with the dragon shifters, ship captains, and General Harden. Leo's and Rupert's children sat in the middle of the mosaic floor, examining the octopus and dolphins pictured there.

Maeve was ensconced on the octopus throne, her sisters standing on the dais beside her. Five queens, Brody thought. They'd come a long way from being orphans at the convent on the Isle of Moon. Maeve looked tired, though, and strained. Her gown was still stained with blood from the cuts she'd received from shattered glass. Around her shoulders, she was wearing an old shawl.

She raised a hand, and a hush fell over the room. "I am Maeve, daughter of the Seer and Queen Cahira. The powers they possessed have all come to me."

Whispers circled about the room.

Maeve had all their powers? Brody thought back to what the Seer had once told him, that his daughter would inherit his gift when he died. That was the way it worked with his ancient race. And Cahira had come from the same race.

Brody gulped. Was Maeve now a sea witch?

She stood and moved to the edge of the dais. "Leofric of Eberon, please step forward."

Leo advanced slowly toward the dais, giving his wife a questioning look.

Luciana nodded with tears in her eyes.

"As you know, Alfred had the same power as you," Maeve said. "But he was also able to touch people." She reached a hand toward Leo and closed her eyes to concentrate. Soon, her hand began to glow. She opened her eyes and planted her hand on Leo's chest.

He jolted as her power flowed through him.

"It is done." Maeve removed her hand from his chest. She reached up to touch his cheek, but he jerked back.

"No," he protested. "It's not safe."

"It is." She rested a palm on his cheek. "See? Take off your gloves, Leo. And hug your children."

He stepped back, his eyes glistening with tears. "I-I don't dare. I couldn't . . ."

Maeve removed his gloves, her hands touching his. "Your power has been turned off for now. In time, you will learn to turn it on or off at will."

Leo turned to face his children. Still, he hesitated.

He has lived with the fear of harming his children for too long, Brody thought as limped toward Leo. "You can test it on me." He grabbed Leo's hand.

Leo blinked back his tears as he shook Brody's hand. "Have I ever thanked you for all you've done?"

With a smile, Brody clapped him on the back.

"My turn." Nevis gave Brody a shove and clasped Leo's hand in his own. "I'm not sure you've ever thanked me, either."

Leo laughed. "Thank you both." He moved toward his children and lowered himself onto one knee. When he extended his arms, they ran toward him, squealing and wrapping their arms around his neck.

With tears running down his face, Leo embraced his children. Then, with a choked laugh, he rose to his feet, still holding them as he spun in a circle.

Eric and Eviana laughed and buried their faces against his shoulders. Luciana ran toward them and flung her arms around them all.

Leo glanced at Maeve, who still stood on the dais. "Thank you."

She nodded, then wiped a tear from her cheek.

The other kings gathered around Leo, each wanting to shake his hand.

"Since our wives are sisters, I consider you all my brothers," Leo told them. "May we always live in peace."

The other men agreed, and everyone cheered.

Luciana stepped back onto the dais to stand with her sisters.

Maeve raised her hands, and everyone grew quiet. "Gabby and Gavin, please step forward."

Gabby rushed toward her with Gavin trotting alongside her. The tabby cat jumped up onto the dais and meowed.

"This may hurt," Maeve whispered as she cradled the cat's face in her hands. She closed her eyes, concentrating until her hands glowed. Gavin hissed, but remained still.

Soon, his whole body began to glow. And grow larger. The fur disappeared, and his shape changed. With a cry, his human form snapped into place.

Gabby fell to her knees while all the other Embraced children cheered.

Maeve whisked off her shawl to cover Gavin. He sat up, blinking as he gazed around. He stretched out his hands and looked at them. Then he extended his legs and wiggled his feet. He peeked under the shawl and his eyes widened. Opening his mouth, he attempted to talk, but only hoarse noises came out.

"Gavin!" Gabby threw her arms around him.

Brody could tell they were twins. They both had golden-red hair and amber-colored eyes. But he had to wonder—if Maeve could lift Gavin's curse, could she remove his?

"It may take a while for you to learn how to talk again," Maeve warned him.

Gavin nodded and slid his legs off the dais so he could stand up. He promptly fell back on his rear.

Gabby laughed and helped him up, wrapping the shawl around his hips. "He'll have to learn how to walk on two legs again, too."

As Gavin hobbled back toward the other Embraced children, they gathered around him to give him hugs.

Maeve took a deep breath. "Before I continue, I want to say this." She looked at Brody. "No matter what happens, I will always love you. If you remain cursed, I will love you. If you're a dog, an eagle, or a seal, I will love you. I will always fight for you and never give up."

Tears filled his eyes. He strode to the dais, or tried to as well as his wounded leg would allow. "I love you, too."

"I'm not sure this will work," she whispered. "But if it doesn't, I'll keep learning. And trying."

"It's all right." He grabbed her hands. "No matter what happens, we have each other."

She nodded, then closed her eyes to concentrate.

How could he have ever doubted her? His sweet Maeve. He felt the power surging through her hands, then shooting into him. More and more energy, sizzling through his muscles, slithering through his veins, exploding in his head.

With a whoosh, the energy dissipated, leaving him so weak, he fell to his knees.

"Are you all right?" Maeve jumped off the dais to kneel beside him.

"I don't know." He couldn't be sure that the curse was gone until his allotted time ran out. Or didn't.

"We'll have to wait and see."

He scoffed. "After that confession of yours, you expect me to wait? Marry me, Maeve. Whether I'm a prince or a dog, be my wife. No matter what."

With a smile, she nodded. "And whether I'm a seer or a siren, be my husband. No matter what."

He kissed her, and everyone in the room cheered.

Epilogue

Three weeks later, on the Isle of Mist . . .

Maeve smiled as she strolled hand in hand with Brody toward the Seer's house. It was a glorious day, and she glanced up at the sky, thanking the goddesses once again that she'd inherited her mother's powers.

Ever since that day in the throne room, Brody had been himself. All day. And all night, she thought with a blush.

Within a week, they had gone back to the Isle of Moon to get married. By the second week, they'd both been crowned king and queen at Lessa Castle. Their kingdom now consisted of three islands, and lately they'd gone back and forth between the Isles of Moon and Secrets to take care of business.

Young families from the Isle of Moon who desperately wanted a parcel of land to call their own had volunteered to colonize the Isle of Secrets. As for the children, Nevis and Elinor had taken charge, and with Luciana's help, they were slowly finding the parents of some of the younger ones.

Farah and Irene had gone to Woodwyn with Sorcha and her husband. Farah was going to be a glass artist, and Irene was eager to work in the gardens at Wyndelas Palace.

Quentin had announced he wanted to be a dragon. Silas had tried to explain that it was impossible, but the boy had refused to listen. That night, Maeve had dreamed of Quentin, seeing him in the future, flying in the form of an eagle. Apparently, his Embraced gift would be the ability to shift into birds, and eventually, he would become the messenger between all the kings, the job that Brody had held in the past. Silas and Gwen had grown fond of the boy, so they had happily taken him back to Norveshka with them. Maeve was happy, knowing that one day Quentin would be able to fly with the dragons.

Rupert had volunteered to train Darroc to be a ship's captain. Bettina and Catriona had become Maeve's ladies-in-waiting. And Elam hadn't wanted to part from Nevis. Maeve felt sure that eventually all the children would be happily situated.

She glanced back at the bluff where she and Brody had just paid their respects to the Seer. His cairn was there, the same one she had seen in her first dream. And a second cairn was close to it, for Maeve had buried her mother next to the Seer. It had seemed fitting, since she suspected her father was the only person Cahira had ever truly loved.

Brody led her through the broken gate into the disheveled garden.

"My father lived here for seventy-five years?"

Brody nodded. "And most of that time, he was completely alone. I was with him for six years. And Trouble, or Gavin I should say, was with him for two."

"Did he ever know Gavin was a shifter?"

Brody paused by the door, thinking. "I don't think he did. After he got involved with the Circle of Five, he lost most of his power of foresight."

"Then how did he continue to make predictions?"

Brody grinned. "I was spying all over the mainland and passing the information back to him."

She scoffed. "How many people were paying you to spy for them?"

"Only Leo." Brody shoved open the creaky door. "I helped the Seer for free. After all, he raised me." He stopped to look around the room. "He saved me. I was ten years old and cursed. I'd just seen my father and brother die. The Seer gave me love and taught me to keep fighting and never give up, no matter what."

"No matter what," Maeve repeated, recalling those same words they had said in the throne room.

She glanced around the tiny one-room cottage and tried to imagine living here alone for seventy-five years, the only person on the island. "I have a feeling you saved the Seer as much as he saved you."

Brody nodded. "I'm sorry you never got to meet him."

She ran her hand along the scarred table. "It is sad, but at the same time, I'm glad you were with him."

Brody strode over to the bookcase and reached behind some books. "Here it is." He pulled out an old journal. "When you read this, you'll feel like you know your father."

She took the journal and cradled it against her chest. "Was this his bed?"

"Aye. That is where he died."

She sat on the bed and touched his pillow. "Thank you, Brody. Thank you for being here with my father. Thank you for always fighting and never giving up."

He sat beside her. "No matter what."

She smoothed her hand over the worn leather of the journal. As much as she wanted to know her father, she was afraid the reading would be painful. "I'll read it when I'm alone."

"I understand."

She glanced up at her husband. Now that he was always human, he was eating and sleeping regularly. And the result had left him more handsome than ever. "Are we truly alone on this isle?"

He nodded. "There might be a few deer left that Gavin didn't have for dinner."

"Ugh." She grimaced.

With a smile, he brushed her hair from her brow. "Why do you ask? Do you have something in mind?"

After three weeks, she knew exactly what that twinkle in his pretty blue eyes meant. Luckily for him, her thoughts tended to steer in the same direction. "I seem to recall a promise you made to me."

"Which one?"

"Something about making love to your siren in the deep blue sea."

"Ah." Another twinkle in his eyes. "I just happen to know where there's a sandy cove and a cave."

"And a deep blue sea?"

"Very deep. Very blue."

Maeve slid the journal beneath her father's pillow. She would read it later. For now, she wanted to celebrate being alive and being with this beautiful man she loved with all her heart. "Then you will take me there immediately."

His eyes widened. "That sounded like an order."

"It was."

He stood and bowed. "As you wish, Your Majesty."

She jumped to her feet and kissed him. "It's good to be the queen."

Connect with Us

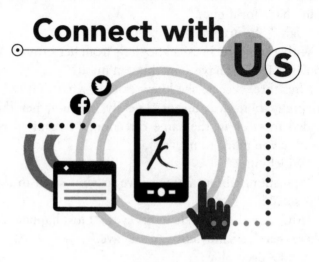

Visit us online at
KensingtonBooks.com
to read more from your favorite authors, see books
by series, view reading group guides, and more.

Join us on social media

for sneak peeks, chances to win books and prize packs,
and to share your thoughts with other readers.

facebook.com/kensingtonpublishing
twitter.com/kensingtonbooks

Tell us what you think!

To share your thoughts, submit a review,
or sign up for our eNewsletters, please visit:
KensingtonBooks.com/TellUs.